To Roger and Stella,

with every good wish from

Ray and Sue Tilly

THE SUN AND THE MOON OF ALEXANDRIA

THE SUN AND THE MOON
— OF —
ALEXANDRIA

Ray Filby

The Book Guild Ltd.
Sussex, England

The Book Guild Ltd.,
25 High Street,
Lewes, Sussex

First published 1993
© Ray Filby 1993
Set in Baskerville
Typesetting by Kudos Graphics
Slinfold, Horsham, West Sussex

Printed in Great Britain by
Antony Rowe Ltd.,
Chippenham, Wiltshire.

A catalogue record for this book is
available from the British Library

ISBN 0 86332 773 7

To my wife SUE

who has encouraged me in writing this story, has painstakingly read the proofs and tolerated my spending many hours on a word processor to produce this volume.

CONTENTS

1

Apollos Contemplates the Pyramids

The young man sat in the meagre shade provided by a large rock which protruded from the hot Egyptian sands. He leaned against the rock and contemplated the pyramids. They were utterly awesome. How magnificently they bore witness to the greatness of one of the most ancient civilizations of the world. When did the people of the Nile organize themselves into a social structure which supported stable government? Were they the first nation to discover the secret of writing as the means of conserving newly acquired knowledge for future generations? Had the inhabitants of the land watered by the Tigris and Euphrates established their famous civilization ahead of the Egyptians? The young man had studied the developments of human civilizations from the earliest times, but the scholarship of the first century was unable to unequivocally identify which of the early great civilizations of the world could really claim to be the first.

The young man's name was Apollos. Apollos was the only son of a wealthy Alexandrian merchant. Being the only son of a household of some opulence had provided Apollos with considerable advantages. He had a keen mind and had been able to take full advantage of the excellent tutors which his parents had hired to give their son the very best possible start in life. Apollos had learnt to read and write at a very young age. He had readily absorbed the mathematics which he proudly realized had been developed more by the Greeks than by any of the other world civilizations. Apollos' ethnic origins were Greek and mathematics was therefore something special to Apollos because it was knowledge that his own Hellenic culture had contributed to enlighten the

9

world. However, Apollos was fascinated by the study of civilization itself, rather than particular facets of civilization like mathematics or language.

From the time his tutors had described to him the great pyramids, Apollos had longed to see them for himself and at last he had been permitted by his family to make the journey alone from Alexandria to Giza. Although many of the treasures of the library at Alexandria had been destroyed in a fire which had occurred a century earlier, the library still contained sufficient volumes of interest on which Apollos could feed his mind. Apollos had seen pictures of the pyramids in this library. He had marvelled that they had been constructed so that every face was an equilateral triangle. The illustrious Greek, Euclid, who had systematically developed the elements of geometry some three hundred years earlier in his home town of Alexandria, had long been revered by Apollos as a paragon of all that was best in Greek culture. Had ever such a logical mind walked the earth before? What an insight into the beauty of relationships between simple shapes had been provided by Euclid. How amazing that every triangle was associated with families of circles which passed through its vertices or touched its sides or passed through special points of symmetry in the lines which bisected the angles of a triangle or which defined its heights. Yet here, before the great pyramids, Apollos' eyes drank in the evidence of geometric genius which predated Euclid by centuries, no not centuries but millenia, for the scholarship concentrated in the great library at Alexandria, reliably dated the pyramids as being built no less than two thousand years before.

But it was more than the geometric regularity of the pyramids which impressed Apollos. He was awestruck at their size. He had been told they were large, but it was not until he gazed up at the man-made mountains which dwarfed his mortal self into insignificance, that he had any realization of the vast scale of these remarkable edifices. And to think these had been made by men. What armies of slaves must have drudged, not just to pile these stones to so great a height, but to carve them from some distant quarry, to transport them to this site, to dress the faces and define the angles of these vast building blocks, and then locate them with such precision, to produce the regular geometric shapes at which Apollos now marvelled. All this had been done at temperatures which would make even light manual work extremely arduous. Alexandria was a warm city, but the Mediterranean breezes afforded some protection against the extremes of continental temperature variation. Although not so many miles from Alexandria, Apollos had found the summer heat of Giza quite oppressive. The sun scorched down from a cloudless sky, baking the sand to temperatures which the touch of bare skin could not tolerate. The cooler sand in the shade of the rock against which Apollos now sheltered, gave him some relief against the discomfort of the unaccustomed heat. This distraction removed, Apollos was able to allow his mind to dwell on the monument he now beheld. The awesome size, the precise geometry, the intensive labour which had constructed the pyramids were all independently remarkable, but why were they there? Apollos' tutors had told him about the Zigurrats of Mesopotamia, the great palaces at Nineveh, the hanging gardens of Babylon, the Colossus that bestrode the harbour at Rhodes, so that even the greatest of ships could pass between his legs. However, none of these monuments to man's effort and ingenuity remained. Even the Colossus which had been built not so long ago by the ethnic group to which Apollos owed his affinity, had ignobly crumbled at the onslaught of an earthquake. The pyramids on the other hand, had stood since the dawn of recorded history, and as Apollos regarded them now, he felt sure they would stand to the end of time.

Apollos' tutors had told him why they were there. The pyramids had been built as tombs for the great Egyptian kings of long ago, the Pharaohs, Rameses and Amenhotep, Seti and Ammenemes. What made these men so different? How could any mortal be so special that the major part of the output of the then greatest nation on earth should be devoted to providing their Pharaoh with so splendid a tomb in which to lie in state till the appointed time to meet his God? Apollos realized that men are often motivated by subconscious driving forces, and Apollos considered that it was out of service to their God, rather than their king, that the Egyptians of ancient times laboured so assiduously to erect the pyramids. It is instinctive in man that this life is not the whole and is only part of human existence. It is instinctive in man that his eternal destiny is controlled by a being, immeasurably greater than himself. As they built the pyramids, the Egyptians were subconsciously reinforcing their inner conviction that this life was but a small part of the total human experience, and a greater being was there to receive them from decay to a more fulfilling existence beyond the grave. Apollos' thoughts were running along monotheistic lines. He realized that the ancient Egyptians, like his own people, worshipped a plethora of Gods. Apollos had been in Egyptian temples and stood before the huge polished statues of the Egyptian deities, the jackal-headed Anubis, the falcon-headed Horus. How impressive they had seemed in the silence and solemnity of those shrines. Outside they seemed totally irrelevant.

The ancient Pharaohs would no doubt, be prepared to meet Ra, the great Egyptian sun God. The Egyptian tradition held that Ra was born afresh every day as a baby, climbed to his Zenith of manhood at midday and reached old age in the evening, prior to his death at nightfall. Apollos' people, the Greeks, also worshipped the sun god, but the nature of Helios was different from Ra. Helios did not die at the end of every day's traverse from east to west, but sailed under the cover of night back to the starting point of his celestial journey to resume the cycle at day break. Apollos himself had been named after another Greek sun God, but one identified with sunlight, and the growth and fertility this promotes, rather than with the objective sun. From childhood, Apollos had been taught the legends of his own Gods. He had found them confusing, inconsistent and totally incredible. The Gods of the Romans were merely the Greek Gods in different guise. Apollos had studied the Egyptian Gods from the ancient writings at the Alexandrian library and found their associated legends to be no better than the superstitious beliefs of his own people. Their belief that each Pharaoh was a son of the sun god, Ra, rather than of the previous Pharaoh, was inconsistent with the Egyptian tables of the dynasties of their kings. Apollos had the instinctive conviction that there was a God, but his logical mind had rejected the polytheism and idolatry of his own people and the other imperial powers of antiquity. Guided by the wisest of his tutors, Jerahmeel, Apollos had become a Jew. The Jew's God, Jehovah, was credible. The history of the Jewish people provided ample evidence that this God worked with mighty power in the life of his nation. He was consistent. He provided ideals and a moral code to live by. If, as tradition had it, the pyramids were built by Jewish slaves, then knowledge of Jehovah not only predated the legends which gave rise to the Greek and Roman deities, but Jehovah was known even before the Gods of that most ancient of civilizations, the Egyptian's.

Apollos suddenly awakened from his contemplations. The shadow of the rock against which he sheltered, stretched before him so far, that Apollos could no longer see the broad ribbon of sand which had seemed like a burning plain during the afternoon, discouraging him from leaving his shade to approach the magnificent monuments which had fed Apollos' thoughts and provoked him to philosophise on the rationality of ancient religion. At those latitudes, the sun set quickly without affording the buffer of a lengthy twilight when preparations for nightfall can be made at a leisurely pace. Apollos rose to his feet. A few moments later he could see the first stars twinkling from a sky which a short while earlier had been a pale blue dome of light. Apollos looked eastwards and could just see the lights which indicated that the people of Giza were now returning home to prepare their evening meals. Apollos started to walk towards the town where he was staying at the better of the two inns which provided food and shelter for travellers. The soft sand which had radiated a scorching heat during the day, was now comfortably warm as it broke over the edges of Apollos' sandals onto his feet. As Apollos' eyes became accustomed to the increasing darkness, he could see beyond Giza, the lights from the Roman fort on the site which was later to become modern Cairo. Apollos peered in a south-easterly direction to see if he could make out the lights of the city of Memphis, at a distance of about fifteen miles. He could not make out with any certainty the location of that ancient metropolis. The air temperature had dropped rapidly over the last few minutes. Apollos gave a shiver and quickened his pace towards his lodging. He was well content that he had been able to both satisfy his long standing desire to see the pyramids, and to prove to his parents that he was fully capable of independently making journeys of some distance on his own. Tomorrow he would set out on the return journey to his native Alexandria.

2

Cambiades and Aspasia

Cambiades and Aspasia lived in a spacious villa in the Greek quarter of the city of Alexandria. Alexandria was then one of the most cosmopolitan cities of the ancient world. Its main communities were the indigenous Egyptians, the Jews and the Greeks. Latterly, a significant number of Romans had settled there to carry on the business of running the Empire of the then dominant power of the world. The Romans chose to live in villas, not dissimilar from that of Cambiades and Aspasia, located in the Greek quarter of the city, which they preferred to the less pretentious accommodation available in the Jewish and Egyptian sectors. Today, one sensed that Cambiades and Aspasia were both preoccupied. Cambiades fidgeted as he gazed out of the window on to the splendid view of the harbour to be had from the elevated site of his villa. Aspasia perpetually moved round the room, adjusting furniture and ornaments.

'Apollos promised he would be back on the 21st day of this month and it is now well on into the afternoon with not so much of a sign of him,' fretted Aspasia. 'You know that I was against the whole idea of him travelling all that distance alone. I knew that was the last I would ever see of my son as he left here with the Ethiopian caravan. No doubt he is now floating in the Nile with his throat cut if the crocodiles have not already eaten him,' she continued, exaggerating her unease to communicate some sense of anxiety to Cambiades. Cambiades never seemed to worry about anything!

Aspasia was a motherly kind of woman. She was somewhat portly, but was well dressed in clothes which were fashionable for Greek women of her age, and hence, looked elegant in spite of her weight. Apollos was the only child of Cambiades and Aspasia, and although this had brought him certain advantages, he was more in danger of being smothered by his over-protective, doting mother than contemporaries who came from larger family groups.

'If you're so sure he's not coming back, why are you fussing about everything being ready for his return?' answered her husband in an uncharacteristically irritated tone. The truth of the matter was that Cambiades was as anxious as Aspasia. Although it was not in his nature to signal his inmost feelings so plainly, Aspasia's restlessness was undermining Cambiades' attempt to maintain a calm front, regardless of his inner emotions. Cambiades was a handsome man in his late fifties. He had become wealthy through the cloth trade which had been his father's metier before him. Cambiades owned two large warehouses near the harbour at Alexandria, and also employed thirty or so Egyptians to work at his looms in another building in the Egyptian quarter of the city. Although enlightened enough not to make use of slave labour which could be bought from some of the Roman galleys which called into port, Cambiades took advantage of the fact that work was in sufficiently poor supply for the Egyptians, that he could pay low wages. To be fair to Cambiades, he paid his workers better than many of his competitors, but business was business, and he would not have been able to maintain his life style if he paid wages which eroded his profit margins to too great an extent. The fact that Cambiades was normally gentle and easy going owed much to his position of wealth and security.

Aspasia bit her lip at Cambiades' reply and carried on fussing about without continuing the conversation. Cambiades realized that he had spoken hastily through irritation and his reply to Aspasia with its taunt of illogicality was unfair. He tried to make amends.

'We know that Apollos is both sensible and capable,' he said. 'Now that he is in his mid-twenties, he has every right to travel as he sees fit without the need to feel he is being restricted by over-anxious parents. He assured us he would stay with the caravans as he journeyed from town to town.

No harm could come to him if he abided by what we both know to be his good common sense. After all, Memphis and Giza are not the other end of the world. They are merely a few miles down the river. Why, when I was barely out of my teens, I made much longer journeys than that, and a world of good it did me. In a few years, Apollos will have the responsibility of running the business. He won't have much opportunity for travel then. We have to let go, Aspasia, if Apollos is going to be able to grow up into the confident and independent man we want him to be. Mark my words, we will see him home, well before sunset.'

These words had a calming effect on Aspasia, and she ceased from her preoccupation with tidying and rearranging the furniture, to come and sit with Cambiades and look out over the harbour. Had there been a window which would enable a sighting to be made of the caravans as they travelled up from the south, she would probably have sat there, but no such view was available from their villa.

Cambiades and Aspasia were justifiably proud of their son. He was good looking, a fine athlete and an able scholar. However, Apollos' special accomplishment was his eloquence. He could marshall his ideas well and express himself so clearly that none could ever win an argument with him. He delighted in opportunities for public speaking. He was greatly admired, especially by the young women of both the Greek and Jewish communities with which he mixed. This had not really been good for Apollos. Thoroughly spoilt by his parents, fully aware of his gifts and beauty, Apollos had become a rather arrogant and conceited young man. Cambiades had not been pleased at Apollos' decision to become a Jew. While having nothing against any Jew in particular, Cambiades did not like the Jews in general because they had so often got the better of him in business deals. Cambiades was not a religious man, but he and Aspasia were part of the Greek set who worshipped at the Temple of Poseidon.

The Temple of Poseidon was a magnificent building appropriately sited on the Alexandrian sea front. Cambiades was too rational to believe in the Poseidon of mythology, son of Cronus, and brother of Zeus and Hades. However, there was obviously some great power which controlled the sea, at times causing it to rage in fierce storms, while at others, settling the sea into the calm and peaceful source of cooling breezes. Surely the God of the sea had shown his power in deciding crucial naval encounters, giving the emergent Greek nation victory over the Persian aggressors at Salamis, and again at Mycale. In more recent times, Poseidon had allowed Augustus to scatter Mark Anthony's fleet at Actium, so sealing the doom of Cleopatra and ending the Ptolemaic line which had ruled Egypt for three centuries. Thus, Egypt was now part of the Roman Empire, and the Romans were showing themselves to be more efficient administrators than the Ptolemies. A Roman prefect at Alexandria saw that Roman law was upheld and taxes were rendered unto Caesar. However, it was for cultural and social reasons, rather than out of any deference to the god who ruled the sea, that Cambiades identified with those who adhered to Poseidon. Perhaps the Greeks no longer held centre stage in world affairs, but they had a great tradition. Cambiades believed that Greeks of standing should identify with temples dedicated to Greek gods as a way of perpetuating that tradition.

From this it can be seen that Cambiades had no deeply religious motive for wishing Apollos to stand with him in the ritual deference offered up to Poseidon. It was just that by becoming a Jew, Apollos seemed to be turning his back on his own kind. However, to a doting father like Cambiades, Apollos could do no wrong, and Cambiades secretly thought that Apollos realized that he would achieve undoubted commercial advantages through being a Jew, when the time came for Apollos to run the family business. Such thoughts did Apollos a· grave injustice. Cambiades realized that much of the blame for his son's conversion to Judaism lay with himself, because he had hired Jerahmeel to be tutor to Apollos. Of all Apollos' tutors, Jerahmeel was the one most admired by Cambiades. He exuded an aura of peace and confidence. Every word he spoke had the ring of wisdom. He was the sort of person who inspired complete and utter trust in all who met or had dealings with him. He was the one tutor whom Apollos could not outstrip in mental agility, and was therefore, the only one who retained his respect. Small wonder that Apollos had become converted to the faith of Jerahmeel. As far as Cambiades was concerned, the only fault in Jerahmeel was that he was a Jew. However, Cambiades was not anti-semitic, and he was aware that potential commercial advantages might accrue in time as a result of Apollos being converted to the ethnic group which controlled the most influential trade rings in Alexandria. He was content to allow this consideration to outweigh any displeasure he may otherwise have felt, through cultural rather than religious reasons, at his son's conversion to a non-hellenistic faith.

Aspasia broke the silence as the couple sat and mused on their son during that summer's afternoon.

'I suppose Apollos' wish to travel and see the world of which he has only heard about must have been brought on by his being unlucky in love. I can't see what Apollos saw in the girl anyway!'

The girl referred to by Aspasia, was Demeter, daughter of Parmenion and Camporina, two friends of Cambiades and Aspasia of very long standing. The truth of the matter was that Aspasia could see very well what Apollos saw in Demeter. Words which would more accurately have conveyed Aspasia's sentiments as an over-doting mother, would have been an expression of incredulity that any girl should be so foolish as not to take the opportunity of forging a liaison with her son. Although Apollos could have had any young woman of his fancy, fate had decreed that the one woman he desired had no interest in him. Demeter had no great intellect. She was spoiled and conceited, but by the fashion of the day, she was very beautiful. Although her face was fairly expressionless, she had the features and figure which anyysculptor would gladly have used as a model if commissioned to create from marble, a goddess to become the focus of some Grecian shrine. Apollos' infatuation for Demeter was of an adolescent nature, although nonetheless, a powerful emotion that Apollos felt deeply. Demeter was aware that Apollos was handsome and clever, but he had no interest in the social events which were her delight, or the fine clothes that can prove a preoccupation for women of any culture. For her part, Demeter had no interest in listening to Apollos' learned monologues, and was bored with the philosophy and religious theories which constituted so much of Apollos' conversation. Although in many ways Demeter was a silly young woman, and Apollos was a clever young man, in this instance, Demeter's judgement was sound, and Apollos' youthful desire was foolish. Demeter and Apollos were not suited to make a life-long match.

Aspasia continued, 'Now that Demeter is soon to be betrothed and will leave Alexandria, Apollos will soon take his mind off her. That should put an end to his restlessness and this continuous desire to travel.'

This was merely wishful thinking on Aspasia's part.

'I have not the slightest doubt that Apollos will soon put Demeter to the back of his mind,' replied Cambiades, 'but that won't end his urge to travel. For years he has wanted to see great things in the world beyond Alexandria and we have continuously persuaded him to stay at home. It is largely our fault that the wanderlust is now so strongly embedded in him. We did promise him that if he could make this short journey alone to prove that he was a capable and self-sufficient traveller, able to plan his route and reach his destinations at the scheduled times, then he could make that tour which has been his ambition for the past four years.'

The tour to which Cambiades referred was a journey back to Greece, but not travelling the easy route by ship across the Mediterranean. Apollos wished to travel up the Eastern coast of the Mediterranean, through Judaea, where a visit to Jerusalem was a main objective. He planned to visit the Phoenician cities of Tyre and Sidon, and then pass through Asia Minor, the part of the Greek empire which had been the legacy of the Seleucids, as Egypt had been to the Ptolemies. Antioch in Pisidia was to be included in the itinerary before passing through the Balkans to visit the homeland of the Greeks, Macedonia and Thessaly, Achaia and Thrace. Apollos thrilled at the names of the great Greek cities, Athens and Sparta, Corinth and Thebes, which had cradled the birth of European civilization. How much he had read about the nation in which his own family was rooted. How he longed to go there himself to witness its sights and breathe its air, to walk through its cities and experience their atmosphere. Apollos had studied the history of his people. He enjoyed thinking on the epic battle at Marathon where a few hundred Greeks routed a vast Persian army. He mentally gloried in his knowledge of the decisive naval victory the Greeks had gained at Salamis. Apollos had charted the course of the Pelopennesian wars and the astounding campaign of conquest launched by Alexander the Great. Greek heroes like Lysander and Epaminondas, Leonidas and Alcibiades, were household words to Apollos. He had great regard for the Greek philosophers, Aristotle, Plato and Socrates. Apollos held the poet Homer in great esteem, as he did the men of maths and science his nation had raised up, especially Pythagoras and Archimedes. The Greek most revered by Apollos was the Athenian, Pericles. Oh, to tread the ground and savour the sights of the city where this paramount statesman held sway. Would the world ever again see his equal?

No, nothing could desist Apollos from returning to the source of the culture of which he was so proud, and Cambiades knew this full well.

'It is the strength of this desire in Apollos that gives me every confidence that he will make good his promise to return here before the day is out,' continued Cambiades. 'You know well that before leaving here, he had made a firm arrangement to accompany Jerahmeel the next time he journeyed to Judaea because he knows full well that we will not permit him to journey alone over that scale of distance. Mark my words Aspasia, Apollos will travel to Greece before the year is out. His wanderlust will not be sated until he has made this tour of his dreams!'

A commotion was heard in the room behind. A servant hurried into Cambiades and Aspasia's lounge to inform them that Apollos was back. The anxiety that had hung over the couple was immediately dispelled. They rushed into the room where Apollos had made his scheduled entrance to embrace their beloved son and to enjoy his raconteur's gift as he relayed to them his adventures en route, and the wondrous sights on which he had feasted his eyes since leaving them a month or so earlier.

3

A Soirée at the Home of Cambiades and Aspasia

A few days later, Apollos' return from his journey provided
the excuse for Cambiades and Aspasia to entertain friends
of the family at their home. For the most part, they were the
wealthy Greeks of that quarter of Alexandria who held in
common a nominal allegiance to the god, Poseidon. Some
of them had brought their grown-up children, young people
in their late teens and early twenties whose privileged home
background and leisured life-style had made them somewhat passive. They generally seemed to prefer sitting
round, listening to their elders talk, and sometimes contri-
buting themselves to the conversation, rather than sailing
boats round the Pharos or performing feats of strength and
agility at the stadium. The young men tired of the fact that
Apollos could easily outrun and outjump them, and those
who could out-throw him with shot, discus or javelin, were
of a lazy disposition and not prepared to put in the training
which would enable them to improve on their talents.

The only non-Greek at the gathering was Jerahmeel,
Apollos' tutor, who had the happy ability of commending
himself to any company. He was not a forceful man, and
fully prepared to hold his peace while others talked, but
when making his contribution to a conversation, he did so
with a clarity of expression which provided the evidence of
a very fine mind. When Jerahmeel resolved a point at issue
with words of wisdom which few ever chose to dispute, he
had a gentle manner too in making his points, so that no
previous speakers felt they had in any way been upstaged by
a cleverer man. Jerahmeel was therefore very welcome at
such gatherings where he functioned very much as a social
lubricant, obviating many a contentious issue which in

22

other company could have led to rancour and discord. Jerahmeel was tall, lithe and agile, but no longer a young man. His hair was grey and many would have estimated his age at approaching seventy, whereas in reality he had not quite turned sixty. Jerahmeel had travelled more than most of the Greeks in that gathering and this had given him an experience of the world which lent added weight to the words he spoke.

The neighbours of Cambiades and Aspasia, Parmenion and Camporina were also at the gathering. Their wealth was built on the spice and perfume trade. Parmenion had perfected formulae for preparing scents and soaps which were easily made from local materials and sold well in the market. Parmenion was therefore, well able to supply his younger daughter with toileteries which she used extravagently. Demeter's preoccupation with her beauty required an abundant supply of creams and soaps and cosmetics. Demeter was not at the gathering as she still had much to do in preparation for her betrothal party, which was soon to take place. However, Parmenion and Camporina were accompanied by their other daughter, Diana, a young woman some two years older than Demeter.

Diana contrasted strongly with her sister. She did not have the classical Greek features of Demeter, and by the standards of that society, was not considered a beauty. No one entertained romantic notions about Diana in the way they did about Demeter. Standards of beauty are a fickle measure, changing at the whim of those whom societies are prepared to cast in the role of Paris to be the arbiters of feminine loveliness. In another day, another age, it might have been Diana and not Demeter who was deemed to epitomise beauty. However, the identi-kit picture used by the Alexandrian Greeks to define feminine attractiveness fitted Demeter and not Diana. Whereas Demeter had had suitors in plenty, none had paid court to Diana.

The absence of romance in her life mattered very little to Diana. Unlike her languid sister, Diana was a very active and positive person. She took a great interest in things and in people. She conversed well and freely. She took special delight in things that were small, and in detail which many would overlook. Whenever her parents bought anything for her, Diana had always responded with genuine and unaffected delight, no matter how inexpensive the gift. Demeter was so often off-hand in the manner in which she received presents. Diana was very much involved in helping her mother run the house. She was aware of the material privileges she enjoyed, and was involved in the charitable works to which wealthy people with a social conscience who live in a society where poverty is evident, are invariably called. None of the Greek young men who were her contemporaries held attraction for Diana, and Diana had no particular wish for marriage.

Had Diana been strictly honest with herself, she would have had to admit that Apollos was a young man for whom she felt some admiration. The fact that he was handsome did not weigh heavily with Diana, but she was impressed with his mind, his intellectual honesty and the very special power of oratory which Apollos delighted in displaying whenever the occasion arose. However, Diana was mature in her judgement. Apollos had many serious faults. His conceit and arrogance were perhaps the result of his being over-indulged by his parents, but there was something more disturbing. Apollos was religious without being good! He had come to the conviction that the Greek deities were worthless and that Jehovah of the Jews was the only credible God, purely as a result of his own rationalism. He had been helped in this process by Jerahmeel who had been delighted to see his gifted protegé adopt his faith, but Apollos' faith was experienced at head rather than heart level. It did not impinge very much on the way Apollos lived his life or behaved towards others. Like most spoilt children, Apollos had an evident selfish streak in his make-up. Diana considered these to be faults Apollos had derived from his environment, especially his home background, and believed they would be cured as he reached an age of greater maturity. His intellect, his gift of oratory, his enquiring mind on the other hand, were rare, congenital gifts, and there was no one in Alexandrian society, save perhaps the ageing Jerahmeel, who had in any similar measure, these divinely bestowed attributes. Diana's regard for Apollos was a secret she kept firmly locked in her own mind. She knew that he was besotted with her sister. She was aware that Apollos had no romantic interest in her. Indeed, Diana believed that she had no romantic interest in Apollos either, and that their relationship was what we might describe today as Platonic friendship. It is likely that Diana thought this way, merely to conceal from herself her depth of feeling for a young man who, although selfish, was undoubtedly, very special.

Mention needs to be made of one other person present at that gathering because of his crucial contribution to the outcome of later events. Anaxagoras was a humble shop keeper. He sold mainly household wares, pots and pans, brushes and lamps, nails and wood, oils suitable for both cooking and for fuelling the types of lamp in common use at the time. Anaxagoras must almost have seemed a hanger-on in that company. He was not a prominent member of the Poseidon cult. Unlike Jerahmeel, he had no intellectual graces to contribute to that society. Being a bachelor in his early forties, there were no family connections which would link Anaxagoras with the group assembled at the home of Cambiades and Aspasia. Anaxagoras was a very big man. Big men are not necessarily clumsy, or indeed strong, but Anaxagoras was both of these. That evening, Anaxagoras had already knocked over a fully laden table and spilt a jar of wine. This was a common enough sort of occurrence whenever Anaxagoras was around, and was indeed a community joke. One might have expected Anaxagoras to have been shunned as a guest by Alexandrian hostesses, but he would invariably be invited to such gatherings. His clumsiness often led to an event which injected levity into gatherings which were becoming far too solemn, and they always provided a distraction from some small failing or oversight that the host family may have made in preparing to entertain friends. Anaxagoras' clumsiness of body was also reflected in a clumsiness of speech. Anaxagoras had that unhappy knack of saying the wrong thing at the wrong time. Occasionally it caused embarrassment, but usually mirth. Why then should this apparent social misfit be so commonly found in fashionable Alexandrian company?

The truth of the matter was that Anaxagoras was extremely well liked. He was one of those very genuine, very honest persons, completely lacking in any form of malice, always ready to help out when difficulties arose, regardless of the inconvenience to himself. Many in that company had been glad of Anaxagoras' services when someone of exceptional strength was required to meet an emergency. When wheels had fallen off wagons, Anaxagoras had often been able to bodily lift the wagon until supports could be found to place under it in preparation for inserting a new axle and remounting the wheel. He had lifted looms which had fallen on workers, threatening to crush them and rescued animals from collapsed barns. Anaxagoras had also been available for less spectacular jobs, when no great strength was needed, but just a helpful neighbour who was on hand to give assistance when emergencies arose. Always cheerful, always reliable, Anaxagoras had a special contribution to make to that society.

As the company gathered and settled down to eat, conversation naturally turned to Apollos' recent journey. This was nothing terribly spectacular or exciting, but Apollos had the gift of describing every last detail of what had happened in an amusing and interesting way. He described with much embroidery and elaboration, how a dispute as to which caravan a particular camel belonged had been settled by getting the camel to identify his master from the rival claimants. He described in such graphic detail, the relative merits of the available inns in Giza that the company rocked with laughter and declared that if they had to journey south, they would avoid Giza and stay at Memphis. Those who had actually been to Giza knew that Apollos spoke with only slight exaggeration. The climax of Apollos' account was his description of the pyramids which he was able to embellish with interesting historical perspective, of which only Jerahmeel in that company would have been previously aware.

Conversation then turned to other things. The women left the company as the food was cleared away by the servants and met in their group while the men gravely considered a current cause for concern in Alexandria. Refuse from a tannery was polluting water in a canal which had been dug from the Nile aqueduct to water the homes and farms of Egyptians who had no other direct access to fresh water. The canal had served this purpose for centuries. The tannery was fairly new. The homes being affected were Egyptian and the tannery was Greek. The parties in the dispute had come close to blows but so far, no violence had erupted. The Greeks who owned the tannery belonged to the cult who worshipped Gannymede, and the snobbery of the Greek social system placed them in a lower class than those who worshipped Poseidon at the magnificent sea-front temple. The distinction of Greek cults was not appreciated by the Egyptians. They regarded the canal issue as yet another example of the Greek classes exploiting their poorer Egyptian neighbours, a source of friction which had existed from the time that Ptolemy had inherited the Kingdom of Egypt from Alexander.

At that gathering, it was generally agreed that the Greeks should give way and respect the Egyptians' ancient water rights. However, it was pointed out that none of them had any influence with the followers of Gannymede, and a series of anecdotes was recounted which generally cast discredit on the Gannymede cult. Jerahmeel, who was the only one who could claim to be completely neutral to the dispute, counselled that the Greeks should collect together enough money to enable their compatriots to move their tannery to a less contentious site. He knew that such a measure was well within the financial means of that company. However, the company failed to appreciate the potential danger of this situation escalating and they discussed all sorts of other remedies which would not hit their pockets. Ultimately, this was a problem that the Greeks of the Gannymede cult should solve and the company gathered at Cambiades' house decided that they had no direct responsibility to settle the matter.

The soirée drew to a close, and Cambiades and Aspasia's guests returned to their homes, satisfied they had spent an enjoyable and profitable evening together. As he left and thanked his hosts for a most pleasant evening, Jerahmeel complimented Apollos on his account of his trip to the pyramids. He asked Apollos to make a special point of being at the synagogue meeting on the sabbath, then bade him farewell.

4

Sandas-cum-Barama

Apollos made his way to the synagogue in the Hebron district of Alexandria. The Hebron district was one of many similar areas in the Jewish quarter of Alexandria. Each district had its own synagogue. The Hebron synagogue was the one with which Jerahmeel had special associations. It was to the rabbis at this synagogue that Jerahmeel had introduced Apollos when in his late teens. Apollos was then struggling to find a religion which satisfied the spiritual aspect of his life, having rejected Poseidon and all other gods of the Greeks as mere folly. It had been hard for Apollos to come to terms with the fact that his own people, the Greeks, who had contributed more to the knowledge of the human race than any other civilization on earth, had remained immature and superstitious in the matter of religion. The Jews on the other hand had discovered the true God, or as they would have claimed, had been chosen by Him, and their contribution to the human race, their rational system of laws, their music, their poetry had all been inspired and born from the special relationship with their God, the one and only God. The Jews did not have a history which could boast of great territorial expansion as the other great powers of antiquity, the Assyrians, the Babylonians, the Persians and the Greeks, or indeed, the Romans who were now rapidly establishing an empire which looked likely to be the greatest yet. On the other hand, the Jews had a resilience, a cohesion, a sense of divine purpose which had enabled them to maintain an identity as a people of some significance from the dawn of civilization, while other nations had waxed to a spectacular zenith, and then crumbled as their military might failed and their empires dissolved. The Jews unashamedly attributed the persistence of their nation to their relationship with Jehovah, the one true God, and it seemed as if they would remain as a special and distinct people to the end of human history.

Apollos had not readily been accepted as a proselyte to the Jewish faith. Judaism was, strangely, not a religion which actively sought converts. The obstacles placed by the rabbis to Apollos becoming accepted as a full member of the synagogue, only served as a challenge to make the young man more assiduous in his study, and Apollos had a great capacity for this. The truth of the matter was that he very quickly threatened to outstrip even the rabbis in his knowledge of the faith and the Jewish scriptures. The rabbis could not fail to be impressed by this candidate for Jewish status, and with the influential backing of Jerahmeel, Apollos was admitted to the faith. He was now a Jew of some standing, a recognized scholar at the synagogue, and his oratorial gifts made him a popular speaker at its meetings.

Apollos arrived in good time for the synagogue meeting and was greeted by Dathan Barjoseph, the President, as he entered the building. The Hebron quarter of the city could not boast of the splendid houses and villas to be found in the predominently Greek suburbs like the one in which Apollos lived. The synagogue was an unpretentious but neat and well appointed building which nestled in well with the environment of small Jewish houses and shops which constituted Hebron. Jerahmeel arrived a short while later accompanied by a dark skinned African in spotless white robes. This African, or more precisely, this Ethiopian, was well known in Alexandria. He was Sandas-cum-Barama, the travelling ambassador of the Candace, as the Queen of Ethiopia was known. Sandas was a grave looking man, well respected in the lands and cities where his diplomatic missions led him. He was indeed a diplomat of some distinction, following a line of diplomats who had been able to curb the desire of the imperial powers of the ancient world to expand their territory beyond the southernmost frontiers of Egypt. Preservation of national territorial integrity by diplomatic means was no mean feat in those days where military might was right, and proud generals and emperors would take their armies wherever they were confident they could crush military opposition. Ethiopia however, had maintained its independent national status for centuries.

Sandas was not a Jew, but he was welcome as a guest at this synagogue, not just because of his status as a prominent international statesman, but because he showed special interest and understanding of the Jewish faith. For some centuries, the nation of Ethiopia had sought to share the special spiritual knowledge of the Jews without committing the country to undergo complete proselytisation to the Jewish faith.

The worship at the synagogue followed its usual form, and at the set time, Dathan Barjoseph introduced Jerahmeel to speak to the congregation of fifty or so devout and sincere Jews gathered in that place.

Jerahmeel began, 'You know how I have told you that on my last visit to Judaea, there was a buzz that once again, great prophets were bringing the word of the Lord to his people. I went to the Jordan and witnessed the activities of one called John who was roughly clothed in goat and camel hides.[1] He warned of wrath to come and he baptized in the river, those who responded to his message. I journeyed to Galilee where I witnessed a Nazarene called Jesus performing great miracles. This Jesus spoke words of wisdom of which I never heard the like before. Five days ago, I met Sandas-cum-Barama, whom you all know well. Sandas was paying his duty visit to the Roman consulate here in Alexandria, which is his custom as he returns from his diplomatic missions to Judaea, Syria and the provinces in Asia Minor. I will take up no more of your time, for I want you to hear the news that Sandas brings back with him from Judaea.'

Jerahmeel sat down and Sandas rose to his feet and slowly and deliberately walked to the front of the assembly. He turned and faced the congregation upon which a hush had fallen as all leaned forward, listening expectantly for what Sandas would have to say. Sandas, ever the master of presence, paused for several seconds before he started to speak, and then addressed the assembly with a solemnity

30

which was characteristic of this phlegmatic Ethiopian, his rich mellow voice reverberating through that building.

'It is well known among your people that since the days of our Candace, whom you know as the Queen of Sheba, we in Ethiopia have been beholden to your nation for sharing with us great wisdom. The Queen of Sheba visited your King Solomon to avail herself of the wisdom for which he was famed, and she was not disappointed. Since that time emissaries from my country have visited yours to learn of your wise men and prophets, and to read your holy books. As one of the most senior, most experienced members of the Ethiopian court, I now have the privilege to be the Candace's travelling ambassador, and this office carries the charge that I must visit your country to learn more of your nation's wisdom, and bring this wisdom to my own people. We have studied and learnt from the wisdom of other nations, the sages of Edom, the philosophers of the Greeks, the lawgivers like Hammurabi, King of Babylon, but the wisdom of your people is different. It is not the wisdom born of the minds of men, it is the wisdom of God. This wisdom can sometimes seem like folly to those who will not wait and meditate on deeper meanings from divine messages which must be carefully considered before they can be comprehended.

'I have often heard your God speaking to me as I read and meditate on your holy books. Sometimes, that message fills me with immediate joy. Sometimes, the message hurts and pains me, but I am ever conscious of your God, using both experiences of joy and pain, of hope and despair, to build me up and bring me closer to him, to draw my mind into line with his own, and to show me great and wondrous mysteries.

'As I journeyed from Judaea on my way here to Egypt, I read words from the prophet Isaiah which I did not understand, but which caused me pain.

"Like a sheep that is taken to be slaughtered,
like a lamb that makes no sound when its wool
   is cut off,
he did not say a word.
He was humiliated, and justice was denied
   him.

31

> No one will be able to tell about his descen-
> dants,
> because his life on earth has come to an end."[2]

'The thing that has caused me pain through my life is that I shall have no descendants, no progeny to continue my name and enjoy my heritage. Here am I, one of the most highly ranked and esteemed individuals of my nation, but because of my office, because I have authority above other men, because I am in charge of the treasure of my Queen and the financial affairs of my nation, I am made a eunuch to hold that responsibility. My nation follows this practice because it still has much wisdom to learn in the ways of running its affairs. Thus, as your God spoke to me through the words of his prophet, of one who would have no descendants, he caused me pain.'

A tear trickled down Sandas' ebony cheek, but strangely it did not seem the tear of sadness, but the tear of great emotion. Sandas continued,

'As I rode on that desert road to Gaza, apparently quite alone, and knowing that God was speaking to me through these words, but not understanding what their meaning was, I cried aloud for a messenger to be sent to bring me an interpretation. A man of whose presence I had been hitherto unaware, came up to my chariot and spoke to me. He was a man of your own people, a man with gentle countenance and gracious in conversation. His name was Philip.[3] He told me that the words I had read from the prophet Isaiah had been fulfilled by one he called his friend, a prophet like no other prophet before. This prophet had taught his people, he had performed great signs among them, and he had not married or had children. He had not been made a eunuch by men as I had, but spiritually, he had become a eunuch of his own volition for the sake of the Kingdom of Heaven. He would have a progeny, but not born of his body. This prophet's progeny would be born of the Spirit conveyed by his words.

'Philip told me that this prophet's name was Jesus, a name meaning, "I will save my people". Philip shared with me some of the wonderful things that this Jesus had taught. He told me that this Jesus had been unjustly put to death

32

through the machinations of your own chief priests in Jerusalem, fulfilling part of the prophecy of Isaiah that I had been reading. With joy in his face, Philip told me that this had all been in accordance with God's plan, and that Jesus had risen from the dead after three days. Philip had seen and met him. This Jesus was none other than God's Son who returned to his Father forty days later, but before he returned, he commissioned his disciples to tell all people that he had died to take the world's sins upon himself, so that all who believed this and gave their allegiance to him, would themselves rise from the dead into his Kingdom which is in another world.

'Philip spoke with such conviction. He had clearly been sent by God to meet me there on the Gaza road, for there could be no other explanation for this coincidence. There and then I decided that this Jesus should be my King, not as Candace is my Queen, but King to rule my thoughts and guide my mind, a King to receive me to himself when this life is done. I asked what I should do to demonstrate my allegiance to this King, and Philip said that I should be baptized in the name of God the Father of this Jesus, in the name of Jesus, son of God, and in the name of the invisible Spirit of God, who was there with us then, guiding our conversation and actions. At that moment another remarkable coincidence occurred. On that desert road, it had not rained for months, but at that very moment, we found a pool of the clearest, most refreshing water I have ever seen. Philip baptized me in that water, and then he was taken from me but the Spirit of whom Philip spoke remained with me. The Spirit cleansed and reorientated my thoughts. Who am I to wish for sons and daughters when my new master Jesus had none, but those born by the Spirit? I will have progeny, and they too will be those the Spirit gives me through the words he enables me to speak. I pray that the words I have spoken tonight will commend this Jesus to you, so that you too may decide to serve him as your King, and so embrace the hope of eternal life.'

Sandas returned to his place and Dathan Barjoseph brought the meeting to a close. The gathering was subdued as they bade courteous farewells to Sandas-cum-Barama. Jerahmeel conducted Sandas back to his lodgings and then returned to discuss the implications of what Sandas had said with Dathan and the senior members of the synagogue who remained behind.

Sandas' words had received a very mixed reception. A few considered that as Sandas himself was not a Jew, he had no understanding of the traditions of the Jewish faith, and his words were best forgotten. On the other hand, many present had been strangely moved as Sandas had spoken with such evident conviction and sincerity, and they wanted to know more of this prophet, this Jesus, who was reputed to have returned from the grave. One present had independently heard this news from a friend who worshipped at a synagogue in another part of Alexandria. This synagogue had also been recently visited by another traveller from Judaea. That traveller had been no Ethiopian, but a fellow Jew of good standing at his synagogue.

'We have a great problem,' said Dathan, 'because if this Jesus is the Messiah, and that, I think, is the unmistakable implication of Sandas' message, then he must be endorsed as such by the High Priests in Jerusalem. If they put him to death, they will scarcely do that.'

Some discussion then followed but without reaching any conclusion. The synagogues in lands away from Judaea tended to ascribe greater authority to the Jerusalem High Priests in matters of religion than did those in the Judaean homelands. However, all present were sufficiently well versed in their scriptures to know that infallibility was not a High Priestly attribute.

'As you know,' concluded Jerahmeel, 'young Apollos and I are soon to visit Judaea. We will see what we can learn of this Jesus and bring you news on our return.'

It was by now very late. The oil was beginning to fail in the lamps which had been lit some hours earlier. With the customary hugs and declaration of 'Shalom, peace be with you', the meeting dispersed and each returned to his own home.

5

The Betrothal Party

A week or so after the portentous revelations of Sandas at the Synagogue of Hebron, a very different sort of social gathering was held at the home of Parmenion and Camporina. The occasion was to celebrate Demeter's betrothal. It was an event from which Apollos would rather have absented himself, but that would only have looked like sour grapes. Apollos dutifully attended the celebration with his parents. Apollos was not the only rejected suitor present, for Demeter had been much sought after by the handsome young Greeks who were Apollos' contemporaries, by virtue of her fashionable beauty. However, Demeter's choice had fallen on a Roman, none other than the young Prefect of Alexandria who was the senior Roman administrator in the City. It had every appearance of being a splendid match. Claurinius, who was not yet thirty, had risen to a post of this seniority, thanks largely to the influence his father wielded in the Roman senate. A glittering career lay ahead for Claurinius.

It is unnecessary to inform the reader that Apollos did not like Claurinius. It is rare to find rejected lovers who like their successful rivals. Although there was so much about Apollos which made him attractive to the other sex, Claurinius had other advantages to which Apollos could not aspire. As a Roman, Claurinius was seen as a dashing young officer in the most successful army of all time. He cut a handsome figure in his Roman armour and extravagantly plumed helmet, his scarlet cloak streaming behind him as he strode imperiously through the colonnaded rooms of the Roman administrative centre in Alexandria, which had previously been one of Ptolemy's palaces. He spoke with the easy self-confidence of one who regarded himself as an influential member of the master race. His conversation often turned to Gaul or Germania, where he had been for a very short period before his posting to Alexandria. Claurinius spoke in such a way that his hearers would derive the impression that he had been responsible for many great military victories against the barbarian hordes that had annihilated Varus' legions some twenty years earlier. The truth of the matter was that Claurinius had never wielded a sword in earnest on the battlefield. His role had been more in the nature of a field officer who organized signals and dispatches.

However, Claurinius had done well as an administrator in Alexandria. There were tensions between Greeks and Egyptians, between Greeks and Jews, and between Jews and Egyptians, which Claurinius had been able to avert from developing into anything serious enough to suggest that Alexandria was in any way a disorderly metropolis. There was no need therefore for his seniors in Rome to have any disquiet about the efficient way in which Claurinius had administered the City. In a few days, Claurinius would be leaving Alexandria with his bride to be, for Rome, where he was to hold a commission in the Praetorian Guard. If he fulfilled his duties well, he could soon expect promotion, and who could say to what position he might rise. Sejanus, who had until recently been the commander of the Praetorian Guard, had been tipped by many to become the next emperor. However, Sejanus had foolishly tried to accelerate his promotion by taking unscrupulous and devious actions. This led to his downfall. It remained to be seen whether Claurinius would rise to become Commander of the elite Praetorian Guard, and if he would have learnt from the error of Sejanus' ways as he climbed young ambition's ladder.

The occasion of Demeter and Claurinius' betrothal was an enormous social success. Claurinius arrived with some fellow officers clothed in their traditional Roman togas. Although arrogant in uniform, off duty, these young men made good and jovial company on this occasion. Wine flowed freely. Anaxagoras was there, inadvertantly adding to the mirth. Although few could laugh when he told the latest in-jokes about Tiberius Caesar while in the company of the emissaries of Rome, it was a different matter when he grabbed at the curtains to save himself as he tripped up over a carelessly placed cushion, and several guests became enveloped in the falling velvet as the curtain rail became dislodged from its supports.

The usual speeches were made. Camporina wept and embraced her daughter, so soon to leave for Rome where the full wedding would take place in the Imperial splendour of the capital. Claurinius knew that his parents would have probably preferred him to take a Roman bride, but he knew Demeter would commend herself to them very well. He had an instinct for recognizing a woman with the decorative qualities that would make a successful hostess in Roman society. The ability to entertain lavishly was an essential accomplishment for any who had ambitions to climb to positions of eminence in the Roman establishment. Romans like Claurinius' parents also had a special regard for the Greeks. This admiration was not based on the fact that the Greeks had had a history and tradition of being a great warrior nation. The Etruscans, the Carthaginians and the Gauls were peoples, who like the Greeks, had been overcome by Roman might. Like the Greeks, these nations also had great traditions as being great warriors, but these nations had contributed very little of culture to the world. The Greeks on the other hand had contributed to the knowledge and art of the world on a scale that Rome could never hope to emulate, in spite of her undoubted military might.

As the evening drew on, Apollos found himself sitting next to Diana, and he suggested that they should go out to enjoy the cooler night air. They walked up to the higher ground behind their houses and looked out over the harbour. Although it was night, light from the Pharos on the little island just beyond the shore, illuminated the boats moored in the harbour, and the night fishing vessels could be seen plying the inshore waters. Diana and Apollos spoke of the magnificence of the Pharos which Ptolemy had had built to enable Alexandrian waters to be safely navigated. Then their conversation turned to other things. They spoke of Apollos' recent visit to the pyramids and of the ancient

Pharaohs. They talked about his coming tour of the lands of the Eastern Mediterranean and his destination, Greece, the homeland of their common culture. On all subjects raised, Diana could talk as easily and fluently as Apollos. Here was a young woman whose intellect matched Apollos' own, or one might say, exceeded it, for Diana's intellect balanced book knowledge with a common sense which Apollos lacked at that stage in his life.

Then, in an entirely unpremeditated moment, they made love. Diana had not until that time, recognized the strength of the feelings she had for Apollos which she had suppressed for so long. The discomfort she felt as a virgin lover was insignificant in the joy and peace she felt at being able to give herself to one she had admired, and indeed, secretly loved, for so long. It was different for Apollos. He fantasized that it was Demeter and not Diana that he was holding in his arms.

Oh, foolish girl to give, not just her love, but herself, to one with so little promise of commitment to her. Foolish, foolish girl to depart from the prudence that had hitherto been a hallmark of her life, and which had served to give her control over her own destiny.

Oh, foolish young man to abuse the love that was being given to him, by filling his mind with thoughts of another who could never be for him. Foolish, foolish young man to fail to recognize that he held in his arms, a pearl of great price. Apollos would never again find a woman who was Diana's equal, and yet he was using her as he had used women of the street before, and this time he did not have to pay for his pleasure.

Apollos and Diana remained, lying on the bank overlooking the harbour for about half an hour. Then they returned to Diana's home. The last guests were on the point of departing. Apollos and Diana had not been missed. Apollos kissed Diana and then walked the short distance back to his own home.

6

Departure for the Grand Tour

While Diana slept the peaceful sleep that night of one who had experienced great emotional relief in self giving, Apollos' was fitful and restless. While the fact that Demeter was now irretrievably lost to him, caused him mental pain, he had had ample opportunity to prepare himself to bear this disappointment. Although selfish, Apollos was not without conscience, and his conscience was undoubtedly disturbed by the knowledge that he had abused a family friend for whom he had no romantic feelings, but who had shown that she held him in considerable affection.

The next day when Apollos and Diana again met, Apollos could see even more clearly, the affection that Diana felt for him. Apollos also knew that Diana was pregnant. How could Apollos know this? Diana herself did not suspect this, and would have no reason to for a month or so. Did Apollos have prophetic insight? More likely, his conscience was causing him to be irrational.

Apollos considered the consequences of Diana's pregnancy. In that society of high class, respectable Greeks, he would be expected to marry the girl. That would spell the end of his cherished wish to visit the Greek homeland of his ancestors. Apollos cursed his foolishness at taking advantage of an innocent young woman to relieve the mental and emotional tensions he had felt the previous night. He should have paid for the services of one who would professionally know how to avoid such consequences. Apollos' mind remained cast in a selfish mould and he decided that he would make arrangements with Jerahmeel to depart within the month for this grand tour on which he had set his heart.

Jerahmeel was surprised when Apollos approached him about being prepared to commence this tour so soon after returning from his trip to the pyramids, but it suited Jerahmeel well to depart as soon as possible. Since Sandas-cum-Barama had addressed the gathering at the Hebron synagogue, Jerahmeel had experienced an inner urge to return to Judaea to discover at the roots the significance of the events of which Sandas had spoken, and to ascertain their affect on the Jewish people. Jerahmeel therefore agreed with Apollos that he would be ready to leave in a fortnight.

Cambiades and Aspasia were rather shocked when Apollos announced to them his intention. Aspasia became very emotional at the prospect of her beloved son leaving so soon, especially as he had only just returned from his first major trip away from home. That trip had only involved an absence of a few weeks, but this tour would last at least two years. Cambiades, calm and rational as ever, comforted Aspasia with the argument that the sooner Apollos left, the sooner he would be back with his wanderlust sated, ready to settle down to take his share of the responsibility in running the family business. Cambiades dissuaded Aspasia from her conviction that she would be witnessing her son depart, never to set eyes on him again. Cambiades and Aspasia had witnessed the young warriors muster to depart for battles to be fought in distant realms. How Cambiades and Aspasia had felt for the parents of these young men, departing from their homeland in the prime of life, for the prospects of again seeing their sons were poor. However, Apollos' departure was different. Apollos was not departing as a warrior to face dangers in battle. Roman rule had brought peace and stability to the lands bordering the Mediter-ranean, and now was as safe a time as any to travel. The thought with which Cambiades was finally able to calm Aspasia's fretful state was the fact that Apollos was being accompanied on this journey by Jerahmeel. Yes, Jerahmeel was sensible, wise and shrewd, a seasoned traveller who held the respect of all who knew him. Apollos would be safe with Jerahmeel as travelling companion and guide.

The preparations were soon made. Although they could have afforded to take a horse each, Jerahmeel advised against this.

'Although progress may be slower on foot,' he counselled, 'you see much more. Horses can give rise to so many inconveniences. They are expensive to feed and stable, and if they go lame, they are a considerable liability.'

This advice was sound. Apollos was in no hurry to cover great tracts of ground. He wanted to feel free to see things at a leisurely pace. He would enjoy the exercise of walking. There were mountains he wished to climb, and horses can only be taken up fairly gentle hills. So it was, they departed without horses, knowing that the extra physical effort they would have to put into making their journeys would be more than compensated for by the convenience and freedom they would experience if unencumbered with beasts. Jerahmeel obtained letters of introduction from Dathan Barjoseph, the president of the Hebron synagogue. Both Apollos and Jerahmeel could be unhesitatingly endorsed as able scholars and speakers who could be relied upon to bring a message of wisdom or scholarship to any synagogue they might visit. Jerahmeel knew that this ability would provide the pair of them with many free meals and good night's lodging.

The day came for their departure. The first part of the journey would be made on one of the boats which sailed along the Mediterranean coast, saving Apollos and Jerahmeel the problem of crossing the many distributaries which traversed the Nile delta, had they chosen to travel east from Alexandria by a land route. Many family friends and members of the Hebron synagogue came to give the couple a good send off. Predictably, Aspasia wept. Diana felt pangs of sadness as she saw them depart, but at the same time, she experienced an inner peace as she knew the Apollos she loved was going to fulfil the dream of his life.

The small boat left the harbour. Apollos and Jerahmeel knew the master quite well. They had paid him to take them as far as Gaza.

7

The Desert Inn

The small boat tacked in an easterly direction, sailing parallel to the Egyptian coast. The current created as the Nile discharged its waters from numerous distributaries into the sea, forced the boat away from the land, but the master steered the boat so that the coastal villages which had grown up along the flat lands of the Nile delta remained in sight. The only other passengers on this small boat were an Arab merchant and two Roman soldiers who were probably bearing dispatches to garrisons in the Roman provinces on the eastern shore of the Mediterranean. Apollos lounged back on the cushions the boat's master had laid out on the deck for the comfort of his passengers, enjoying the warmth of the sun and the sense that he had embarked on what he anticipated to be the greatest experience of his life.

The whole of the first day of this sea journey was taken up in traversing the sea front of the Nile delta. Then the coast line took on a very different character. It was virtually uninhabited and rather more rugged. In the distance, the hills of the northern part of the Sinai peninsular could just be made out against the blue sky. Jerahmeel spent the time in giving Apollos as much advice as he could on the art of safe travelling.

'The great secret is not so much to have the resourcefulness to get out of difficulties when they arise, but rather, to have the foresight and instinct to anticipate and elude any dangers before they are encountered,' he solemnly advised. 'Always take the opportunity of filling your water flask with fresh water whenever this is available, and if any occasion arises when we have to separate, we must be sure always to arrange a place and time to rendezvous. Our money will last longer if we accept any offers of hospitality from the faithful at the synagogues we will attend on our journeys, but on the occasions when we have to stay at an inn, it is not necessarily good policy to put up at the cheapest hostelry around.'

This latter piece of advice Apollos could readily endorse from his limited experience of travel for a few miles down the Nile.

After three days, the boat arrived at a village on the coast, just outside Gaza. After thanking the master and paying their dues, Apollos and Jerahmeel made their way into the garrison town of Gaza. Apollos was glad to be on firm ground again, but was disappointed in Gaza. Compared with Alexandria, Gaza was a dirty and smelly place. The streets were not well laid out and the buildings were generally in a poor state of repair. Even the religious buildings did scant credit to the gods they professed to honour. The temples to the Greek and Roman gods were made of cracked, discoloured marble and the synagogues were scarcely distinguishable from poor quality dwelling houses. Only the Star of David above the portal identified Jewish places of worship. The most impressive shrine was the temple dedicated to the worship of Dagon, the Philistine deity, but even this was in need of repair. Jerahmeel and Apollos speculated on how far this edifice might have resembled the one which Samson had pulled down upon the mocking Philistine nobility as the final suicidal act of a tragic life.[4]

As evening was drawing in, our travellers had no alternative but to stay in Gaza. They found an inn on the outskirts of the city which, although noisy, was considerably cleaner than the ones in the town centre, and they arranged to eat and sleep the night there. They talked about how they would continue their journey as they enjoyed their evening meal. Apollos had assumed that they would follow a coastal route up to Ashdod, before cutting inland to reach Jerusalem, but Jerahmeel had other ideas. He did not think Apollos would benefit much from touring the cities founded by the Philistines, and planned to take a longer and more difficult route which involved travelling inland from Gaza across the Shephelah to the Negeb, where they would stay at Beersheba before heading north through the hill country of Judah. This route would enable Apollos and Jerahmeel to visit some of the towns which had been famous in the history of the Jewish people, as the pair made their way to Jerusalem. Apollos was glad to fall in with Jerahmeel's experience and knowledge of the area. Apollos was to learn much more of Jerahmeel's travel lore over the next few days.

After they had paid the Gaza innkeeper the following morning, our two travellers spent a little time looking round Gaza. The Gaza which Apollos and Jerahmeel now surveyed, was probably a few kilometres away from the site of the Gaza which had featured in Jewish history. This early city had long since been destroyed. Apollos was quite interested in looking at the sights of the town and felt confirmed in his view that this place compared unfavourably with his native Alexandria. Jerahmeel who had been there before was more interested in the bustle of the market centre where he entered into conversation with one or two stall holders and farmers who had driven cattle into town to sell. From these interchanges, Jerahmeel had picked up the fact that a small caravan would be leaving late morning for Gerar, a town about fifteen miles inland.

'It's always best travelling in company in these parts if the opportunity comes up.' Jerahmeel wisely advised Apollos. Thus, before the sun had reached its zenith, Apollos and Jerahmeel found themselves walking the dusty path to Gerar in the company of a dozen or so camels and a few asses with their drivers, bearing market produce for the small town of Gerar.

Gerar itself was unimpressive, but Jerahmeel was keen to remind Apollos of its importance at the time of the patriarchs, Abraham[5] and Isaac[6]. They had been treated as equals by Abimelech, the King of the Philistines, who had lived there. Jerahmeel was also proud to recount the story of the great military victory at Gerar of Asa, King of Judah, over the invading Ethiopian army of Zerah[7].

After spending the night at Gerar, the travellers set out the next morning for Beersheba. No caravans were travelling in this direction, and the flat land of the coastal plain

44

soon gave way to more hilly terrain. They were in the province of Herod's tetrarchy, known as Idumea, the land of the Edomites. Apollos had noted in Jerahmeel, a trace of racism which was quite inconsistent with his otherwise well balanced outlook on life. Jerahmeel had been uncomfortable in the Philistine towns, and he had no great liking for the Edomites. To Apollos, who was a Jew by conversion and not by race, this seemed quite illogical. So much intermarriage had taken place since the days when the primaeval tribes, descended from the patriarchs, had warred over lands defined by the fertile crescent, that only the Jews could claim anything like racial purity. Apollos was sceptical about the true ethnic origins of those identified by Jerahmeel as Philistines or Edomites, Moabites or members of the tribe of Midian. Historically, these peoples had been the enemies of the Jews, but over a thousand years had elapsed since Joshua had crossed the Jordan, driving out the Canaanite tribes before him. Jerahmeel seemed quite comfortable with both the Egyptians and the Greeks in Alexandria, and historically, these had also been peoples at enmity with Israel, Egypt at the time when Moses led his people from slavery at the Exodus[8], and more recently, the Greeks who had been stalwartly opposed by the Maccabean princes[9]. There was one ethnic group for whom Jerahmeel had a particular loathing, and the couple were soon to discover that in this case, Jerahmeel's instinct had not been entirely misplaced.

The two travellers continued on the road which was becoming more clearly defined as it was forced to follow the valleys between the increasingly steep hills. Jerahmeel stopped as the road entered a narrow ravine. He looked at the ground where the unmistakable print of horses hooves could be seen.

'These are not the tracks of people making a journey,' said Jerahmeel thoughtfully. 'Look, they are going all over the place. If we were near a town, I would say that these were horsemen, out riding for a day's sport, but Beersheba is many miles away yet. The only people who might have horses to ride around in these parts are bandits, and the ravine ahead is just the sort of place where they might ambush unwary travellers.'

45

Apollos felt a tingle of excitement run down his spine at this first hint of danger and real adventure on their journey. 'The first rule of safe travel,' continued Jerahmeel, 'is to avoid danger, not to get out of it once it is upon you and it is too late to escape. I suggest we leave the road and climb as high as we can get along the hills to the south. It will not be as difficult as all that. I can usually find out the tracks followed by the shepherds and goatherds who look after their flocks in the hill country.'

The couple left the road, and ascended the hill to the south. Although much older than Apollos, Jerahmeel was extremely fit, and was still going strongly when Apollos had to call out to him to rest awhile so that he might recover his breath. Jerahmeel was able to identify footpaths in the upper hills which travelled to the east. At one stage, they saw a wisp of smoke arising from some fire, lower down the hill. As they drew level with this, they could see beneath them, a group of twenty or so men, sitting around tents set up on a sheltered piece of flat land, well above the road, which could just be seen even further beneath. Although several hundred yards away, it was clear that these men were dressed in bright clothing. Jerahmeel insisted that this proved they were not shepherds, or any who might have legitimate reason to camp on these hills, but bandits. Apollos felt particularly glad of the company of his experienced fellow traveller at this time.

They continued along the footpaths which Jerahmeel could discern, just below the ridge of the row of hills which stretched eastwards. The going was heavy, but Apollos felt exhilarated by the freshness of the cool air which was blowing from the north west, and he savoured the scent of the mountain flowers and grasses which generated a sweet aroma which he had not experienced in the sultry climate of his native Egypt. After a few miles, the land became flatter as the hills merged to form a sort of plateau, and the road which seemed so far beneath them, had climbed over the last mile or so to continue its route across the plateau. The couple made their way back to the road, and stopped to eat the food with which they provisioned themselves at Gerar. They finished the last of their water, and continued on the road they knew would lead to Beersheba.

The sun was now getting low in the sky behind them, and Jerahmeel urged Apollos on, so that they might reach Beersheba before nightfall. It was with some relief that Beersheba came in sight before sunset. Jerahmeel identified the first building they approached, half a mile or so from the huddle of small houses and shops which marked the beginning of the town proper, as an inn. Jerahmeel had stayed there before when he had visited Beersheba a few months earlier.

The tired travellers made their way through the low door into the hallway of this inn. Although it was not yet quite dark, some of the lamps had been lit to show a rather untidy room with a few crude tables and benches arranged around the edge of the room. The only people in the room were a group of half-a-dozen heavily built men who were sitting round one of the tables drinking what Apollos imagined must have been a fairly potent brew, and making a lot of noise in the process. The best adjective to describe these men was shaggy. Their thick woollen clothes were badly cared for. They all had very long, black, greasy hair, and sported thick, uncombed beards. Their raucous laughter subdued a bit as Apollos and Jerahmeel entered and they eyed the travellers up and down. One of these men left the table and went out to a room at the side, returning a moment later with a slightly less shaggy individual whom Apollos assumed to be the inn-keeper. The inn-keeper dropped the dirty cloth he was carrying on the table and came over to our travellers, eyeing them up and down in much the same way as the men round the table had done.

'No doubt, you travellers would like a room for the night?' he asked obsequiously. He spoke in Aramaic, a language Jerahmeel knew well, and which Apollos could just about follow, but hardly speak. 'Ten drachmas for a room is the best price you'll find in these parts.'

Apollos could sense that Jerahmeel was uneasy, but this disquiet was not displayed in the way he spoke.

'It is indeed a good price.' Jerahmeel answered. 'I have stayed here before and enjoyed the fare. The last time I came, Zoheth was inn-keeper. Has he moved away.'

The inn-keeper looked uneasy and paused before he answered.

'Zoheth is my brother,' he replied. 'I am looking after the inn while he is away visiting his wife's relatives in Hebron.'

Apollos was taken back by what Jerahmeel said next. It was as well that Apollos was not confident in speaking Aramaic, or he may have said something which could have left the pair in difficulty. Three of the shaggy men who had been drinking had got up and had moved to stand by the door.

'Our two companions who are carrying the main part of our merchandise have just gone on ahead of us because they thought they would get better stabling for the camels in Beersheba town. Zoheth's stables have always been good enough for me, and as you say, ten drachmas is a better price than we can hope to negotiate for accommodation elsewhere. They can only be a hundred yards or so down the road by now. We will catch them up before they make other unnecessarily expensive arrangements and bring them back to stay at this inn.'

Jerahmeel turned to Apollos and using a nonchalant tone which belied his anxiety, spoke to him in Latin.

'Say nothing but just play along with me for now. I will shortly explain to you what may seem strange behaviour.'

Apollos realized that Jerahmeel had switched from Aramaic to conceal his communication from those present in the room and had not even used Greek, as that was a lingua franca in the eastern Mediterranean countries of which these Aramaic speaking peasant folk might have had some knowledge.

The inn-keeper nodded to the men by the door and they made way as Jerahmeel and Apollos left the inn, Jerahmeel walking with a relaxed swagger. Jerahmeel hastened his gait as soon as they were a few yards from the inn door and were swallowed into the darkness of the Beersheba road and the lights of the inn were left behind. Apollos was very tired at the end of the unaccustomed exercise that this hard day's walk had been and was not unnaturally irritated that the welcome prospect of food and rest had so suddenly been snatched away by Jerahmeel's strange behaviour. Apollos was prudent enough to wait until they were out of earshot of the inn before giving vent to his displeasure.

'Calm yourself down and let me explain why I acted and

spoke as I did to get out of that inn at the first possible moment,' said Jerahmeel in a tone he judged would best placate his tired companion. 'As soon as we entered that room, I realized that all the men sitting around were Amalekites.' (Apollos knew that of all the ethnic groups for which Jerahmeel felt antipathy, it was those he labelled Amalekites which aroused the greatest antagonism.) 'The man who claimed to be inn-keeper was an Amalekite like the others and therefore, certainly not the brother of Zoheth. Zoheth was not married the last time I came this way, which was barely six months ago, so I give no credence to the story that he was away visiting his wife's relatives. The tariff of ten drachmas for a room is a ridiculously low price. I don't know what that man posing as inn-keeper is about, but he is obviously a liar, and up to no good. I felt immeasurably safer and more secure as soon as we had left the inn and put a bit of distance between ourselves and that place. I had a suspicion that we may have been in a den of thieves, or worse, and that is why I told the tale about having two friends just ahead of us, carrying the main part of our merchandise. If robbery had been these men's aim, it was only the prospect of deriving an even greater gain from our companions, which would prevail upon those villains to allow us out of the inn at all, once we had been trapped inside.'

Apollos listened with almost incredulous amazement at Jerahmeel's bizarre assessment of the situation at the inn. His irritation subsided and he felt truly thankful to be accompanied by so shrewd and sagacious a travelling companion. By the time Jerahmeel had finished explaining his course of action at the inn, they were already in the outskirts proper of Beersheba. It was not long before they found an inn which was clean and bright, and inculcated no suspicious vibrations in Jerahmeel. After enjoying a good meal together, our travellers turned in and were soon enjoying the deep and tranquil sleep which is the pleasant legacy of a day's energetic walking in the fresh air of hill country.

8

Beersheba

The following morning, Apollos and Jerahmeel woke, well rested after a comfortable night in this well appointed inn. After enjoying a good breakfast of barley bread, olives and eggs, they paid the inn-keeper and went off to explore Beersheba. The town had a number of interesting associations with the patriarchs. It was the principle town of the territory which had been allocated to the tribe of Simeon when the land was divided after Joshua's conquest of Canaan[10]. Abraham had settled in Beersheba, immediately after returning from his expedition to Mount Moriah where God had provided him with a ram to sacrifice in place of his young son Isaac[11]. Jacob had stopped at Beersheba when on his way to Egypt to be reunited with his beloved Joseph, and had offered sacrifices there[12]. Beersheba lay on the caravan route from the north to Egypt. This overland route was different from the journey following the rather rougher terrain by which Apollos and Jerahmeel had approched the town, travelling from Gaza and Gerar, after cutting off the corner of the Mediterranean with a sea crossing. The reason for the importance of Beersheba on the caravan routes lay in its plenteous water supply. It was not a natural oasis but derived its water from a number of huge wells which had been dug by Abraham[13]. They had been filled in by the Philistines, probably after some territorial dispute whose details are lost in the mists of antiquity, but had been cleared a generation later by Abraham's son, Isaac. The ancient meaning of the name, Beersheba, was 'The well of the Seven'.[14]

Jerahmeel directed Apollos to these wells which lay on the edge of the town. The wells were impressive indeed.

50

The largest was some four metres in diameter, and had involved excavating through a considerable thickness of solid rock to expose looser earth and stone. This had been dug away to a depth of some twelve metres or so to reach the fresh subterranean water.

When our pair of travellers reached the wells, they were surprised at the intensity of activity, as chains of men were passing buckets of water which had been drawn up by ox teams, harnessed to turnstiles which were ingeniously designed to raise and lower buckets from the cool water beneath. The bucket chains were filling water-carrying wagons, which again, were drawn by oxen. Jerahmeel had visited these wells before, and he realized that rather more water was being drawn than was required to meet the normal domestic needs of Beersheba. Jerahmeel and Apollos were soon to be given an explanation of why so much water was being drawn.

Apollos' attention fell on a distinguished looking man wearing a green turban and a bright yellow robe. He was standing on a large rock on the other side of the well, and appeared to be supervising the bucket chain. After a while, he looked up and seeing Jerahmeel and Apollos on the other side of the well, had a quick word with one of the other men who was standing nearby and evidently involved in the water transportation activity. This man climbed on to the rock and took over the supervision of the bucket chain while the man in yellow quickly made his way round to Jerahmeel and Apollos. He was obviously well known to Jerahmeel and the pair warmly embraced.

'What a pleasure to see you in these parts again, Jerahmeel,' beamed the man in yellow, his face radiating a most lovely, unaffected smile. 'What brings you to Beersheba at this time of year?'

Jerahmeel explained that he was accompanying his friend on a journey of exploration and discovery, and introduced Apollos. The man in yellow was called Benaiah. He was president of one of the synagogues in Beersheba.

'I have never seen so much water being drawn out of the Beersheba wells,' said Jerahmeel, 'and I have visited these wells many times before.'

Benaiah explained the activity.

'We are expecting a visit from Caleb of Jezreel in the next week or so. Caleb is one of John the Baptist's disciples. Since John was executed by that butcher, Herod[15], Caleb has been continuing John's ministry of baptism. He does not restrict his activities to the Jordan valley, but travels the length and breadth of Israel. In places where there are small rivers, or at Galilee, or towns by the great sea, there is no problem in conducting baptism, but here in Beersheba, although water is plentiful, it occurs naturally in the wrong place for baptism. The fresh water lies deep in the wells, and the stream which flows by Beersheba is far too shallow to enable a baptism to be performed. The men of our synagogue are therefore filling a cistern on the hillside which Caleb will be able to use to baptize those who respond to his message when he comes. The rock is impervious, and as it is not so hot at this time of year, the water will not evaporate too quickly. By the end of the day, we expect to have gathered enough water for Caleb to conduct an impressive series of baptisms in the cistern on the hillside which many will witness and from which, great truths will be learned.'

Benaiah then turned his attention to the well being of Jerahmeel and his companion.

'Where are you staying, and how long do you expect to be in Beersheba? Will you be able to stay until Caleb arrives? You know you are welcome to stay with Haggith and myself. I have already made arrangements for Caleb to be accommodated at the home of Shaphan, for he has by far the finest house among those who attend our synagogue.'

Jerahmeel thanked Benaiah warmly for his offer of hospitality. He explained that their time was their own, and that they would be delighted to stay if something as significant as a baptism was being arranged. Inwardly, Jerahmeel thought that this would not only be of interest and educational value to Apollos, but would be of great spiritual benefit to him. Jerahmeel had been baptized by John in the River Jordan during one of his earlier tours of Israel, and he had always looked back on this as one of the most significant experiences of his life. Benaiah had also been baptized by John and was delighted that the opportunity of sharing this experience would soon be available to fellow members of his synagogue who had not travelled far from Beersheba.

Jerahmeel then told Benaiah of where he had stayed the previous night, and also, of the inn on the outskirts of Beersheba at which they had declined to stay.

'I had no idea that Zoheth was married,' said Jerahmeel, 'or that he had a brother. Indeed, the man claiming to be his brother had the appearance of an Amalekite, and I in no wise believe he was in any way related to Zoheth.'

Benaiah knew of the inn of which Jerahmeel spoke, and knew that the inn-keeper was called Zoheth, but knew little else about the man.

'Many of the shepherds whose flocks pasture on the hills to the south are Amalekites,' he said. 'They tend to use inns on the edge of town, rather than come right into Beersheba. Well,' he said to Jerahmeel, 'You know how it is between our people and the Amalekites. We don't mix well, although we don't show them the discourtesy that the folk up north display towards the Samaritans.'

After checking that his presence was no longer needed to assist with the water transportation project, Benaiah accompanied the two travellers to his home where they met his wife, Haggith, a hospitable and homely woman whom Apollos estimated to be in her late forties. She warmly welcomed Jerahmeel and graciously received Apollos into the comfort of their well appointed home.

'I do hope you will speak at one of our sabbath gatherings,' she said to Jerahmeel. 'You throw such light on the teachings of the Law and the Prophets. Large portions of Scripture take on a whole new meaning after you have expounded them. I expect Benaiah has told you that Caleb of Jezreel is coming to conduct a baptism here in a few days. Many say that he has an even more impressive presence than John, if such a thing were possible. I have never met John or Caleb,' she said, 'but I know that Benaiah has rather special memories of his own baptism. The news of John's execution came as a great shock to us all. They do say that terrible things are happening in Jerusalem now, and those in power are persecuting the prophets more vindictively now than they were persecuted, even in the days of the bad kings of Israel. That Herod seems to think that because his father, the so called, Herod the Great, rebuilt the Temple in Jerusalem, his family should be regarded as great benefactors to our people. In my book, I think the Herods are worse than Ahab, Manasseh and Ahaz rolled into one. But what would you expect of a line of Edomite princes, made rulers over Israel. They are just opportunist adventurers who know how to curry favour with Rome. The Herods have built temples to the Roman gods to please their Roman patrons, so Herod's motives for building the Jerusalem Temple are certainly suspect.'

Haggith was one of those women, who, once started on a hobby horse, was difficult to stop, or indeed, get in a word edgeways. After a while, Benaiah was able to excuse himself from the company to see to some business in town. When Jerahmeel was able to achieve conversational initiative, he gave Haggith a more detailed introduction of Apollos, and flattered the young man by telling Haggith that if she had considered his own teaching on the Law and the Prophets to be of interest, then she would certainly find that Apollos' teaching on the history of their people, even more so.

Benaiah had barely been gone half an hour when he returned in a very excited state.

'You are fortunate to have had your wits about you last night,' he said to Jerahmeel. 'Beersheba is astir with the news of a terrible crime that has been committed at the inn where you called last night. Zoheth, the inn-keeper, his three servants and seven travellers have been found murdered in the inn. The discovery was made early this morning by the boy who delivers the bread. The motive was obviously robbery. There was no sign of your Amalekites who must have left in the middle of the night when they reckoned that no more travellers would call that night. You and Apollos had better come to the town magistrates to tell them all you know.' Benaiah said to Jerahmeel. 'You are almost certainly the only people who would be able to identify these criminals if they ever get picked up, but my guess is that they will be miles away by now, hidden in some remote cavern. They won't come back this way but will spend their ill gotten gains in some distant town.'

Jerahmeel and Apollos made their way to the Magistrate's house in the middle of town. Apollos was not unnaturally impressed at how reliable Jerahmeel's instinct had been the previous night. He was learning fast the dangers that faced the unwary who took it upon themselves to travel in those times. The Magistrate into whose presence Benaiah took Jerahmeel and Apollos, was clearly agitated. The gruesome events of the previous night could have consequences for himself. Better arrangements would be called for to protect outlying inns and homesteads in that normally peaceful town and the resources available to the Magistrate were woefully meagre. Beersheba came just outside the boundary of the Idumea and was of no great interest to the Romans. Hated as were the Romans, a garrison of Roman soldiers provided the means of enforcing and maintaining law and order, but there were no Roman soldiers at Beersheba. Technically, Beersheba was the responsibility of Aretas, King of the Nabataeans, but this Jewish town and its administration were of no real interest or importance to the Arabs who, by and large, were nomadic, and had not developed good machinery for the administration of urban settlements.

Jerahmeel and Apollos furnished the Magistrate with all the details he needed, the time they had arrived, the appearance of the inn, any signs of violence, the numbers and descriptions of the people they had encountered there. It was only on the latter point that Jerahmeel and Apollos could contribute anything very positive. The general description of the men they had encountered was straightforward to furnish. They were of quite distinctive appearance, and as a group, would be readily recognizable in a crowd. However, it seemed most unlikely that these men would be found among the townsfolk of Beersheba. Their modus operandi was one of hit-and-run, and Benaiah's assessment that by now, these villains would be hidden up, far away in the hills, was almost certainly accurate. While Apollos was able to give a general description of the men, he was surprised at his own inability to furnish much detail. Jerahmeel again impressed by being able to state the colours of the clothing worn by men in the group, and any particular distinguishing marks, scars, jewelry worn, skin discolorations. As they had only been in the inn for a few minutes and there had been eight or nine men present, the detail Jerahmeel provided showed him to be a highly observant individual.

The Magistrate's clerk wrote all of this down, and the Magistrate thanked the travellers. He wanted to know the purpose of their journey and how long they would be staying in Beershaba as they would obviously be needed to provide identification, should any suspects be picked up in the next day or so.

The next couple of days passed pleasantly enough as Jerahmeel and Apollos explored Beersheba and the surrounding hills. Hill country was new to Apollos, and he delighted in the cool breezes and the fresh air which contrasted with the rather sultry Alexandrian climate. Jerahmeel renewed his acquaintance with the members of Benaiah's synagogue. They took a great interest in Apollos and were fascinated to hear about Alexandria and the way Apollos had become a Jew. There was much talk of the coming of Caleb of Jezreel, and the older ones who had the opportunity to travel, reminisced about the splendid preaching they had heard on the Jordan's bank as the Baptist harangued the crowds. Apollos and Jerahmeel enjoyed the comfort of Benaiah's home and Haggith's cooking. Haggith enjoyed mothering her guests who were temporarily filling the vacuum which her own family had left since starting their own families in other parts of Beersheba.

Then news came that a suspect had been picked up in the nearby hills. He was waiting under guard with the Magistrate, and Jerahmeel and Apollos were sent for to provide identification. They were shown to this man, sitting sullenly in the room which led off the Magistrate's office. His thick, uncombed, black beard and shaggy hair gave him an appearance which immediately reminded Apollos of the occupants of that ill-fated inn. He wore the same type of woollen garments which were shabby and frayed, as had been the clothes worn by the men in the inn. Any Jew who was familiar with the people who lived in that area would have identified this man as a typical Amalekite. So similar was this man to those that Apollos had seen in the inn, that Apollos felt sure he must have been one of them, but which one? It was not enough to say that he was just like those men. To provide positive identification, Apollos would have needed to identify this man as being a particular individual he had seen on that night, beyond reasonable doubt. This, Apollos could not do. In the time that had elapsed since the two travellers had left the inn, the features of the men Apollos had seen had merged in his mind into a single picture.

'I think this is one of the men,' Apollos said hesitantly, 'but I cannot give absolutely positive identification. I think that I would say the same about any man who had that sort of hair and wore those sort of clothes.'

The Magistrate turned to Jerahmeel who was studying the man carefully. The man looked impassively at the two who had come to identify him. Jerahmeel looked thoughtfully at this Amalekite for what seemed like five minutes, although time always passes slowly in tense situations like this. It was clear to Apollos who knew Jerahmeel well, that his attention was not merely taken with the man he had come to identify, but that he was wrestling with private thoughts of his own. Jerahmeel finally spoke.

'No,' he said to the Magistrate. 'This is definitely not one of the men we saw in the inn, the night we came to Beersheba.'

The Magistrate was satisfied that Jerahmeel was positive enough in his assertion and immediately arranged for the man to be released. It seems that he was found shepherding his sheep on the nearby hills. He had vehemently denied that he had been anywhere near Beersheba during the previous week, and the only reason he had been brought in was that his general description fitted that which had been provided by Jerahmeel and Apollos a few days earlier. However, such a description could have fitted many of the shepherds, classified as Amalekites, who looked after flocks in that area.

As they returned to Benaiah's house, Apollos asked Jerahmeel how it was that he was so positive that this man was not one of those they had encountered at the inn. Jerahmeel explained that this man had some particular features, a prominent scar on the left side of his forehead, and his left ear pierced to carry a gold ear-ring. There were other less conspicious but distinctive features which Jerahmeel had also observed. Jerahmeel asserted that

57

general characteristics like black hair and a particular style of clothing could not be used to make positive identification among a group who shared these characteristics. It appeared that Jerahmeel had observed some characteristic identifying feature in each of the men they had seen in the inn, and none of them had the particular features which uniquely characterized the appearance of the suspect who had just been released.

Apollos mused on Jerahmeel's explanation as they approached Benaiah's house. At last, Apollos realized the question which was worrying his mind about Jerahmeel's explanation.

'Since you were able to make this identity from features you must have recognized almost as soon as you saw this man, why did it take you so long to make your conclusive statement to the Magistrate?' asked Apollos.

'I would rather that you had not asked that,' said Jerahmeel, 'but I will give you an honest answer. The man was obviously an Amalekite, and I have been brought up to believe that all Amalekites are fundamentally bad. I know that is irrational and indeed wrong, but it is surprising how deeply prejudices, instilled into one at a young age, can cloud one's judgement in later years. I found myself thinking as I saw that Amalekite, that although he had not committed that particular crime, he was probably guilty of others, equally heinous. By identifying him then, I could have had him punished for the other misdeeds for which he had eluded punishment, even though he would have been charged with something of which he was innocent. Fortunately, the logic of my mind was able to over-ride the irrational prejudice I have against Amalekite people. I have learned something about myself today, Apollos. I am ashamed that my mind came so nearly to cause me to act falsely on so serious a matter. I am glad that the final words I spoke were honest and that I didn't send an innocent man to the gallows.'

They entered the home where they were staying, and the events of that morning and Jerahmeel's admission were soon forgotten as they enjoyed the meal Haggith had prepared for them.

9

Caleb of Jezreel

A few days later, Caleb of Jezreel arrived in Beersheba as expected. He was a younger man than either Jerahmeel or Apollos had anticipated, and they estimated his age as about thirty. Caleb was tall, slim and handsome, his ascetic features tanned as a result of his outdoor life-style. He wore a camel skin coat, a distinguishing feature of the senior disciples of John the Baptist, who were continuing his ministry. Caleb's long hair marked him out as a Nazarite. In spite of this and his main garment being of rough camel skin, his general appearance was neat and tidy. His coat was fastened with a rather splendid leather belt, and his hair was tied back. His beard also seemed to be well trimmed and combed. This was rather unusual for a Nazarite who would normally allow neither beard nor hair to be cut in any way. Caleb was a rather quiet man in normal conversation, although he had the reputation of being a great orator. He certainly did not have the overbearing personality which insisted on speaking louder and longer than anyone else in his company. Such a trait was fairly common among those who sought to establish self-eminence in spiritual leadership. However, although a quiet man, Caleb had great presence. He had a penetrating gaze and a certain directness in his conversation. Apollos and Jerahmeel quickly decided that this was a man they would both like and trust.

A very special meeting was held at Benaiah's synagogue that sabbath. It was attended not only by the regular members, most of whom were already known to Jerahmeel and whom Apollos had met socially over the last few days, but many members of the other two synagogues in

Beersheba had also come by invitation. The small synagogue was well packed, the men sitting in the main section of the building and the women in the gallery. Being on the very edge of the Kingdom of Herod, indeed just outside its recognized borders, Beersheba was in danger of losing touch with mainstream religious developments in Judaea, and the visit of a man of Caleb's reputation who was well known as a principal lieutenant of John the Baptist, was a most significant event for Beersheba.

Benaiah was quite obviously full of a joyful pride as he stood to welcome the congregation, and extend a special welcome to the members of neighbouring synagogues who had joined them for this occasion. He then bade a special welcome to Jerahmeel and Apollos whom he described as great scholars from Alexandria. Finally he expressed to Caleb the sentiments of joy and gratitude that all present felt for his making a journey, well beyond the region where his ministry was usually centred, to spend time with them in Beersheba.

After the opening prayers and psalms, Apollos was invited to give the first address. Benaiah had made this arrangement as a result of Jerahmeel's recommendation. Like most who knew him, Benaiah trusted Jerahmeel's judgement implicitly. Apollos had spent the last couple of days thinking of what he would say.

Apollos opened his address with the usual pleasantries, complimenting the Beershebans on the warmth of the welcome he, a stranger in their midst, had received. He then launched into a message he drew straight from the history of those whose attention he now held. He spoke of the patriarch Abraham who was probably the person to whom Beersheba owed its foundation. Apollos reminded the congregation of the great promise that Abraham had received from God himself, not just that his descendants would be more numerous than the sands of the seashore and the stars of the sky,[16] but that all nations of the earth would be blessed by his seed.[17] Apollos asserted that this meant that God's special spiritual blessings were not to be exclusively reserved for the natural descendants of Abraham, but that these descendants would share great blessings among the other nations of the earth. Apollos then declared himself to be a member of a non-Jewish nation, a Greek, who had experienced rich blessings from the teachings of the Jewish faith, and had indeed, himself become a proselyte Jew.

Apollos then reminded that predominantly Jewish congregation of other gentiles who had received some measure of blessing from the Jewish nation, who in return, had brought benefit to the Jews. Abraham had honoured the great priest King of Salem, Melchizedek, after Abraham's victory over King Chedorlaomer who had taken captive his nephew, Lot. Melchizedek had in turn, blessed Abraham.[18] Apollos spoke of Moses who, when living as a fugitive from Pharaoh, had received shelter from Jethro, Priest of Midian and had married Zipporah, his daughter.[19] During the Exodus, the wisdom of Jethro had been invaluable to Moses, and acting on his father-in-law's advice, Moses was able to establish a system for administering justice to his people which provided the framework for governing Canaan after Joshua's conquest.[20] Apollos spoke of Ahaseurus, King of Persia, who married the beautiful Esther, with consequential benefits to both Jews and Persians.[21] He reminded them of Rahab of Jericho who had sheltered Joshua's spies,[22] and of Ruth the Moabitess, who accompanied Naomi back to Israel after her bereavements.[23] As Ruth and Rahab had been respectively, great and great-great grandmothers of David,[24] the greatest of Jewish kings, it followed that David had both Canaanite and Moabite blood flowing in his veins. Apollos referred to many other scriptural examples of gentiles who had been blessed by the Jewish nation and who had, in turn, brought blessing to the Jews.

Apollos then involved the congregation in making his point. He asked them if they could think of any family or clan in the history of the Jews who were specially commended for their zeal in promoting the worship of Jehovah. An older man in the congregation who was well versed in scripture gave Apollos the answer he wanted. 'Why, the Rechabites, for they supported King Jehu of Israel when he had to contend with the profanity of Baal worship,[25] and the Rechabites of Judah were specially commended by the greatest of the prophets of Judah, Jeremiah, for their exemplary life-style when the rest of the nation was in a state of decadence.[26'] Another in that congregation remembered that the Rechabites had been prominent in building the walls of Jerusalem under Nehemiah when the Jews returned from exile.[27]

Apollos then pointed out to the Jews of Beersheba that the Rechabites, a family whose name was a watchword for Jewish zeal and piety, were not descendants of Jacob (who was also known as Israel, hence the generic name, Israelite) but were Kenites.[28] Unlike the twelve tribes who were Israelite, the Kenites were of Midianite origin. The Kenites, who specially associated themselves with the tribe of Judah,[29] were great smiths, and thus, Apollos explained, they enabled the Israelites to forge the weapons and armour, without which the conquest of Canaan could never have been undertaken.

Apollos concluded his address by emphasizing that he was not trying to illustrate that Israel owed its existence to the contribution of foreigners, but on the contrary, many foreigners like those he had just mentioned, had derived great spiritual blessings from Israel. The fact that these foreigners had unreservedly contributed their skills and resources to the benefit of Israel, indicated their recognition of the measure with which they had been blessed. 'I, like the Kenites, am not of Jewish stock,' said Apollos, 'but I am fully conscious, as were the Kenites, of the blessings that the faith of your nation has afforded me. I am now proud to be counted as a Jew, and it is my wish, my prayer, that I may be able to contribute from my resources of youth and health and strength to the well being of your nation, no less than the others of whom I have spoken, who made return for the blessings your nation afforded them. My dearest hope is, that the promise made to your father Abraham may soon be fulfilled, and that in his seed all nations of the world may be blessed.'

Apollos then left the lectern from which he had spoken and returned to sit by Jerahmeel. He felt a warm glow of pleasure at the murmur of approval which went round the congregation. This approval was earned, not only by what Apollos had said, but from the manner he had delivered his address. A talk based on the history of their nation was more interesting to the Jews assembled there, than a detailed exegesis of the Mosaic law, which was their usual diet of sabbath instruction, and Apollos had considerable skill in the way he projected his spoken word. He knew just how to emphasize the important points, and recognized the moments when a pause added to the power of his message.

Benaiah thanked Apollos warmly for his words and invited the congregation to stand and sing the eighty-seventh Psalm. He had chosen a short psalm which fitted in so well with Apollos' message.

The Lord built his City on the sacred hill;
More than any other place in Israel he loves the City of Jerusalem.
Listen, City of God to the wonderful things he says about you:
'I will include Egypt and Babylonia when I list the nations that obey me;
I will number among the inhabitants of Jerusalem the people of Philistia, Tyre, and the Sudan.'
Of Zion it will be said that all nations belong there and that the Almighty will make her strong.
The Lord will write a list of the peoples and include them all as citizens of Jerusalem.
They dance and sing,
'In Zion is the source of all our blessings.'[30]

During the last verse, Benaiah bowed to Caleb, and returned to the congregation while the Baptist's disciple climbed to the lectern. An expectant hush enveloped the congregation as the psalm ended. Caleb said a short prayer and motioned the people to be seated. Caleb paused before he started his address, and then spoke in a strong, resonant voice.

'I had no idea what Apollos was going to say tonight,' he began, 'but I trusted that God would give him words on which I could build a message. When I visit congregations who are preparing for baptism in repentance for their sins, I invariably find that God gives the speaker who precedes me, words on which I can build to identify sins of the community for which repentance is called. The fact that I can base my address on the previous speaker's words, words of which I know nothing until I hear them uttered, enables me to speak without the congregation thinking that I have involved myself in gossip before my address, to acquaint myself of specific, prevalent sins of the society among whom I have been called to visit and exercise a short ministry.

'The words which Apollos spoke concern a sin of the Jewish people which sorely vexed my master John. Has not a tradition developed among the Jewish people that their importance to God lies in the fact that they were descended from Abraham, and that all who do not share this progenitor are cursed? How angry was my master, when those who expressed such convictions came for baptism. He declared them to be a viper's brood for placing their reliance on such an external matter as having Abraham as their common ancestor.[31] Do not our scriptures show how often our people fell into sin and displeased God? Did the mere fact that they could claim descent from Abraham, cause the Lord to withhold the punishments which so many of our compatriots earned during the sad and sinful episodes of our nation's history? Has not our friend, Apollos, so eloquently revealed to us the blessings brought to our nation by gentile converts who understood the spirit of our tradition, rather than setting great store by blood kinship with a great ancestor? The history of our kings surely gives us dramatic revelation that the offspring of a good king may be an evil man, and an evil man may sire a son who is open to the workings of God in his life? Was not Manasseh the son of the good King Hezekiah? Was not that good King Josiah, son of the idolatrous Amon who was rejected by his people?[32]

'No, we are not made right with God merely through the privilege of kinship with His special people, but by loving the Lord God above all else, and seeking to demonstrate this love in the quality of our lives. How well Apollos drew our attention to the contribution to our spiritual heritage which was brought by others who are not of our race. He spoke of the Kenites. Was not Sisera, the Canaanite general who sought to destroy our nation, slain by Jael, wife of

Heber the Kenite, in the days of Barak the Judge and Deborah the Prophetess?[33] And notice how a woman rather than Barak the Judge, is credited with destroying the enemy of God's people. This was prophesied by Deborah.[34] Do not the Jewish people sin, not only by despising those of other races, but by affording women lower status than men in society? How many of the names that Apollos mentioned, who shaped the destiny of our nation, were not only gentile, but women. Esther of course was of Jewish stock, but Zipporah, Rahab and Ruth came from other nations. The mother of the tribes of Ephraim and Manasseh was the daughter of an Egyptian priest,[35] and Tamar, the mother of the tribe of Judah, was a woman of Canaan![36]

'As Jews, we identify certain nations as being specially inferior, because they were our enemies in the past. Even now, we still despise and distrust the people of these nations, although centuries have rolled by since the times we contested ownership of the promised land with them. We deride the Philistines because they were Israel's enemies at the time of the Judges and during the reign of King Saul, yet who was one of King David's most loyal commanders when his kingship was threatened, as Absalom his son rebelled against him? His most faithful commander was Ittai the Gittite, and he was a Philistine!'[37]

Apollos felt a glow of pride that the words he had spoken earlier had provided a foundation which was enabling this acclaimed servant of God to launch an address which was clearly identifying a moral shortcoming of many of those present, and it was to discover such shortcomings that men of good intent had come to that gathering. For a while, Apollos basked in the euphoria of having made this contribution to Caleb's ministry. Caleb continued.

'As I have travelled the length and breadth of Israel, I have observed examples of love and loyalty and sacrifice among people whom the Jews despise, which greatly exceed anything I have encountered among our own people. In the north, the Samaritans care for their sick and look after the elderly of their society in a way which is quite touching. Indeed, in their way, the Samaritans worship the same God as we do, and can claim kinship with the ten tribes who were carried off and destroyed by the mighty Assyrians.

Yet, because some of their forefathers intermarried with the other nations that dwelt in Israel, they are treated as if they were lepers by those who claim to be pure blooded members of the tribes of Benjamin, Levi and Judah! In Jerusalem, I see the sick and feeble Jewish people turned out on to the streets, the lame and blind forced to beg for a crust, and elderly parents being evicted from their homes by sons who are avaricious for the financial gain which will accrue from the sale of their parents' houses!

'There are no Samaritans living among you in Beersheba, but I can see the way you interact with those in this community who are not of our faith. Those you describe as Midianites,[38] Edomites and Amalekites,[39] are regarded with contempt, although they themselves do not make such distinctions. Such barriers to friendship and harmony do not exist between these peoples. If you study your scriptures well, you will find that all these people can claim that Abraham was their ancestor, yes, even the Amalekites, no less than you Jews. As I travelled to your town, I lost my way and could well have added two days to my journey, but I was given shelter and food and a bed for the night and good directions the following morning by a shepherd who lives in the hills to the north. I wished God's peace and blessing on that man and his family, a man, who by his dress and speech, you would call an Amalekite!'

Apollos was conscious that Jerahmeel was feeling distinctly uneasy as Caleb spoke and unerringly homed in on what Apollos considered to be the only flaw in Jerahmeel's makeup. As Caleb continued, Apollos himself soon felt uneasy, and the complacency he had felt as Caleb had started to build his address on Apollos' earlier words, soon evaporated.

'I have mentioned to you, how much the Jewish nation owes to people of gentile stock who have thrown in their lot with God's people, and you will be aware from examples that both Apollos and I have quoted, how many of those were women. How sadly Jewish people underrate the contribution that women have to make to the society of God's people. Some will merely regard women as beings of no account in God's plan for eternity. Others will regard them as beings who are there purely for the service of man and for the gratification of his carnal desires. Yes, even men who are highly regarded and hold leadership roles in the Temple or in synagogues, will think nothing of consorting with prostitutes, their sole concern being that others may not know this. God is not mocked. He sees what is done in secret. There are others capable of sound and logical thought, who can clearly assess the fundamental principles of right and wrong, who will seduce a virgin with no thought of the shame and disgrace that can be brought on to her and her family, with no thought for who will bear the expense of the upbringing of any child so conceived, with no thought for the fact that such a child who has come into the world as a wholly innocent victim of their lust, will be deprived of the honourable home background which is every child's birthright. Does not every child have the same human dignity as any one of us, and the same rights to the expectations we take as granted?'

Caleb exposed other sins which existed in the world at large, and those who lived in Beersheba knew that their community was not exempt from such shortcomings. Too many were preoccupied with material wealth and possessions. Some were prepared to go any length and to compromise moral principles to achieve status and social prestige. Some had acquired the invidious ability of being able to deceive without telling a direct lie. A particular sin which Caleb had encountered in his journeyings through Israel and which was perceptible to a limited degree among the more senior members of the synagogues represented at that meeting, was a form of supercilious pride. How proud were some of the leading and most religious Jews of their ability to outwardly maintain the law of Moses to the last scruple, even if this display meant making life thoroughly miserable for themselves and those around them.

'Have you not realized,' expounded Caleb, 'that the Law we received through Moses, was not a law of limitations and restrictions which would curtail our potential for fulfilment as people? The Law we received represents God's guide lines for living fulfilled, well balanced and happy lives, and so many of our people have distorted the application of the Law so that it has become a vehicle for promoting human pride. In so doing, they have made it an instrument which brings misery, instead of the joy intended by God.'

As Caleb drew his address to a close, most of those present, including Jerahmeel and Apollos, were aware of some aspect of their lives which fell seriously short of the ideal.

'I know none of you well,' said Caleb. 'I have not spoken of specific sins which I can associate with any of you as individuals. Indeed, in the short time I have been in Beersheba, I have received nothing but kindness and courtesy from all of you, and the limited acquaintance I have of you, could lead me to think of you all as paragons of virtue. Alas, I know that no one is entirely virtuous. Alas, the burden of my ministry, as was John's before me, is the uncomfortable task of making you aware of things about yourselves which you would wish expunged from your beings. The joy of my ministry lies in the fact that through the rite of baptism. I can provide you with the opportunity to declare to God in public that you sincerely wish these sins to be washed away and removed from you. Think well on what I have said. Repent of your sins. In three days I will baptize in the cistern in the hills just to the north of Beersheba, all those consider that they have genuinely repented, so giving them a sign that they may make a new start in living lives to be increasingly dedicated to the Lord our God. This ministry which was entrusted to my master, John, and which I seek to continue, is to prepare God's people for the coming of the Messiah. Indeed, he may have already arrived. Be prepared therefore, for the time when he will surely reveal his presence in your midst!'

Caleb left the lectern and sat down. The meeting closed with a quiet psalm and Benaiah led the congregation in a final prayer. A subdued and thoughtful people left the synagogue that evening. All had been affected in some way by Caleb's words, and they quietly wended their way home to reflect on truths about themselves of which many had become painfully aware that night for the first time. Many wondered too, at Caleb's reference to the Messiah. They had had news of great upheavals in Jerusalem from caravans that passed through Beersheba en route for Egypt, and there was much talk of Messiahs, but such news had had little impact on Beersheba. Beersheba was almost regarded as a religious backwater by those who lived to the north. The final news which had reached Beersheba of most of those who had created a stir by their claim of Messiahship, was that they had turned out to be no more than imposters and had met an inglorious end.

10

Baptisms

Three days later, a large crowd gathered around the cistern in the hills just to the north of Beersheba. The cistern was a natural hollow in the rock, about fifteen metres long and six metres wide. It had been filled to a depth of just over one metre by the men of Benaiah's synagogue with clear well water. The day had dawned, glorious and sunny, and the afternoon was comfortably warm. A faint murmur could be heard from the crowd who were patiently and quietly sitting on the hillside, overlooking the cistern. Rather more noise could be heard from the children who had accompanied their families, and were happily playing on a grassy slope, just below the cistern. Children seem to be impervious to solemn atmospheres which accompany events of great religious significance, but the children were not too noisy. While they remained in safety on the grassy slope which was in full sight of their parents, no one sought to interfere with the fun they were obviously enjoying. They rolled down the grass and clambered back to the line of rocks which defined the perimeter of the large solid rock formation in which had been created the artificial pool where the baptisms were to take place.

Those who had come to be baptized were sitting together at one extreme of the pool. For the most part, they were wearing white or very light coloured clothes. Jerahmeel and Apollos were sitting in this group. They had been deeply affected by Caleb's address the previous sabbath. Although Caleb had pointed out that those who had been previously baptized by John should have no need to experience a second baptism unless they were conscious of a serious spiritual regression since their baptism, Jerahmeel felt that the irrational racism which coloured his mental outlook was a sin of which he had not previously repented. He had become very aware of this aspect of his nature during Caleb's address and welcomed this opportunity for making a clear cut demonstration of repentance. He confided to Apollos that he had been very close to compounding the sin of his mind by committing a sin which could have had tragic consequences. Jerahmeel had been on the verge of positively identifying the Amalekite shepherd as one present at Zoheth's inn, merely because of his irrational distrust of all Amalekites.

Apollos confided in Jerahmeel that he had been promiscuous in Alexandria, and indeed, could possibly have fathered children, although to the best of his knowledge, no child had been born as a result of his immoral behaviour. Apollos thought privately to himself that apart from Diana, the women with whom he had had intercourse were prostitutes and knew how to avoid pregnancy. Apollos considered that his misgivings that Diana was pregnant, which caused him to hasten his departure from Alexandria, were quite irrational. It was surely well known that a virgin cannot become pregnant on her first experience of intercourse. However, Apollos felt deeply sad and ashamed at the way he had treated Diana. So much had happened since leaving Alexandria, that Apollos had scarcely had a moment to think of those at home. Demeter was now no more than a pretty girl of whom he had entertained fantasies in the past. Apollos remembered his parents, and thoughts of Diana now began to fill his mind. What a splendid young woman she was. Apollos had become aware of the richness of her mind and intellect as they had talked together on the hillside on the evening that Demeter and Claurinius celebrated their engagement. 'Diana deserves the love and affection of a far better man than myself,' thought Apollos to himself as they waited for Caleb of Jezreel to appear and commence the baptism. Apollos felt in great need of this opportunity for repentance. He had behaved in Alexandria in a way which directly contravened the moral code of the faith which he had not only embraced, but of which he had been accepted as a teacher!

Caleb was not in view of the company present. He was

spending some time praying with a few of the synagogue leaders behind a bluff on the hillside. At the appropriate moment, Caleb and these elders emerged into view. A reverent hush fell on the crowd. The leaders sat down on a patch of ground which had been reserved for them. This was the cue for which a twelve year old boy had been briefed to respond. He stood and sang the fifty-first psalm in a clear treble voice.

> Be merciful to me, O God, because of your constant love.
> Because of your great mercy wipe away my sins!
> Wash away all my evil and make me clean from my sin!
> I recognize my faults;
> I am always conscious of my sins.
> I have sinned against you – only against you – and done what you consider evil.
> So you are right in judging me;
> you are justified in condemning me.

As the sweet notes of the boy's voice reverberated around the hillside, Caleb carefully lowered himself into the water and stood waist deep, facing those who were to be baptized.

> I have been evil from the day I was born;
> from the time I was conceived, I have been sinful.
> Sincerity and truth are what you require;
> fill my mind with your wisdom.
> Remove my sin and I will be clean;
> wash me, and I will be whiter than snow.
> Let me hear the sounds of joy and gladness;
> and though you have crushed me and broken me, I will be happy once again.
> Close your eyes to my sins
> and wipe out all my evil.
> Create a pure heart in me, O God,
> and put a new and loyal spirit in me.
> Do not banish me from your presence;
> do not take your Holy Spirit away from me.

Give me the joy that comes from your salvation,
and make me willing to obey you.
Then I will teach sinners your commands,
and they will turn back to you.

Those waiting to be baptized stood and made their way to
the edge of the pool, opposite the point where Caleb had
lowered himself into the water. The rock formation was
such that the water shelved gently where candidates for
baptism waited, and they would be able to make a dignified
entry into the pool, and wade into the deepening water until
they reached the point where Caleb was standing.

Spare my life, O God and save me,
and I will gladly proclaim your righteousness.
Help me to speak Lord,
and I will praise you.
You do not want sacrifices, or I would offer
them;
you are not pleased with burnt offerings.
My sacrifice is a humble spirit, O God;
you will not reject a humble and repentant
heart.[40]

As the echoing last notes of the psalm faded into silence,
Caleb looked heavenwards and raised his arms.
'Heavenly Father,' he prayed, 'Look graciously now upon
your repentant subjects gathered here. May the sacrifice of
humility which they are now undertaking be pleasing in
Your sight. May they sense the balm of Your gentle,
forgiving love, for however we have sinned, whoever we
have hurt, whatever we have failed to do, the pain and
anguish has been felt by You. May all who are baptized in
repentance today rise from the water, spiritually refreshed,
and able to start new lives, dedicated to Your service and
the love of their fellow men and women. May the strength
to serve You faithfully be available to each one of us, so that
our lives henceforth may redound to Your glory. Amen.'
Caleb looked towards those awaiting baptism, and he
lowered his arms, so that they were outstretched as if in
welcome to that gathering. One by one in prearranged

73

order, they entered the water and waded towards Caleb. As they reached the baptist, he gently placed his hands on their shoulders and spoke quietly a few private words to each. Some had had the opportunity of receiving counsel from Caleb on the sins which weighed on their heart, and Caleb's words were invariably appropriate to the needs of the individual to whom he ministered. To Jerahmeel, Caleb expressed the wish that henceforth, men and women of every race, nation and tongue would be blessed by the wisdom borne of Jerahmeel's years and understanding. Apollos was blessed with the hope that his relationships with women would be honourable, and that his children would know the security of having parents who kept sacred the bonds of faithful love. After he had spoken his personal words, Caleb prayed in louder voice,

'Father, forgive this your servant who has come to you in penitence and faith, trusting in your everlasting love and mercy.'

Caleb then pressed gently on the shoulders of each candidate who allowed him or herself to be submerged. After a second, Caleb released the person being baptized and embraced them as they emerged from the water. As each baptized individual returned to the edge of the pool, Benaiah was waiting to hand them a towel, while the next candidate was making a dignified approach to Caleb. The baptisms were completed in about twenty minutes and Caleb concluded the ceremony with a short blessing. Those assembled then returned quietly to their homes.

Over the next few days, Caleb made a point of visiting as many of the families who had received his ministry as he could, before leaving Beersheba to continue his work in other parts of Israel. He duly called at Benaiah's home and Jerahmeel and Apollos were able to raise a number of burning issues with Caleb. Jerahmeel reminded Caleb that in his address in the synagogue, he had spoken of the coming Messiah, and had hinted that he may already have arrived. Jerahmeel then told Caleb of the message that had been delivered by Sandas-cum-Barama at the Hebron synagogue in Alexandria, and of the Jesus of whom Sandas had spoken.

'I know of Jesus,' said Caleb. 'This Jesus was a cousin of

my master, John the Baptist. John particularly directed the attention of two of my friends to this Jesus whom he called the Lamb of God. They had been disciples of John like myself, but after spending some time with this Jesus, they became his disciples.[41]

'After John had been imprisoned by Herod, we visited John as often as the authorities allowed. He was not unnaturally depressed, but not so much by his imprisonment, but impatience to see the appearance of the one for whom his ministry had been preparing the people. He had believed that this Jesus was he, but while isolated in prison, it seemed that nothing special was happening. This Jesus was not establishing a new age of justice when tyrants like Herod would be overthrown and those unjustly imprisoned would be released. After a while, he asked myself and Amos, another disciple, to find out Jesus and directly challenge him as to whether or not he was the Messiah. This we did, but Jesus did not give us a direct answer. Instead, he asked us to spend the day with him and his disciples. What wonderful things I witnessed that day. This Jesus healed all manner of illnesses, even giving sight to those who had been born blind and restoring hearing to those who were deaf. At the end of the day, Jesus told us to report what we had seen to John. This we did, and we observed a great peace come over our master. A few days later, John was executed, but we know he met death as a happy man.[42]

'I cannot say with certainty that Jesus is the Messiah. I know that he was crucified. Like yourselves, I have heard reports that he rose again from the dead, but he no longer appears to be around in Israel. If he was the Messiah indeed, then be sure that nothing in heaven and earth will be able to prevent his becoming known to people of good will, and it is my prayer that the people I have baptized, both here and in other parts of Israel as I continue my master's ministry, will be better fitted to receive him. If he is not, then no matter, God can be trusted to send us soon the promised Messiah. Each of us must patiently wait on the hand of God who will accomplish everything as promised in good time.'

The following day, Caleb bade his final farewells and left

Beersheba. It was not only those who had been baptized, but all who had heard him, and everyone in Beersheba who had enjoyed his company during those very wonderful days, felt specially blessed at his ministry.

11

Hebron

A fortnight later, Jerahmeel and Apollos decided that they should now move on. Much as Apollos had enjoyed the hospitality of Benaiah and Haggith, he was anxious to continue his exploration of the exciting world he was discovering since he left Alexandria. They cleared their departure with the Magistrate. He had little hope that the murderous gang who carried out the audacious crime at Zoheth's inn would ever now be found, and he saw no reason why Jerahmeel and Apollos should be detained in Beersheba. They bade farewell to the good friends they had made in the very short time they had been in that town. For Jerahmeel, there were a number of old friends as well as new acquaintances in this group. Very special thanks were afforded of course to Benaiah and Haggith. The couple graciously insisted that the special scholarship that Apollos and Jerahmeel had brought in the teaching they gave at Benaiah's synagogue, more than repaid what they modestly called, 'the poor hospitality they had been able to offer'. Apollos had spoken but the once during Caleb's visit, but Jerahmeel had given words of encouragement, comfort and wisdom on each of the sabbaths which had followed Caleb's departure.

Although Apollos enjoyed speaking and had an eloquent and entertaining style of imparting knowledge, Caleb's ministry had made him think carefully on his own spiritual standing. Although he had undergone a baptism of repentance, this did not remove the fact that he had flouted the Law of Moses while proclaiming himself to be a convert to Judaism. Apollos considered that to continue to function as a teacher in the synagogues they visited would confound his

77

promiscuity with the further sin of hypocrisy, and Apollos confided in Jerahmeel that, for the time being at any rate, he should not preach at synagogue gatherings. This was something that Jerahmeel understood, and he was inwardly glad to see that this tour was not just a finishing school to consolidate Apollos' academic knowledge, but that moral character development was taking place in his young protegé.

Our travellers left Beersheba behind them, and made their way northwards, directing their steps towards Hebron which they would visit en route for Jerusalem. The name Hebron had a comforting ring to Apollos and Jerahmeel, for their own synagogue in Alexandria was in a district named after this ancient city in Judaea. Their journey was now through even more rugged hill country than they had traversed on their trek to Beersheba. They frequently left the road when it appeared it would enter some narrow gorge and any dangers ahead could not be seen. Jerahmeel had a wonderful sense of direction, and could invariably find his way back to the road after they had circumnavigated potentially treacherous sections of the recognized route to Hebron. The journey was predominantly uphill, and by late afternoon, both Jerahmeel and Apollos were feeling very weary. They had neither passed nor met many other travellers during the day, and there had been very few villages on their itinerary. It was with great relief that most elevated city in Israel at last came into view. Hebron, formally known as Kiriath-arba, was located at an altitude of some nine hundred metres. The normally white walls of the buildings of Hebron, nestling in the hills of the Judaean uplands, glowed pink as they caught the rays of the setting sun. Jerahmeel and Apollos had no difficulty in finding a comfortable inn where they arranged to spend the night.

The following day, they commenced their sight-seeing of this city of antiquity, a city which was ancient[48] even before the patriarch, Abraham,[43] had established his camp in its vicinity, some thousand years earlier when it was a Hittite settlement. Jerahmeel conducted Apollos to the venerated field of Machpelah, just beyond the city boundary. Here were the tombs of Abraham and Sarah,[44] of Isaac and Rebecca,[45] and of Jacob[46] and Leah.[44] Outside the cave which was the sepulchre of the most ancient patriarchs and matriarchs of the Jewish nation, were other impressive tombs with inscriptions which indicated that they were the last resting place of other great names in Jewish history, Apollos identified a tomb for each of Israel's sons, including Joseph who had been embalmed in Apollos' native land of Egypt.[47] Apollos and Jerahmeel silently revered these monuments which represented such a precious link with the past. In the silence of that cemetery, they experienced an atmosphere of purposeful peace as the mortal remains of those who had striven in their lifetime to establish a nation whose destiny was to be dedicated to God, rested near the most elevated settlement of significance in the land that God had promised he would give to Abraham and his descendants.

Hebron was a significant settlement indeed. After they had imbibed their fill of Machpelah's sombre but peaceful atmosphere, Apollos and Jerahmeel returned to the business of Hebron's bustling centre. They spoke together of the portentous events which had taken place at Hebron, of which Apollos had up to the present, merely book knowledge, but could now add the experience of ambience and atmosphere. During the invasion of Joshua, Hebron had been a city of the Anakim,[49] an Amorite tribe. Hoham, their king had been slain with Adonizedek, king of Jerusalem and three other Amorite kings after they had suffered a defeat at the hand of Joshua at the battle of Gibeon. This battle had been accompanied by miraculous events which indicated that God was on Israel's side. The hours of daylight were extended to give the Israelites time to complete their victory, and the defeated Amorites who fled after the fight, were caught in an extraordinary hailstorm in which more men were killed by giant hailstones than had fallen in battle.[50]

The district around Hebron had been allocated to the namesake of the baptist who had ministered at Beersheba, Caleb, when the land of Canaan was divided out after the conquest.[51] Caleb and Joshua were the only two of the twelve spies who had been sent by Moses to reconnoitre the promised land, who had returned to the Israelite camp at Kadesh-barnea, confident that God would give victory to the Israelites when they entered Canaan. The region around Hebron had been explored by the twelve spies, and Caleb had been prominent in its ultimate conquest.[52]

Hebron had indeed been King David's capital in the early days of the Jewish monarchy. It was at Hebron that David had been annointed, firstly, King of Judah,[53] and then, two years later, King of all Israel.[54] However, Hebron would also have had unhappy connotations for David, for it was here that his favourite but rebellious son, Absalom, raised his standard.[55]

In its more recent history, Hebron had been occupied by the Idumaeans, but it had been recaptured by Judas Maccabaeus.[56]

During their wandering through Hebron, Jerahmeel again realized his happy knack of bumping into a devout Jew who remembered him from a previous visit he had made to Hebron. The result of this encounter was that Apollos and Jerahmeel were again offered accommodation in a comfortable household. This saved our travellers the expense of remaining at the inn, and Jerahmeel's ministry at the synagogue was regarded as more than ample recompense for this hospitality.

Jerahmeel and Apollos remained at Hebron for about a month before proceeding to Jerusalem.

12

Arrival at Jerusalem

Our travellers set out early from Hebron on a day which
dawned cooler than normal for the time of year. Although
the hill country of Judaea was difficult terrain for wayfarers
on foot, the refreshing breezes from the north west found
our travellers journeying with light and jaunty step on the
road which led them to the ancient and famous city of
Jerusalem. This road was much busier than the roads they
had followed on their way to Beersheba and Hebron. With
so many fellow travellers about, there was no part of the
route about which Jerahmeel deemed a detour via the
shepherd tracks through the hills to be necessary to ensure
safe passage. Their route took them through Mamre, Alulos
and Thekoa. By mid-morning, they were passing the
fortress called Herodium and had made Bethlehem by midday. Here, they rested for an hour or so, and then joined the
increasingly busy road to Jerusalem, passing through
Bethany and Bethphage in the middle of the afternoon.
These villages were no more than a mile or so from
Jerusalem. Although journeying from the south, the
road conducted Apollos and Jerahmeel to the north of the
City. The Tyropoeon, Hinnom and Kidron valleys made
Jerusalem very difficult to approach from the west, south
and east. These features had enabled the city to be built as
an almost impregnable fortress. It had defied the onslaught
of Joshua's invading army of Hebrews whom God had
fashioned into an almost invincible and irresistible nation
through the Exodus experience of forty hard years of
nomadic life in the semi-desert of Sinai. This Jebusite city
had not finally come under the control of the Jews until the
reign of King David.[57]

Apollos felt a thrill as the city walls came into view. Although Jerahmeel had been there before, he too felt some stirring as the city which was the very heart of his nation was sighted. What battles had been fought to control that metropolis. During the time that good kings ruled in Judah and the inhabitants had been faithful to His laws, God had preserved the city from both Syrian[58] and Assyrian[59] attack. He had delivered it to the Babylonians when the nation had sunk to idolatory and decadence,[60] but the Persians who replaced Babylon as the world super-power, allowed Nehemiah to re-establish Jewish control over the city.[61] The rival Greek dynasties, the Ptolemies and the Seleucids, who had inherited Alexander the Great's empire, contested its possession. Judas Maccabaeus led a revolt against the Seleucid king, Antiochus IV Epiphanes and re-established Jewish sovereignty.[62] The Maccabaean dynasty known as the Hasmonaeans had ruled the city until Pompey established Roman control some hundred years before the time that Apollos and Jerahmeel were now entering the city. Even the Romans had lost control of the city to the Parthians, but with Roman help, the so-called, Herod the Great, had retaken the city and had ruled Israel as a puppet king who owed allegiance to Rome. Herod's successors still ruled under Roman patronage.

Jerahmeel and Apollos entered the city by a gate which led to the Bethesda quarter. They were considerably jostled as they made their way through this narrow opening in the massive city walls through which large numbers of people were continuously passing in either direction. A pair of Roman sentries stood each side of the gate, scrutinising the continuously moving crowd who seemed to be quite oblivious of the sentries' presence. Every now and then, they would pick on a man and take him into the guard house, and after a few minutes they would reappear, releasing the man to rejoin the crowd. Jerahmeel explained to Apollos that Jerusalem had a reputation of being a hot-bed of rebellion against Roman rule. The Romans were always having to suppress minor revolts. The men who had been detained in an apparently random manner from the crowds which passed through the gates, were merely searched to ensure that they were not bearing concealed weapons.

Apollos had been impressed at the very scale of the city walls. How could any army penetrate these impregnable ramparts? Even more impressive sights awaited within. Hard by the wall, towering over all other buildings around, was the huge Antonia fortress. Jerahmeel explained that this had been built by Herod and so named to curry favour with the then most influential Roman in the eastern part of the Empire, Mark Anthony. This name was well known to Apollos. Indeed, it was almost a household word in his native Alexandria where his scandalous relationship with the Ptolemaic queen, Cleopatra, had affected the destiny of Egypt and had resulted in its becoming more firmly absorbed into the Roman Empire. The Roman army of occupation in Jerusalem was garrisoned in this fortress of Antonia, and soldiers could be seen regularly entering and leaving the building, usually in groups of three or four.

A wall stretched from this fortress, and Apollos could see that this wall defined a very large courtyard. Within this courtyard was another impressive building whose gilded walls and towers reflected the rays of the setting sun to appear even more resplendent than it might at other times of day. Apollos did not need to be told that this was none other than the celebrated Temple, but not the Temple of Solomon. It merely occupied the site where that former glory of Israel had once stood. Jerahmeel explained that this Temple had also been built by Herod, but in Jerahmeel's view, for political rather than religious reasons. Being an Idumaean, and hence, an Edomite in the eyes of Israel, Herod was regarded as a gentile. Even the gesture of building a magnificent temple had not endeared Herod to the Jews, for in many ways, he was a tyrant, and everybody knew that he owed his position entirely to having the support of the hated Romans. Herod the Great had made a political marriage to a Hasmonaean princess, Mariamne, knowing that Maccabaean blood would give his progeny the credibility with the Jewish people which he was denied. However, a descendant of Herod the Great who had inherited a part of his father's kingdom, Herod Antipas, was no descendant of the Maccabaeans, but of Malthake, a Samaritan wife of his much married father. Herod Antipas was more unpopular with the Jews than even his father.

Among the crimes which offended the Jews, were his disgraceful treatment of his first wife, Arnon, a Nabataean princess, his illegal marriage to Herodias, his half-brother's wife,[63] and his beheading of the prophet whom Caleb of Jezreel followed, John the Baptist. Herod Antipas had been succeeded by his nephew, Herod Agrippa I who in turn was succeeded by the king who currently ruled, Herod Agrippa II. As a great-grandson of Mariamne, Herod Agrippa II could claim that Hasmonaean blood, flowed in his veins. Herod Agrippa II was generally accepted by the Jewish people in a way his predecessors had not been. Apollos was intrigued by this history lesson which Jerahmeel was delivering about the dynasty which now ruled Israel. Apollos had been told much of this before, but found the fact that the kings all seemed to bear the name Herod made matters confusing.

'The Temple is a place we must visit another day,' said Jerahmeel to Apollos as they struggled through the crowds which thronged this teeming city, where all around them seemed to have the intense urgency of attitude associated with those whose preoccupation and main concern in life was to make money. 'I do not have the friends and contacts in Jerusalem that I have in Beersheba and Hebron who will afford us the hospitality of free lodging. Jerusalem tends to be an expensive place to live, and we will need to move away from the Temple quarter if we are to find reasonably priced accommodation before nightfall.' After investigating one or two potentially inviting inns, they found suitable hostelry, enjoyed a meal, and rested early in preparation for another day of exploration in a city which Apollos anticipated was going to be the most exciting yet.

13

The Temple

Jerahmeel told Apollos that a visit to the Temple would be
the climax of their visit to Jerusalem, and suggested that
they should delay this until they had first made a general
exploration of the City. This plan suited Apollos well, and
the pair spent the best part of the day, wandering through
the narrow streets. They prudently kept the main part of
their money in money belts which they wore beneath their
outer clothing. Apollos had never been through such
crowded streets before. Our two travellers were continuously jostled as they passed along the main business
thoroughfares, in much the same way as they had been the
previous day when they had passed through the narrow city
gates through which hundreds of visitors and citizens
continuously poured. Small wonder that Jerusalem was
notorious for pick-pockets and sneak thieves.

Our travellers made a circuit of the outer walls of the City
and mentally compared and contrasted the gates which
pierced this defensive fortification. Apollos was surprised
to find the City contained other internal walls. Jerahmeel
explained that these represented successive defensive
boundaries of the City as Jerusalem had grown over the
centuries. The present walls probably represented the limit
to which its perimeter could expand. The deep valleys
which contributed so much to the City's defences, prevented further growth on three sides at least of the
metropolis as it stood at present. Apollos and Jerahmeel
found the House of the High Priest, and the Palace of King
Herod, before finally making their way to the Temple.

The Antonia Fortress stood at the north-western corner
of the rectangular wall which defined the Temple area. Our

travellers passed through this wall to find the interior of the boundary wall, lined with rows of columns which supported porticos, forming a sort of cloister. This cloister afforded shelter to the many activities which were being carried out within the Temple area. Money changers were converting currency into the Temple coinage, the only legal tender within the perimeter defined by the boundary wall. Those who changed their money used it to buy sacrificial animals which could be purchased from stalls under the porticos, further round the cloister. In other parts of the colonnade which surrounded the Temple courtyard, meetings were being held, schools were being conducted, and some groups were praying and singing. The whole place had as much bustle and business going on as Apollos had witnessed in the too modern active city without.

The Temple proper was on raised ground in the centre of the area, and surrounded by a balustrade. Notices around this balustrade in Greek and Latin warned the unwary foreigner that it was a capital offence for a gentile to enter the Temple. Apollos and Jerahmeel went into the Temple. They had to wait a moment or so for their eyes to adapt to the lower light level. The inside of the Temple was quiet, but there was still much activity. Although many white robed priests could be seen within the Temple, none seemed to be able to pass the time in idleness. Their attention was being continuously sought by those coming into the Temple building. There were parents, bringing young male babies for circumcision, having with them the required sacrificial offering which they had bought in the outer courtyard. The social status of the parents could be deduced from their offering. Most had only a white pigeon to offer. Some came in with a sheep or a goat. One opulent family came in with a magnificent white bullock. The animals were taken away for slaughter. Four priests could be seen around the huge altar of undressed stones at the centre of the edifice, tendering on pitchforks huge pieces of meat from sacrifices to the flames that rose from a steadily burning fire at the centre of the altar.

Apollos was absolutely enthralled at what he saw. He had been in great temples before in his native Egypt, and they were all impressive in their way, meticulously clean, silent, designed to direct the gaze and attention of anyone entering them to some huge statue at a focal point in the edifice, representing the deity in whose honour the temple had been constructed. However, Apollos had rejected polytheism and idolatory, so that all these temples had been regarded by Apollos as sham and irrelevant. This Temple in Jerusalem was different. It had atmosphere, genuine atmosphere, which made him feel deeply conscious of the presence of the omnipotent, unseen God who required no statue to symbolise his presence. Apollos and Jerahmeel spent some time in silent prayer, before wandering around the Temple to explore as much as was permitted lay-people, or more precisely, lay-men to visit, for women were allowed in the outermost court only. The Priests' Court and special holy places were not accessible to Apollos and Jerahmeel. Indeed, within the holy place behind a great curtain, often referred to as the veil, was enshrined the Holy of Holies, which the High Priest alone could enter but once a year on the Day of Atonement.[64]

Jerahmeel had visited the Temple many times before. While he had probably been as awestruck on his first visit as Apollos was now, Jerahmeel mentally reacted rather differently to Apollos at the scene they now witnessed. The experience of a devout and sincere life had developed within Jerahmeel, an acute spirituality which enabled him to appreciate realities in very fundamental terms. Jerahmeel mused on the status games he saw enacted in that space. The seniority of the priests could be readily determined by the degree of elaboration of their embroidered ephods. The higher priests even had great precious stones sown into this garment. The more junior priests were paying deferential service to the more senior members of their caste, obsequiously bowing as they fetched and carried the objects which the high priests signified with gestures and nods that they needed. The junior priests had the mundane tasks to perform, fetching and carrying, turning the giant pieces of meat from the sacrifices which were being roasted in the dancing flames which sprang from the huge stone altar, and carrying out the ceremonial ablutions.

The poorer families, bringing infants for circumcision,

could be readily identified as they had no more than a white dove to offer for sacrifice, and these would be directed to junior priests.[65] The well dressed family with the magnificent, young white bullock was being attended to by a senior priest. Two senior priests supervised the chest into which visitors placed their alms. Jerahmeel felt that he could almost detect these priests' contempt at the meagre offerings made by the many poor people who passed by that chest, tossing in coins which they could ill afford to give.[66] Every now and then, one whom Jerahmeel could recognize as a pharisee would come to give alms. The pharisee would often be preceded by a servant who held the box containing his gift aloft so that all around would be aware that a spectacular offering was to be made. One pharisee was particularly conspicuous. His face was partly concealed by the phylacteries which hung from his forehead, but could be seen to be contorted in an agonized grimace. Jerahmeel knew that this was a public indication of the pain he was experiencing as a result of fasting. His gift was obviously appreciated by the priests sitting by the alms chest. As it was deposited, they both stood and obsequiously bowed, and this gesture was echoed by the pharisee, who then turned and shuffled his way back to the Temple entrance, aware of the admiring stares of the poorer folk, who deferentially made way to allow him to pass.[67]

'What does God make of all this?' thought Jerahmeel to himself.

A question which had burned in Jerahmeel's mind since the day that Sandas-cum-Barama had spoken at his home synagogue in Alexandria, which had been raised again with Caleb of Jezreel at Beersheba, concerned the attitude of the Jewish priests in the Temple at Jerusalem to this Jesus who was reputed to have risen from the dead. Although it was undoubtedly clear that they had opposed him at one time, because they had been instrumental in arranging for him to be executed, the fact that he had been able to prove his credentials by returning from the grave must surely have caused them to revise their opinion of this prophet. Jerahmeel had expected that it would have been the easiest thing in the world for him to simply go up to a junior priest and ask his question directly. However, Jerahmeel had an overwhelming premonition that to do so would court disaster. Jerahmeel knew full well how fanatic some Jews could be over religious matters, especially issues which affected the status quo or appeared to conflict with centuries of tradition. The implication that the priests had made a serious mistake in the way they had treated a messenger from God who had proved his credentials in a rather special way, could seriously threaten their vested interest in maintaining their status as the ultimate and absolute authority on all matters pertaining to religion. Jerahmeel remembered the notices in Greek and Latin at the entrance to the main Temple building, warning gentiles that to enter was a capital offence. Even though he was a Jew of good standing, Jerahmeel was aware that offending Jewish religious scruples could provoke a fanatical response out of all proportion to the perceived offence. He therefore deemed it would be unwise to mention the name Jesus to a priest in that most sacred place, for to do so might well bring upon himself the sort of fate that a gentile found in that place might expect to experience.

After spending about an hour in the Temple, Jerahmeel and Apollos made their way out into the bright sunlight which bathed the Court of Gentiles. This was the name given to the area which was outside the main Temple building but within the cloister which defined the rectangular Temple precinct. Apollos, who had remained in awestruck silence as they had explored the Temple interior, expressed a wish that they might return again to the Temple, especially if a special religious event or festival was taking place. On such occasions, processions were formed which all Jews present could join, and these processions often entered the Court of Priests, which was one of the areas prohibited to visitors on normal days.

14

The Synagogue of the Freedmen

Jerahmeel did not have contacts in Jerusalem like those that had proved so useful to our travellers in Beersheba and Hebron. There were many synagogues in Jerusalem, and over the years, Jerahmeel had worshipped in several of them. However, in a big metropolis like Jerusalem, the population turned over fairly rapidly, and synagogues changed their character as their presidents came and went. Thus, there was no particular synagogue for which Jerahmeel felt a lasting affinity. Which synagogue Apollos and Jerahmeel might choose to attend for sabbath worship was therefore an open question. Observing that they came from Alexandria, the innkeeper at the hostel where they were staying suggested that they might try the Synagogue of the Freedmen. The congregation there consisted largely of expatriate Jews from North Africa, particularly, Cyrene and Alexandria, who conversed more happily in Greek than Aramaic.

So it was, Jerahmeel and Apollos made their way to the Siloam district of Jerusalem where they easily found the imposing Synagogue of the Freedmen, on a main road, opposite the Fountain Gate. They arrived early which gave Jerahmeel an opportunity to present his credentials in the form of the Dathan Barjoseph's letter to the President of the Synagogue of the Freedmen. The President received the travellers courteously enough, but there was no great warmth in his welcome. The Synagogue soon filled with sabbath worshippers who were, by and large, from the more wealthy classes. It appeared that the synagogue was so named because it had been founded many years earlier by Jews who had formerly been Roman slaves, but had worked sufficiently hard to be able to purchase their freedom. As the innkeeper had told them, there were many Greek speaking Jews from Alexandria and Cyrene in that congregation. One strange and rather off-putting characteristic that the members of this synagogue seemed to share, was an extreme intensity of expression. They were obviously very sincere and ultra devout, but a smile scarcely crossed their lips to lighten the heavy and serious visage that most of them bore. It did not take Jerahmeel long to recognize that although religious ardour was evident in good measure, humour was a characteristic lacking in that gathering.

The candles in the seven-branched candelabra were lit and the service commenced. The Synagogue of the Freedmen was a beautiful building on which meticulous care had been bestowed. The service was an elaborately ritualistic event, quite different from the sort of service which Jerahmeel and Apollos had been used to in their native Alexandria. While Jerahmeel did not find this service particularly to his taste, Apollos appeared to thoroughly enjoy the experience. For him, the ritual, the candles, the incense, recaptured an element of the magical atmosphere he had imbibed at the Temple.

At the appropriate time, the President of the Synagogue bade welcome to Apollos and Jerahmeel and half a dozen or so other visitors to the service. This was evidently a popular synagogue with visitors to Jerusalem, but everything was very formal. There was no opportunity given for Jerahmeel to respond to the President's welcome or to say anything to those gathered there. In a less pretentious gathering, Jerahmeel's letter of introduction would have been recognized by a synagogue president as an indication that an exceptional teacher was in their midst. The main address was given by an elderly Jew whose face was sad and sombre, even by the standards of that gathering. Jerahmeel recognized that he was a pharisee. The teaching was a turgid exposition on an aspect of the Law concerning rights of property ownership. The address was fortunately short.

After the service when Jerahmeel and Apollos had the opportunity to converse socially with those present, Jerahmeel found an opportunity to raise the question which had been burning in his mind to have resolved since he reached Jerusalem. He asked them how they rated the prophet, Jesus, of whom he had heard, and whom he believed, had ministered in Jerusalem. Jerahmeel was surprised by the vehement anger with which his query was greeted. He was told that this carpenter had been a dangerous and evil man. He had used evil powers to perform magic effects and to speak entrancing words so that many were deceived. He had sought to undermine two thousand years of the religious tradition of the Jewish nation by flouting their laws and encouraging others to do the same. He even claimed to be the Messiah, although everyone knew he came from Galilee. Galilee did not even have the reputation to be a birthplace of a prophet, let alone the Messiah.

The President of the Synagogue explained that one of legacies of Moses and Aaron which enabled the nation to determine whether or not the credentials of a so-called Messiah were valid, was the Levitical priesthood. Caiaphas, the High Priest, had declared against this Jesus after his case had been heard by the Sanhedrin, and the man was duly executed for blasphemy. It seems that a member of the Synagogue of the Freedmen who was a bystander in the crowd who watched the criminals pass by, had actually been pressed into service by the Roman officials to carry this man's cross after he had collapsed on his way to execution. There was no doubt that the Romans had done their job thoroughly. Jesus was well and truly dead. Knowing the rumours that might have reached Jerahmeel's ears, the President spoke of the followers that this Jesus had left behind.

'If anything, this man's disciples are more dangerous than Jesus himself. They make wild claims that he came back from the dead, although none of us have ever seen him. They state that entry into the next world can be achieved in his name. Many of this man's followers are among the dregs of society who have done nothing to secure themselves a place in the next world. It obviously suits them to believe that he has power to bestow on them the rights to enter heaven as a gift. They go further and claim there is no other way to heaven. The congregation of our synagogue know full well that this is utter nonsense, for our members above all men have had to work for everything they have in life. Many of them were slaves who worked hard to buy their own freedom. Since then, they have continued to work harder than others in our society who were born free. As a result, they have established successful businesses and become fairly wealthy men. They not only work hard for things in life, but by scrupulous observation of all that the Law demands of us, have done all that is necessary to make themselves fully acceptable to God. How can a sham prophet whose followers claim that he can give free entry to heaven be taken seriously by men like those who attend this synagogue?

'The followers of this Jesus ascribe to him, greater authority than that vested in the Aaronic line of priesthood. However, their real danger lies in their fanaticism. When we brought one of their number before the Council, he persisted in his wild claims, even though he knew he was courting a death sentence. He was duly stoned.[69] Another of Jesus' disciples was beheaded by Herod[70] and many have been imprisoned, but still they persist in championing this lost cause, heedless of the fact that by offending the leaders of our faith and misleading the people, they are courting prosecution and worse.

'When the genuine Messiah comes, he will lead the nation to renew the traditions established by Moses and the prophets who followed him. He will prove his credentials by establishing our people as a great nation, greater than it was in King David's day, so that even Rome will look puny in comparison. The wonders which accompany the true Messiah will leave none in doubt that his claim to be the deliverer of his people is valid.'

The President ended abruptly and the meeting dispersed. Apollos considered that the President had spoken with sound logic and considered at that time, that there would be no point in further pursuing enquiries about this Jesus. As they walked back to their inn, Jerahmeel said little and seemed rather sad. He had genuinely believed that while in Jerusalem, they might have had verification of something which would have represented the greatest event in his nation's history. These hopes were now firmly dashed.

15

James

Over the next few days, Apollos and Jerahmeel continued
to explore the sights of Jerusalem. Apollos was thrilled by
all he saw, and they returned several times to the principal
buildings and sites with important connections. At least
once a day, they went to the Temple and each time, they
discovered some new feature of interest which they had
missed on earlier visits, or they experienced some new
aspect of worship as different events were celebrated in the
Temple. Apollos was absolutely enthralled at the music, the
ritual, the processions, the garments worn by the priests,
the atmosphere generated in that uniquely holy place.
Jerahmeel on the other hand, appeared to be preoccupied.
He no longer seemed to take delight in revealing to Apollos
the treasures and traditions of his nation's history which
were so familiar to himself, and which this tour was giving
him the opportunity to share with his prize pupil. His mind
was clearly on other things and he no longer conversed as
freely as he normally did when there were new things to
explain and new sights were being experienced.

Then, one week after they had attended the service at the
Synagogue of the Freedmen, they encountered a group
which was to lead Jerahmeel into making profound and
exciting discoveries. It was quite early on the Sabbath day.
Apollos and Jerahmeel were paying their diurnal visit to the
Temple. They spent longer than usual in the outer
courtyard, the Court of Gentiles as it was known. There
seemed to be more than customary business in that bustling
courtyard. Almost every bay of the cloister which formed
the perimeter of the courtyard was taken up with some
activity. As Apollos and Jerahmeel came to that part of the

courtyard bounded by the arcade known as Solomon's Cloister, they stopped by a group who were worshipping and singing in a very lively manner.[71] They had seen this particular group in Solomon's Cloister on previous visits to the Temple but this time they waited to watch and listen. As they watched, they could not fail to see that these were people who radiated joy. As they listened, they heard the name Jesus mentioned many times in the prayers and in the hymns that were sung. After a while, Apollos made to move on but Jerahmeel indicated that he wanted to stay.

Twenty minutes or so later, the prayers came to an end. The group made to leave the Temple Courtyard, and separated with warm embraces. Jerahmeel stopped one young man as he was leaving and asked about Jesus of whom he had heard them sing and pray. The young man was delighted to have been approached. He introduced himself as Amariah. He explained that they met regularly to worship Jesus who was the promised deliverer of their people. He spoke of the wonders that Jesus had performed. He told them of Jesus' death and his rising again three days later. Amariah realized that he was telling the couple more than they could easily take in, in that bustling environment, and he suggested that they should come round to visit his community. Here they would meet others who knew this Jesus very well, as they had been his personal friends and relations while he lived on earth. Jerahmeel was keen to go at the earliest possible opportunity, and Amariah invited them to come that evening. The opinions so forcibly expressed at the Synagogue of the Freedmen the previous Sabbath, had caused Apollos to mentally write off Jesus as a false prophet of no importance. Apollos had been particularly looking forward to attending the Synagogue of Freedmen again that Sabbath. At that moment, Jerahmeel's priorities were different. Without saying anything which could have proved offensive to Amariah, Apollos indicated that that evening, he wished to attend the same synagogue that he had been to the previous week. It was finally arranged that Apollos should go to the Synagogue while Jerahmeel would return to the Temple late that afternoon. Amariah would be there to meet him and conduct him to his community.

When Jerahmeel arrived at the Temple, he found Amariah already waiting. Amariah greeted Jerahmeel with a warm and open smile. Amariah then accompanied Jerahmeel to the upper quarter of the City, eventually arriving at an apparently small house in a secluded side street which lead off another narrow street. Amariah knocked three times in a rhythm which indicated to Jerahmeel that this was some sort of coded signal. The door was opened by a young woman whom Jerahmeel recognized as a member of the group who had worshipped in Solomon's Cloister that morning. Once inside the house, Jerahmeel realized that appearances had been deceptive. The house was really quite large and stretched back a long way. As they walked down the corridors and climbed the stairs, Jerahmeel realized that a quite significant number of people were living here. They cheerily greeted Amariah as he passed them. Jerahmeel noticed that on many of the doors, there had been painted both the Star of David and another logo which crudely resembled the outline of a fish. Amariah knocked at one of these doors and entered as a voice called from within. Jerahmeel followed and was greeted by the occupant of the room, a strikingly handsome man who was about forty years old. Amariah had already briefed this man of how he had met Jerahmeel. Amariah introduced the two men, Jerahmeel as an enquirer after Jesus whom he had met that morning at the Temple, and the other, as James who was both brother of Jesus and the leader of their community.[72] Amariah courteously bowed, bade his leave and went out, leaving the two men to talk together.

Jerahmeel soon felt relaxed in James' company. James first asked Jerahmeel about Alexandria and showed great interest in Jerahmeel's account of the places they had visited on their way to Jerusalem. Jerahmeel passed over his letter of introduction from Dathan Barjoseph, and James was clearly impressed by the eulogy that the President of the Synagogue in the Hebron district in Alexandria had written in support of Jerahmeel. James was particularly interested in learning about what Jerahmeel had heard of Jesus. Jerahmeel told James of Sandas-cum-Barama's visit to the Synagogue he attended in Alexandria, and he described Caleb of Jezreel's account of the day he had spent with Jesus when Caleb was a disciple of John the Baptist. Jerahmeel was a straightforward person and he instinctively sensed that James was a man of complete integrity. He therefore decided that it was politic to report to James the negative comments which had been made concerning Jesus when he attended the Synagogue of the Freedmen, the previous sabbath. James gave a wry smile when Jerahmeel mentioned that one of their own number had actually carried Jesus' cross when he was on his way to execution.

'I wonder why they should have made special mention of that?' mused James.

Jerahmeel suggested that this was to prove that they had first hand evidence that Jesus really was executed.

'Yes,' said James, 'I am sure that this must have been the reason, but this is one fact about which there is no dispute. So many in Jerusalem witnessed that execution, including some of Jesus' disciples. Even his mother, who is also my mother, saw Jesus experience that terrible death. The thing which surprises me about their mentioning the member of the Synagogue of the Freedmen who carried Jesus' cross, is that he left that Synagogue when the news broke that Jesus' had come back from the grave. This man was called Simon.[73] Simon, his friend Lucius,[74] and Simon's two sons, Rufus and Alexander, had previously been staunch members of the Synagogue of the Freedmen, but they were utterly convinced by the accounts they heard of Jesus' resurrection and became members of this community.

'The members of the Synagogue of the Freedmen became very vindictive when they discovered how many people were joining our community, and they started to persecute those who were most eloquent in speaking of Jesus. Some they imprisoned. The Synagogue of the Freedmen were even responsible for bringing one of our members before the Council and having him sentenced and summarily executed. The persecution of the members of our community forced most of them to leave Jerusalem, but Jesus' special disciples remained in Jerusalem. As former members, Simon and Lucius were also likely to be victims of the jealous rage of the Synagogue of the Freedmen. They therefore left Jerusalem and have gone to stay with a community like our own in a city in the north.'

That James should so freely converse with Jerahmeel was an indication that he reciprocated Jerahmeel's recognition of a completely trustworthy individual. Jerahmeel was a stranger, but James had unerring judgement of the character and quality of the people he met.

'Do you not feel yourself and others of your community to be at risk?' asked Jerahmeel.

'Undoubtedly we are,' replied James, 'but we have a spirit of boldness and courage. Immediately after Jesus had been crucified, his disciples were a sorry and scared bunch of men, hiding from the authorities in obscure upper rooms and inconspicuous houses. Then, on the day of Pentecost, that is six weeks to the day after Jesus had risen, the disciples received a divine gift of great power.[75] This power enabled them to boldly proclaim the fact that Jesus who died, rose again to give all men the assurance that they too could receive the gift of eternal life. With this assurance, we have no fear of anything the authorities can do to us. The worst that they can do is to have us executed, and that will merely bring us to the better life that exists with Jesus beyond the grave, although, we do indeed enjoy now in this life, the unseen but very real company of the spirit of Jesus whom we can talk to as a friend.

'I told you of the execution of one of our members as a result of an intrigue carried out by the Synagogue of the Freedmen. The man's name was Stephen. He was an absolutely splendid fellow, and had been chosen as a deacon of our community because of his outstanding abilities in administration. This freed the special disciples of Jesus whom we call apostles, to exercise the great gifts for preaching and teaching which they received on the day of Pentecost. However, Stephen too proved to be a great preacher, and this is why he was marked out for execution by those who fear our community. Stephen was stoned, but his death was a triumphant experience. Stephen's dying words expressed his ecstasy as he saw Jesus on the right hand of God, welcoming Stephen to his kingdom as he passed from this life.[69]

'Stephen's death was not futile, for many became believers when they saw the manner of his death and the radiance of his countenance as the heavenly light fell upon it. One of those who took an active part in his stoning, a pharisee named Saul,[69] became a believer a short while later. He took on the new name, Paul, and what a tower of strength he has been to the movement which seeks to convince the world that Jesus' death and resurrection means the end of the power of final death. What a wonderful friend and inspiration Paul has been to me, indeed to all of us.

'However, those with hard hearts refused to be moved by Stephen's death, and more persecution followed. The next to be executed was one of Jesus' most loyal and faithful disciples, a man with the same name as myself. James was executed by Herod,[70] that is Herod Agrippa I. This Herod, like his uncle, Herod Antipas, who had John the Baptist executed, was prepared to sink to any depths to gain popularity with those whom he believed to be important to his own security. Divine retribution was to follow. Within weeks, Herod himself was mysteriously struck down dead when he tried to delude the people and speak as if he were some kind of divine messenger.[76]

'While none of us fear persecution, or even death, the spirit which guides us is not one of blind folly. The spirit which directs us, told us to send our best speakers to other cities to spread the word there. The apostles have therefore left Jerusalem and are proclaiming in distant towns and cities the truths that Jesus revealed to us.

'Stephen's great friend and fellow deacon was a man named Philip, a great teacher as Stephen had been. He too had to leave Jerusalem during the persecutions. I realize that this was the Philip who happened to be on the Gaza road as the Ethiopian, Sandas-cum-Barama passed by.[3] I had not known of this until you told me of Sandas-cum-Barama, and the things he said to you at your own synagogue in Alexandria, but praise God, he places his people in the right place at the right time. Look, how God has now brought you here where you can learn from those who knew Jesus during his life-time on earth.

'We continue to face the threat of persecution, but still, many are becoming believers in Jerusalem. Now that our most outspoken preachers have left the city, those who find us a threat have difficulty in knowing how to prevent our communities in Jerusalem from growing. They know where we live. As you have seen, our bolder members even worship Jesus in the Temple cloisters, but the authorities cannot continue to arrest hundreds of law abiding citizens for no other reason that that they worship God in a different way to themselves. The new king, Herod Agrippa II, is fair and just in the way he administers the law. In any case, apart from myself, there is no one now in Jerusalem, whom our enemies would recognize as being sufficiently prominent in our movement to be worth targeting for persecution. We don't even feel uneasy, for the spirit which gives us boldness, also gives us peace.'

James paused here. He knew Jerahmeel would have many questions to ask, but he felt inwardly confident that this very genuine man would soon become a believer himself.

'I had felt despondent during the last week,' begun Jerahmeel, 'for the hopes that had been rising in me over the past months that something special had happened in Israel, had all but been totally dashed by what I had heard at the Synagogue of the Freedmen. However, I now feel exhilarated, for what you have said puts many things in perspective, but there is still much that I do not understand. Everything seems to hinge on the fact that Jesus rose from the dead. It could be said that as his brother, you have a vested interest in this claim being accepted as valid. No one before has risen from the dead. You spoke of the deacon, Stephen, seeing Jesus in the next world at the moment of his death, but if Jesus rose from the dead, why is he not here among you now?'

These were just the questions that James had expected to be raised.

'During the time Jesus taught on earth, I had no vested interest in his success. It is a human failing that although we will readily ascribe greatness to strangers, we are reluctant to accept that someone in our own family is special beyond ourselves. Jesus was a marvellous elder brother. He was always resourceful, considerate, level headed and industrious. Many things happened in our family which would have caused most elder brothers to become very angry but Jesus always remained calm. He had an interest in the synagogue and its teaching which went much further than that of a normal, devout Jewish young man, and it was clear that he had a leaning to be a spiritual teacher himself, perhaps to become the president of a synagogue. However, he was also a very able craftsman. He was a carpenter as my father Joseph had been. My father died when our younger brothers Joseph, Simon and Judas were still very young. Jesus therefore remained at home as the family breadwinner until Joseph and Simon were old enough to earn their own living.

'One day when we attended a wedding as a family at Cana-in-Galilee, the wine ran out. My mother knew that Jesus was always resourceful and she asked him to retrieve the situation. Jesus asked the servants to fill the jars with water which they did. When the water was drawn, it was no longer water, but the finest wine I have ever tasted.[78] It was clear to all of us then that Jesus was not just resourceful, but that he could perform miracles. I think that in asking him to help at this wedding, my mother had unwittingly precipitated Jesus into a new way of life. From that time on, Jesus gave up his carpentry to preach. He proclaimed great truths about God as no one had done before. He also performed more miracles. Jesus healed the sick, fed hungry crowds and even calmed raging storms. You mentioned earlier that no one before had risen from the dead. It is true that no one except Jesus has risen without a servant of God being on hand to perform the miracle. You will of course remember that the prophets Elijah and Elisha brought back the dead to life.[79, 80] Jesus performed such miracles himself. Just before his own death, Jesus brought back to life his friend Lazarus whose body had already started to decompose in the tomb.[81] In performing this miracle, it was as if Jesus was giving his disciples a sign that he had power, even over the grave, so that they should not despair when he himself was shortly to die. However, frail humans as we all are, the disciples failed to recognize this sign.

'I suppose that I resented Jesus leaving home for that left me with the responsibility of looking after Mary, our mother. There were times when we had news of Jesus being in danger of being crushed by great crowds who thronged around him. On one occasion when he seemed to be trapped by the crowds in a house, my mother, my brothers and I tried to extricate him from the danger, but he seemed to be rather disparaging about us, implying that the crowds who had come to listen to him were more like a real family than we were,[82] and my resentment grew.

'After he had been preaching and fulfilling a most spectacular ministry for about three years, Jesus was arrested by the religious authorities who were jealous of his success. They had him crucified, causing my mother untold anguish. She was there at the foot of the cross when he died. My mother had told us that when she had taken Jesus as an infant up to the Temple, an old man had recognized Jesus to be the Messiah, but told my mother that sorrow like a sharp sword would pierce her heart.[83] She had thought that this merely meant the sorrow she experienced when Jesus left home to preach, but the full force of this prophecy came home to her, that dreadful Friday.

'Three days later, three women went to the tomb with spices to embalm the body, but returned with disturbing but exciting news. The stone which sealed the tomb had been rolled away.[84] The grave clothes were still there, but not scattered as they might be if someone had torn them from the body. They were folded in position, almost as if the body passed through them, leaving them behind on the slab.[85] One of the women, Mary Magdalene, reported that she had met Jesus, alive in the garden. Then other disciples came back with reports that they too had met Jesus. Because many of them had preconceived ideas that Jesus was dead, he was not always recognized immediately. However, even before he was recognized, his presence had the effect of instilling great peace and joy to the disciples who experienced his company. Then through his actions, through the words he spoke, it became clear that this was Jesus, risen from the dead. Sometimes Jesus would appear to just one or two disciples, sometimes to many gathered in a company. Sometimes he would appear in a room which had been securely sealed against intruders, and at others, in the open air, or on a road, or by the sea shore, or on a mountain. For several days, many of us had these wonderful experiences of meeting the risen Jesus, yes, Jesus appeared to me too, although I had been no great support to him in

102

his life-time.[86]

'Because I am privileged to be an eyewitness, I obviously have no reason, no need to doubt that Jesus rose from the dead, but then, so many, many people saw Jesus during those few days that no one need be in any doubt that Jesus had conquered death. The evidence of eyewitnesses is overwhelming. Jesus even allowed the most sceptical of his disciples to feel the wounds, mortal wounds by which he had died.[87] Yes, Jesus was pierced to the heart after he had hung on the cross for several hours, and the way the blood and water poured from that wound showed that he was already dead. During these appearances, Jesus told his disciples to go to a hill in Galilee at a certain time. There, he commissioned them to go through the world, telling everyone the news of his resurrection and to explain the implications of this event for all people.[88] Then they saw Jesus taken up to heaven in a cloud.[89] He had asked the disciples to remain together in the upper room which they shared until he had sent them someone else to help them continue his work.[90] That person came on the day of Pentecost in the form of the Spirit which I described to you. This Spirit entered into each disciple and was accompanied by mystic signs, great tongues of flame which rested on the disciples and the sound of a mighty rushing wind.[75]

'This person, this Spirit was not what the disciples had expected, but was more valuable for the task which lay ahead than a person in human form. A person in human form could only be at one place at one time. This Spirit, which is none other than the power of God, enabled the disciples to speak in different tongues. This Spirit enabled them to perform great miracles, just as Jesus had done, during the time he was on earth. Before that Day of Pentecost, the disciples had been a timid, anxious group, fearing perhaps that the priests would subject them to the same fate as Jesus if they were caught. On that Day of Pentecost, the disciples were able to go out and boldly proclaim with this new power, that Jesus had risen from the dead. They spoke so effectively that thousands became believers, there and then. There was no longer any need to fear the priests, the Romans, death or persecution, for the disciples then had both power and the certain knowledge that Jesus had conquered death for them, giving them the assurance of life in the next world with him. Although this Spirit came in a special way on that Day of Pentecost, this Spirit still comes to those who believe, whom God wishes to equip with special power to proclaim this wonderful news.'

James paused again. Had he spoken too long and given Jerahmeel more than he could assimilate, but Jerahmeel was excited, eager to ask questions, eager to hear more.

'If what you say is true, and I have no doubt that it is, for your words have a ring of conviction and authority, why is there so much opposition to your community? Perhaps the priests cannot bear to lose face, as they would have to in admitting their mistake, but why should people, like the congregation of the Synagogue of the Freedmen be so against the people of your community who are able to declare that they have irrefutable evidence that Jesus came back to life after being crucified? Have the members of the Synagogue of the Freedmen been presented with any valid contradictory evidence?'

James answered Jerahmeel's question.

'If we were distorting facts and spreading deceit, they would have found it very straightforward to disprove our claims. The priests had merely to produce the body of Jesus. This should after all have been an easy thing for them to do. They had put a guard of soldiers on the tomb. However, a guard of soldiers cannot thwart the almighty power of God and there was no corpse to display. The priests had to resort to bribing the soldiers to say that they were asleep and that the disciples had stolen the body while they slept. If this statement had been other than a fabrication which the guards were instructed to make by their superiors, the guards would have been executed for dereliction of duty. In any case, if the guards were asleep, how could they know that the disciples had stolen the body? If we had stolen the body, and just made up our stories of seeing Jesus alive, we would know that we were spreading a deception. Whatever motive there might be ascribed to us for this deception, we would not be prepared to face danger and death to perpetuate what we would realize was no more than trickery. However, we are fully prepared to face death for truth, especially a truth which guarantees that mortal death on earth is not the end of life, but rather, the beginning of a new more glorious phase of life.

'As you say, the priests would lose face, if they accepted our story and acknowledged that they had made a mistake. More than that, they would lose their authority, their status and their power. These are poor reasons for denying truth, but they are compelling reasons for people welded to the values by which the world lives and subscribing to the standards by which the world judges others.

'What of the members of the Synagogue of the Freedmen? They resolutely oppose our message because they sincerely but incorrectly misinterpret our Scriptures. Although they are at enmity with our community, I admire them for their sincerity, but with the exeception of men like Lucius and Simon and his sons, they will not use their minds to see that Jesus' interpretation of Scripture can be the only right one. They cling to preconceived ideas of how the prophecies of the Messiah will be fulfilled, and fail to see that what has happened, although different from their preconceived ideas, not only wonderfully fulfills all that the prophets said, but is also in line with the teaching of Moses.'[90]

Jerahmeel interrupted.

'Surely, there is a difficulty here. The men of the Synagogue of the Freedmen were able to quote from the prophets, passages which seemed to indicate that the Messiah would be a King, and would reign for ever over his Kingdom. The Jesus you have described does not fit this prophecy!'

James continued.

'I have learnt much about the interpretation of prophecy over the last few years. The prophecies were delivered so that we cannot take them at face value, but we have to search for their meaning and their fulfilment. Indeed, if prophecy were too explicit, it would provide a pattern which the unscrupulous might easily imitate to deceive others. In reality, it is not until a prophecy is fulfilled that the full force of the original words of the prophet can be appreciated. Careful thought and study has shown to me that Jesus' fulfilled all the prophecies of the Messiah, completely and absolutely, including the prophecy that he would be king,[91] – no – more than that, Lord of lords, and King of kings. Jesus told us that his kingdom was not of this world.[92] When we ask ourselves, what is the nature of a king, we can see exactly what Jesus meant. The nature of a king is to be obeyed. A worldly king establishes his authority by force, punishing those who disobey, but we obey the instructions that Jesus gave us on earth, and still gives us as we speak to him in our prayers, because we love him. Jesus is in fact, the King of our lives. What's more, we have had news that in some other cities, some of their leading men and even their kings, have accepted Jesus as King of their lives, too. Thus, Jesus is already, King of kings, and his kingdom will continue to grow and will last forever. The interpretation that the members of the Synagogue of the Freedmen, and others put on that prophecy, requires that their Messiah will have to be human with an infinite earthly life span. Such a prophetic outcome poses more problems than resurrection from the dead!'

Jerahmeel nodded his head. This made sense and satisfactorily resolved one of his difficulties. He raised another.

'Young Amariah told me that Jesus' resurrection on the third day was a fulfilment of prophecy, but I cannot recall which of the prophets explicitly stated this?'

James explained this.

'Many of the prophecies are concealed and often remain unrecognized until their fulfilment. Hosea's prophecy of the resurrection is like this.

'"After two days, he will revive us, on the third day, he will raise us up, that we may live before him."[93]

'One of the most remarkable concealed prophecies, which we did not appreciate until its fulfilment, is found in the twenty-second psalm. This psalm describes the crucifixion of Jesus in detail.[94] There is one prophetic book which is totally unlike the others in its content and style, the book of the prophet Jonah. This book tells a story that many of us find it hard to accept at its face value in a literal sense. It is more like a story written to conceal many mystic meanings. During his time on earth, Jesus was often challenged to prove his credentials with a sign, that is by performing a public miracle to convince an audience of sceptics. He would not perform such a miracle, but he promised them

106

the sign, the sign of the prophet Jonah. As Jonah was inside the whale for three days before coming back to land,[95] so Jesus told them that he would be in the depths of the earth for three days.[96] That sign has now been fulfilled. Jesus himself gave us the key to discovering the prophecy concealed in the book of Jonah. It is perhaps also significant that Jonah went to Nineveh, the capital of Assyria, a pagan nation which the Israelites regarded as incorrigibly evil. However, it is recorded that the men of Nineveh repented and escaped the judgement in store for them. On the other hand, the Israelites frequently ignored God's prophets. This mirrors the situation we see today in Israel. Most of those in Jerusalem have rejected Jesus, but the gentiles are accepting with gladness the news that the apostles proclaim to them.'

Jerahmeel posed another question.

'The President of the Synagogue of the Freedmen stated that Jesus claimed that no one could come to God, except by him, but this President claimed that the members of his Synagogue had in fact earned their way to God through their scrupulous adherence to all the Law demanded of them. Is this claim justified?'

James sighed.

'This is the most contentious issue of them all. Yes, God provided the Israelites with the Law through Moses, to give a guide to the way to live a righteous life, but as circumstances change, so must the law. A law written for nomads is not necessarily appropriate for farmers, or for city dwellers. In any case, however hard we try to conform to all that we think the Law demands of us, we can never succeed in this to the extent that we may claim to have lived perfect lives.[97, 98] Only perfection is good enough for God. As Jesus taught us, he showed us how much we all sin in our thoughts,[99] and these are as important to God as our deeds. Our thoughts are all part of our real selves which define our true being. Can beings with such unclean and dishonourable thoughts aspire to share company with the all knowing, perfect God in the next world? Through Scripture, God has shown us the way he must be approached. One of the earliest stories of Scripture was the story of how God accepted the herdsmen, Abel's offering of a sacrifice from his flock, but did not accept the offering of fruits grown from the ground, which Cain provided.[100] The message indicates that the shedding of blood is required to become right with God. Thus, the rite of sacrifice has been practiced by many religions besides that of the Jews, but sacrifices are only an imperfect and temporary way of expressing sorrow and contrition to God. However, God guided us into the ritual of sacrifice, so that we would recognize what Jesus did. In dying, he was the perfect sacrifice. This was all foretold in the book of Isaiah, but I am sure that the prophecy of the Messiah as the suffering servant who has borne our griefs and had our sins laid on him,[101] was not one which you would have heard quoted at the Synagogue of the Freedmen. They may have told you that our community does not observe the Law. This is not true. We observe the Law but we do not seek to make ourselves right with God through the Law. Our righteousness comes rather through having Jesus as King of our lives. Everything we do is done to please him. As he loved all those around him, so we seek to reflect this love in our dealings with our fellow men. Rigid adherence to laws in situations for which they were not designed to apply, can result in innocent people being hurt or injured, but this never arises if all one's actions spring from genuine love.'

A light dawned in Jerahmeel's face.

'Thank you, thank you James for explaining all these things to me. There is still much I need to know and learn, but what you have said has resolved difficulties which were churning in my mind. I feel that I am ready now to become a believer in this Jesus myself. It is late and I am sure I have taken up more of your time than you had expected.'

James showed obvious delight at Jerahmeel's response, and invited him to come around again the following day. He asked Jerahmeel to bring his young friend too.

'The Jews who are not of this community celebrate the sabbath as their special holy day, but we celebrate the first day of the week. This is because Jesus rose from the dead on that day. Here tomorrow, you will see a form of worship which is quite different from anything you have experienced at a synagogue.'

James warmly embraced Jerahmeel, and Jerahmeel left

that house. Jerahmeel declined the offer James made, that Amariah should guide him home. Although it was beginning to get dark, there was enough light for Jerahmeel to mark his bearings so that he could find the house again. Then, with a joyful step and light heart, Jerahmeel made his way back to the inn where he was staying with Apollos.

16

The Jerusalem Church

Jerahmeel hurried the last few hundred yards to the inn. The moon shone brightly and the air was cool. At that hour of the evening, Jerahmeel encountered few passers-by in those narrow streets which had teemed with bustle and activity during the daylight hours. Small groups made their way home from synagogue meetings which had finished late. Some were pausing to chat at the points where their routes home separated, clinging to the last remaining hours of sabbath fellowship with protracted conversations before they finally had to part to return to their homes. On that calm and peaceful evening, Jerahmeel was the only one who hurried. He was concerned that Apollos would have arrived at the inn some time earlier and would experience anxiety that Jerahmeel's return to the inn was late. However, Jerahmeel arrived at the inn a short time before Apollos made his entry.

That evening, Apollos had had rather the opposite experience of Jerahmeel. Jerahmeel's mention of Jesus the previous sabbath had stimulated the members of the Synagogue of the Freedmen to revive their sentiments of opposition to what Jesus of Nazareth stood for. The address had been directed against false prophets who sought to lead the people of Israel who had been faithful to the teachings of Moses and the true prophets, away from the traditions of their fore-fathers. At the end of the meeting, the synagogue elders had enquired of Apollos after Jerahmeel. Apollos gave an evasive reply. A long conversation then followed to which Apollos found himself in the unaccustomed position of being almost a passive listener rather than an active participant. The elders reminisced about the struggles they had engaged in over the years to save the people from becoming the victims of false prophets or false Messiahs. Jesus and his followers were portrayed as one of many such would-be misleaders of Israel. From this conversation, to which Apollos listened intently, it appeared that the false Messiahs invariably contravened prophecies in important respects, so destroying their credibility.

Now that they were back at the inn, Jerahmeel and Apollos were both tired. They had so much to discuss and tell each other about their respective conversations of the evening, but neither were in the state or mood for a long dialogue at that hour. They sensibly decided to retire and save their news for the morning.

The following morning, Jerahmeel started their discussion. They both loved a good argument and were well matched debaters. Jerahmeel had been convinced the previous day that Jesus was the Messiah while Apollos had been led to the conclusion that Jesus was just another false prophet. Jerahmeel could not answer all the well rehearsed arguments with which the Synagogue of the Freedmen had indoctrinated Apollos, for Jerahmeel had learnt all he knew of Jesus from a single evening's session with James. Jerahmeel had the perfect excuse to suggest to Apollos that that day, they should visit the community which James led, to have their difficulties properly resolved. Jerahmeel took Apollos, through the narrow streets to the house he had visited the previous night, and they arrived mid-morning at about the time James had expected them.

The door of the house stood open. Several young people whom Jerahmeel deduced were from the community, stood near the door, welcoming the people making their way to the house, whom they recognized. Amariah was among those in the welcoming party. As he saw Jerahmeel and Apollos approach, he smiled warmly at them and came to meet them.

'You created a marvellous impression with James,' said Amariah as he conducted the pair into the house. He had obviously heard about the conversation the two had had at the house the previous evening.

Amariah conducted them to a large room which Jerahmeel had not seen on his first visit. The room was

111

scrupulously clean and set out for worship. A table covered with a white cloth provided a focus at the centre of the room. The table was bare but embroidered into the cloth at its corners, Jerahmeel noticed the Star of David and the Fish Motif he had seen on some of the doors the previous day. A number of people were already in the room. The younger people were sitting on the floor near the table, while the older people sat on benches arranged around the edge of the room. These older people, who were mainly women, considerably outnumbered the younger ones present. Jerahmeel speculated to himself that this imbalance might be in some way a consequence of the persecutions that community had faced in earlier years. The younger more active people, being the main target of those who found this community a threat, would be the ones most likely to feel forced to move away to safer towns and cities.

Apollos and Jerahmeel found a seat on the edge of this gathering. After a few minutes, three men, one of whom, Jerahmeel recognized as James, took their place behind the table. After a few moments a hush settled. James stood, welcoming all those present and identifying Jerahmeel and Apollos as guests. He spoke initially in Greek and repeated the welcome in Aramaic. The community then sang a Jewish hymn which was well known to Apollos and Jerahmeel. Prayers and psalms followed in much the same way as they might have done at a conventional synagogue. At the appropriate point in the service, one of the two men with James picked up a scroll and read from the prophet, Isaiah. He read in Hebrew. Every few verses he stopped, allowing first James to translate into Aramaic and the other man, into Greek. One verse received special emphasis.

Therefore will I divide him a portion with the great, and he shall divide the spoil with the strong; because he hath poured out his soul unto death, and he was numbered with the transgressors, and he bare the sin of many, and made intercession for the trangressors.[102]

James then spoke on this verse, explaining how Jesus had fulfilled this prophecy, for when he died on the cross, Jesus was in the company of two convicted felons. As he suffered, Jesus prayed for those who crucified him, and for those who suffered on the crosses with him. James made much of the fact that one of those malefactors who fully deserved his punishment, and for whom it was too late to make any sort of amends, now that he was firmly nailed to a cross, recognized that Jesus, the man without sin, was soon to enter his kingdom. He prayed that Jesus might remember him when he came to his kingdom, and Jesus promised that that night, he would be with him in paradise.[103] James explained that although that man's sin would normally have excluded him from paradise, Jesus being without sin, could bear that man's sin himself, so fulfilling the prophecy. James explained that the rites of sacrifice for the forgiveness of sins which the Jews had practiced for years, were ordained by God through Moses and the prophets, so that people would understand the perfect and sufficient nature of Jesus' sacrifice when this prophecy was fulfilled at the appointed time. James lamented that the Jewish people had failed to recognize the significance of Jesus' death, although the sacrifice of his life had been accompanied by other mystic signs to convey to the people its special meaning. The sky had become supernaturally dark to signify that a sombre event was taking place.[104] Then as Jesus died, the veil in the Temple which symbolically represented the barrier between man and God, through which only the High Priest was allowed to pass but once a year, was rent in two. The rending occurred not from the bottom to the top as a man in the Temple might have torn the curtain, but with no person near that veil, it was rent from top to bottom as an act of God.[105] People who were known to have died years before, were seen walking the streets alive to signify that death had been conquered.[106]

James ended by rejoicing that Jesus himself had been seen alive three days later, and that so many of those who were present in that gathering with him that morning shared the experience of having seen the risen Jesus. He rejoiced that many of those who had not been privileged to actually see the risen Jesus, had still come to know him as the one who had borne their sins, as he had the sins of the dying thief. He rejoiced that they also knew Jesus now as a

113

living person, who although unseen, could communicate with them and guide them through life.

James' words and his manner of delivery were impressive enough to make an impact on the most apathetic of listeners. Jerahmeel noticed the animated and eager expressions on the faces of so many in that gathering, and realized that they were empathising with a first hand experience of their own. The reason why all did not initially display this emotion soon became clear. James sat down, and his words were translated into Greek by one of those with him for the benefit of the non-Aramaic speakers in that congregation. Jerahmeel was impressed with the accuracy of the translation, and that the message lost none of its force. He was glad that the translation had been made while Apollos was in that gathering, for although Apollos had a working knowledge of Aramaic, Greek was his native tongue, and it was through this medium that he would derive the force of that message.

After the address had been translated, they sang another hymn, and a young woman in the congregation, after catching James' eye, was motioned to stand. She spoke of the sordid life style in which she had passed her days until the time she had been introduced to that community. Then, with a radiant joy, shining from her face, she spoke of how she had met Jesus, not in the flesh, but in the spirit, and of how she, no less than the dying thief on the cross, had been given the assurance that Jesus had taken her sins so that one day she too would join him in paradise. At the present, her days were joyful, for she was no longer preoccupied with living for selfish pleasure and gain, but derived far greater happiness from the things she could do for others.

The meeting ended in a way which was completely different from any synagogue service. A young man brought in a plate of freshly baked bread and a large flagon of wine, and placed them on the table before James. James held aloft, first the bread and then the wine, and reminded the congregation of how Jesus had used bread and wine on the last evening of his life as he celebrated the Passover with his disciples. Jesus had used these as a dramatic visual aid to indicate to those with him, the sacrifice so soon to be made of himself.[107] This sacrifice would provide a means of

114

cleansing from sin which would be enduring in a way which no sacrifice of an animal in the Temple could be. Two more young men then came up from the congregation, each with an empty plate and flagon. James broke the bread into two equal pieces, placing a piece on each plate and he shared the wine between their flagons. One of these young men then left the room, followed by about half that congregation. As the last person in this group left the room, the other young man led out the rest of the congregation. James indicated with a gesture that Jerahmeel and Apollos should follow this group. James and the two men who had shared with him the leading of the service, were the last to leave that room.

The company proceeded to another large room which was laid out as a refectory with two long tables. The two groups sat at each table and the young men who had led the processions placed the bread and wine on the tables to be shared by those seated. These young men went out of another door, soon returning with plates and bowls of food which comprised a simple but tasty meal. Jerahmeel and Apollos said little to each other as they ate, but absorbed the atmosphere of that gathering. The people ate quietly and spoke in subdued tones, but everybody seemed relaxed and happy. Apollos could not help but notice how attentive all were that their neighbours were receiving adequate shares from the bowls of food being passed down the table. As he listened to the conversation, Apollos realized that the division of that company into two groups was not random. The people on the table where Apollos and Jerahmeel sat, spoke to one another in Greek, while those on the other table held their conversation in Aramaic.

The meal ended. James stood and said a prayer of benediction. The gathering dispersed.

17

Apollos Meets James

James came over to Apollos and Jerahmeel and asked them if they would like to join him and the elders. They went upstairs to the room where Jerahmeel had met with James on the previous evening and James introduced Josiah and Jason, the men who had presided with him over that morning's gathering. Jason had been the one who provided the Greek translations. Jerahmeel introduced Apollos.

Jerahmeel started the conversation by first expressing gratitude on behalf of Apollos and himself that they should have been privileged to be invited to share that time of morning worship, and indeed, the wonderful meal also, which seemed like a continuation of the worship. He told those elders how his heart had warmed the previous night through the conversation he had held with James, and that he now had the conviction that Jesus was indeed the Messiah whom he had longed for but never expected in his life-time. He explained that although he had shared as much of what he had learnt as he could with Apollos, he did not know nearly enough to answer the many problems that Apollos had naturally raised over a situation which would so radically change the conventional Jewish approach to their faith.

James nodded. He was glad that Jerahmeel had expressed the teaching he had received from him as a change that the Jews would need to make to their faith, rather than as a totally new faith. James continued the conversation by asking Apollos to talk about his reactions to what Jerahmeel had told him and to particularly raise the matters which gave difficulty.

Jerahmeel inwardly winced as Apollos spoke of what he

had learned from those he described as the wise men of the Synagogue of the Freedmen. He stated that they were scrupulous in testing the claims of a would-be Messiah against the ancient prophecies, and that they had found Jesus to be lacking on a number of counts. For example, it was clear from the prophecy of Micah that the Messiah would be born in Bethlehem,[108] but Jesus hailed from Nazareth, a city which was not mentioned in Scripture. Nazareth was situated in an area which was conspicuous in Israel for its failure to raise a prophetic voice.[109]

James appeared unruffled at this challenge to the doctrines he proclaimed.

'I must compliment the Freedmen on their careful and accurate reading of Scripture,' James began. 'I am indeed a Nazarene and would not lay claim to the gift of prophecy on the grounds of my birthplace. The lands of Zebulun and Naphtali have been sterile soil for the raising of prophets.'

James paused at this point. He had shrewdly described his Galilean homeland in terms of the ancient tribal allocations, for he considered it likely that this young scholar, reputed to be well read in the Scriptures, would have been familiar with the passage from Isaiah's prophecy,

> The land of the tribes of Zebulun and Naphtali was once disgraced, but the future will bring honour to this region, from the Mediterranean eastwards to the land on the other side of the Jordan, and even to Galilee itself, where the foreigners live.
>
> The people who walked in darkness have seen a great light.
>
> They lived in a land of shadows, but now light is shining on them.[110]

However, James did not labour this point by making any mention of the prophecy. He relied on Apollos having good recall of Scripture. James continued.

'Although I was born in Nazareth, my elder brother, Jesus, was born in Bethlehem. It happened when Augustus Caesar called for a census of the Roman Empire to be made. Quirinius was governor at the time and you will find a detailed account in the official records. I have not searched the records, but for all I know, Jesus, infant as he was, may be listed by name. As my father, Joseph, was a descendant of David, Bethlehem was his clan hometown, and he had to return here for the registration required by the census.[111]

'I describe Jesus as my elder brother, but strictly, he was my half brother. Jesus was conceived out of wedlock, and Joseph was not his father! Did not the Freedmen tell you this?'

Apollos shook his head.

'My word,' smiled James. 'What the Freedmen might make of that piece of information. I tell you this because it will provide you with a means of authenticating what I am saying, it is a further fulfilment of prophecy, and it will explain in some way, why Jesus was different from other men, from all other men.

'I was an adolescent when some domestic problem had come up regarding Jesus not claiming some property which might legally have been deemed his by right. Joseph had told me that Jesus had no human father, but had been conceived by the spirit of God. An angel had appeared to Mary, my mother, and had told her that she would have this son, who would be none other than God, living in human form on earth.[112] This was a fulfilment of the prophecy of Isaiah,

> Behold, a virgin shall conceive and bear a son and shall call his name Immanuel, which means, God with us.[113]

I knew that the Hebrew word, translated as virgin in the Aramaic which was our domestic language, could also mean no more than a young woman of marriageable age, but I knew my mother well enough to know that she would be incapable of any immoral act. However, I still challenged my father as to why he was prepared to accept Mary's account of the angelic visitation without further proof. Joseph told me that he had all the reassurance he needed, for an angel had appeared to him in a dream and confirmed what Mary had reported.[114]

'Arrogant young man that I was, I suggested that there was a difference between a direct appearance of an angel and one fantasized in a dream, for our minds can enable us to dream what we want to see and hear. Joseph was not angry as he indeed had every right to be at my impudence, for he had the perfect answer. He told me that God interacts with every individual in a different way. God communicates with each person using the medium which is most appropriate to them. In Joseph's case, it seems that God invariably sent his angels to speak through dreams. This was after all, the way God had spoken to his namesake, Joseph, in the times of the patriarchs. Dreams which were the mere fabrication of his internal mind could not have communicated to my father, Joseph, information which would make him aware of unexpected danger. However, while Jesus was still a very small boy, Joseph had been told by an angel in a dream, to leave Bethlehem where they had lived since the birth of Jesus, for great danger threatened. A mere dream is forgotten at daybreak, but a message from God is heeded by a man of God. Immediately, Joseph arranged to evacuate Mary and Jesus, and they went to Egypt.[115] Within days, Herod's soldiers had slaughered all the boys in Bethlehem of less than two years old.

'Herod, a man of evil, heeded the message sent from God to guide some wise gentiles to pay their respects to the infant king born in Israel. They had, mistakenly, sought him in the king's palace, so giving Herod wind that a special king had been born. Herod, a devil's disciple if ever there was, also heeded the prophecy God had entrusted to Micah, that this ruler in Israel should be born in Bethlehem, but foolish man that he was, Herod could not thwart the purposes of God. He did that unutterably awful deed of killing all the Bethlehem infants to be sure that whoever this potential ruler might be, living in obscurity in Bethlehem, he would be snuffed out before reaching maturity.[116] Herod's deed was in vain, for my father, Joseph had already conducted Jesus and my mother to safety.'

James knew from what Jerahmeel had told him of the journey which he and Apollos had made thus far, that they had passed through Bethlehem. Some forty years on, the inhabitants of Bethlehem still rankled over that atrocity of Herod, and James wondered if the travellers had picked up snatches of conversation in Bethlehem which would have confirmed some aspects of what he had just told them. Unfortunately, in their hurry to reach Jerusalem, Jerahmeel and Apollos had spent very little time in Bethlehem. No matter, James sensed that the way to convince Apollos against the indoctrination he had derived from the Freedmen, was to emphasize the way that Jesus' life fulfilled prophecy.

'The events which followed the departure of Joseph and Mary with Jesus to Egypt,' continued James, 'were foretold by the prophets. Hosea had declared

"I called my son out of Egypt."[117]

and Jeremaiah had written of the massacre of the innocents,

"A voice is heard in Ramah, lamenting and weeping bitterly: it is Rachel weeping for her children, refusing to be comforted for her children, because they are no more."[118]

The life of Jesus so perfectly fulfilled prophecies, not just obvious prophecies but also verses which we had overlooked in our studies of Scripture as young people, that these verses have suddenly come to life and taken on new meaning and significance.'

James paused, awaiting a reaction from Apollos. Apollos was impressed with what James had said, but was not prepared as was Jerahmeel, to become a believer.

Apollos thanked James for his discourse, and conceded that James had made a good case for Jesus being the Messiah in fulfilment of prophecy. However, he could not accept the interpretation which he was hearing put on the significance of Jesus' life and death.

'How can he take our sins away?' queried Apollos. 'The teaching of the Law is plain. This Law must be obeyed. Of course we will fail from time to time, but when we are judged, those of us who have taken care in the observation of the Law will prove on balance, to have succeeded more often than we have failed, and so be justified. God after all, cannot expect a person to do better than his best.'

Jason and Josiah then spoke. Josiah had been brought up

to obey the law from childhood, but now recognized the futility of trying to fulfil the law. The harder Josiah tried to observe its scruples, the more unpleasant and objectionable he had become as a person, and surely, this could not have been what God intended. Jesus' sacrifice had released Josiah from the obligation of making a fetish of slavishly following a detailed code of onerous duties which detracted from leading a fulfilled life. Instead, as a servant of Jesus, he could now enjoy life by fulfilling that service in the love and care he showed to those around him. Jason was a Greek like Apollos, and had been brought up to worship the same pagan idols as Apollos had in childhood. Jason had not been attracted to what he called Old Judaism as Apollos had been, because Old Judaism seemed to be a particularly nationalistic religion, reserved for the exclusive use of one ethnic group. New Judaism, which had come in the wake of Jesus, the Messiah, had resolved these difficulties. It was based on the Law and the prophets, but enabled these to be interpreted to lead men and women to a liberating rather than restrictive way of life. Also, there was no attempt to make New Judaism, the exclusive privilege of ethnic Jews. On the contrary, New Judaism sought to provide a meaning for this life and the hope of eternal life for every class and race of men and women.

Apollos was thoughtful but not convinced that he need make any fundamental change in the beliefs he had adopted over the years as a result of much study and thought.

James said a short prayer, and Jerahmeel and Apollos returned to their inn.

18

A Special Baptism

A strain entered into the marvellous relationship which had existed between Jerahmeel and Apollos, and which had made the journey through Israel such an interesting and pleasant experience up to that point. They now had something meaty to discuss but something over which they had adopted opposite viewpoints. Apollos reminded Jerahmeel that earlier in his life, he had already changed his religion as a result of Jerahmeel's influence. He had valued the change, but he had made the change for life. Apollos insisted that New Judaism, as described by James and the elders at the community they had visited, was not just a further step of evolution in the Jewish faith. It was a completely new religion, even if it did have its roots in Old Judaism.

Jerahmeel was swayed very much by the experience that Josiah had recounted. Jerahmeel was painfully aware how seriously he (and for that matter, Apollos also) was failing to fulfil the demands of the Jewish Law. Jerahmeel could see how all of Scripture prepared mankind to recognize their personal sinfulness and to see that Jesus' death could be grasped as having the significance of a perfect sacrifice to cover sin in a way that no other sacrifices could. However, Apollos would have none of this. He insisted that it was obvious that all men would be judged on their own merits, and not on someone else's.

Jerahmeel was disturbed when Apollos announced a few days later that he was going out to visit some new friends he had made at the Synagogue of the Freedmen. Although Jerahmeel knew that Apollos would not have objected if he accompanied him, he was not explicitly invited, and

Jerahmeel sensed that Apollos would rather pay this visit without him. Jerahmeel thought to himself of the persecutions which James' community had experienced in the past at the hands of members of the Synagogue of the Freedmen,[68] persecutions which had resulted in imprisonment and even death for some of those who belonged to that lovely community which had made him so welcome and to which he felt such an affinity.

Apollos left the inn and shortly afterwards, Jerahmeel made his way to the community which had so influenced his thoughts. The door was shut and Jerahmeel knocked. There was no reply. He knocked again. The door still did not open. A short while later, a young man whom Jerahmeel recognized as a community member, came up the street and asked Jerahmeel what he wanted. Jerahmeel explained that he urgently wished to speak with James. The young man recalled that Jerahmeel was a guest who had attended their love feast a few days earlier. He knocked at the door with what Jerahmeel recognized to be the same rhythm which Amariah had used on the first occasion he had visited the house. The door was immediately opened as if the knock was expected. Jerahmeel deduced that the young man had left the community by some other door, so that he could ascertain in the street, the identity of the one who knocked, before the caller was admitted.

Jerahmeel was conducted to James' room but had to wait about twenty minutes before James could leave whatever community task he was involved in to join him. James smiled warmly as he returned to his room and recognized his visitor. The men embraced. James could see that there was a look of anxiety on Jerahmeel's face.

Jerahmeel spoke of Apollos, the strain which was developing in their relationship, and the fact that he had just gone out alone to visit some contacts in the Synagogue of Freedmen. James looked grave.

'We are not as isolated from the world in this community as we may seem to be,' began James. 'We find it necessary to gather intelligence on the activities of those who may be the enemies of this community. I have had news that the Synagogue of the Freedmen may be planning some further onslaught against us. We are well prepared. If any tried to force an entry through our main door, that is, the way in which you entered, we could evacuate this building very quickly. We have passages and ways out of this house which lead out to many other streets in the maze which this part of Jerusalem has become. We therefore have no immediate fears that we would be unable to escape from the limited resources which the Synagogue of Freedmen can now bring against us. However, the situation which exists with Apollos and yourself is disturbing on a number of counts. When do you plan to leave Jerusalem, and where are you headed for?'

Jerahmeel explained that they had really seen all they needed of the sights of Jerusalem, but that he had hoped to learn more of New Judaism. They were headed for Greece, but had no detailed itinerary in mind.

James suggested that they should make for Antioch as soon as possible. He described in most glowing terms, a community like his own in that city. He explained that visits were often exchanged between members of the two communities, and that one of the Jerusalem elders with rather special gifts, a learned man called Agabus,[119] was currently at Antioch. James then identified some differences which existed between the situations in Antioch and Jerusalem which would enable Jerahmeel to avoid the personal tensions which he was now experiencing with Apollos.

'I regard our community here as being a rather special sort of synagogue,' said James, looking pensive as he spoke. 'You heard Josiah speak of our faith as New Judaism, and I think and pray that in time, this outlook upon the new age in which we live, may be accepted by all Jewry, so that Old Judaism may be absorbed into New Judaism. You will realize from what I have said to you, that all our beliefs are founded in the ancient faith of Israel, and we can see how clearly my brother, Jesus, is the fulfilment of the prophets and of the hopes of our nation. Although it is absolutely clear that New Judaism is for all men on earth, it is the greatest wish of my brother who lives with us now in the spirit with as much power as when he lived on earth, that his special people, our people whom God chose out at the dawn of history, the Jewish nation, should come as a whole

124

to recognize the fulfilment of their destiny. How earnestly we pray that they would embrace the only sure and certain way to eternal life available to them. Many in Jerusalem have already turned, and synagogues throughout the province of Asia and in Greece are turning with joy and thanksgiving to the new life which Jesus has brought. However, our religious hierarchy, the pharisees and the sadducees, the priests and the scribes, have a worldly vested interest in the old order, and stubbornly cling to their old attitudes, even though the spirit of Jesus must be working in their minds and demonstrating the truth to them.

'New and Old Judaism cannot happily coexist as separate ways to God, except in communities which are so drained of spiritual vigour that they have become totally apathetic. That is why there is such tension here in Jerusalem, and why we live under the continuous threat of persecution. Away from Jerusalem, in places like Antioch, the communities of New Judaism have a free and independent existence. If you go to Antioch, you will not find a strong synagogue, like the Synagogue of the Freedmen, rooted in Old Judaism, able to bring the established power of the civil authorities to restrict the free expression of those who have discovered Jesus for themselves as the fulfilment of their faith. If you take Apollos to Antioch, he will be able to experience the atmosphere of New Judaism in a free and strong community, unhampered by the machinations of frightened and jealous men, anxious to maintain their worldly status against the threat which comes from the enlightened thought which Jesus brought to mankind. I think that even now, Apollos was convinced in his mind by what he has learned of Jesus in the last few days, but I was wrong to expect him to be won by clear argument. We know from experience that converts are won through their hearts and not their heads.

'Here, in Jerusalem, I have avoided breaking irrevocably with Old Judaism. I am encouraged that some of our younger members have courage to retain the link with the roots of our faith by openly worshipping Jesus within the Temple courts. You will have noticed that the Star of David displayed in this building, still declares that we are part of

125

the faith of Israel. Hasten the day when all Israel may enjoy that faith in its fulness as we do now.'

James paused and Jerahmeel asked a question to satisfy his curiosity about the symbols he had seen in that building.

'Yes, James, I have seen the Star of David. It is painted on your walls, carved into your doors and embroidered into your linen, but there is another symbol which is strange to me. It looks like a fish. Sometimes I see it painted in the middle of David's Star, and sometimes it is engraved alongside. What is its significance?'

'Many of Jesus' early disciples were fishermen, and the fish is a simple logo to represent our movement. It has a rather special meaning too, which you will appreciate as a Greek speaker. Your word for fish is ICHTHYS, which is an acronym, Iesous CHristos THeou HYios Soter, Jesus Christ, of God the Son, Saviour,' explained James.

Both James and Jerahmeel paused, each thinking of the next step to be taken, awaiting for the spirit to give some guidance. James suggested that they should pray together as they weighed the issues. James prayed for the communities which recognized the Messiahship, the Divinity, the saving grace of Jesus. He prayed that all Israel should soon be united in this faith. He prayed for God's protection on the members of this community in Jerusalem. He prayed that Apollos would soon be among those whose faith was grounded in the traditions of Israel, who would come to acknowledge that his beliefs had been fulfilled in Jesus. Jerahmeel thanked God that the fulfilment of prophecy which he had looked for for years had now been accomplished. He re-echoed James' prayer for Apollos. He prayed that the zeal of the congregation of the Synagogue of the Freedmen might be directed in ways which would lead to enlightenment. He prayed for guidance about what he and Apollos should do next.

As they finished praying, Jerahmeel's face lightened. He knew what he should do next.

'I shall make plans to leave with Apollos for Antioch as soon as possible. I take it that it is Antioch in Syria where the community like this is to be found?'

Antioch on the Orontes, capital of the province of Syria,

was the largest and most important of sixteen Antiochs founded to perpetuate the name of the Seleucid king, Antiochus. Jerahmeel had taken a decision which appeared obvious from the discussion that had just been held with James. Two factors had caused Jerahmeel to be hesitant about following this suggestion. Jerahmeel had felt a peace and joy which arose from his contact with James and that special community in Jerusalem, such as he had never known in his life before, and he was reluctant to leave such a fountain of inner peace after so short an acquaintance. Secondly, Jerahmeel had doubts about whether Apollos would follow his suggestion about continuing their journey. Since their recent difference on matters of faith, Apollos had seemed to be in a controversial mood, and tended to snap at anything Jerahmeel proposed. Jerahmeel realized that Apollos mind was in a state of some torment. He was encountering a serious challenge to some deeply held convictions. However, Jerahmeel now confidently made the decision to follow James' suggestion. The short time of prayer that Jerahmeel had shared with James had resulted in the anxieties in Jerahmeel's mind becoming wonderfully resolved. He was confident that the community at Antioch would be a source of the same inner peace that he had derived from that home in Jerusalem. He was confident that Apollos would acquiesce with his suggestion to leave Jerusalem.

James looked well pleased with the confidence with which Jerahmeel announced his decision.

'As we prayed, indeed, before we prayed, I had a strong conviction that you have come to a very clear decision in your mind that Jesus is indeed the Messiah and our Saviour, and that you would want to make a clear declaration of this,' suggested James, looking intently at Jerahmeel.

'Indeed, yes, indeed, yes,' replied Jerahmeel, repeating his words to emphasize his conviction.

'The way we confirm membership of this community, no, not just of this community, but the wider community of all who acknowledge Jesus as Lord of their lives, is for the believer to be baptized,' explained James. 'This was the final command of Jesus to his followers before he was taken into heaven, that they should make new disciples and baptize them.'[88]

'As I have explained when I described our journey here,' answered Jerahmeel, 'I was baptized by Caleb of Jezreel at Beersheba, and some years earlier, I was baptized by John in the River Jordan.'

'Baptism in the name of Jesus is rather special,' continued James. 'John's baptism was a sign of repentance, but the baptism in Jesus' name, while involving repentance, also symbolizes forgiveness in a way which John's baptism could not. As those who are baptized are immersed, it is as if they enter the water with their sins clinging to them, symbolically dying as they are under the water, to emerge with their sins left behind. It is a picture of sins being nailed to Jesus' cross as he died, so that those who have been baptized can start a new life in the strength of the risen Jesus, strength to defeat the power of sin in the new life which lies ahead. I speak of baptism in Jesus' name, but in obedience to Jesus' command, new disciples are baptized in the names of the three aspects of God, the Father of Jesus who created all things, Jesus himself, who won forgiveness and eternal life for us, and the Spirit of God which continues to live with us now in a very real way.'

'May I experience this baptism?' entreated Jerahmeel.

'This would be an answer to my prayer,' answered James. 'There is no reason why you should not be baptized now as you have professed sincere belief in Jesus. Wait here awhile.'

James left the room, and came back a few minutes later. He gave Jerahmeel a loose white garment to change into, and led him into an inner courtyard of that house. Some of the younger members of that community, the ones who had served at the meal Jerahmeel had attended with Apollos and who were called deacons, were removing some planks which covered a pool about three metres square. Steps led into the water. About twenty members of the community had gathered round the pool. Jerahmeel recognized Amariah, Josiah and Jason. As James and Jerahmeel stood on the edge of the pool, the community sang a hymn. James entered the water and beckoned Jerahmeel to follow. James immersed Jerahmeel three times as he declared baptism in the name of the Father, Son and Holy Spirit. As Jerahmeel left the water, the community gathered round him to shake his hand or embrace him. Jerahmeel felt an overwhelming sense of well-being and confidence. The group went back indoors. Jerahmeel changed back into his clothes and joined the group for a simple meal. There was an atmosphere of great peace and contentment. Threats of persecution and dangers from without seemed quite irrelevant during that most happy and joyful time. Then with further embraces and handshakes, Jerahmeel bade farewell to that community whose fellowship he had enjoyed for such a short time, but which had had such a profound effect on the outlook with which Jerahmeel now faced life.

Before leaving, Jerahmeel returned with James to his room. James gave Jerahmeel two documents. One was a letter of introduction to the community at Antioch. The other, James described as a specially valuble gift. He explained that one of the members of that community who had been a lesser disciple of Jesus while he lived on earth and had witnessed so much of Jesus' ministry, had written a biography of Jesus. This was such a marvellous account that members of the community were making copies. They had only made a dozen copies so far, but James felt he could confidently entrust one to Jerahmeel to give him a much more complete picture of Jesus' life and work. The young man who had written this book was called John Mark. James told Jerahmeel that John Mark travelled a great deal with his Uncle Barnabas, founding new communities like the ones in Jerusalem and Antioch. James had heard that Barnabas and John Mark were bound for Antioch, and he expressed a hope that Jerahmeel might meet him there.

'When you find the community at Antioch, do make a point of telling their leader, Simon, of what has happened while you have been in Jerusalem, for Simon too was a member of the Synagogue of the Freedmen before he joined our community,' advised James. 'You may be surprised when you first meet Simon to discover that he is a negro. Although he has a Jewish name, his parents came from Ethiopia, the land of Sandas-cum-Barama who gave you the first hint that something special had happened in Israel.'

These were James' last words to Jerahmeel. After saying

his farewells, Jerahmeel returned to the inn. He arrived there some time before Apollos rejoined him.

As Apollos walked in, Jerahmeel greeted him with the suggestion that as they had seen just about all there was to see in Jerusalem, perhaps they ought now to continue their journey northwards. Apollos immediately agreed.

19

Antioch

The following day dawned cloudy and overcast. The travellers paid their dues at the inn, complimented the host on the comfort they had enjoyed at his establishment and set off on their way. Although denied the bright sunlight which they had enjoyed on their journeyings thus far, they were glad of cooler weather for the difficult walking conditions which the hilly terrain around Jerusalem would present. They wrapped their cloaks well round themselves to gain protection against the damping drizzle which the swirling gusts attempted to penetrate to their inner clothing. Such weather conditions would represent a depressing start to most journeys, but the emotional states of our travellers were affected by factors quite independent of the weather. Apollos was depressed, but he would have been depressed at the beginning of that trek had the sun shone brightly and had the air been freshened by a light, dry breeze. Apollos' depression arose from the mental conflict that raged unresolved in his mind as he sought to intellectually resolve the contradictory religious stances he had encountered from the communities whose worship he had shared in Jerusalem. No such problem clouded Jerahmeel's mind. His step was buoyant and he felt boundless energy surging through his limbs as they climbed the steep pathways which led away from the capital of Judaea, into the hills which defined the Jordan valley. A torrential downpour could not have dampened Jerahmeel's elevated spirits.

The first part of the journey passed in silence. As the terrain became easier and the couple were able to saunter at an easy pace along the downhill stretches, Apollos and

Jerahmeel began to regain their rapport and conversation began to flow. Jerahmeel allowed Apollos to lead in the conversation and they touched on a number of topics. Matters of religious controversy arose but no rancour entered into the dialogue. Jerahmeel had a natural skill at averting a challenging of aggressive question with a gentle but powerfully adequate answer. The couple avoided talking on one topic for too long, and found many interesting diversions along the route. They speculated on the business and circumstances of other travellers who seemed to be following the same route as themselves away from Jerusalem. Apollos remarked upon and admired the contours of the hills in terrain so different from his native Egypt. They discussed their itinerary. Apollos was content to allow Jerahmeel, seasoned traveller that he was and knowing the places of interest worth visiting in this land, to lead in the choice of route and stopping places.

There is no need to recount in great detail the next part of the journey of Apollos and Jerahmeel. Very little happened which has much bearing on later events. Their route took them through Jericho, Archelais and Phasaelis. They passed by the fortress of Alexandrium and followed the course of the River Jordan northwards until they reached the Sea of Galilee. They briefly looked at the lakeside towns of Magdala, Gennesaret and Capernaum before continuing northwards through Chorazin to Caesaraea Philippi. The places through which they passed were all quite fascinating in different ways, and Jerahmeel was able to reveal to Apollos from the store of information which he had picked up on earlier visits, details of special interest which the young traveller would have otherwise missed. This phase of their journey took about six weeks.

During these travels, Jerahmeel read the biography of Jesus written by John Mark, which he had been given by James. He found it a most moving account which complemented what he had learned about Jesus from James and the community in Jerusalem. Apollos was naturally curious about the document which Jerahmeel took out to read whenever they were comfortably settled in to an inn for the evening. When Jerahmeel had read the biography twice, he allowed Apollos to read this account. The life and work of Jesus challenged Apollos, but he could not reconcile the ministry of Jesus with the interpretation that Apollos had put on his Jewish faith.

Whenever the sabbath fell, Jerahmeel and Apollos attended the synagogue of whichever town or village they were passing through. Jerahmeel was usually given the opportunity to speak in answer to the greeting extended to the travellers, and he proclaimed the news he had heard in Jerusalem, that the long awaited Messiah had come, had been crucified, but had risen and ascended. Jerahmeel had always been a good speaker, but Apollos was conscious that Jerahmeel spoke with even more confidence and eloquence on these occasions than he had in the past when he had expounded passages from the Law of Moses, or attempted the difficult task of making obscure passages from the prophetic books seem exciting and interesting.

The reaction to Jerahmeel's short homilies were mixed. A few of the older members of these synagogues were openly hostile. Several with open minds, who had already heard similar messages from other sources, expressed an intention of going to Jerusalem to learn more of this. The majority, who had also heard this news from other sources, remained apathetic, content with the status quo, and reacted with neither hostility nor enthusiasm. Jerahmeel's talks increased the turbulence in Apollos' mind, for although he had great confidence in Jerahmeel's judgement, for the time being, Apollos was not prepared to be swayed. The part he had taken in the discussions he had held with Jerahmeel en route had caused him to argue himself more firmly into the camp which rejected the claim that Jesus was the Messiah and the interpretation put on the significance of Jesus' death and resurrection by James and his Jerusalem community.

Jerahmeel and Apollos stayed at no place for very long during this phase of their journey, for both were anxious to reach other objectives. Jerahmeel was impatient to get to Antioch and meet the community there, which James had described in such glowing terms. Apollos was anxious to make Greece. From Caesaraea Philippi, the pair joined up with a caravan, travelling west to the Mediterranean port of Tyre. At that city, Jerahmeel and Apollos made enquiries about boats leaving Tyre for other Mediterranean ports and two days later, they were able to secure a passage on a small ship, north bound for Antioch.

The voyage took about three days, the ship's northbound voyage being interrupted by stops at Tripolis and Laodicea to deliver and collect freight which merchants in those cities had arranged to have transported in this vessel. At last they sailed into Seleucia Pieira, Antioch's sea-port, whence our travellers were able to proceed to the centre of Antioch, a few miles from the coast.

Antioch was the capital of the Roman province of Syria and was the third largest city in the Empire. This was the first truly Hellenic city which they had visited since leaving Alexandria, although many Roman features were now prominent. The city had been taken by Gnaeus Pompey some hundred years earlier, and during the course of the century, the Romans had built an imposing forum, some magnificent temples, and two complexes of baths named after Caesar and Caligula respectively. For the most part however, the city had a Greek profile. The Greek love of culture was reflected in the museums and libraries in the city. Jerahmeel did not know whether the theatres were of Greek or Roman origin, but the magnificent palace was clearly Greek. Apollos inwardly smiled as he discovered that the principal Greek temple was dedicated to Apollo. The River Orontes which flowed through Antioch, passed by the circus which was the venue for the popular Roman sport of chariot racing, and separated into two branches which met again a few hundred yards downstream, forming a large island. The Palace was situated on this island.

The lay-out of the roads of Antioch contrasted with the disorganized maze which the narrow streets of Jerusalem had become. The main street of Antioch was a broad avenue called the Road of Herod, running east–west. The other streets in the centre of town ran either parallel to the Road of Herod, or north–south, so that the street plan of Antioch took the form of neat rectangular blocks.

The first preoccupation of Apollos and Jerahmeel was to find board and lodging. Having found an unpretentious but clean and neat inn in the northern suburbs of the city whose terms were modest, the travellers were able to indulge their lust for sightseeing. Jerahmeel identified to himself, a house on the banks of the River Orontes which James had described to him as the home of the Antioch community who followed the way of New Judaism. The symbol on the door which James assured Jerahmeel would unambiguously enable the house to be identified, was neither the Star of David nor the Fish which were used by the Jerusalem community, but a stark cross whose significance was obvious.

When the sabbath arrived, Apollos was surprised to find that Jerahmeel made no attempt to find a synagogue for worship. The following day, Jerahmeel took Apollos to the house with the cross on the door at a time which Jerahmeel knew from the description James had given him, would be in good time for the main act of worship of this community.

20

The Church at Antioch

The door of the house was open. Two young men were waiting by the door to welcome worshippers as they arrived. Jerahmeel introduced himself and Apollos as travellers from Alexandria who had recently passed through Jerusalem. He mentioned that they had attended meetings of the community run by James which proclaimed the New Judaism which followed the teachings of James' brother, Jesus of Nazareth. Jerahmeel explained that James had commended this community and its leader, Simon, to them, and that he had a letter of introduction from James.

The young men's faces which were friendly and cheerful, brightened further as Jerahmeel made this introduction. As our travellers had arrived early for the worship, Simon himself was not yet there to meet them personally, but one of the young men said he would take the travellers to meet Manaen, the owner of the house, first, and they would meet Simon later.[121]

As Jerahmeel and Apollos were conducted through the spacious corridors and up the marble staircase of this house, they realized that it was a home of some opulence. This mansion on an imposing site, overlooking the River Orontes, was very different from the house where the Jerusalem community lived. Jerahmeel and Apollos were to discover a number of other very significant differences between the community at Antioch and that at Jerusalem. It has been already mentioned that the emblem adopted to represent this community was a cross, rather than a fish, and a cross could be seen in many places in the house. It was sometimes found painted on doors or walls, sometimes, as a free standing cross, made of wood, mounted on a plinth and placed on a shelf or a table. The community at Antioch did not all live in this one house behind doors which were only opened with caution. The city of Antioch had a refreshing atmosphere of freedom, and people could enter and leave this house without the fear of becoming victims of a persecution which the community's enemies might revive at any time. Thus, most of the community lived in houses in other parts of the city, and came to this house as a meeting place and a worship centre. Those at Antioch who followed the teachings of Jesus, spoke of themselves as a church rather than as a community. Being predominantly Greek speaking, they spoke of Jesus as Jesus Christ rather than Jesus the Messiah, and the members of the church were referred to as Christians.[122]

There were few people in the building at that time. The first person they encountered as they were led down the broad corridor to which the marble staircase gave access, was a very well dressed, aristocratic looking gentleman. This was Manaen. After introducing the travellers as visitors from Jerusalem, the young man left to return to the front door of the house. Jerahmeel gave his letter of introduction to Manaen who nodded and smiled as he read its contents and then returned it to Jerahmeel. Although of aristocratic bearing, Manaen was most gracious and friendly, and Jerahmeel and Apollos soon felt at home. It appeared that Manaen was a very wealthy gentleman who had connections with royalty. He had actually been brought up with Herod Antipas, but he had no great admiration for this tetrarch with whom he had shared his childhood. Although technically the owner of this impressive house, Manaen regarded this as an asset to be shared with his fellow Christians, and a small number of Christians in Antioch who had no alternative home, lived in the ample accommodation afforded by Manaen's mansion.

After the introductions and a short time spent chatting, Manaen conducted Apollos and Jerahmeel to a large and beautiful room on the ground floor where the worship was to take place. The room was lined with marble columns and the worshippers who were now beginning to arrive in significant numbers, sat on benches arranged around a table in the centre of the room. This was reminiscent of the table which had formed the focal point of the room where worship was held in the Jerusalem community. There was the same scrupulously clean, white cloth on the table. On this cloth stood a wooden cross. Manaen showed Apollos and Jerahmeel to their seats and said that they would be introduced to Simon at the end of the formal worship. He explained that Simon would be anxious to learn about the current state of affairs in Jerusalem, and there would be no sense of rush, if the telling of this news was kept until after the time of praise and prayer.

As the meeting room filled, Apollos and Jerahmeel surveyed the gathering. The Jerusalem community had had a very high proportion of middle aged to elderly widows among its members, but at Antioch, the church reflected a much better representation of the city's population. There were elderly people there, but the congregation was predominantly young with the women only just outnumbering the men. There were family groups, young married couples, and single people of all ages. Jerahmeel had assessed that the majority of the community in Jerusalem were poor. At Antioch too, a high proportion of those present did not appear to be wealthy, but there were a significant number whose magnificent dress marked them out as belonging to the upper classes. These did not sit in a group as was often the case at synagogues but appeared to be well distributed through the congregation. Another difference between this gathering and a synagogue lay in the fact that men and women sat together and not in segregated groups. Jerahmeel's eye was adept at identifying racial types and ethnic groups. While a very significant number present were Jewish, there were many Greeks, a few Romans, Medes, Parthians, several with dark skins who obviously originated from Africa and a number whom Jerahmeel could not categorize. Although there were a significant number of children in the gathering, the room had a quiet and peaceful aura. If any small child became fractious, the mother left the room with the infant, returning when the child seemed settled. The congregation was remarkably punctual. There were no arrivals during the final five minutes before worship began.

As in Jerusalem, three people entered to take their places

behind the table from whence they led the worship. One of the trio remained standing as the other two sat. He welcomed the congregation in Jesus' name. This man was a negro and Jerahmeel guessed that this was Simon. He was to discover that the rather tall man to Simon's right was called Lucius[121] and the hoary sage to the left, who appeared to frown from a face framed with flaxen hair and a long white beard, was named Agabus. Agabus had a deceptively frightening appearance. In reality, he was a very kindly, paternal man who was greatly loved by the children. He was aptly described as a sage, however, for he was a man of great learning, wisdom and insight. He also had the gift of prophecy and four years earlier, Agabus had predicted that over the next thirty years, the world would experience two years in which there was a serious food shortage. The first of these would be on a fairly minor scale, but enough to make people uncomfortable. This would prepare people to learn how to live when food was short for the second year of food shortage which Agabus predicted would be a major famine.[119] The year of minor famine materialized a year after Agabus's prediction. It had made life rather uncomfortable throughout the Roman Empire for several months. The world was still awaiting the year of major famine which Agabus had prophesied would take place.

After the introduction, the congregation stood to sing a hymn and then settled while Simon remained standing, to deal with formalities which needed to be completed before the worship could continue properly.

'Today is a most exciting occasion for us at Antioch,' Simon declared, speaking with alacrity and enthusiasm, 'for we have visitors in our congregation who can give us news of old friends and tell us how the church is faring beyond Antioch. First, I have been told that we have visitors from Jerusalem.'

Simon's eyes expectantly scanned the congregation and he beamed as Jerahmeel and Apollos stood. The rest of the congregation turned and looked expectantly at the pair. Jerahmeel spoke.

'I bring you greetings from James, from Josiah and Jason, and from the community at Jerusalem. They are faring well and have been a source of great blessing to me, for when I first visited them, I knew little of Jesus, although I had heard rumours that a great prophet had come. James told me so much of his brother that I realize he is indeed the Messiah, or as you say in Antioch, the Christ. Indeed, I would want to say more than that he is the Christ. I feel I know him now as a person, unseen perhaps, but with me now, with all of us now, present in this place.'

The congregation nodded their assent at this point, and many verbally reinforced Jerahmeel's claim.

'Indeed we do!' 'What a joy to know Jesus!' 'Thank you Lord for being here!'

'Before I left Jerusalem,' Jerahmeel continued, 'James most graciously gave me a gift which I greatly treasure. It is a copy of a biography of Jesus, written by John Mark, one of his disciples. I have read this through and through, and have heard Jesus speaking to me so clearly through its stories and through the teaching it conveys.'

Jerahmeel sat down and Apollos resumed his seat next to him. A murmur of approval went through the congregation. Several present held aloft documents like the one in Jerahmeel's possession. It was clear that not only was John Mark well known in Antioch, but that copies of his biography of Jesus were being made and circulated there, as in Jerusalem.

Simon beamed more widely than ever.

'It barely seems a month ago that John Mark and Barnabas were with us in Antioch before returning to Cyprus, but I believe we have a visitor from Cyprus who can give us news of our beloved Mark and Barnabas.'

Again, Simon scanned the congregation. A well dressed man on the opposite side of the room stood to speak.

'Barnabas and John Mark send you their greetings,' he began. 'They returned safely to Cyprus three weeks ago,[123] just before I left to sail for Syria. They spoke warmly of the support and love they received from you here in Antioch and hope to return here soon. They will not stay long in Cyprus, for the churches there are in the hands of faithful and capable elders, and the churches continue to enjoy the support and favour of the governor, Sergius Paulus.[124] Barnabas and John Mark hope to go to Egypt where they plan to spread the good news of Jesus Christ to the people of Alexandria. They would value your prayers.'

The man sat down as the congregation reacted with excited approval. Apollos felt the first pang of homesickness since leaving Egypt at that unexpected mention of his home-town. It was some time before the enthusiasm that overflowed from that congregation settled back to the reverend calm which Simon needed to be easily heard but as he raised his arms, quiet was restored. Simon warmly thanked the visitor from Cyprus for his news. Simon then invited visitors from Macedonia to give them their news. Two men in another part of the room stood. The spokesman introduced himself and his companion as cloth-merchants who were travelling to the cities at the eastern end of the Mediterranean in pursuance of their business. He told the congregation that they were citizens of Philippi and brought greetings to them from Paul and Silas. At the mention of these names, there was again an excited buzz, but this gave place to anxious silence as the visitor spoke of how Paul and Silas had been imprisoned after performing a miracle which released a girl from a sooth-saying spirit. The man who spoke was a good raconteur, and he instilled great excitement in that congregation by describing the earthquake which broke down the prison and would have enabled Paul and Silas to escape. However, they remained in the broken prison until the jailer arrived. This jailer was so impressed with their bearing and fortitude that he allowed them to explain to him, what made them so different from other men. The man from Philippi then told the Antioch congregation how the jailer and his family had become Christians.[25] The man continued by telling them of how he himself and his companion were invited to a house in Philippi where they too became Christians after hearing Paul and Silas speak. The Macedonian described the flourishing church which now met regularly at the house in Philippi. He expressed every confidence that the forty members of that church would by now, have swelled to fifty or sixty during the months that he and his companion had been away.

There was again, an enthusiastic response from the congregation which Simon had to allow to subside before he was able to invite the congregation to pray in response to the news they had received that morning. After a short bidding prayer, other prayers were offered spontaneously by different members of that congregation. The prayers were full of praise and thanksgiving for the churches in Jerusalem, Cyprus and Philippi. Some prayed for the safety of the church leaders and for God's protection on them and special mention was made of James in Jerusalem, Paul and Silas in Europe, Barnabas and John Mark who were about to embark as missionaries to Africa. The prayer time was very orderly, no two people attempting to pray simultaneously. The prayers were mainly offered in Greek but some prayed in other languages which Jerahmeel, travelled as he was, had not heard before. These prayers had a lilting musical quality to them and almost invariably, they were closely followed by someone speaking in Greek and giving what Jerahmeel felt sure, was a translation of the prayers, spoken in tongues, unfamiliar to Jerahmeel.

After the prayers, the congregation sang a joyful hymn, and then sat down as a scroll was handed to Agabus. Agabus read from the scroll, the well known story of how Moses had constructed a serpent out of brass which was displayed on a tall post in the middle of the Israelite camp. Those who had been bitten by the venomous snakes, plaguing the Israelites at that stage of their wilderness journey, made a rapid recovery from the snakebite which would have otherwise proved fatal, when they looked up to catch sight of Moses' serpent.[126]

The study of history was a particular interest of Apollos, and he was regarded as an expert in Jewish history by the members of his synagogue in Alexandria. Apollos enjoyed listening to this familiar story which grounded the unaccustomed form of worship he was experiencing in the Antioch Church, back into something of which he really felt part. However, Apollos' eyes had not been opened, as had Jerahmeel's during his visit to James when in Jerusalem, to discover the prophetic force of events which could pass off to unenlightened listeners, as mere historical incidents. Apollos was to discover that the incident of the brazen serpent had prophetic significance.

As Agabus finished reading, he carefully rerolled the scroll and placed it on the table. He sat down and Lucius stood, conscious of expectant eyes and ears, waiting for what he was to say. Lucius elaborated on that wilderness miracle, stressing the response of faith required of those who had been bitten by the venomous serpents, to struggle to a position where they could look up to a symbol, ordained by God to restore life where there would have otherwise been death. He then reminded the congregation that they were approaching the time when they would celebrate the anniversary of Jesus' death. He told them of how Jesus had proclaimed, long before anyone in his company had any premonition that he would die on the cross, that he would be lifted up like the serpent in the wilderness, so that those infected with a poison which would lead to death, might look up to him and be restored to life. Lucius explained that because all of us have been infected with the fatal venom of sin, we were all destined for a death which was final and absolute, but that God had ordained a sign, like the uplifted serpent, which would be the means of eternal life. He explained that in these latter days, it was not necessary to physically look up and see the crucified Jesus. Sufficient for us to know that he died on the cross, and look up to him with our mind's eye, realizing that God had given his Son to die out of his love for the world, so that everyone who believed this in a way which meant their lives were dedicated to serving Jesus, should not experience irrevocable death, but have the assurance of eternal life.[127]

Lucius sat down and the congregation sat several moments in hushed silence before Simon stood to continue proceedings. This was the sign for two deacons to bring in a flagon of wine and a plate of bread. Unlike the service at the Jerusalem Church, only one flagon and one plate were used at Antioch, but Simon said much the same thing as James in Jerusalem, reminding those present of the way Jesus had used the bread and the wine at his last Passover meal with the disciples to dramatically demonstrate the significance of his impending death. Simon then re-emphasized the reminder that Lucius had given them, that the anniversary of Jesus' death would fall on that coming Friday.

'I was an eyewitness of Jesus' crucifixion,' stated Simon, speaking slowly and in solemn tones. 'I invite everyone present to join with me here on Friday, bringing any others with you who would discover a meaning to life, and I will tell you of what I and my sons heard and saw on that day.'

Simon sat down, and there was again a time of silence. Then the deacons of the Antioch church quietly brought in tables and benches which they neatly arranged round the edge of that ample sized room. They brought in plates and bowls of food, and flagons of wine and laid them on the tables. This took no longer than five minutes, silence being maintained during this period. When the tables were fully laid, the ten deacons stood at the end of the room. Simon, Lucius and Agabus then stood and Simon stretched out his hands towards the tables. This was a sign that all was ready and the people then started to talk quietly among themselves as they waited for the deacons to conduct them to their places. As the tables filled, Simon went to the tables, adding bread which he had broken at the end of the worship, to the plates of bread which were already on the table. Agabus followed with the flagon, pouring wine from this into the partially filled flagons already on the tables. When everyone was seated, Simon returned to the central table, and silence was again observed as Simon said a short word of thanks. The meal then started. Conversation flowed freely and Jerahmeel and Apollos enjoyed the congenial atmosphere, generated in that gathering.

21

Simon of Cyrene

Jerahmeel and Apollos spent a leisurely week, sightseeing in the lovely city of Antioch. Jerahmeel counted the days to Friday, in anticipation of what he confidently expected to be a rather special address from Simon. During the meal which they had shared with the Antioch Christians, Simon, Lucius and Agabus had circulated among those present at this love feast, as the Christians called it, making a special point of becoming personally acquainted with the visitors. Simon had pressed Jerahmeel and Apollos to come to that meeting house again on the Friday. Agabus was particularly concerned to hear of the well being of the Jerusalem Church with which Jerahmeel and Apollos had so recently been involved, explaining that that was really his home church. It appeared that Agabus spent a lot of time away from Jerusalem, visiting other churches. He was endowed with a special gift of prophecy which was proving invaluable in helping to consolidate churches, recently founded by other Christians whose special spiritual gift was evangelism. Lucius had a special gift for teaching the mysteries of the Kingdom of God.

The Friday arrived. Jerahmeel and Apollos made their way to Manaen's house and were greeted by two young men at the door. They remembered Jerahmeel and Apollos as the Jerusalem visitors of the previous Sunday and warmly welcomed them. They made their way to the meeting room which was already half full. There were no children present on this occasion and the atmosphere was generally subdued. The central table had no white cloth as it had on Sunday, and the dark wooden cross contrasted starkly with the lighter wood of the highly polished table.

Apollos and Jerahmeel waited silently in that hushed, expectant gathering for about ten minutes. Simon entered and took his place, standing by the table rather than behind it. The congregation rose. Simon stood for a few moments, his head bowed in silent prayer. He raised his head and nodded to a young man at the side of the room who responded to this signal by singing a Psalm in a clear tenor voice. Jerahmeel and Apollos recognized this as the twenty-second psalm.[94] Those in the congregation who knew the words and the rather doleful melody to which the Psalm was set, joined in the singing. The Psalm ended. Simon motioned the people to be seated.

'Many of you know me as Simon of Cyrene, for that is the town where I was brought up. Many of you have wondered at my Jewish name, for as you see, I am not of Jewish stock but a negro, and that is why I am also called Simon Niger.[121] My parents were merchants from Ethiopia. Although the Ethiopians have not adopted the Jewish faith, that nation has a high respect for the wisdom that has come from Israel. They know the history of the Jews, almost as well as their own, for Jewish history is well documented. My parents gave me the name of Simon, after the patriarch of one of the twelve tribes, although my parents did not adopt the Jewish faith themselves. I could not accept as rational, either the religion of my own people, or that of the Greeks who were the principle inhabitants of Cyrene. The religions of the Romans, the Phoenicians and the Egyptians, like that of the Greeks, were based on idol worship. I rejected such religions but found the faith of the Jewish merchants who lived in my town both rational and satisfying. I therefore became a Jew myself, although I had to make considerable efforts before they would accept me as a proselyte, and I am very indebted to Lucius who befriended me and supported me during those difficult times in Cyrene.'

Apollos mused as Simon described his conversion to the faith of Israel, that this handsome negro had gone through an experience, very similar to his own. Jerahmeel had played much the same part in Apollos' acceptance into the Jewish faith as Lucius had for Simon.

'After many years of happy marriage, I was widowed and left with two sons, Rufus and Alexander, whom you have met. They are no longer with us in this city as their work has now taken them to that other Antioch, Antioch in Pisidia. As my sons were well into their teens when their mother died, they were of an age when they could share so much with me, and they brought me much comfort at that time of sadness. Lucius and I decided that we would travel with them to the land of Israel, to learn more of our faith from the prophets and priests who lived at the heart of God's special nation. We therefore travelled to Jerusalem where we found a synagogue whose members, like ourselves, came from the cities of North Africa, principally from Alexandria and Cyrene, and who spoke Greek as we did. They called this the Synagogue of the Freedmen,[68] for many had been Roman slaves who had worked to purchase their freedom. We felt proud to become members of this synagogue, for its members were zealous and devout to an extraordinary degree.'

Jerahmeel was already aware that Simon was a former member of this Synagogue, but Apollos felt a sudden pang of disquiet and surprise as he discovered another unexpected element of life, common to himself and Simon. The mention of that Synagogue reminded Apollos of the controversy which had arisen between himself and Jerahmeel since they had stayed in Jerusalem, although, recently, Jerahmeel had not raised religious issues with Apollos. Jerahmeel wisely considered that the influence of the Church at Antioch would steer Apollos in the way Jerahmeel wanted him to go, rather better, if he refrained himself from raising matters of personal controversy with Apollos.

Simon continued.

'After we had been in Jerusalem for nearly a year, the time came for that greatest of Jewish festivals, the Passover, and I went into the City with Alexander and Rufus, to join in the festive spirit of the holiday. However, I was to experience an event which I found extremely disturbing.

'Jerusalem was crowded with pilgrims, all in a holiday mood. After we had visited the Temple and the markets and walked round the city walls, we joined a jostling crowd who were lining two sides of a road, waiting for a procession. As Roman soldiers were pushing the crowds back on each side of the way, we could not cross over, and we waited to see the procession pass by. From the crowds' talk, we soon found that the spectacle we were about to witness, was criminals on their way to execution.

'Three Roman soldiers on horseback were the first part of the procession coming into view, slowly riding abreast up the narrow way. The closely packed crowd swayed back on each side of the road to allow these symbols of Imperial power to force their way through the densely packed throng. They were followed by three men, staggering under the weight of huge wooden crosses, each man being whipped on by burly Roman legionaries, and behind them came a platoon of well armed Roman soldiers, marching to the slow beat of a bass drum. As this procession passed, the Romans who had been marshalling the crowd fell into rank at the rear of the platoon, and the crowd was then able to mill across the narrow street, filling in the space behind the slowly moving procession.

'My attention was fixed on the first man carrying a cross. Although he was richly dressed in a scarlet robe, I could see that he was in a terrible state. He was obviously much more exhausted than the other two prisoners, and congealed blood lay around his forehead, beneath a vicious ring of plaited thorn twigs which had been forced down, over his head to his ears.[128]

'Just as the procession reached the point where I stood with Rufus and Alexander, this man collapsed and a double drumbeat brought the platoon of soldiers to sharp halt. The commanding horseman wheeled round to see what had happened. It was obvious that the lictor who was lashing away at the collapsed man with a vicious hide whip, would be unable to get him back on to his feet by this means, and he stopped his frantic activity as the equestrian commander raised his hand. The commander then scanned the crowd, and his eyes came to rest on my face, conspicuous I suppose, because it was black.

' "Here, Cushi," he shouted, "Take up the cross." [129]

'The crowd parted to let me and my boys through. My hackles had risen at being addressed as "Cushi",* but my

---

*Nigger is a modern equivalent.

148

pity for the collapsed man welled up as the dominant emotion in my heart at that moment. My sons helped me to take the weight of the cross on my shoulders, and we moved forwards as the slow relentless beat of the drum sounded up. I don't remember much more of that journey. Although I regard myself as a strong and fit man, the cross proved an almost intolerable burden. I don't know how I managed to complete the journey, and climb the hill called Golgotha, which was the place reserved for the execution of these unfortunate men. When I finally got the cross to the top of the hill and relieved myself of the load, I turned to look at the man who had collapsed. He was not able to speak to me because I was quickly ushered away by the soldiers, but as our eyes met, his glance conveyed a gratitude which immediately made me feel that the last mile I had walked under the cross's load, was the most worthwhile thing I had done in my life.

'I stayed with Rufus and Alexander to see this man meet his end. We had known the Romans to be cruel people, but actually witnessing an execution brought home to us, how very cruel man can be to his own kind, and we felt sickened to see how many of those around us were relishing the agony. I was specially surprised to find the priests whom I had hoped to meet during my pilgrimage to learn more of Jehovah, jeering and taking special delight in the execution of the man who had worn the red robe. I could see the soldiers using this robe as a prize for a game of dice they were playing, oblivious to the suffering of the men, suspended from the crosses above them.[133]

'We waited as this man spent his last hours of suffering and listened to his words. He had refused the drugged wine offered before the nails had been driven through his hands and feet,[130] but as the day wore on, he declared, "I thirst!", and a sponge soaked in vinegar was held to his lips.

'The sky grew strangely dark as if an intense storm was imminent, and he cried out in anguish, "My God, my God, why hast Thou forsaken me?"[132]

'These words I recognized from the 22nd Psalm. Other words from this Psalm which I had studied carefully from the Jewish scrolls during my search for God in Cyrene crossed my mind.

149

All who see me jeer at me, make mouths at me and
wag their heads.
My strength drains away like water, and all my
bones are loose.
My mouth is dry as a potsherd and my tongue
sticks to my jaw.
A band of ruffians rings me round and they have
pierced my hands and feet.
They share out my garments among them and
cast lots for my clothes.[94]

'I realized that I was witnessing the fulfillment of the
Scriptures I had studied over the past years. Suddenly as
this man gave a great cry and declared "It is finished!",
everything fell into place in my mind. The meaning of the
Scriptures I had studied so carefully all became clear. I had
no need to meet the priests to learn of Jehovah. I had met
my God face to face. It was none other than He who had just
yielded up his life there on the cross.'

Simon paused. The congregation remained silent, reflecting on the sombre event Simon had just described. Many
present who had been members of the Church at Antioch
for some years had heard Simon describe this before, but
the eyewitness account of that most momentous event of
history lost none of its impact by the retelling.

'All of you know that that was not the end of the matter,'
continued Simon, 'for great developments followed that
sacrificial death on that tragic Friday, no not tragic, but
triumphant Friday, for the final cry, "It is finished!", was a
cry of exultation. I will speak to you of the marvellous
sequel to this event when we meet as usual on the first day
of the week, but let us tonight and tomorrow, contemplate
the suffering which our God endured on our behalf on that
day. I wish you all now, good night and God's blessings be
with you until we meet again.'

Simon took his seat behind the table, his head bowed as
he sat in silent meditation. As Simon had been speaking,
the dusk had gathered but no lamps had been lit. The room
which had been bright an hour or so earlier was now getting
quite dark. This contributed to the atmosphere of the
occasion and somehow, gave added impact to Simon's

message. The congregation filed silently out of the room and when they reached the street, they went their separate ways to their homes.

22

A Walk by the Orontes

The following day was spent quietly but pleasantly. Jerahmeel and Apollos walked to the city's sea-port, Seleucia Pieria, which was further than a devout Jew should have walked on the Sabbath, and they watched the ships sailing to and fro around the harbour. Although the Jewish merchants were not working on the Sabbath, it was a normal day for gentile traders, and activity around the port was not perceptibly different from any other day of the week. Not all the traffic was commercial. A platoon of Roman legionaries embarked on a war galley, an impressive trireme which bore the name *Romulus*, and carried a splendid eagle as its figurehead. Our travellers watched this galley row into deep water and out of the harbour entrance, before hoisting its square sail to use the gentle south-westerly breeze to assist the efforts of the rowers. The regular beat of the drum which kept the galley slaves in step, could still be heard when the sea-bound ship was at least two hundred metres from the jetty from which Jerahmeel and Apollos watched the navigation of ships using the harbour of Antioch's sea-port.

After having spent an enjoyable and thoroughly lazy day, Apollos and Jerahmeel made their way back to their inn in Antioch's northern suburbs. As with the previous Sabbath, Jerahmeel made no attempt to find a synagogue at which they could have worshipped, and Apollos did not challenge this departure from Jerahmeel's normal habits of Sabbath observance.

The following day, they returned to the Church which met at Manaen's house. This now seemed quite familiar to them, and they no longer felt that they entered as strangers when greeted by the young men on door duty. The atmosphere was a total contrast to the subdued mood which had pervaded the house, two evenings earlier. The people arriving for worship were evidently in a festive mood. Vases of spring flowers had been placed on tables standing by the pillars at the front of the room, and the central table was again covered with a clean white cloth.

At the appointed time, Simon, Lucius and Agabus took up their positions behind this table to lead the worship. This started with Simon declaring that 'Jesus Christ is risen today!' and receiving the response, 'He is risen indeed!'

The service followed much the same pattern as the previous week, but there were no new visitors to be invited to bring news and greetings from other churches. After the prayers, Simon addressed the congregation. He continued the account of his experiences in Jerusalem from the point where he had finished the previous Friday. He described the sadness and depression that he and his sons had felt for some weeks after witnessing that awful death on the cross at Golgotha. Then Simon gave an account of how he and his sons went out into the Jerusalem streets on the first day of the week, six weeks later, to find a great commotion going on. The disciples of the man whom Simon and his sons had seen crucified, were proclaiming to the world that their master, Jesus, who had died on the cross, had risen from the dead three days later, that they had seen and spoken to him over the past few weeks, and that they had eaten with him and felt the wounds in his body. Simon described how some in the crowd were deriding those disciples with drunkenness until Peter spoke with great power and conviction. Simon referred to this disciple as 'Our dear, beloved friend, Peter,' from which Apollos and Jerahmeel deduced that Peter was personally known to the Church at Antioch. Simon told the congregation of how Peter had refuted the charge of drunkenness, for no wine would have been available at that hour in the morning.[75] Peter then quoted from the Prophets and the Psalms[134] to show the people that, not only was all they were saying about Jesus a fulfilment of prophecy, but the very event the crowd was witnessing at that moment, had been foretold by the prophet, Joel.[135]

Peter's great sermon had a profound impact on the

crowd, and Simon described how he and his sons, and also Lucius, were among the three thousand who became believers that day. Simon went on to describe the joy he had experienced at this marvellous resolution of the anxiety which had filled his mind since witnessing the crucifixion of Jesus. Simon then described what had followed after he became a believer, the persecution he had experienced, his rejection by the members of his synagogue, and the establishment of the Church in Jerusalem. He stated that this was initially under the leadership of the apostles, and later led by James when the apostles travelled to other cities as the persecutions continued. Simon exulted in the way that God had worked even through persecution, for although many had to leave Jerusalem to avoid the vindictive intolerance of the Jews who were trapped in their own traditions, the Church in Jerusalem continued to grow and flourish, and those who had left Jerusalem, had founded churches in other cities. Simon concluded with an expression of the joy and satisfaction that he and Lucius had experienced at having played a significant part in founding the church at Antioch, for that Church had gained such a reputation for its love, the zeal of its members and the good works it performed, that it was a constant source of pride to those privileged to lead it.

The service ended as the previous week, the formal worship giving place to the love feast which was now becoming a familiar meal to Apollos and Jerahmeel. Simon, Lucius and Agabus circulated as before. When they came to the table where Jerahmeel and Apollos were eating, they expressed a wish to get to know them better, and to find an opportunity to have a more detailed account of the state of affairs the travellers had discovered in Jerusalem and the way the church was faring in that turbulent city. It was arranged that our travellers would spend the afternoon with Simon and Agabus.

It was a delightful afternoon for walking, and the four took a stroll along the banks of the River Orontes. Simon walked with Jerahmeel, and their conversation proved most valuable to Jerahmeel, both in confirming the understanding of the Christian faith he had gained so far, and in clarifying points on which Jerahmeel felt he needed further instruction. Apollos and Agabus followed a few yards behind. Agabus sensed that Apollos had misgivings about the Christian faith and steered the conversation round to talk about these. He asked Apollos about his spiritual journey through life and found his account of how Apollos had adopted the Jewish faith very significant. Agabus then asked Apollos directly, what he thought of Jesus. Apollos paused before replying.

'The teaching of Jesus, presented in John Mark's biography, marks him out as a spiritual teacher beyond any other who had lived before. His miracles indicated that he was rather a special prophet, and the incontravertible evidence that he had risen from the dead, lends weight to the claim that Jesus is the Messiah, the Christ.'

'None the less,' went on Apollos, 'he is not quite the Messiah that had been expected from prophecy, which foretold that the Christ would be a ruler in the line of King David who would receive the acclamation, King of Kings and Lord of Lords.'[91]

Apollos realized that he did not really need Agabus to resolve a problem which had already been sorted out for him.

'Jerahmeel has cleared up this difficulty for me,' continued Apollos, 'by explaining that kings and rulers in future times will obey the instructions they recieve from Jesus by the interpretation they put on his teaching, not because they are forced to by a worldly autocrat, but because they want to out of love for Jesus. In that sense, the reign of Jesus will last for ever.'

'However,' continued Apollos, 'It does seem to me that you Christians are revering him as more than a great prophet, more even than as the greatest prophet that ever lived. Jesus is regarded as if he were God himself, living for a time as a man upon this earth, before returning to heaven. This does seem a rather extravagant claim. John Mark gives a very detailed account in his biography of the deeds and words of Jesus, and Jesus does not make any direct claim to be God himself!'

This was a fair question and Agabus sought to answer it on the basis of what he knew Apollos would already be aware of in the writings of the prophets.

'If Jesus was the Messiah, the Christ, and the prophets had foretold that the Messiah would be none other than God himself, would it not be logical to recognize that divinity was concentrated in the person of the Messiah?' asked Agabus.

'James in Jerusalem drew my attention to the prophecy of Isaiah, that a virgin will conceive and bear a son who will be called Emmanuel, which means God with us,'[113] replied Apollos, 'but I have met many bearing the name Emmanuel and I do not regard them as God incarnate, just because they bear a name with a rather special meaning.'

'The prophecy you refer to,' answered Agabus, 'does not mean that Emmanuel will be the Messiah's name, but rather, that he will be known as God with us. The Messiah's name was not Emmanuel but Jesus, which means "he will save his people". However, Isaiah's prophecy was fulfilled in Jesus, because, as you rightly say, we do regard Jesus as God with us. But Isaiah gave a much more direct prophecy of the divinity of the Messiah.

> A child is born to us!
> A son is given to us!
> And he will be our ruler.
> He will be called, "Wonderful Counsellor,"
> "Mighty God," "Eternal Father," "Prince of Peace."
> His royal power will continue to grow;
> his kingdom will be at peace.
> He will rule as King David's successor,
> basing his power on right and justice,
> from now until the end of time.
> The Lord Almighty is determined to do all this.'[91]

Apollos nodded his head slowly as Agabus quoted this prophecy.

'Why then,' asked Apollos, 'did Jesus not say he was God outright and avoid all this speculation and controversy?'

Agabus smiled through his white beard.

'When our forefathers in their wisdom, wrote out the burdensome laws they expected the Jewish people to adhere to, they included a statement that it would be blasphemy for a man to claim to be God. Generally of course, this is true, but they did not anticipate the problem that this rule would create for God himself when he fulfilled prophecy and came on earth to live as a man! However, even without this rule, I do not think that Jesus would have made a blatant statement of his own divinity. It was very much in Jesus' nature to speak and act in a way which caused men to reflect upon the manner of man he was, and to discover his identity for themselves.

'As you read John Mark's biography of Jesus,' asked Agabus, 'did you form the impression that he was in any way an arrogant man or perhaps a little dishonest?'

'On the contrary,' replied Apollos, 'he was a man of complete integrity. He was neither dishonest nor arrogant, but that alone cannot bestow upon him the attribute of divinity!'

'Near the beginning of John Mark's account, we are told of how Jesus healed a paralysed man who had been lowered to him through a hole which his friends had made in the roof,' Agabus reminded Apollos. 'Do you remember the rather special thing that Jesus said to that man, which was the key to his being restored to health?'

Apollos thought hard. His face lightened.

'Why, yes, he told the man that his sins were forgiven.'[136]

'We may be able to forgive another, sins they have committed against ourselves,' answered Agabus, 'but who but God can proclaim a general forgiveness of sins? A foolishly arrogant man might make such a meaningless claim, maybe, but Jesus was not that sort of man. And then, Jesus' declaration of forgiveness proved to be much more than mere empty words, but a pronouncement of real power, for the man was healed indeed. He took up his bed and walked!'

Agabus paused, leaving Apollos to think on this before continuing.

'No, Jesus was not an arrogant man, neither was he a dishonest man. Jesus' honesty went beyond the honesty of even good men who will remain silent when others speak words of deceit, being satisfied if they themselves do not consciously speak falsehood. However, when Jesus heard falsehood spoken, even by men who were greatly revered by society, he would not remain silent but corrected words which would mislead others. I will now tell you an incident which was not recorded by John Mark. After Jesus had risen from the dead, the last of his special twelve disciples, the apostles, to see the risen Jesus was a hard-bitten realist called Thomas. When Thomas did meet the risen Jesus, he insisted on verifying that he was seeing no ghost or imposter. Jesus allowed Thomas to actually place his hands in the wounds he had sustained in his hands, his feet and his side as he hung upon the cross. Thomas was convinced and he spontaneously declared that Jesus was his Lord and his God.[87] Thomas had discovered what Jesus wants all of us to discover for ourselves. Jesus did not refute Thomas' declaraton. We can therefore come to only one conclusion, if we acknowledge that Jesus had complete integrity and would not have remained silent when a false statement was being made which would seriously mislead others!'

Apollos paused for some time before answering and Agabus remained silent, allowing Apollos to gather his thoughts.

'It does seem to me that prophecy is being used to substantiate a claim that Jesus death was sacrificial and that the only way to secure eternal life is to accept that this sacrificial death is sufficient to cover our sins. While I can accept Jesus as the teacher, the Messiah, the perfect example for us to follow even, I cannot accept the interpretation put on the sacrificial nature of his death. Every man must be judged on his merits, and although none of us would claim to have lived perfect lives, our success in conforming to the instructions God has left through the law, yes, and in following Jesus' example, will hopefully outweigh our failures when we come to be judged.'

'I could not expect to survive judgement,' answered Agabus, 'on the basis of the quality of my life, for I know that although I can present to the outside world a tolerably upright and noble image, God must be aware of much that is wrong with my make up, so much, that in my natural state, I could not hope to enter into the radiance of God's presence. I would not even be able to tolerate living with my fellow men if they could read every thought of my mind and could see the mixed motives which govern my actions.'

'Our thoughts are our own business,' answered Apollos, 'and should not influence the verdict as we are judged.' 'This is not the case,' said Agabus as he continued the debate. 'Our thoughts are very much a measure of the sort of people we are, and God knows every thought which passes through our minds. You will have read the teaching that Jesus gave which is recorded in John Mark's biography, that the things which defile a man are not the things which enter his body through eating, but the things which are already in his mind. If Jesus is to be accepted as Messiah on the basis of his teaching, then this doctrine must be seen as an important aspect of revelation he gave us. John Mark's account by no means includes all the teaching Jesus gave on the importance of our inner selves being right with God, and not just our outward deeds. On one occasion, he declared that nursing a grudge against our brother was morally as bad as committing murder, and looking upon a woman as an object of lust was as bad as adultery.[99] I am conscious that I cannot rid myself of sin, and I am thankful that Jesus' sacrificial death will cover my sin if I dedicate my life to him as his servant. I have indeed done just that, and Jesus has given me more than I could have expected in return. He has given me strength to overcome much of the sin in my life. He has given me assurance of eternal life with him. He has given me joy in this world such as I never dreamed of before knowing Jesus. He has also given me rather special gifts besides which I try to use in his service.'

Even after this testimony which Agabus presented in a manner which Apollos recognized, projected great feeling and sincerity, Apollos was not prepared to accept that another's sacrifice was the price of his sins. Agabus challenged Apollos as to what he considered to be the significance of sacrifices offered in the Jewish Temple. Apollos suggested that these provided a tangible demonstration of the supplicant's penitence. Agabus answered that unless there was something special and sacred about the shedding of blood to take a life, God would surely have found another tangible and constructive way by which a person could give something to show penitence, for a loving God can surely take no pleasure in the shedding of an innocent animal's blood. Agabus maintained that the rite of sacrifice had been ordained at the beginning of civilization, so that mankind would understand and recognize the significance of the special sacrifice that the Messiah, God living as a man, would make of himself on behalf of mankind, when that event occurred.

Apollos was beginning to find himself out of his depth at this stage of the discussion, for the significance of sacrifices was an aspect of his religion which he had never properly thought through. However, the discussion ended without Apollos taking that vital step of faith which Agabus knew was required for a person to become truly Christian.

After the foursome had walked for an hour or so by the quietly flowing river, they realized they had come far enough. They were now in the gently rolling countryside, some way beyond the outer limits of the city of Antioch and they sat on a grassy slope to rest awhile before making the return to the metropolis. On the return, Apollos walked with Simon and Jerahmeel accompanied Agabus.

'What are your plans for the next week of so?' asked Agabus.

'Our ultimate destination is Greece,' replied Jerahmeel, 'for that is the land that Apollos has set his heart on seeing. However, I would rather stay for some further time here in Antioch. I myself have been unable to convince Apollos of the claims that Jesus has on his life, but the church here at Antioch is so powerful in its worship and teaching. I feel sure that Apollos will come to know Jesus through its ministry.'

Agabus then made a suggestion which at first surprised Jerahmeel, but he recognized that Agabus had rather special prophetic gifts which gave weight to his counsel.

'Men and women are won for the Lord Jesus through their hearts and not their heads,' said Agabus. 'Apollos is a young man with a fine intellect, but I realize that he will not be won for Christ by argument. When I saw Apollos, I had a strange stirring within, and the Spirit told me that that young man would become a great champion of the church. However, the Spirit also told me that he would not be won as a servant of the church in Antioch. I prophecy that Apollos will be won for Christ by you yourself, Jerahmeel. However, this prophecy, like most prophecy, is conditional.

160

Apollos' conversion will be dependent on your showing steadfast love towards him and being unfaltering in your witness. Yes, Jerahmeel, you will win Apollos for the Lord, but the Spirit tells me, his conversion will cost you dear.'

The four men separated when they returned to Manaen's house in the middle of Antioch. They made their farewells with warm embraces. Simon and Agabus went into the house and Apollos and Jerahmeel returned to their inn in the northern suburbs. Apollos was surprised when Jerahmeel suggested the following morning that the time had come for them to continue their journey to Greece, but was pleased to fall in with this plan. Two days later they left Antioch.

23

Troy

Apollos and Jerahmeel set off overland, travelling in a westerly direction towards the Aegean Sea. This would give them the opportunity of visiting a number of notable Hellenic cities before crossing to the Greek mainland. Apollos followed the route suggested by Jerahmeel. Unbeknown to Apollos, the route chosen was not entirely based on Jerahmeel's previous experience of travelling in this region, as had been the itinerary followed thus far on their journey of exploration from Alexandria. Jerahmeel was following a route which had been suggested to him by Simon, as they had walked by the Orontes the previous Sunday afternoon. It was a route which closely followed the missionary journeys of Paul, and therefore, passed through cities where Christian churches had been founded. Their journey took them through the provinces of Cilicia, Cappadocia, Galatia, Pisidia and Asia. They stopped for a few days at the cities of Tarsus, Derbe, Lystra, Antioch, Colossae, Laodicea, Philadelphia, Sardis and Ephesus. In the case of Antioch and Laodicea, our travellers were visiting cities bearing the same name as two other cities they had recently visited. Jerahmeel explained to Apollos that the Seleucid kings had a propensity to secure a form of immortality by founding cities and naming them after themselves or their relatives. No fewer than sixteen Antiochs had been founded by Seleucus I Nicator and named after his father, Antiochus. The Laodiceas had been founded by Antiochus II and named after his wife, Laodice.

Jerahmeel and Apollos found that Ephesus was a particularly interesting city, and they decided to stay here for two weeks. Jerahmeel had no great difficulty in identifying the church at Ephesus, and Apollos and Jerahmeel linked up with the Christians at Ephesus, as they had done at the other cities on their route. At Antioch in Pisidia, they had met Simon's sons, Alexander and Rufus who were stalwart workers for that church. At all the churches, there were significant variations in the form of worship, but Sunday services followed much the same sort of pattern as Jerahmeel and Apollos had experienced at Jerusalem and Syrian Antioch. There was much talk in these churches of Paul, Barnabas and Silas who had been responsible for winning the first converts to Christianity in many of these cities and founding the churches. These young churches were by and large, healthy and vigorous, although differences could be perceived in the enthusiasm and energy with which they sustained their faith. Jerahmeel was the spokesman for our pair of travellers. Apollos said little but listened hard and learnt much. However, much to Jerahmeel's disappointment, he showed no inclination to make a profession of accepting the Christian faith.

Ephesus was situated at the mouth of the River Cayster. On one side of the city was the sea, and behind it rose the grassy slopes of the Koressos mountains. A magnificent highway ran through the city to the harbour where the caravans and merchant fleets would meet to trade and exchange their wares. The city had all the hall-marks of wealth and opulence. Its streets were paved with marble, and its civic buildings included baths, theatres and libraries. The principle building of interest lay nearly two miles to the north-east of the City centre. This was the famed temple to the goddess, Diana. Apollos felt a pang as he visited this pagan shrine, for although he felt no affinity for the form of worship practiced, the name reminded him of the Diana he had so hastily left in Alexandria. He wondered if the pain he felt was merely homesickness.

In spite of his knowledge and familiarity with the legends of the Greek divinities, it was not until that moment that Apollos thought of the link which existed between his name and Diana's. Diana, the chaste huntress, goddess of the moon was the daughter of Zeus and Leto, and twin sister of the sun god, Apollo, whose birth she preceded by one day. As Apollos read the inscriptions on the walls of the Temple, he realized that the form of the legend of Diana's origin and her function, was different from the definitive Hellenic version he had studied in the library at Alexandria. At Ephesus, Diana was revered principally as a fertility goddess, and the Ephesian legends linked her in some way with the Amazons.

The Temple building was magnificent. It was adorned with fine sculptures and splendid paintings depicting incidents from the Ephesian version of the legends of Diana. Apollos had visited great temples, both in his native Egypt, and in the cities he had visited while on this grand tour. None could compare in scale or magnificence with the Temple of Diana. From a religious standpoint, only the Temple in Jerusalem could generate an atmosphere which touched Apollos spiritually. Having rejected idolatory, the pagan temples projected a form of religion which was irrelevant to Apollos, but nonetheless, he could not fail to admire the adornments of the Ephesian Temple and feel awestruck at its great size. Apollos estimated that the Temple of Diana was at least ten times larger than any other temple he had visited. The focal point of the Temple was a huge statue of Diana which, it was claimed, had not been sculptured by mortal man but it had fallen from heaven. Apollos and Jerahmeel returned to visit this pagan shrine many times during their stay in Ephesus.

As Jerahmeel and Apollos toured the commercial centres of the city and the markets, they were surprised to find the number of traders who dealt with Diana cult objects, mainly replicas of the statue of Diana they had seen in the Temple. It was claimed that Diana was worshipped all over the world, and adherents to this Goddess who made a pilgrimage to the city, would be specially blessed if they returned with a copper or silver replica of their patron goddess.[137]

Jerahmeel and Apollos entered into a discussion on the commercialisation of religion. Jerahmeel felt sure that the true God had some blessing for the innocent, although misguided men and women, who had in the past, financed from their hard earned resources the original building of the temple, and for those who today, provided for its continued upkeep. They did so out of genuine devotion, because they knew no better way to God. However, he agreed with Apollos, that evil men exploited the genuine thirst for spiritual experience of ordinary people, and considered that some of the priests, no less than the sellers of Diana idols, fell into this category. Jerahmeel then pointed out that a faith, centred on the true God, was not immune to such human abuse, and considered that Jewish priests, like their pagan counterparts, could often be prompted by worldly rather than spiritual motives. It was on the tip of Apollos' tongue to suggest that perhaps the elders of Christian churches might also be prone to the same temptations. However, Apollos had grown in maturity over the past few months. His mind was now tuned to recognize the tactless thought which could be so easily transported from the mind to the tongue. He was now able to mentally arrest the process, and so avoid causing the offence that he had created with thoughtless remarks in the past.

When Apollos and Jerahmeel had exhausted the sights of Ephesus, they continued northwards on their journey to Greece. They followed the coast, stopping for a few days at the cities of Smyrna, Pergamum, Adramyttium, Assos and Troas. Apollos was particularly excited when they reached Troas, for this was near the site of the famed city of Troy, so celebrated in the literature of Greece's greatest poet. He had read Homer's *Iliad* and the *Odyssey* through and through. Apollos had anticipated that a visit to the site of Troy would be one of the climactic moments of his tour.

On the first morning of their sojourn in Troas, Apollos and Jerahmeel walked the few miles from Troas to the reputed site of Troy. A local shepherd pointed out a grassy hill as the accepted site where stood the ancient fortified city. No ruins were evident, not even a trace of a city wall. Apollos and Jerahmeel climbed the hill. There were no other visitors. A fresh breeze blew in from the open sea which the travellers could just see from their vantage point. As they surveyed the plains around this hill, Apollos reminisced on all he had read in Homer's epic poems. Was this the point from where the fair Helen saw the thousand ships which bore the Greek armies, pledged to win her back for Menelaus? Did King Priam scowl down from the Trojan ramparts as he watched Agamemnon establish his camp and deploy the warriors who maintained the siege? Were these the plains where the Trojan hero, Prince Hector, exchanged mighty blows with his Greek adversaries and slew Patroculus, only to meet his own death in turn at the hands of the valiant Achilles. From what point did Helen's abductor, Prince Paris, draw his bow to loose the shaft which pierced the vulnerable heel of the hitherto indomitable Achilles? What cunning schemes did Ulysees bring to bear upon the beleaguered Trojans? How did the Greeks manage to deceive the Trojans into importing through their gates, the monstrous wooden horse which sealed their doom? This horse concealed the warriors who were able to destroy from within, the city which Agamemnon's host had failed to overcome from without, and so end the seven years' siege.

And what part did the gods play in all this? Legend had it that the Amazons supported the Trojans, who were also favoured by the powerful deities, Leto, and her children, Diana and Apollo. As Apollos' mind took this turn, he realized that he was only surveying the site of empty, even if fascinating, legend. Perhaps there was no Troy, and the legends were merely myths. Apollos felt deflated. Jerahmeel, who had visited so many of these places before, seemed to radiate a new life and power from the things he was learning and the new contacts he was making on this tour. Apollos was discovering that things he had expected to be special, were turning out empty. Even the faith into which he had struggled to be accepted, was now meeting a powerful challenge. The Jewish faith, in the form that Apollos believed it should be practised, almost seemed to be being written off by the Christians, as an anachronism.

No matter. In two days time they would cross the Hellespont and on to Greece. The Macedonian, Alexander had crossed the Hellespont three centuries earlier on his victorious march to Persia, and there was no doubt that Alexander had existed as a Greek hero. Apollos reflected to himself that the real objectives of this journey would be discovered in Greece itself.

166

24

The Church of Alexandria

A few weeks after Apollos and Jerahmeel departed on their extended tour of Israel, Asia Minor and Greece, Diana was aware that she was pregnant. Diana confided in her parents whose initial reaction was one of incredulity. Diana was so sensible and reliable. Although her parents often wondered at why she had been overlooked, Diana had no suitors to their knowledge. This was the last sort of problem that Parmenion and Camporina had expected, for Diana was not just an intelligent young woman, she complemented this gift with the more practical attribute of common sense. The question was immediately raised as to who was the father. Parmenion was reassuring.

'Cambiades and Aspasia are an honourable couple,' he told Diana. 'They will make sure that Apollos does the right thing by you when he returns from Greece. Apollos is a fine young man. You could make many a worse match than Apollos.'

Inwardly, Parmenion had misgivings. He was aware of the superficial attraction that Apollos would have for most young women, although of course, his younger daughter, Demeter, had not responded to Apollos' charm. However, he wondered if Apollos was really good enough for Diana. Did he have the qualities of fidelity and steadfastness, which Parmenion regarded as important qualities for one entering into marriage? Apollos may have been clever and handsome, but he was also somewhat selfish and arrogant, and these were not qualities which he would want in a husband for his beloved Diana. Although Parmenion and Camporina treated their daughters as equal, they found it difficult not to hold Diana in greater affection than

Demeter. As Demeter was cold and aloof, so conversely, was Diana warm and affectionate. Diana was in every way, a daughter in whom they felt great pride.

'Of course,' advised Parmenion, 'there is no need for you to marry Apollos if you don't really love him. We are wealthy and can provide well for both you and our grandchild.'

Again, Parmenion had inward misgivings. The last thing he wanted was to force his daughter into a loveless marriage, but although he now had ample means, would these be sustained sufficiently long to see Diana's child to maturity and independence? Parmenion was now over fifty, and although that may seem no great age, life expectancy, even for the privileged classes in those days, was more like sixty years, rather than the Biblical life-span of threescore years and ten. There were problems too with business. Friction was growing between the three main ethnic communities in Alexandria, the indigenous Egyptians, the Jews and the Greeks. The Egyptians were no longer proving reliable and trustworthy workers in his perfumeries where soaps and scent were manufactured. The Jewish traders were bartering more keenly and eroding Parmenion's profits to such an extent that he was considering going out of business altogether.

Camporina was not at all enamoured with the prospect of Apollos becoming her son-in-law.

'That young man is tarred too much with the shortcomings associated with vanity,' she complained privately to Parmenion. 'He may look nice and sound clever, but he argues for the sake of displaying his learning and basks in the admiration he receives, without appreciating the less spectacular but more valuable qualities of others around him. I like Cambiades and Aspasia, but they have spoilt their son so that I don't think he will make the affectionate and loving husband that Diana deserves. Why could not Diana have found some wealthy merchant or even a Roman Consul, as Demeter's husband has every chance of becoming?'

Parmenion listened to his wife's outburst without comment. Her aspirations for Diana were of course unrealistic, but then, who would have thought that Demeter would

168

marry a Roman with such promising career prospects. However, wealth and a glittering career were not synonymous with being loyal, affectionate and supportive. It was these latter qualities which Parmenion would have wished for, in the one to whom he gave his beloved Diana in marriage.

Parmenion went around to see Cambiades, and Cambiades' reaction was as Parmenion expected. Cambiades was not so blind to his son's faults that he would reject any suggestion that Apollos had seduced a young woman. There was no other family with whom Cambiades would more wish to be linked by marriage ties than that of his old friends, Parmenion and Camporina. Cambiades was concerned that he had no idea when Apollos would return. He expected him back within two years, but not much earlier. There was therefore, very little chance of arranging for the marriage to take place before the child was born. Communications were also a problem. Cambiades and Aspasia were receiving letters from Apollos, enthusing over the new sights he was seeing and the new people he was meeting. Although this news of Apollos' well-being was reassuring, Cambiades and Aspasia had no way of sending letters back as they never knew where Apollos would be next. Cambiades promised any financial help that might be required to give the child the best possible start in life. Although Cambiades spoke easily as one who had been accustomed to wealth and opulence throughout his life, he too had the same economic misgivings as Parmenion. Conflict between the ethnic groups in Alexandria was adversely affecting his business as it was Parmenion's.

When Cambiades told Aspasia the news, her first reaction was to be immediately defensive of her son.

'How do we know this is true?' she challenged. 'It is all too convenient to bring a paternity charge against a young man when he is away and it is known that he won't return for a long time to answer for himself.'

However, Aspasia soon recognized that her spontaneous reaction was emotional and ill considered. She knew Diana well enough to know that she would not groundlessly cite Apollos as the father of her child. As Aspasia considered the situation, she could think of no one she would have preferred as a daughter-in-law more than Diana, and she started to look forward to the prospect of becoming a grandmother. Apollos had seemed so restless of latter years that Aspasia had wondered if he ever would settle down within her life time. The prospect of having grandchildren was something she had barely dared hope for. Well, now Apollos would have to settle down and take a responsible part, not only in the family business, but in raising a family. But when would he be back? How could they summon him back? The letters they received were reassuring, but while Apollos was moving from place to place, they had to endure the agonizing frustration of one way communication only!

Diana found her father a great support and comfort over the next few weeks. He was reassuring and spoke enthusiastically of the joys of parenthood. He did not hide the fact that Diana would have to make great sacrifices and go without so many things that a single young woman of her age might have expected from life, but he assured her that the rewards would more than outweigh the sacrifices.

Camporina was not so tactful. It is perhaps too easy for a parent who is over-concerned for the physical and social well-being of their son or daughter, to give vent to their concern in a way which causes alienation between the generations rather than family consolidation. Camporina asked Diana far too often how she could have ever allowed such a thing to happen. She wondered if ever they could go again as a family to worship at the Temple of Poseidon, for none of the respectable Greek families who honoured that deity had had children in their families born out of wedlock. Diana tolerated such remarks for longer than most daughters, but in the end, she gave vent to her feelings about Poseidon and those who worshipped him, in an uncharacteristic outburst of sarcasm.

'If it embarrasses you to have me in your company when you go to worship your silly sea god, leave me at home!' exclaimed Diana. 'Indeed, I am surprised that you should wish to worship such a creature, as he would appear to conflict with your principles on the matter of bearing children out of wedlock. Just consider the amorous adventures of this son of Cronus and Rhea. By the Pleiade,

170

Alcyone, he bore Aethusa, Hyperenor and Hyrieus, and by the Harpy, Celaeno, he bore Lycus and Eurypylus. He seduced Chione who bore him Eummolpus. He actually raped Pittheus' daughter, Aethra. It was by Poseidon that Hippothous was born to Cercyon's daughter, Alope, and it was also by Poseidon, that Nauplius was born to Danaus' daughter, Amymone. He made the goddess, Gaea, mother of the giant Antaeus, and even seduced the Gorgon, Medusa, in the Temple of Athene, and there were more. Goddesses, mortals, nymphs, they were all the same to Poseidon. He went the whole way in all his amorous adventures. Why should you be angry at your daughter's one moment of folly when you worship so promiscuous a God?'

Camporina had only a vague knowledge of the myths which defined the personalities of the Hellenic Gods. She knew that Diana had such a keener mind than herself and was not prepared to enter such an argument from which she could only emerge the loser.

Camporina tossed her head.

'Don't be silly, Diana,' she said. 'I hadn't meant to imply that you embarrass us. You know that we worship Poseidon as the power which controls the sea and don't pay much attention to those silly stories. The God who rules the sea must be a great God indeed. Look how he has used the sea to protect our people and promote their destiny.'

Diana said no more. She felt rather ashamed at having allowed herself to be provoked into this outburst. She knew her mother really had her best interests at heart. However, from that time, Diana never again entered the great Temple of Poseidon.

One day as Diana sat alone outside their house, Anaxagoras passed by. Diana was alone because Parmenion and Camporina were at the Temple, paying their weekly respects to Poseidon. It is not unlikely that the opportunity to socialise with other wealthy Greeks, was a reason for visiting the Temple which outweighed the importance they placed in worshipping the sea god.

'You look sad, Diana,' began Anaxagoras. 'Are you not attending the Temple?'

'I see the Temple as totally irrelevant to my life,' answered

171

Diana. 'In any case, a girl in my condition is not really fit company for the honourable people who meet to worship Poseidon. But why aren't you there, Anaxagoras?'

By now, Diana knew that everybody in the Greek community with whom she mixed, were aware that she was pregnant.

'I too find Poseidon irrelevant and you may have noticed that I have not been to that Temple for months,' replied Anaxagoras. 'For years, I have had no real religion, no set of beliefs to give meaning to my life, but now I have found a religion which is meaningful in a way the other faiths practised in Alexandria are not. Those who follow this religion meet on the first day every week in the Jewish quarter of town, but we are not really following the Jewish faith. This new faith is challenging and exciting. We believe in one God only, like the Jews, but not in the same way. We believe that God sent his son to come to earth to live as a man to show us what God is really like. I am not clever enough to explain everything about him, but we have some wonderful teachers where I go to worship. Will you come to hear about this God, Diana?'

'Yes, I would like to,' replied Diana, who was feeling very alone and isolated and was glad of this invitation, 'but I don't think people who worship any God will want to have much to do with a girl like me.'

'That is where you are wrong, so wrong,' said Anaxagoras. 'This God is a God of love who shows special concern for those who feel rejected by others. As I said, I am not clever enough to explain to you much about him, but if only you will come to where I worship, you will learn from those who have a wonderful way with words, and who can project God's love in the way they speak.'

Anaxagoras did not need to be clever to communicate that there was something special about his new-found faith. He spoke with such enthusiasm and sincerity that Diana felt she just had to go and hear what this new faith was all about. Parmenion and Camporina were surprised when Diana announced that she was going to a meeting in the Jewish sector of town, but they raised no objection. They knew that Apollos had adopted the Jewish faith and assumed that she was going to become acquainted with the

172

faith of the one they expected to become her husband. They were reassured that she would be accompanied by Anaxagoras who held a special place in the affection of the Greeks living in that part of Alexandria.

On the first day of the week, Diana and Anaxagoras went to the meeting at what appeared to be a synagogue. Indeed, the building was a synagogue, but disruptions had occurred in its worship during recent weeks as a result of the visit of two Jews from Cyprus. These men brought with them, news that the long awaited Messiah had come. This caused quite a stir in the Jewish community of Alexandria. Some Jews accepted the news with enthusiasm and excitement, glad that the destiny of their nation had been fulfilled. Others indignantly rejected the so-called Messiah as an imposter. Jews fell into one of two categories, those who joyfully accepted the proclamation of the Jews from Cyprus and those who violently rejected it. None were indifferent or undecided. Since the president and senior members of the synagogue where this message had first been proclaimed, received the news favourably, the Jews from that synagogue who could not go along with a crucified Messiah, left to join one or other of the orthodox synagogues in Alexandria. Jews from these synagogues on the other hand, who had long awaited such news, joined the synagogue which the Jews from Cyprus had made their headquarters. Many from Hebron synagogue which Apollos and Jerahmeel had attended made this transfer, their minds having already been prepared for such news by the visit of Sandas-cum-Barama. However, most of the Hebron Synagogue awaited the report that Jerahmeel and Apollos would bring from Jerusalem before making a decision on this matter.

Diana had never been inside a synagogue before, but there was nothing about this building which caused her any great surprise. A Jewish visitor would have experienced more surprise, because changes had been made over recent weeks which did not conform to normal Jewish practice. The synagogue was crowded, but not all present were Jews. It was made clear by the visitors from Cyprus that the news they brought, although principally for the Jews, was to be shared with all men and women. About one-third at that gathering were thus, non-Jewish. Egyptians and Greeks

173

made up the gentile section of that congregation in nearly equal proportion. Also, men and women were present in nearly equal numbers and were not segregated. Alongside the Star of David which decorated one wall, a fish and a cross had been painted. Diana and Anaxagoras managed to squeeze into seats near the back of the building.

Soon after they arrived, the President welcomed the congregation and expressed delight that there were more than ever present at the meeting. After a psalm had been sung, the President introduced the visitors from Cyprus who were evidently well known to most but not all at that gathering. The visitors from Cyprus were none other than John Mark and Barnabas of whom Apollos and Jerahmeel had heard news when in Antioch.

John Mark spoke first. He seemed to be a rather diffident, shy young man, but once he had got going, he was an excellent raconteur. He told the congregation of incidents in the life of this Messiah, this Jesus, which John Mark had either witnessed or heard about from close friends, when he was a mere youth in the land of Judaea. All the stories John Mark told showed Jesus to be a special friend of individuals who were social rejects for one reason or another, lepers,[143] tax-collectors,[138] prostitutes,[142] adulterers,[139] beggars,[141] or members of racial groups despised by the Jews.[140] In every case, Jesus had been able to bring about a profound change. In some cases, he healed those he encountered, of disfiguring or debilitating diseases. In other cases he completely changed the individual's attitude to life, so that, for example, greedy tax-gatherers who had made themselves rich by extortion, became generous benefactors to the poor. This Jesus often found he could commend gentiles for having a better grasp of spiritual truth than the Jews who had had the benefit of generations of teaching from the writings of Moses and the prophets, and in one case, this led to a Phoenician woman's daughter experiencing a miraculous cure.

Then Barnabas stood to speak. Diana had never before encountered a person with such presence. He spoke in a clear confident voice, and projected such authority, but at the same time, appeared extremely gentle and kind. Barnabas made it clear that this Jesus was not an ordinary man but much greater than the greatest of prophets or most exalted of kings. He was none other than the Son of God. He would save for eternity, all those who would entrust the control of the rest of their lives to him.

Diana came away from that meeting in a very pensive mood. All that had been said had given her considerable food for thought. She realized why Anaxagoras had been so enthusiastic at having discovered for the first time in his life, a credible religion. However, Diana was not one to be swayed by the emotions of the moment. She believed that she too might be on the verge of discovering a worthwhile religion which would give her something infinitely greater than herself to live for, but Diana decided that she must learn more about this Jesus before making a commitment.

25

The Riot

Diana went to that synagogue with Anaxagoras for the next few weeks. She discovered the members of this religion called themselves Christians and when they met as a body, they referred to themselves as a church. There was an atmosphere of love and caring in that community which Diana had never experienced before. By and large, the Jews in the community were highly respectable people, but many of the Greeks and Egyptians had been social misfits in some way or other. One or two had reputations for drunkenness. One Egyptian had served a prison sentence for robbery, and a Greek had been in prison because of inability to pay his debts. All testified to having received forgiveness for the pain they had caused others through their sins and their crimes, and they spoke of the relief at being able to start new lives in Christ, with the power that he gave to live life in a better, more positive and worthwhile way. Diana noticed that there was no obvious differentiation between the various classes and ethnic groups in that community, whatever their background or previous life-style. If anything, it almost seemed as if those who had most to be ashamed of in their past, were specially loved because of the change that their new faith had brought about in their lives.

Diana found that there were opportunities to meet members of this community at times, other than the first day of the week. Although Sunday meetings were always joyful occasions, they were so crowded, and week by week, more and more people seemed to squeeze into that synagogue building. There were mid-week occasions when she was able to meet with small groups of these Christians and raise the many, many questions she wanted answered before she felt confident that Christianity was for her, and that the claims made on behalf of this Jesus were valid. Diana soon realized that hard proof was not really necessary. The joy, the vitality, the love of this community was infectious and she really wanted to be part of it. The groups she met with were aware that they could not always give Diana satisfactory answers to some of the searching questions she posed, but they arranged for Barnabas and John Mark to be present at some of the mid-week meetings which they knew that Diana would attend. On these occasions, Diana always felt her questions were more than adequately answered, either from John Mark's eye-witness evidence, or from Barnabas's mature wisdom and understanding of how Jesus Christ was relevant to the human situation.

Each week, new members of that community, who wanted to publicly declare that they had decided to commit their lives to Jesus Christ, were baptized. The baptisms were carried out in Lake Mareotis which bordered the south-eastern quarter of Alexandria. These were most moving ceremonies. The baptisms were invariably conducted by either John Mark or Barnabas, assisted by those who had formerly been senior members of the synagogue, and were now recognized as elders of the Church. Diana made the decision that she too would like to make this public declaration, and one spring morning, she was baptized with five other new members of the Alexandrian Church. Anaxagoras had been baptized himself, some time earlier, and was delighted to be Diana's sponsor on this occasion.

The sadness and shame that Diana felt at the worry she had caused her parents, mollified as a result of Diana's association with this community where she felt more than accepted. Diana realized that she was loved and belonged in a special sort of way. She made friends with people with whom she had not previously had the chance of mixing when her social circle was predominantly made up of people from the wealthy Greek classes. There were Greeks at this Church, but Diana took great delight in the friends she made among the Jews and Egyptians. As everybody spoke Greek, these ethnic differences were not very

177

apparent in the way that community gelled. As friendships and even marriages were made which transcended ethnic origins, the Church became increasingly, a united group of Christians, rather than representatives of three separate cultural groups who met together to worship.

Sadly, this unity of spirit and purpose did not exist in the Alexandria beyond the Church. Friction between the ethnic groups turned to strife. The Greek and Jewish owners of businesses suffered severe losses because of the unreliable nature of the largely Egyptian workforce. They seemed powerless to prevent theft from their businesses by their employees, who considered stealing to be fair game from those whom they regarded as having exploited them for generations. The Jewish traders retaliated by putting up prices, and this provoked a riot in which Jewish stalls and shops were destroyed and looted. The Roman authorities had some difficulty in restoring a semblance of order with the limited soldiery available to police a city which had always been regarded from Rome, as peaceful and law abiding, and in no need of a powerful garrison like that established in Jerusalem.

While the Christians met in their haven of peace, the city seethed with rancour and intolerance. Then an incident occurred which was to have far reaching effects on Diana and Anaxagoras. The Egyptians who relied on water from the canal which was being polluted by the Greek owned tannery, started to experience illnesses which they attributed to the foul water. The Greek tannery owners ignored representations from the Egyptians. Then two Egyptian children died. This marked the flash point for serious community violence. The enraged Egyptians gathered in a mob and attacked anything they recognized as Greek. They burnt down the tannery and the Temple of Ganymede where many of the Greeks in that quarter of the town worshipped. Several Greeks were killed while attempting to protect their property. The violence escalated, and the mob turned their attention to the quarter of the city where the wealthy Greeks lived in the affluent suburb around the Temple of Poseidon. The fact that the Greeks living here had nothing to do with running the contentious tannery was not a factor to which the frenzied mob paid much attention.

178

The Temple of Poseidon suffered the same fate as that of Ganymede. Shops were looted, houses destroyed and Greeks clubbed to death. The violence was so sudden, its intensity beyond anything which had been experienced before in Alexandria, that the Roman authorities were quite unable to contain the damage. It appeared that the mob had assembled almost spontaneously in the middle of the afternoon. By early evening, the violence had run its course and the mob dispersed and returned to their homes in the Egyptian quarter of the city, leaving a trail of mayhem and destruction.

All this happened on the first day of the week, on Sunday, and from the standpoint of their safety, Anaxagoras and Diana were fortunate to have been at their Church. The noise of the mob could be heard from the Church, but at that meeting, no one was aware of the intensity of the violence or the target at which the riot was directed. What a shock awaited Anaxagoras and Diana as they left their Church in the Jewish quarter and made their way back to the Greek quarter near the sea. Anaxagoras's shop had been destroyed and looted, but worse was in store for Diana. Her home had been burnt. Her parents had both been killed. Cambiades and Aspasia had suffered the same fate. The Greeks who were known to Anaxagoras and Diana, who had survived the onslaught, were too shocked, too busy clearing up their own debris, to be of any help and comfort to Anaxagoras and Diana. Diana was distraught.

Roman soldiers were supervising as best they could, the clearing up operations. The dead bodies had been transferred to a makeshift morgue, an open patch of ground where they had been laid out and labelled. Diana had the grisly task of confirming that her parents were among the dead. They had already been identified by other acquaintances who had escaped a similar fate. More bodies were brought in as Anaxagoras and Diana were conducted down the rows of corpses by a Roman soldier. Diana wept at the sight of her parents, laid out side by side. The sun had just set, and torches had been lit to provide sufficient light for this macabre task to proceed. The flickering light added to the ghastliness of the horrific spectacle.

Anaxagoras had suffered no personal bereavement as

179

Diana. He felt specially responsible for Diana's well being at this time, and this helped him put the loss of his shop out of his mind.

'We must return to the Church,' he advised. 'There will be someone there who can help us.'

This was obviously sound advice, and they walked in silence, back to the Church they had left earlier that evening, Diana leaning heavily on Anaxagoras's arm.

When they returned to the Church, they found that most of the Christians who had dispersed after the meeting earlier that evening, had reassembled, aware that something terrible had happened but having heard only vague and garbled accounts of what had occurred. Anaxagoras put them more fully into the picture. Although an atmosphere of concern and alarm pervaded the group gathered outside their Church building, the Jewish quarter of the city was at least calm. Diana was in a state of shock and had started to tremble. A Jewish couple stepped forward and put protective arms around her. They indicated to Anaxagoras that they would take her to their home and departed. Two more Greek members of the Church returned from the Poseidon quarter in a distressed state. They had gone back to what should have been their home after the time of worship, only to find it had been severely damaged and all but totally destroyed. They were offered shelter for the night in another Jewish home. A group of men asked Anaxagoras if they could do anything to help. It was noticeable that a significant number of those volunteering were Egyptian. Anaxagoras suggested that they should return and see what could be done.

When Anaxagoras arrived back at the Poseidon quarter with the twenty or so Christians, it was almost dark. The torches which had been lit and fixed to stands gave some impression of the destruction, but it was clear that no repairs could be carried out until daylight. There were several Greeks wandering around in a dazed fashion, some of them openly weeping. The Christians asked if any needed shelter for the night and these offers were gladly accepted by those who had nowhere else to go. They seemed to hve been suddenly plunged from affluence to destitution. The party returned to the Jewish quarter. The unfortunate Greeks went to various Christian homes to pass the night. Anaxagoras was offered shelter at the home of an Egyptian family whom he had come to know well since attending this Church.

26

The Birth of Selenece

Anaxagoras' first concern the following morning was for Diana. He went straight round to the house where she was staying and found her still dazed but composed. She was naturally confused and uncertain about what should be done next, but Diana still showed gratitude for the kindness and concern she was being afforded by the couple with whom she was sheltering.

Once he was satisfied about Diana's well-being, Anaxagoras returned to the Greek quarter and took stock of the situation. His own shop was destroyed beyond repair, and he recovered what possessions were worth retaining from the wreckage of what had once been his home and source of livelihood. Roman soldiers were in evidence, guarding the sites against further looting. A centurion was seated at a table near the site of the Temple, taking down notes from Greeks who were anxious to give the authorities as much information as they could about the previous night and those they considered responsible for the riot. However, in situations like that where law and order had completely broken down, it was difficult for the Romans to obtain reliable identification of those involved in the previous night's looting. The mob was almost entirely made up of Egyptians, personally unknown to the Greeks living in that part of Alexandria. The more energetic Greeks, whose homes and shops had not been completely destroyed, were beginning to carry out repairs to their property. There was obviously a lot of work to be done.

Anaxagoras returned with his pathetic bundle of salvaged belongings to the home where he had stayed the previous night. He reported on the situation and news went round the bush telegraph giving the Christians fuller knowledge of the situation. That afternoon, a group of Christian men again met at their Church building, and Anaxagoras indicated what help they could give to the distressed Greeks. An hour later, they reassembled with tools and trolleys of wooden planks, and made their way to the Poseidon quarter. Their help was greatly appreciated and a significant start was made to the major repair project which faced that community.

Later that day, the Roman authorities were satisfied that all the bodies had been found and identified, and gave clearance for their burial. The Roman Prefect who succeeded Claurinius wrote his report to Rome. He inwardly cursed Claurinius for providing such glowing accounts of the peace and tranquillity of Alexandria so that the city had been left with a totally inadequate garrison to cope with, let alone prevent, the sort of disturbances he had had to deal with in recent weeks. To have a city degenerate into a riotous state within months of taking over duty would not enamour him to his superiors in Rome. Although it was true that Claurinius had not paid sufficient heed to the reports of his intelligence officers and had painted far too rosy a picture of the way the city was running under his administration, to be fair to Claurinius, violence of this degree of intensity could not have been anticipated at the time he had left Alexandria.

A mass funeral was arranged for the twenty-five or so victims of the violence the following day. They were buried in the Necropolis cemetery on the outskirts of the Greek quarter. Diana attended this sad ceremony with Anaxagoras, glad of his support at that time of intense grief for her.

Barnabas came round to visit Diana. His words were so very reassuring and comforting. How aptly was this apostle named, Barnabas, which means Son of Consolation.[144] He asked Diana what help he could give her and if she had begun to think of her immediate future. She told him that she felt she could no longer stay in Alexandria, not just because of the painful memories that would linger with her in that environment, but because she felt there was a possibility that she could develop a bitterness and resentment towards those who had killed her parents. At that time, she still felt emotionally numbed by the experience, but did not want to remain exposed to a temptation to abandon the attitude of love and forgiveness she had learnt was an essential part of the Christian way of living. Barnabas gave a nod of approbation at the attitude Diana's intentions conveyed. Barnabas's effectiveness as a comforter lay very much in his capacity to listen rather than talk to the bereaved. Diana told Barnabas that her sister was married to the former Roman Prefect of Alexandria and she thought that she should go to Rome to be with her. Before she left, Barnabas prayed for Diana, that she would be given strength to bear the traumatic event which had overtaken her, and that God would guide her into making the best decision for her immediate future.

That night, Diana thought carefully about her plans for the future. She instinctively knew that Demeter would not be particularly pleased to have her unmarried sister with her baby, staying with her in the palatial splendour to which she was becoming accustomed in Rome. She knew her sister had no great love for children and could well resent the intrusion of Diana on to her scene, if this cramped the social style which she was developing to further her husband's career. Diana then thought of her aunt and uncle who used to live at Alexandria, but who now lived at Ephesus. Diana was very fond of them and knew this fondness was reciprocated. They had no children of their own and although now relatively elderly, Diana felt sure that she would be welcome to stay with them.

Without either Diana or Barnabas being conscious of the fact, Diana's decision was an answer to the prayer that Barnabas had shared with Diana the previous evening. As Barnabas did not meet with Diana again before she left Alexandria, Barnabas remained unaware of the change of plan.

Anaxagoras too was concerned to know of Diana's plans for the future. She told him of her relatives in Ephesus. Anaxagoras asked how she would travel to Ephesus, for a woman could not make that journey on her own, especially in Diana's condition. He also wanted to leave Alexandria. They both wanted to leave that city and its unhappy memories as soon as possible. As Diana was in the later stages of pregnancy, it was important that they should not delay the journey. Anaxagoras was more than happy to accompany Diana to Ephesus as he had no connections to draw him to any other city on the shores of the Mediterranean. Ephesus was not only a Hellenic city, it was also known to have a flourishing church and it was this factor that confirmed in both their minds that Ephesus was the right place to start new lives.

Anaxagoras discovered that a ship with room for passengers was due to sail to Ephesus at the end of the week. He booked a passage for himself and Diana. The next few days were spent in making fond farewells to their Christian friends who had been so supportive to them during this time of adversity. They had few belongings to pack but had sufficient money to sustain them for the voyage and provide for their immediate needs when they reached Ephesus. The following Friday, they set sail. A favourable southerly breeze was blowing, enabling them to make Ephesus ten days later.

Diana did not know immediately how to locate her aunt and uncle, but the church at Ephesus proved fairly easy to find. The news of the calamitous events at Alexandria had already reached Ephesus, and the Christians were full of sympathy for Diana and Anaxagoras and they were put up in separate houses. With the help of the Christians, Diana was able to find her uncle and aunt. As she had rightly anticipated, they were delighted to see her, although distressed at the cause of her departure from Alexandria. Diana was made most welcome to share their home and six weeks later, Diana had a baby daughter. She named the child Selenece. The welcome demands of the baby served to take Diana's mind off the painful memories of that dreadful night in Alexandria. Selenece was dedicated at the Ephesian church when she was three months old.

27

Claurinius' Commission

Claurinius and Demeter embarked for Rome within a week of their betrothal party. A Roman war galley, a trireme named *The Jupiter*, was made available to the young Roman administrator of Alexandria for this journey. Demeter needed about twenty chests to pack her belongings, mainly clothes, which she would need as she started her new life in the capital of the Empire. Claurinius needed a similar number of chests for his military gear, the things he had acquired for himself and the presents for his parents which he had bought during his tour of duty in Alexandria. The ship did not have a hold as such, but space was found to store these chests in spare cabins on this ship. It took about two days for a small work party of burly legionaries to get the ship loaded and the baggage securely stowed.

At last the day dawned for the couple to depart. Parmenion and Camporina bade fond farewells, but were comforted by the thought that they would be going to visit Demeter in her new home in Rome in a few months, once she felt established in this new environment. *The Jupiter* sailed from the Royal Docks. The pilot used the rowers to navigate the ship around the famous Pharos, and hoisted the sail once *The Jupiter* had made open water. The stiff easterly breeze filled the square sail and soon took the ship out of sight.

The Jupiter's voyage took her to Cyrene on the North African coast, some seven to eight hundred kilometres west of Alexandria, and then across the Mediterranean to Syracuse on the eastern coast of Sicily. The ship then sailed northwards, through the straits of Messina and made Ostia at the Tiber's mouth a few days later. After leaving directions with the centurion in charge of the legionaries on the unloading and delivery of the chests they had brought from Alexandria, Claurinius and Demeter took a small boat up the Tiber to the heart of Rome. News of *The Jupiter*'s arrival had preceded them, and Claurinius's parents were there to meet their son and his bride as they disembarked from the boat that had ferried them up the Tiber. Senator Quintus Albinian and his wife Drussiliana were proud of their son and welcomed him warmly. They graciously received Demeter and complimented Claurinius on his choice of bride. They then made their way to the Senator's spacious home and shared news. Quintus brought Claurinius up to date with Roman politics and gave an account of which personalities appeared to be currently important in the political, imperial and military circles which controlled the destiny of Rome and its Empire. Demeter was at first a little overawed at the opulence of her in-laws-to-be whose home exceeded anything she had expected. The home she had left in Alexandria was splendid by Alexandrian standards, but everything in Rome seemed to be that much bigger and grander than anything she had been used to before. However, it did not take Demeter long to become accustomed to Roman ways and enjoy the obsequious service of the slaves who would hasten to perform her least bidding. A few days later, Claurinius and Demeter were married at a splendid ceremony, appropriate to a couple of their social status, and took up residence in a well appointed house near to the home of Claurinius' parents. The house was nothing like as large or pretentious as the Senator's mansion but was comfortable and spacious and more than adequate for the immediate needs of Claurinius and Demeter.

A few days later, Claurinius took up his new post as a senior officer of the Praetorian Guard, where he held a rank immediately below that of the guard commander. Rome was passing through a relatively peaceful phase and the Praetorian Guard's duties were largely ceremonial. This suited Claurinius well. He did not have to become involved in the action which became the preoccupation of the Praetorian Guard, whenever there was civil unrest, or some political faction was seeking the violent overthrow of a

Caesar who threatened their vested interests. This left Claurinius free to cultivate the influential contacts which Quintus had indicated to his son would prove valuable in furthering his career.

Meanwhile, Demeter was learning from Drussiliana, the ways and customs of ancient Rome, and soon felt competent to entertain Roman dignitaries and the families which carried influence in the affairs of ancient Rome. Drussiliana was impressed with the way her new daughter-in-law was coping. Any doubts she may have harboured at her son's choice of a bride who was not a member of the Roman aristocracy were soon dispelled. The daughters of their friends knew little of life outside Rome. Demeter was at least able to display a knowledge of part of the Empire about which most of those who came to visit the home of Claurinius and Demeter would be interested to learn. The scandalous relationship between Mark Anthony and Cleopatra was still sufficiently recent history, that the Romans were fascinated to know more about the country which had been the centre of events which had split the Empire for a time.

For several weeks, life proceeded in an idyllic fashion for Claurinius and Demeter. Although he had enjoyed his tour of duty in Alexandria, Claurinius was glad to be back at the hub of things where momentous decisions were taken and where opportunities for advancement were plentiful. Although Demeter naturally missed her parents and her familiar home in Alexandria, she quickly became accustomed to the luxurious Roman lifestyle she was now enjoying, and looked forward to the time when her parents would be able to visit her. How impressed they would be at the splendours of upper-class life in Rome.

A situation then occurred which was to have repercussions on Claurinius' career. Concern was growing in Rome that certain merchant ships were not returning to Ostia and other Italian ports on their expected arrival dates. This became a matter for anxious conjecture. One popular theory was that these ships were falling prey to pirates, but with no definite news, this was mere speculation. Indeed, this suggestion seemed almost unthinkable. Pompey had cleared the Mediterranean of pirates a century earlier, and

188

now that sea was virtually a Roman lake, completely bordered by Imperial territory. If pirates were at large, from where could they operate? Then, one day, the story was confirmed by a sailor who had been picked up, clinging to timbers from a wrecked ship, drifting in the southern part of the Adriatic Sea. Two pirate vessels had appeared out of nowhere it seemed, rammed his ship, looted the contents, massacred the crew and sailed away as the ship sunk.

Such news called for action. Three war galleys were hastily prepared to sail. The command of this fleet was awarded to the young officer of the Praetorian Guard who was becoming so well known in influential circles in Rome. There were no officers, experienced in naval warfare, in Rome at that time, and Claurinius had so impressed his guests with accounts of his exploits in Germania, that he seemed to be the man with the necessary dash and flare to free the sea-ways of this unexpected menace. He would have the pick of the soldiery, currently encamped in the north of the country, and experienced sailors to see to navigation.

Claurinius was not inwardly pleased to be offered this responsibility. Although displaying bravado to his guests who always enjoyed tales of heroic exploits at arms, Claurinius knew that although he might have some gifts at administering a peaceful city or even a province, he was not really a warrior in the true Roman mould. However, Senator Quintus Albinian recognized the opportunity represented by this commission.

'To achieve greatness in Rome, one needs to prove oneself a great war-lord,' Quintus advised Claurinius. 'It was undoubtedly Julius Caesar's military genius which enabled him to become Emperor. Although Augustus was a mediocre general, he showed good judgement in choosing his battles and the frontiers on which to fight, so that he was invariably successful, and at the end of the day, it is the successful outcome of a campaign which holds sway with the people. Tiberius too was an able and successful soldier. Had Germanicus survived, he would have become Caesar, because he recovered the military reverses experienced by Varus. The people know full well that to win victories in Germania requires military ability of a very high order.

Caligula owes his accession to become Roman Emperor entirely to the fact that as Germanicus' son, he basks in the aura of a militarily great father. However, although I would say this to no one but yourself, Claurinius, Caligula is not fit to be Emperor and I do not expect his reign to endure for long.

'I made the mistake of leaving the army when a young man, and although I am now respected as a senator, I can never rank in Roman eyes as one who has brought glory to Rome with military conquests. I can therefore acquire no greater status in the Empire and must rest content as a mere senator. However, Claurinius, there is no need for your career to be limited in the same way as mine for lack of military glory. At present, Rome is hungry for a military success, no matter how small. The Circus Maximus has not had a victory parade for years and the people are crying out for such an event to reassure themselves that they are still the prime military power in the world. Your commission to clear the Mediterranean of pirates is a wonderful opportunity. With a fleet of well armed war galleys, you cannot fail to crush any shipping you encounter at sea. You will return as a victorious admiral. You will have the acclamation of the populace. You will provide the opportunity for a victory parade when you will be able to display the captured pirates at the Circus Maximus. Caesar will raise your arm in honour. The people will remember you as the one who removed the threat to Rome's prosperity. That memory will stand you in good stead when there is another political upheaval, and new power structures are created in Rome.'

Quintus Albinian anticipated his son's triumph with unconcealed excitement and enthusiasm. He had great ambition for Claurinius and in his mind's eye, had mapped his son's route to the highest office the Empire had to offer. Claurinius could not fail to be influenced by the intense and enthusiastic way his father imparted this advice. Yes, what honour he could acquire. What a marvellous stepping-stone in his career would be this commission. Claurinius now looked forward to setting sail with the redoubtable might of Roman soldiery, to rid the Mediterranean once and for all, of any who dared challenge the supremacy and authority of the Eagle.

28

Caligula

There were only three war triremes harboured at Ostia, *The Jupiter* on which Claurinius and Demeter had journeyed to Rome, *The Vulcan* and *The Minerva*. They had not been reserved for any immediate military duty and were therefore commissioned for hunting down and destroying the pirates which were harassing Roman shipping. Each was manned by a team of experienced sailors, and rows of galley slaves whose sullen efforts, enforced by the lash of the slave-master's whip, gave these war vessels some independence from the capricious whim of wind which usually provided the main motivating force to keep these vessels moving swiftly through the sea. However, in addition to the sailors, these ships would need a complement of soldiers, skilled in the military arts which would be required when engaging another vessel in combat at sea. Archers would be needed, men skilled at grappling and boarding a hostile ship, and soldiers who knew how to fire the naval ballista, the nautical equivalent of the Roman catapult which had been deployed so successfully in land battles.

Rome had not been involved in naval conflict for many years and its army did not include among its legions, a designated marine corps. Legionaries who had recently been involved in siege warfare would probably be the most suitable men to successfully wage naval warfare. Claurinius was given five days to select his soldiers. He would need eighty men for each trireme. He was not allowed to select his men from the elite Praetorian Guard, the only soldiers allowed within Rome proper, but he could have the pick of the men from the Fifteenth Legion. These were encamped on the other side of the Rubicon, the customary resting place of army units, returning to the Capital of the Empire to recuperate after a campaign. The Fifteenth Legion had acquitted themselves well in a fiercely fought campaign against the Dacians. They were now rested, and some were even restive, anxious to get back into military action.

Claurinius arrived at the camp of the Fifteenth Legion, bearing his documents of commission which carried Caesar's seal. He was conducted to the Legion's General, Marcus Asianus, who examined Claurinius' documents and was able to assess the sort of men he would need. Marcus summoned three centurions to his tent whom he described to Claurinius as the best in the Fifteenth Legion, Severus, Crispus and Valerian. Marcus Asianus asked them each to describe briefly to Claurinius their recent campaign and the part they had played in the action. Roman centurions were the backbone of the Roman army. They were not commissioned officers who held their rank as a result of aristocratic connections, but were senior non-commissioned officers who had risen to this status as a result of conspicuous ability displayed in the field. Each of those summoned by Marcus Asianus gave a concise account of the battles against the Dacians in which they had been involved. Their accounts left Claurinius in no doubt that these were soldiers of the first order in both ability and valour. After they had spoken, Marcus Asianus asked them to wait outside the tent, and then asked Claurinius if these men seemed suitable, or should he summon others? Claurinius affirmed that these centurions would do very well.

The General then asked the centurions he had selected to return into the tent and he invited Claurinius to explain to them the task he had been commissioned to carry out. Claurinius told the centurions that he would be commanding three triremes whose job was to search out and destroy the pirates which were menacing the merchant ships of the Empire. After giving his centurions the opportunity to ask any necessary questions, Marcus Asianus ordered these centurions to each pick the best eighty men they could, to fulfil the tasks involved in naval warfare. They were to have these assembled on the third hour of Wednesday, that was six days hence, when Claurinius would return to inspect the troops who would serve under him in this venture. The three centurions raised their right hands in the traditional Roman salute, turned smartly to the right and left the tent.

On his return to Rome, Claurinius was told by General Caius Intripio, the commander of the Praetorian Guard and Claurinius' immediate superior, that he could select three captains from the Guard to take general responsibility for each of the ships in Claurinius' small fleet. Claurinius realized that this was an expedient way of thinning the officer ranks of the rather top-heavy Praetorian Guard, and avoiding the further depletion of experienced field officers from the Fifteenth Legion who had suffered heavy casualties in the Dacian campaign. Claurinius chose Julius Messana, who had been his aide while in Alexandria, and two other young men from aristocratic families which had links with his own, Sextus Sindinion and Caius Aurelius.

Early on the Monday morning, Claurinius and his three captains, resplendent in their purple cloaks and white plumed helmets which marked them out as officers of the elite Praetorian Guard, set out in military chariots on the three day journey to the camp of the Fifteenth Legion. On entering the camp, they dismounted from their chariots which were taken to the equestrian compound and Claurinius announced the purpose of his visit to the corporal in charge of the camp guard. Claurinius had been expected, and he and his captains were conducted to Marcus Asianus' tent. The General, standing with his aides, was already waiting to meet him. The pair exchanged the customary military salute and Claurinius introduced his captains.

The General then led the small party to the parade and drill area of the camp. There assembled in three well marshalled companies, were the men selected as the fighting force for Claurinius' small navy. Each company was divided into three platoons, arranged as three ranks with eight men in each rank. Corporals and sergeants stood smartly in front of each platoon, and the three centurions Claurinius had met earlier in the week, stood in front of each company. As the inspection party came in sight, the centurion who fronted the first company shouted 'Hail Marcus!' and the troops came smartly to attention while the centurions raised their right arms in salute. General

Marcus Asianus returned the salute, and the centurions smartly returned to the attention position. As the inspection party approached each company, the commanding centurion introduced himself and his company and then conducted Marcus Asianus, Claurinius and the retinue of aides and captains along the seried ranks.

The assembled men were smartly turned out, with shining cuirasses and burnished helmets, but it was their granite features which marked out these soldiers as seasoned veterans of the Imperial Army. Claurinius stopped to speak to those whose battle scars bore evidence of wounds suffered in fierce conflicts and was impressed at the stoic fortitude of these hardened legionaries. After the inspection, Marcus Asianus invited Claurinius to speak to the men. Claurinius introduced himself and his captains; he told them of the task ahead and that they would be setting sail in just over a week.

As they returned to the General's tent, he told Claurinius that he was well pleased with the selection the centurions had made. As well as fine fighting men, the companies included soldiers who could cook, service weapons and armour, and even carry out many of the repairs which might be necessary to keep a ship sea-worthy after sustaining damage in a battle. Claurinius began now to feel very excited and confident about his commission. He had not felt very enthusiastic when he first received news that this task was being entrusted to him. He was reluctant to leave the luxuries of the congenial Roman lifestyle to which he was rapidly becoming accustomed. However, the force now under his command was surely invincible. Claurinius mentally anticipated the honours which would be heaped on him when he returned to Rome, having successfully fulfilled his mission.

The following day, Claurinius and his captains left the camp of the Fifteenth Legion and rode back to Rome in their chariots. It was arranged for them to meet Caesar in the afternoon of the day following their return to Rome. Caesar wished to bestow his benedictions on the leaders of this task force, embarking on its mission to clear hostile shipping from Roman sea-lanes.

That afternoon, Claurinius and his captains strode

194

proudly up the steps of Caesar's palace which they previously knew, only as an important edifice, around which they had the responsibility of deploying the Praetorian Guard. The visit to Caesar proved more of an ordeal than Claurinius or his captains had anticipated.

They arrived exactly on the hour at which they had been summoned and were met by a palace servant who conducted them to Caesar's audience chamber. This was a large hall, lined with a colonnade of marble columns, mounted by capitals, exquisitely carved in the Corinthian style. A marble stairway at the far end of the hall led up to a portal from which Caesar might be expected to make a grand entrance. The stairway extended across the whole of the far wall and consisted of two flights of ten steps. A flat area about three metres deep separated the upper and lower flights. A throne or pair of thrones could be accommodated on this flat area but no thrones were in place on this occasion.

Waiting in the hall in immaculate white togas, were Caesar's retinue of attendants. Claurinius recognized some as friends of his father who had won imperial favour. A few slaves scurried about the sides of the hall, arranging couches, bringing in bowls of fruit, and placing goblets full of ruby red wine on tables around the edge of the hall. Claurinius had the sense that everybody there was uneasy and on edge as they waited for Caesar to make his entry.

They waited for five minutes, ten minutes, quarter of an hour. Nobody spoke. As the minutes ticked by, the attendants began to shuffle nervously. After twenty minutes, a trumpet sounded. Everybody stiffened. A portly man in a crumpled toga, clasping a half-full wine goblet in his right hand, appeared at the top of the steps. A red stain on the side of the toga was evidently created by wine spilt from the goblet. This was Caligula Caesar.

'Hail Caesar!' went up the cry from the assembled company as they raised their right arms in salute. Caesar surveyed the company and then, half walked, half staggered down the steps. He beckoned an attendant over to him and pointed down the hall at the four Praetorian officers, standing to attention and holding their richly plumed helmets in their left arms. Caesar and his attendant spoke together for a moment. It crossed Claurinius' mind that Caesar did not know who they were or why they had come. Caligula then advanced down the hall with a loping gait, looking sideways at the four officers.

'So you are the valiant men who will rid the seas of Rome's enemies and enable honest ships to ply their trade?'

Caesar sounded quite lucid as he spoke.

'What does Neptune tell you of the menace which haunts and pollutes our seas?'

Claurinius was glad that Caligula Caesar addressed this question to Julius rather than himself. Caesar fixed Julius Messana with a strange gaze. Julius was aware of Caesar's unusual ways which had been euphemistically called eccentricities.

'We would seek the advice of Caesar rather than Neptune on so important a matter,' replied Julius with admirable tact. This reply obviously pleased Caesar and he smiled a leering smile.

'Although it is true that I am a god, there are some secrets which I can only learn by consulting with other gods,' said Caesar and then shouted, 'Be so good as to see if Equinodon will honour us by his presence today!'

Two attendants left the hall while Caesar made his way to a couch at the side of the hall, the attendants standing in that part of the hall parting to make way. Caesar sat down, still clutching his goblet, and bowed his head as if deep in thought. Everybody in the hall remained silent. After a few moments a clatter of hooves could be heard, and Claurinius and his captains witnessed the amazing spectacle of a horse being led through the portal where Caesar had made his entry and down the steps into the centre of the hall. Caesar walked back into the middle of the hall and stood by the horse while the attendants returned to their places.

'This is my horse whom I discovered was a god like me,' explained Caesar. 'The Senate have all paid their respects to this wisest of creatures. However, only I who am also a god can communicate with him. Equinodon, tell us how we are to rid the sea of pirates.'

Caesar held his ear to the horse's mouth as if listening for a reply.

'Equinodon says that you must take a god to sea with you

and the god will guide you into all manner of valiant deeds so that you will annihilate all shipping which does not acknowledge Rome to be the rightful master of the seas.'

Caesar stopped speaking and glowered round the assembled company.

'But where can we find such a god?' he continued. 'I would gladly go myself, and Equinodon here, too, but we must not leave Rome. Who knows what evil will befall the city without out presence to dispel the powers of evil ranged against us?'

Caesar again held his ear to the horse's mouth.

'Equinodon says that you should take Pullusodon!' exclaimed Caesar. 'I made Pullusodon a god, only last week. Invite Pullusodon to honour us with his presence.'

Caesar returned to the couch at the side of the room and again resumed his thoughtful pose. The same two attendants left, returning again through the magnificent portal, this time, carrying a cockerel. It was fortunately an overfed, docile bird and hardly fluttered as it was handed to Caesar who in turn placed the bird in the crook of Claurinius' right arm.

'The destiny of Rome is now secure,' shouted Caesar. 'Drink with me in honour of Pullusodon and our gallant officers.'

Claurinius and his captains stood still while the rest of those standing in the hall scurried round to pick up one of the goblets which had been left by the slaves around the edge of the hall. Caesar held his cup aloft and then took a deep draught. The attendants did likewise. Caesar then threw his goblet to the ground with a loud clatter, spilling the remaining contents. This gesture was followed by those who stood around with goblets in their hand.

'Now leave us, leave us!' shouted Caesar. 'Securing the destiny of Rome has for a while drained me of my power. Leave us, leave us!'

Caesar made his way to a couch by a table, sat down and buried his head in his arms. The attendants silently left the hall and Claurinius and his captains were conducted out by the attendant who had admitted them, Claurinius still clutching the cockerel under his arm.

29

An Encounter With Pirates

The next few days were very busy for Claurinius. He arranged for his servants to pack the military gear he would need for the voyage and to send this on ahead of him to Ostia to be loaded on to *The Jupiter*, along with the ridiculous Pullusodon. Claurinius and his captains went to Ostia to inspect their ships and meet the naval captains and the crews who would be responsible for the navigation of each of the ships. On such a venture, the seamanship of the sailors could be a more important factor in deciding the success of a naval engagement than the valour of the soldiers aboard. While they were at Ostia, the waggons carrying the military baggage of the legionaries trundled up in heavy ox-drawn carts. Claurinius was impressed at the way the baggage had been labelled so that it would be loaded on to the right ship, and was further impressed at the way the sailors stowed the baggage so that each soldier could easily find and identify his own kit. Claurinius was reassured to see the great lumps of rock which had been loaded in the stern of the ship as ammunition for the ballista to fire as missiles during a hostile encounter.

Over the next couple of days, Claurinius bade farewell to his parents and to Demeter. Demeter had acclimatised herself well to Roman life and Claurinius had every confidence that under the protective eye of his parents, she would continue to successfully cultivate the social contacts who mattered in Rome. Already, Demeter was establishing a reputation as a marvellous hostess.

The Saturday arrived and Claurinius and his captains rode to meet the companies of soldiers who had marched from the camp of the Fifteenth Legion. They travelled on horseback rather than in chariots. The three companies were already assembled in marching order. Claurinius formally took over command of these men from the senior officer who had made the journey with the soldiers from their camp by the Rubicon. Claurinius' three captains placed themselves at the head of their companies, and Claurinius rode slowly ahead of this task force as they marched from the parade ground where they had broken their journey, to their embarkation port of Ostia. A modest crowd gathered by the roadsides to cheer on their way, the fighting men on whom Rome's destiny depended. After a steady march, they made Ostia by mid-afternoon. The centurions saw to the men settling into their quarters on board ship. The following morning, the ships, headed by *The Jupiter* which was Claurinius' flagship, pulled out of Ostia and made for the open sea.

They sailed southwards, down the Tyrrhenian Sea towards the straits of Messina which separated Sicily from the toe of Italy, and then turned eastwards towards the southern Adriatic from whence had come the last report of pirate activity. At this stage of the journey, the wind was favourable, and the rowers were only sparingly used to give them exercise but keeping them fresh for rowing at the speed in earnest, should this be necessary in a naval battle. The small fleet sailed towards any shipping which was sighted and boarding parties were sent to such ships which were commanded to heave to by the formidable trio of large war galleys. The boarding parties enquired of the masters of these ships their business, their port of embarkation and their destination. They explained that their mission was to clear the seas of pirates and asked if any such rogue shipping had been sighted. The answer was invariably negative. In his naïvety, it never struck Claurinius that not all shipping using the Mediterranean accepted Rome's undisputed right to control the sea lanes. He could well be providing more information to be passed on to the pirates about his own mission and location, than the scant intelligence he was collecting on the pirates from the ships he encountered during this phase of his mission.

Claurinius had selected Julius Messana as the captain who would be responsible for affairs on *The Jupiter*, and

Valerian as his centurion. Sextus Sindinion had been allocated *The Minerva* and Severus was his centurion. *The Vulcan* was captained by Caius Aurelius with the centurion, Crispus, responsible for the fighting men. Days passed with no news or information concerning pirate vessels. Claurinius began to quite enjoy relaxing on the deck of *The Jupiter* as it gently sailed along the calm waters of the Mediterranean. The sun shone brightly each day, but the gentle sea breezes prevented those on board from becoming uncomfortably hot. Contrary to his sea captains' advice, Claurinius had the deck lamps lit at night and would relax in his hammock in the evening, enjoying the cool air, watching the lights of the other two galleys which sailed in *The Jupiter*'s wake, and listening to the soldiers singing bawdy camp songs to wile away the night hours. Perhaps there were no pirates. If there were, perhaps this fleet would never encounter them. Claurinius rather hoped that this might be the case. He did not really want violent action to interfere with this pleasant sea cruise he was enjoying at imperial expense.

Each day the captains and the centurions would assemble together on one or other of the three ships to discuss activities. There was plenty arranged to avoid boredom setting in. The ship which hosted the staff meeting was invariably inspected in great detail, but the soldiers by training, were tidy in their habits, and there was seldom found anything which could justifiably attract criticism. The three rowing decks were an unpleasant area. The glowering galley slaves were chained three to an oar and kept in time to the drum beat of the galley master for fear of the lash of the slave master who strode the gangway which separated the port and starboard galley teams. There was always an unpleasant stench from the rowing decks and the inspection party seldom stayed long in this area of misery and human degradation. Although some of the galley slaves may have been criminals, the only crime of most of those who reluctantly pulled at the heavy oars, was to have been a soldier in an army on the wrong side of a military conflict with Rome, as this apparently invincible city state steadily expanded its empire by conquest. Occasionally, Claurinius and his senior officers would stay to observe demonstrations of how rapidly the direction of the ship could be reversed by the port and starboard rowers pulling in opposite directions on their oars, or to see the maximum rate at which the rowers could work as the pace of the drum beat was raised to astonishingly high rates.

During the day, various training activities were arranged for the soldiers. Grappling lines and nets were thrown between the ships for the soldiers to clamber across in a mock boarding operation. Target practice was held for the archers and the slingsmen who aimed their bolts and stones at a large lump of wood towed by one of the vessels. These activities were run on a competitive basis. When the wood was recovered, the winning ship could be decided by the number of arrows embedded in the wood which were tipped with the characteristic colour, allocated to each ship. This target was also used to derive a measure of the ballista. The corporals in charge of the ballista teams had to assess the weights of the rocks which were loaded, and the tension in the ropes at the moment they were released to fire the missile, in order to gauge the range a projectile would reach. It was more difficult to judge the range than the direction that these huge catapults would hurl their rocks, but after a few days, the ballista teams knew their machines well and could usually place a rock within ten metres of the target. Use of the ballista for practice purposes was restricted to conserve ammunition, and every few days, the ships would anchor near some suitable shoreline and send small boats ashore to collect suitable rocks to replenish ballista ammunition.

One evening as Claurinius relaxed in his hammock, basking in the light of the deck lamps and listening to the soldiers singing, he saw a red object come flying through the sky. It hit the deck with a crash. The singing suddenly stopped. Claurinius sprang from his hammock. A fire started below the hole which the red hot rock had made through the the deck. Men started running. Deck lights were doused. The ballista teams assembled at their catapults. Archers and slingsmen lined the ships' gunnels, peering into the darkness for the source of this destructive missile. A glow could be seen to starboard as covers were taken off another red rock being loaded into a catapult to be hurled at the Roman ships. The missile narrowly missed *The Minerva*. The fire on *The Jupiter* started to spread.

'Form a bucket chain to douse the fire!' ordered Claurinius.

Grey shapes of hostile ships could now be perceived through the darkness only a few yards from the well lit Roman galleys. A very loud crash was heard. *The Vulcan* had been rammed amidships. Lightly armoured men were swarming from the ramming vessel on to *Vulcan*'s decks. Men were shouting. The clash of weapons could be heard as the legionaries engaged the intruders. A well aimed rock from *The Jupiter*'s ballista hit the wales of the ramming vessel amidships. A second rock hit the ship below the water line. *The Jupiter* was now blazing quite fiercely. A second great crash was heard as *The Minerva* was rammed. A third ship coming towards *The Jupiter* changed course to avoid being caught in the flames issuing from *The Jupiter*'s oar holes. A hail of arrows landed on *The Jupiter*'s decks, wounding several soldiers. The soldiers lining *The Jupiter*'s gunnels returned the fire with arrows and slingshot. *The Vulcan* and the vessel which rammed it were both sinking rapidly. Men were jumping into the water and swimming to one of the other ships. A fire had broken out on *The Minerva*. The hostile pirates were leaving *The Minerva* and swarming back on to their own ship. They were hacking away at the timbers of *The Minerva* into which their ship was embedded. Their rowers were straining to separate from *The Minerva* before the fire spread to their own vessel. The ships parted. *The Minerva* started to list. *The Vulcan* and the pirate vessel embedded into it were soon totally submerged.

The pirate vessels rowed away into the night, leaving *The Jupiter* and *The Minerva* blazing fiercely. *The Minerva*'s list increased as water poured in through the gaping hole left where she had been rammed. Suddenly she went down. The men on deck jumped into the sea, but most were weighed down by their armour and could not swim to another vessel.

The Jupiter's sail caught light and it seemed that the fire was spreading. Fortunately, the ship had not been damaged below the water-line and remained upright and afloat. Now that the distraction of arrows from the hostile ships had departed, everyone's attention and efforts were directed at extinguishing the fires. After half an hour's efforts, it seemed that the fires were at least being contained. Then as water continued to be poured on the flames by the frantically working bucket chains, the flames subsided, leaving glowing timbers which were soon cooled into charred beams by the constant dousing with water.

A grey dawn was breaking in the east. Bedraggled and weary men sat upon the decks. As the sky grew lighter, Claurinius ordered a roll-call to be taken so that casualties could be assessed. *The Jupiter* had lost five of its fighting men, killed, and ten had received arrow wounds. The situation below decks was much worse. In the confined space of the rowing decks, the smoke had had a devastating effect, suffocating most of the rowers. Only twenty or so who had managed to strain at their chains and get near the oar holes had survived. Survivors who had been picked up from the stricken ships were brought to Claurinius. Only two soldiers had managed to slip their armour and swim to safety. The sailors had been luckier and twenty or so seamen from *The Vulcan* and *The Minerva* had made it to *The Jupiter*. *The Jupiter* had also picked up from the sea, a dozen or so men from the pirate vessel which had foundered with *The Vulcan* and who had failed to make it back to one of their own ships. They were clearly frightened, and under threats of being boiled alive or something worse if they did not answer the questions posed they provided their interrogators with all the information they needed.

It appeared that the pirate vessels operated from a concealed cove a few miles from Carthage. Although Carthage, like the rest of the cities which bordered the Mediterranean, was under Roman control, coastal surveillance around Carthage was not all that it might have been to allow such an enterprise to be conducted, almost under the Roman noses. Of all the peoples whom the Romans had subjugated in the building of their empire, the Carthaginians, even more than the Jews, were most resentful of the Roman yoke. For years, Carthage and Rome had vied for supremacy in the Mediterranean. In the days of Hannibal, it had seemed that Carthage might prevail in the Punic wars, but whereas Carthage had one great general, Rome had produced a continuous line of military commanders of surpassing ability, such as the Cunctator, Fabius Maximus, and Scipio Africanus, and in more recent history, Gnaeus Pompey and Julius Caesar. Rome was now the unquestioned superpower of the day. However, the people of Carthage still remembered the glories of their past, and continued to do anything they could to undermine the power of their imperial overlords.

As the sun rose, the extent of the structural damage could be appreciated. *The Jupiter* was no longer the proud vessel that had left Ostia but a battle scarred and charred hulk. What was left of the sail was no more than a tattered rag, but the mast was still intact. The soldiers with manual skills were already making good some of the damage to the woodwork. *The Jupiter* was certainly not beyond repair, but she would need a complete refit at a well equipped naval port to restore her to her original glory. The main problem which confronted *The Jupiter* with no sail and no galley slaves fit to row, was motivating power. Claurinius conferred with Julius Messana, Valerian, and Hadasca, the chief seaman of *The Jupiter*. He first enquired of Hadasca, the location of the ship. Although he had had no time to take careful bearings, Hadasca indicated that he thought they were some kilometres east of Cyprus, and possibly, no more than fifty kilometres from the Syrian coast.

'Is that not the land which used to be referred to as Phoenicia?' Claurinius asked. Julius nodded to affirm this. 'And are not the Carthaginians a Phoenician people?' Claurinius continued. A plan was forming in Claurinius' mind which he hoped might enable him to salvage some advantage from the previous night's disaster and revive his fast fading dream of a triumphant return to Rome. He had to find some way of avoiding coming back to Rome in a wrecked and defeated state. Julius confirmed that the Carthaginians, like many other successful communities which had grown up around the Mediterranean, had been settled centuries earlier by the Phoenicians.

Claurinius then enquired about the prospects for navigating the ship. Hadasca confirmed what Claurinius already knew, that *The Jupiter* was still sea-worthy but needed a sail and a complement of rowers.

'Our surviving galley slaves will have recovered sufficiently to man an oar by tomorrow,' stated Claurinius, 'we have a dozen of the Carthaginian pirates who can also take their place on the rowing benches and we have enough soldiers to pull the remaining oars.'

Julius and Valerian both reacted to this suggestion. Free born Romans would not take kindly to doing work reserved for slaves.

'It will not be for long,' reassured Claurinius. 'When we reach the Phoenician coast, we will capture ourselves some more galley slaves.'

Valerian, who had always been involved in what he considered to be honourable military encounters, looked concerned.

'Syria is a law abiding province in the Empire,' he ventured, giving the region the name by which it was known on Roman maps. 'We cannot make slaves of those who are serving the Empire without giving provocation.'

'Would you question my order!' snapped Claurinius.

Valerian remained silent. He had served in the Roman army long enough to know that a superior officer's orders are obeyed without question.

'Have the men assembled on deck then,' ordered Claurinius. 'I will address them in ten minutes.'

Ten minutes later, Claurinius left his cabin and made his way to the deck where the men were waiting expectantly. He congratulated them on the previous night's efforts. He particularly praised the team who manned the ballista which he claimed had sunk three of the enemies ships and caused the others to flee in terror. Very few of the men knew precisely what ships had been involved in the action, and although they knew they had lost *The Vulcan* and *The Minerva*, they had no idea about enemy casualties, and felt encouraged by Claurinius' words.

'The ships who raided us last night were Phoenician pirate vessels which it is our task to destroy. We made a good start last night in destroying five. *The Vulcan* and *The Minerva* accounted for one each in addition to the three we destroyed.' Claurinius continued to lie and exaggerate as he spoke. Not many of the assembled soldiers were aware that there were no more than three ships in the flotilla of pirate vessels which attacked in the darkness.

'Unfortunately, as you know,' continued Claurinius, 'we lost *The Vulcan* and *The Mineva*. We have also lost most of our galley slaves and our sail. However, we do not intend to remain stranded in the middle of the sea, do we?'

The men grunted assent at this rhetorical question.

'Although we are fighting men, we will have to row *The Jupiter* ourselves to land.'

A murmur was heard among the ranks.

'We will not have to row for long. Phoenicia is barely a day's rowing away. When we reach Phoenicia, we will capture a complement of galley slaves from this nation of pirates and return to Rome in triumph!'

Claurinius' voice rose as he shouted those last few words and this had the desired effect on the soldiers who raised a cheer.

'First however,' continued Claurinius in a lower voice, 'we must commit our honoured dead to the gods.'

The five fallen men of *The Jupiter*'s complement had been laid out on the deck at the ship's bows. Claurinius made his way to this end of the ship, followed by Julius Messana, Valerian and Hadasca and the rest of the company. He recited the usual words used at a military funeral, commending these men of valour to the care of Jupiter, Mars and Neptune. The fallen men's comrades then lifted the bodies carefully on to a chute which had been erected in anticipation of this ceremony, and the bodies slid into the sea. The bodies of the galley slaves in the decks below were also conferred to the waves, but in a less ceremonious manner.

Everybody was now beginning to feel the toll of the previous night's exertions. Claurinius ordered the men to spend a few hours resting. Food was served. Late in the afternoon, Valerian organized the men into teams of rowers. The first team took their places on the benches and the slow eastward journey began towards the coast of the Roman province of Syria which Claurinius had referred to by its ancient name of Phoenicia. Claurinius arranged to have the name of the ship painted out before it came in sight of land.

30

The Philippian Jailer

Once they had crossed the Hellespont, Apollos really began to feel he was on Grecian soil and approaching the climax of the tour. Jerahmeel and Apollos picked up the Egnatian Way, the great Roman road which linked Byzantium on the Bosphorus with Apollonia on the Adriatic Sea, the Macedonian port located nearest to the Italian mainland. A short sea crossing at the narrowest part of the Adriatic Sea, connected the great Roman roads called the Appian and Egnation Ways to provide excellent communications between Rome itself and the city of Byzantium, which for a time was to rival Rome as the centre of imperial power.

Apollos and Jerahmeel journeyed along the northern shore of the lovely Aegean Sea, passing through Thrace and on to Macedonia. Apollos drank in the atmosphere of the Greek civilization as they passed through the cities of Doriscus, Neapolis and Philippi. They spent some time at Philippi where they were made most welcome by the Christian Church. They stayed at the home of Lydia who was a founder member of the Philippian Church and could claim to be the very first Christian convert in Europe.[145] Lydia spoke with unconcealed warmth and affection of Paul and Silas who had brought to that city, a faith which transformed the lives of so many. In particular, they had dramatically influenced the life of the city jailer. Apollos and Jerahmeel met this jailer at the Church which assembled at Lydia's house. One evening, Lydia invited the jailer round to her house to recount to Apollos and Jerahmeel the story which he never tired of telling, of how Paul and Silas had been committed to his charge as prisoners a few years earlier, and the effect this had on himself and his family. Jerahmeel and Apollos had already heard the account in outline from the Philippian Christian who had visited the Church of Antioch, but they knew that the jailer's report of what had happened would have an impact which only a first hand raconteur could give to such a tale.

There were many retired soldiers from the imperial legions living in Philippi, and Flavius Hadrian, the city jailer, was a typical retired legionary. He was a man of the world, used to hardships and the privations of military campaigns. His father, Casca Hadrian, had been a soldier before him, and Flavius Hadrian proudly recounted how his father had fought with Pompey in Egypt and with Julius Caesar in Gaul. Flavius had a special affection for Philippi, not just because that city was now his home, but because Casca Hadrian had been specially commended for valour by Mark Anthony after a great battle fought near Philippi. On that occasion, Anthony's army had defeated the armies of Brutus and Cassius, whom Flavius Hadrian described as those treacherous villians who assassinated great Julius on the Ides of March.

Flavius briefly outlined his own military experience. He knew this was not the main event in which Apollos and Jerahmeel would be interested, but could not resist starting by giving a concise outline of his military credentials.

'I fought in the east under Augustus,' began Flavius, 'where we defeated the Parthians and then the Armenians. When Rome's eastern frontier was secure, my legion was transferred to the command of Germanicus who was fighting a brilliant campaign in Germania. After two years hard fighting, we recovered the territory lost by Varus, gaining control of all the land between the Rhine and the Weser.

'But all that was many years ago. Like so many Roman soldiers who are too old to continue to fight with the regular army but are not old enough to be pensioned off, I have been given another job to do, for which a hardened soldier like myself is admirably suited. I am a jailer. I look after the city prison. I run a tight prison. It used to be said of me that no one who spends time in Hadrian's prison will want to repeat the experience. Perhaps I was harsh, but the

Roman system is a harsh one. The worst calamity that can occur to a Roman jailer is to have a prisoner escape. No excuse is accepted for failing in the duty of guarding prisoners. If my prison was attacked by an army of a thousand men and they only managed to get one man out, I would still be held responsible. If I was lucky, I would be sent to prison myself in place of the escaped convict. However, the usual fate of an inefficient jailer is execution. Well, I had a family to support, so I made quite sure that no prisoner escaped from my jail.

'I well remember the time when I almost did lose a few prisoners.[125] It was a hot summer's day. I only had a couple of prisoners in jail at the time, but from my jail house, I could hear that some quite extraordinary disturbance was going on in town. Well disturbances usually meant trouble, and trouble of that kind usually meant prisoners, so I was not surprised when the magistrates and the city police came to my prison with a couple of men whom they had arrested. They had somehow interfered in the work of some slave girl belonging to a worthy citizen. This had created a riot and these men, who had caused all the trouble, had been brought before the magistrates. When they were committed to me at the jail house, I could see that these two men had already been severely beaten for their crime. However, in spite of the pain they must have felt, they looked calm, even happy. They must have been a couple of real toughies. I wasn't going to take any chances with fellows like that, so I took them to the inner prison, fastened their feet in the stocks and locked the door. "There's no chance of those two getting out," I reassured the magistrates, and they thankfully returned to the City Hall, hoping that, having dealt with one of the worst riots the city had known for years, all would now be quiet.

'I went back to the jail house to get my supper ready. The evening was now drawing in. As I munched away, I was suddenly aware of the sound of singing from the prison. I went to the prison door and peeped through the bars. I was amazed. Those two bloody and bruised convicts were merrily singing away, as happy as if they'd just won the chariot race at the Circus and discovered their prize was a hundred times bigger than they had expected. Every now

209

and then they'd stop singing and talk to the prisoners who were already in the jail when they had arrived. Then they would start up singing again.

'This was a strange carry on. I'd never had happy prisoners in my jail before, but there was nothing I needed to do about that then, so I went back to finish my supper. I could hear the singing carrying on, and after a while the other two prisoners must have learned the tunes, because they started to join in too. The men had good voices and the songs they were singing were not bawdy bar songs. The music they made had a tranquil but at the same time joyous quality about it. I stayed and listened as darkness fell.

'As the faint sound of singing wafted up to the jail-house from the prison below, the breeze which had been blowing that evening stopped and everything became still. The static air was electric and I felt uneasy in the stillness which lasted only a few minutes. Then I heard a faint rumbling, and the room in the jail-house where I sat started to shake. The shaking became more violent. The pots and pans clattered to the ground. The chairs and table toppled over. I was thrown to the floor. Part of the ceiling fell in. A great cloud of dust arose. I started to cough and splutter. The shaking lasted about ten minutes. Then all was still as it had been before. As the dust settled and I controlled my cough, I looked about me. Both the door and the window of my room had fallen out of their locations, and a great crack went from the corner of the ceiling to the opening where there had once been a window. I got to my feet. We had just experienced an earthquake. Although dusty, I was uninjured.

'Suddenly, I thought of the prisoners below. What had happened to them? As I rushed down what was left of the stairs, my worst fears were realized when I saw what had befallen the prison. The thickest wall had been reduced to a pile of rubble. The door had burst its lock. Only one light was still burning. As I clambered over what had been the door into the prison chamber, I surveyed what appeared to be a deserted cavern. The stocks in the middle of the chamber where I had fastened the convicts feet earlier that evening were all broken up, and the doors of all the side cells were either lying on the ground or swinging freely on their hinges. The prisoners had obviously escaped. I would get the blame for not having chained them to myself. I would be executed the next morning. No, I wouldn't give the authorities the satisfaction of making me the scapegoat for their having built the prison badly. I drew my sword. I wedged it between two large pieces of stone from the wall, that had been dislodged by the earthquake. I prepared to throw myself on my sword.

'A voice called out to me from a dark corner of the prison, obscured by fallen masonry from the remaining lamp which still hung from the roof, "Don't do yourself any harm. We are all still here."

'I lifted the lamp from the hook, and made my way over the stones and rubble to the place where the voice had spoken. As I held my lamp up, I could see all four prisoners there. The two who had come in that day whose feet I had fastened in the stocks, smiled warmly at me as the light from my lantern reached their faces. They were obviously special men and I felt afraid of them in a way that I'd never feared an adversary in battle. I fell to my knees before them. I bowed my head. Then I looked up to them again. Although they had survived the earthquake and had not used this opportunity to escape, they were covered in dust, and their bruises and cuts had not been tended. I got to my feet and asked them to come with me to my house where my wife put on some hot water and we set about cleaning them up.

'"What must I do to be saved?" I asked, still expecting that I would be blamed in some way for allowing the jail to fall down while the houses near by, including my own house, had come unscathed through the earthquake.

'"You must believe in the Lord Jesus, you and your family, and you will be saved."

'"Who is this Lord Jesus?" I asked.

'The two men then told us the story that you all know well of Jesus, of how God, living as a man with us on earth, lived a perfect life, and actually suffered a criminal's death. He did this so that we men, who would otherwise suffer death at the appointed time, could have the assurance of another life with Jesus, if only we would trust him and commit the rest of our lives to him. Paul and Silas, those were the names of these special prisoners, spoke with such sincerity and persuasion that I and my whole family had no hesitation in committing our lives there and then to this Jesus. That night we were all baptized, for Paul and Silas had explained that that was the appointed way by which believers should signify that they were abandoning their old life-style with all its selfishness and greed, to live a new life wholly for Jesus.

'The next day, the magistrates came to officially release Paul and Silas. They realized overnight that they had beaten and cast them into prison because they were afraid of the crowd, and not because Paul and Silas had any real case to answer.

'Now, my family and I come regularly to this house on the first day of the week to meet with Lydia and with others who have experienced the same joy that Lydia and my family have, in living only for Jesus. I specially enjoy singing with my new friends, the very same hymns of praise that I first heard Paul and Silas sing that eventful night as I sat in my jail house above the prison.

'Did I change my job when I became a Christian? No. Paul and Silas explained to me that as jailer, I had special opportunities to tell others of the Lord Jesus. I told you when I introduced myself, that few convicts repeat the experience of staying in my prison. The same is still true now, but I am no longer a harsh man. I hope that I am now able to share something special with prisoners who come into my custody for a time, which enables them to start new lives, with new attitudes, new hopes, new priorities. In many cases, I see that new life begin, even before the prisoner is released, for there is no state of man, whether slave, prisoner, or even condemned murderer, that the grace of God cannot change to a new state of inner joy and peace and assurance of life everlasting with Jesus.'

Jerahmeel beamed with approval at the jailer's tale. The best part of the rest of the evening was taken up by Jerahmeel recounting to Lydia and the jailer, the quite different means by which he had made the same discovery as the jailer. Apollos mused in thoughtful silence on all that was said.

31

Philip

From Philippi, Apollos and Jerahmeel continued along the Egnatian Way, through Amphipolis, Apollonia on the Aegean Sea, and Thessalonica. At Thessalonica, they encountered a church which was special in the way that its members lived and planned their daily lives as if the return of Jesus was imminent. For a few, this led to a lethargic lifestyle of just sitting around and waiting for the *parousia*.[146] However, the majority lived in a very positive fashion, treating every day as if it were their last. The return of their Master would not have found them lacking in the zeal with which they were performing his business.

From Thessalonica, our travellers turned south, leaving the Egnatian Way and heading for Beroea, and then on to Mount Olympus. They joined a party making an ascent of this footstool of the gods. Although Apollos and Jerahmeel discounted the ancient stories about the Greek gods as mere myths for the amusement of primitive minds, the isolated grandeur of Mount Olympus was impressive and generated a rather special atmosphere. Apollos had never before experienced such an intense experience of the grandeur and majesty of God, and Jerahmeel found the sensation of the closeness to God, strangely reminiscent of the feelings he had experienced many years earlier, when he had climbed Mount Sinai.

From Olympus, Jerahmeel and Apollos made their way southwards through Thessaly to Achaia and the Peloponnesus. This was where Apollos considered that the centre of Greek culture and history lay. Here were the cities of redoubtable warriors, Sparta, Athens, Corinth and Thebes who competed for dominance in the Peloponnesian wars, but who united to repulse the might of Persia whose empire, in her day, seemed as invincible as that of Rome today. Our travellers route took them to Pharsalus, the site of the battle where the audacious Julius Caesar, with his small army of veterans from the Gallic wars, inflicted a humiliating defeat on the much larger army of his rival Gnaeus Pompey. The flight of Pompey to Egypt after this battle, where he was murdered by one of his own soldiers, gave Julius Caesar the undisputed supremacy in the Roman Empire for which he had striven. As this power struggle had more to do with Roman than Greek history, it was not of special interest to Apollos, but Jerahmeel considered the outcome of the battle of Pharsalus to be of great significance to the Jewish nation. Surely, the hand of God was against Pompey from the time that he had taken Jerusalem and not only entered the Temple, mounted on his horse, but had desecrated that place in a way which Jews found profoundly offensive. He had actually dared to enter the Holy of Holies, the sanctuary which the High Priest alone had the right to enter, and then, only on the Day of Atonement after fulfilling the correct ritual purification. To Jerahmeel's mind, the outcome of the battle of Pharsalus was not so much Caesar wresting supremacy from Pompey, but the fulfilment of divine retribution.

From Pharsalus, our travellers continued to another famous battlefield, the pass at Thermopylae where a small Greek Army had held the numerically greater Persian army at bay. But for a traitor directing the Persians to a route which bypassed Thermopylae, the Greeks could have held off the huge Persial army indefinitely. Even though this treachery had allowed them to be outflanked by the Persians, Greek heroism saved the day, and Apollos and Jerahmeel silently stood to revere what was reputed to be the site where Leonidas and three hundred Spartans covered the retreat of the main Greek army. Although outnumbered by a hundred to one, the disciplined Spartans showed themselves in that engagement to be the finest warriors of their day, perhaps the finest the world has ever known. Although the final outcome against such odds was inevitable and the Spartans died to a man, they gave their Greek compatriots sufficient time to adopt an impregnable defensive position across the narrow Isthmus of Corinth. The Persian army had no alternative but to withdraw when the massive Persian supporting fleet was annihilated by the superior seamanship of the Greek ships under Themistocles at the naval battle of Salamis.

Our travellers continued from Thermopylae, through Thebes, the city which ultimately prevailed in the Peloponnesian wars, and thence proceeded on the coast road to Marathon. Jerahmeel and Apollos passed through this town to survey the Plain of Marathon which lay on the coastal strip beyond the city. Here was fought one of the battles which posterity has revealed to be decisive in its effect on subsequent world history. Again, Apollos and Jerahmeel stood in silence to allow their imaginations to capture in their minds' eye, the scene when no more than a few thousand valiant Athenians under Miltiades, routed a Persian army, reputed to number half a million men, and harried them into a disorderly retreat.

From Marathon, our travellers walked to Athens, the distance of forty-two kilometres (twenty-six miles three hundred and eighty-five yards) made famous by Pheidippides, who ran the distance to bring news to the Athenians of the great victory.

At Athens, which should have marked a high point of the tour, our travellers heard the dreadful news of the riots in Alexandria. Reports were vague and unreliable, and exaggerated accounts suggested that hundreds of Greeks, Jews and Egyptians had been killed in inter-communal rioting. Apollos and Jerahmeel realized that they would have to return immediately to Alexandria. They made their way to the Piraeus to book a passage on the first ship bound for Alexandria. However, the riots had disturbed the normal commerce between the two cities. Although Piraeus was a large and bustling port, at that time, they could find no ship which was making the direct crossing to Alexandria via Crete on a specified date. The only ship which had Alexandria as its ultimate destination was a smallish vessel, the *Trojan Hero*, which would be calling at a number of ports around the eastern seaboard of the Mediterranean. The journey could take two or three weeks. In desperation, they booked a passage on this ship which would sail from the

Piraeus in two days, as there seemed no alternative way of reaching Alexandria in less time.

The *Trojan Hero* made slow progress, sailing in the cross wind. It called first at Rhodes and then at Paphos on Cyprus. At each of these ports the ship had to wait for two or three days for merchants to arrive to collect the cargoes destined for their warehouses, and load new cargoes to be shipped to other parts of the Mediterranean. At Rhodes, our two travellers scarcely heeded the two great feet on the huge pedestals which defined the harbour entrance. These were all that was left of the great statue to the sun god, Helios, which had been fashioned by the sculptor, Chares of Lindos, to stand astride the harbour entrance while ships passed between his huge legs as they entered and left the harbour. In a happier state of mind, the remains of the Colossus of Rhodes, that great wonder of the ancient world, would have been of interest to our travellers. However, the news from Alexandria had left them very preoccupied.

About ten days after leaving Piraeus, the *Trojan Hero* arrived at Sidon, its main port of call, and moored in the smaller of the twin harbours. The captain indicated that they would be at Sidon for four or five days at least. Although Apollos and Jerahmeel had at that time no inclination to indulge their appetite for sightseeing, there was no point in just sitting around on the ship for those few days.

Although the city was technically under Roman authority, it was allowed local autonomy, and only a very small garrison of Roman soldiers was maintained in Sidon to support the agencies, responsible for law and order. The inhabitants of the city were mainly Syro-Phoenician but there was a very large Greek community living in Greater Sidon. Jerahmeel and Apollos made their way from Lesser Sidon, where their boat was moored, to the Greek area of the city. They passed the ancient Temple of Eshmun, the Phoenician God of healing. This would normally have been a shrine of interest to our travellers, but their minds were now preoccupied with other concerns. They wandered rather aimlessly around Greater Sidon for an hour or so when Jerahmeel noticed a large house with a prominent cross displayed on its door. They deduced that this was probably a church and called at the house. They were invited in and made welcome. The first matter raised by Apollos was an enquiry as to whether his hosts had any more detailed news than had been available at Athens, on the state of his home town of Alexandria. Apart from knowing that Alexandria had been ravaged by inter-communal violence, the Sidonian Christians could furnish no further details.

Conversation turned to Christian affairs and the names of acquaintances which they had in common were discovered. Agabus was well known to the Sidonian Christians. They also knew well the ubiquitous Paul of whom Apollos and Jerahmeel had heard so much but had never met. Another special name came up which Apollos and Jerahmeel had encountered before. It appeared that the church at Sidon had been founded by one called Philip who operated from Samaria, but spent much time visiting churches he had founded, right down the eastern sea-board of the Mediterranean, from the Philistine cities of Gaza and Ashkelon in the south, to the Phoenician cities of Tyre and Sidon in the north. The mention of Gaza reminded Apollos and Jerahmeel of the significant visit of Sandas-cum-Barama to their synagogue in the Hebron district of Alexandria. Could this Philip be the same Philip who had baptized the Ethiopian on the Gaza Road? The Sidonians told Apollos and Jerahmeel that Philip was in Sidon at that very moment and would be addressing the Church on the following day, the first day of the week. Jerahmeel and Apollos were warmly pressed to attend this service.

The following day, Apollos and Jerahmeel arrived at the Church at the appointed meeting time. The meeting room was laid out in a similar manner to the many other churches they had attended on their travels, a table laid with an immaculate white cloth being the focal point. Philip presided at the service, assisted by two elders of the Sidonian Church. Philip was a jolly looking man. One sensed immediately that he was a very approachable person. He was obviously much loved by the Christians at Sidon. Philip took as his theme for the address, the free nature of the gift of eternal salvation for each and every person who was prepared to freely receive. Jerahmeel was delighted that he had chosen this topic, for he knew that Apollos still held the view that a place in the next world had to be earned by our efforts in this. Philip emphasized how poor and inadequate were our efforts in comparison with the vast bounty God had showered upon us.

Philip then posed some rhetorical questions.

'How could we live as if we were earning the gift of eternal life from God, for God who had given us everything, could surely be no man's debtor? In the light of the suffering which everyone knew that God's Son had undergone on our behalf to shed the blood which bought us salvation, how could any be so arrogantly foolish as to believe that they were earning salvation for themselves by the quality of their lives? And yet,' continued Philip, 'I know from many people I have met in the many churches I visit, that so many people calling themselves Christian, believe just this!'

Philip then used an illustration which Jerahmeel thought was very telling.

'During my visit here to Sidon, I have been most wonderfully entertained at the home of your elder, Polycrates and his wife, Persephone,' said Philip. 'I have stayed with them before, and can honestly say that I have never eaten better or slept in a more comfortable bed. I know that my visits to Sidon must cost them hundreds of drachmas, and yet I know they do this out of love for me, and love for the fellowship of you Christians whom I seek to serve. I wonder how Polycrates and Persephone would have felt, if after the sumptuous repast I enjoyed last night, I put a drachma on the table and offered it to them as a contribution to the cost of the meal? They would have felt most insulted that I should have debased by such means, the lavish way they have entertained me since I have been in Sidon.'

Philip paused.

'And yet,' he continued, 'and yet, the Christian who offers the meagre quality of his life to God as payment which he believes will purchase his salvation, is debasing God's free gift in just such a way. I am eternally indebted to Polycrates and Persephone for all they have done for me, and they know that they can call upon me at any time to do anything in my power to help them. However, I don't deceive myself that I have in any way bought from them the generosity they have shown me. Just so with the Lord. My life is dedicated to the service of Jesus because I love him, but I do not deceive myself that I can buy the gift of eternal life for which he suffered so terribly on my behalf, because he first loved me with a greater love than I can ever reciprocate.'

Philip did not speak for long, but his point was well taken. Philip was obviously aware that he had given teaching which was needed by some of the Sidonian Christians who had not properly grasped the concept of divine grace, God's free unmerited favour. Jerahmeel knew that this was the very point which Apollos found a stumbling block, and looked across at his young companion. Apollos was evidently deep in thought.

After the service, Jerahmeel and Apollos were introduced to Philip. They were able to mention contacts they had in common in the Christian world. Philip had been one of the original seven deacons of the Jerusalem Church,[147] and had very fond memories of James. Jerahmeel spoke of Sandascum-Barama and found that Philip retained a vivid recollection of the day he baptized the Ethiopian on the Gaza Road. Philip was obviously very taken with Jerahmeel and he expressed a hope that they should meet again before they left Sidon.

As Jerahmeel and Apollos wandered back to the *Trojan Hero*, moored in the harbour of Lesser Sidon, their attention was taken by a large black ship approaching Sidon from the west. The ship was sharply silhouetted against the light of the western sky where a red sun was beginning to set. As the ship drew closer, it could be identified as a massive Roman war trireme, but it bore none of the proud accoutrements usually carried by such ship. Its sail was no more than the remnant of a tattered rag, dangling from its mast. The motivation was provided by the rowers, but no more than twenty or so of the hundred oars were being rowed. The unmanned oars trailed aimlessly in the water as the huge hulk lugubriously ploughed through the choppy sea. Even the oars being used were not keeping smartly to time in the accustomed manner of war ships, driven by teams of harshly disciplined galley slaves, but splashed asynchronously in the water as they wearily returned to commence a new stroke.

As the ship approached closer, it became evident that the black appearance was not just an effect of being silhouetted against the sun. Most of the woodwork was black and charred. The ship had obviously been on fire, probably as the result of some naval battle. By this time, more onlookers had gathered along the Sidonian sea-front to observe this unusual sight. As the vessel approached closer to the land, eyes strained to catch the ship's name but her identity was concealed. The name on the ship's bows was obscured and her figure-head had been smashed to a pulp.

It became clear that the ship was not heading for one of the harbours, but would pass by Sidon, making for some destination further north. The ship laboured its ragged way past the Sidonian waterfront, creaking as the oars pulled against her battered timbers. The onlookers started to move along the front, following the vessel's northward progress, excitedly speculating on this ship's business and the calamity she must have encountered at sea to be left in so sorry a state. Apollos suggested that they might follow the crowd, but Jerahmeel counselled that they should leave the ship well alone.

'There is something ominous and foreboding about that ship,' Jerahmeel cautioned, shuddering as he spoke. 'I have always hated slave galleys and the degrading system which allows men to be used as if their only value lay in their having the physical power to transport other men who considered themselves to be superior, but this ship carries some extra aura of evil beyond anything I usually associate with a slave driven galley. It is something quite intangible. I can't explain it, but I do not want to go near that ship.'

Jerahmeel and Apollos made their way back to their berth on the *Trojan Hero*.

The ship whose passage Jerahmeel and Apollos had just witnessed was *The Jupiter*. *The Jupiter* dropped anchor by the shore, a couple of miles north of Sidon. On berthing, Claurinius first sent Julius Massana ashore with a troop of legionaries to obtain timber and a sail, badly needed materials to effect further repairs on his ship. Julius was also ordered to pay his respects to the senior Roman officer in command at Sidon. Claurinius told Julius to give his name as Sextus Sindinion, captain of *The Minerva* and explain that his ship had been involved in a sea battle with pirates. The main objective of coming ashore was to replenish the ammunition used by his ballista. He had therefore sought out a section of shoreline where plenty of suitable rocks were in evidence. Julius was not happy about this assignment, but he complied with Claurinius' order and proceeded with this mission of deceit.

32

The Black Ship at Sidon

The following morning found Apollos and Jerahmeel sitting by the Sidonian sea-front, idly watching ships being loaded and unloaded, turning their attention to any new arrivals being piloted to any empty berth available, the captains sometimes having difficulty in navigating in the capricious breeze. Then Apollos and Jerahmeel would gaze into the distance at the fully laden vessels which had left port and were sailing to the open sea. The conversation inevitably turned to the time the couple had spent worshipping at the church in Sidon the previous day, and to the address that Philip had given.

'I thought that Philip explained very well that a Christian gives his life to Jesus because he knows that Jesus has bought him salvation. The belief that following Jesus' moral teaching accrues the merit which will earn a place in heaven, is a misconception which disregards the nature of salvation as a free gift,' stated Jerahmeel.

Apollos disagreed. 'I don't see how someone who never knew me could possibly die on my behalf to bear the punishment for my sins, and so have first claim on the allegiance of my life. The only view of judgement which makes any logical sense, is that our misdeeds are tested against our virtues, and salvation will be granted to those whose virtues outnumber their sins.'

'It is not true to claim that Jesus never knew you,' said Jerahmeel, 'for Jesus was not just another man, but God living as a man, to reveal to us in a way we humans might understand, the true nature of God. If Jesus was God, then he indeed knew each and every one of us. If your view of judgement is correct, Apollos, can you really face such judgement with any confidence? You told me some time ago that you may have fathered a child, yet you have taken no trouble to verify this. If you are father of a child, then you have a responsibility to a human who has as much individual human dignity as you yourself, as much right to parental love and care as you received from your doting parents. Such a responsibility can only be discharged by devoting a considerable amount of your time and energy and resources to caring for and cherishing that child. If you have a child, and please God, you haven't, if you have a child, Apollos, and on judgement day, you are charged with neglecting your sacred responsibility to that child, what virtue will you claim to compensate for this serious shortcoming?'·

Apollos sat in silence for some time. Jerahmeel had never challenged him before so directly on this aspect of his morality. He could not defend himself. There was no answer with which Apollos could adequately respond to Jerahmeel's assertion. Apollos hated losing an argument, and specially one on so sensitive an issue. Apollos felt irritated. He was lost for words. After a few minutes he stood up and said the thing which he knew at that moment would annoy Jerahmeel most.

'I am going to see what is going on at the black ship. I know you want to keep away from that vessel so I will come back and meet you here later.'

With that, Apollos turned away from Jerahmeel and walked northwards along the sea front in the direction the ship had been heading the previous evening. He had no idea whether or not he would find the ship or if it had by now moved many miles up the coast. However, the object of expressing his intention of finding the black ship was to annoy Jerahmeel, rather than conveying any genuine interest in this vessel.

Apollos had soon left the main town of Sidon behind him, and was walking along the low cliffs which defined that shoreline. As he reached the top of a rather higher section of cliff, he caught sight of the black ship, moored almost a mile further on. As he continued to approach the ship, he could see more and more of what was going on. Small boats were being rowed to and from the ship. What were they carrying? When he reached the point on the coast opposite the place where the ship was moored about seventy metres out to sea, he found quite a number of people had gathered to observe the activities surrounding this ship. For the most part, they were young men of Sidon with nothing better to do with the day. Apollos joined this group of onlookers.

The boats were being rowed by fully armoured Roman soldiers who were collecting rocks from the sea shore, loading them into their boats, and rowing them back to the black ship. An activity taking place on board ship was the firing of some of these pieces of rock from the ballista. It was almost as if a show was being put on to encourage an audience. The lumps of rock were evidently being aimed at a large piece of driftwood, floating about a hundred metres from the ship. Every time a rock landed within ten metres of the target, a cheer went up from the soldiers on board the ship. A bad shot was greeted with a wail. Those on shore started to join in with the cheers and wails.

Then a fairly large group of soldiers came ashore on four boats. A soldier said something to the group of youths. Whatever he said was greeted with jeers and cat-calls. The soldier's remark had evidently been a planned provocation and the youths responded in just the way he had wanted. With a cry of, 'Come and row the ship yourselves then, Phoenician scum!', the soldiers suddenly rushed at the band of youths and started to knock them around. Some had ropes and nets which they threw over some of the youths. Others were manhandled towards the rowing boats. Many of the youths turned to run, but another band of soldiers appeared as if from nowhere, behind the place where the youths had been standing, so cutting off any retreat. Apollos turned to escape the melée and found himself confronted by a burly legionary. He was an ugly man with a moon-shaped scar on his cheek. The soldier grabbed Apollos with a mutilated hand. He had only three fingers. Apollos struggled to free himself. He found himself knocked to the ground. The Roman still held on to him. Apollos struggled to his feet and buffeted the soldier, but he only injured his knuckles against the armour. He was on the ground again and being dragged towards a rowing boat. He could not break the soldier's grip. Suddenly, there was a lithe figure dressed in brown beside them, entering into the fray. He struck the Roman a resounding blow. The soldier cursed and turned to deal with this new adversary. He relaxed his grip on Apollos as he drew his sword. He slashed at his assailant who gave a cry as the blow found its mark. Apollos grabbed the soldier's ankle and pulled at it with all his might. The soldier fell, and released his grip on Apollos as he tried to break his fall. The figure in brown took hold of Apollos' arm and pulled him to his feet. He dragged Apollos away from the soldier who was now intent on recovering his sword which he had dropped as he fell. All the soldiers around were fully occupied in bundling the young men on to the rowing boats, and Apollos and the brown figure were able to evade further encounters as they made their way out of the struggling group. They started to run back towards Sidon.

After a while, they had put a good four hundred metres between themselves and the affray on the shore. No one was following them. The figure in brown suddenly collapsed. It was Jerahmeel who had followed Apollos at a distance to keep a watchful eye on his protegé and had sprung into action when he saw Apollos in danger as the attack started. Jerahmeel had received a deep wound in his side and was bleeding profusely. Apollos picked up Jerahmeel and carried him as fast as he could in his breathless state, another five hundred metres to the nearest house he could find. The occupants let them in. When they saw the injury, they brought swabs to try and stench the flow of blood and make Jerahmeel as comfortable as possible. They gave him water to drink and brought a blanket to keep him warm. Jerahmeel kept tightly hold of Apollos' hand.

After a while, Jerahmeel started to breathe more easily and started to talk to Apollos.

'Those soldiers have taken the young men to be galley slaves in that odious ship.' Jerahmeel had rightly conjectured the purpose of the unprovoked attack.

Apollos shuddered as he thought of the miserable fate which might have befallen him, had not Jerahmeel come to his aid.

'You have saved me from a fate worse than death,' he whispered gratefully to Jerahmeel.

Jerahmeel continued, 'You have wondered how one person might buy another person's life with their own. I have accepted in a way that you could not, that Jesus bought my life with his. I have now bought your life with mine. You now have the best part of your life ahead of you. Use your life and special gifts in a way that you know will please me.'

Apollos felt alarm at these words.

'You know that there is no one in the whole world that I admire more than you, and my dearest wish is to model myself on you. I pray that you will see me acquire in just a small measure, the exemplary attitudes and wisdom which you display in all your dealings,' replied Apollos.

Jerahmeel forced a smile.

'I haven't long left to see much change in your life from now. I feel my life ebbing away.'

'Don't say that Jerahmeel,' pleaded Apollos. 'The bandages seem to be stemming the bleeding. With rest, you will begin to pick up strength again, and we can give your wound all the time it needs to heal.'

Jerahmeel gave a weak smile.

'I could not ask for a better way to die,' he continued. 'I have no children, Apollos, but you have been more than a son to me. I have taken pride in seeing you develop into manhood, and in enjoying your companionship. No tutor could wish for a more able and ardent pupil than you have been, Apollos, and I have learnt so much from you in all the discussions we have held together. I am glad that my life has been ended in enabling the one I love most in the world to live, and perhaps pass on to others some of the things I have taught him. Do use your gifts to teach others, Apollos.'

'I am sorry I ended our discussion this morning so rudely and abruptly,' said Apollos. 'I have never done such a thing before. I don't know what came over me.'

Jerahmeel squeezed Apollos' hand.

'I was the one at fault in speaking to you as I did,' replied Jerahmeel, again forcing a weak smile. 'I have had a wonderful and fulfilled life. I have travelled and seen more of the world than most others can ever claim to have seen. I have made wonderful friends. I now know my God as a personal friend who has prepared a place for me, and whom soon I shall meet. I have lived the allotted lifespan of most men. I would not want life to just pass from me, but I would want to see it spent in doing some last great thing. This I have done in saving you Apollos. I can leave this world happy in that knowledge, and now my dearest wish is to meet Jesus who I know is waiting for me. Goodbye, Apollos.'

Apollos felt his hand squeezed once again, and then the hand that held his suddenly went limp. Jerahmeel's head fell back. Jerahmeel had left this world to enter the better world beyond.

Apollos remained there for some time, struggling to hold back the tears that welled in his eyes. The Sidonian couple who had given them shelter stood silently in the background. After a time, Apollos felt composed enough to speak to them. Apollos gently lowered Jerahmeel's now cold hand.

'Thank you for affording my friend help and shelter in the last hour of his life,' he said. 'He received his wound when we were attacked by soldiers from the black ship. I will go back to our friends in Sidon, and we will return to collect Jerahmeel, that is my friend's name, before the end of the day.'

Apollos returned sadly to Sidon and made his way to the house where the church met. He told the Christians what had happened. They knew that something calamitous had occurred for the town was in uproar. A group of the Christians made their way back to the house with Apollos and carried Jerahmeel's corpse back to the church where it was prepared for burial.

In Sidon, crowds of people had surrounded the headquarters of the small Roman garrison, and were throwing stones at the ring of soldiers who were defending the place by making a defensive wall with their shields. Parents whose sons had been dragged to the black ship were calling out, 'Is this the way Rome treats law abiding citizens who pay Caesar their taxes?' and were demanding their sons back. A senior officer was obviously trying to speak to the crowd from behind the wall of shields, but for a time could not be heard above the rabble. At last a leading citizen managed to calm the mob sufficiently to enable the

227

commander of the garrison to be heard.

'Rome does not treat its citizens in this way,' he shouted. 'I am appalled as you are by what has happened. I know the name of the ship, and I know the name of its captain. I pledge that I will return to Rome myself to report this incident and have your sons returned. It will take me no more than a few days to arrange for an officer to take over my post. I will return to Rome very soon to ensure that justice is done. Be sure. I am ashamed of what has happened, but we will make amends.'

The angry and hostile crowd gradually dispersed after these words. The Prefect of Sidon was an honourable man, and trusted by the Sidonian people. Their best hope for the return of their sons lay in making representations at the highest possible level in Rome.

33

A Triumphant Funeral

Apollos was distraught at the loss of his friend and mentor. Had he not impetuously left Jerahmeel when confronted with a home truth which was uncomfortable to face up to, and made his way to observe the black ship just to annoy Jerahmeel, events would not have turned out as they did and Jerahmeel would still have been alive. Apollos was not given to displays of emotion, but he wept bitterly that night. Apollos mentally took stock of his life, a life that had been bought for him at so dear a price. He had not really done anything in life which brought great benefit to others. On the contrary, he had evaded responsibilities as he made the decisions and followed the course of action which benefited chiefly himself. His personal selfishness and associated faults of arrogance and pride came very much home to Apollos. How he needed some way to escape the burden which the recognition of his own worthlessness was imposing on him. Jerahmeel's final charge to Apollos had been to live his life in a way of which Jerahmeel would approve. Jerahmeel had given his life for Apollos, and Jerahmeel himself testified that his life in turn had been bought by Christ, who had lifted the burden of Jerahmeel's sin. Apollos was not conscious of much sin in Jerahmeel's life, certainly in comparison with his own. If Jerahmeel needed a saviour, then how much greater was his own need. All that Apollos had learnt of the purpose of Jesus' life and his shedding his blood on behalf of men as individuals, at last came home to Apollos. He had desperate need of a saviour and a saviour was at hand. At that moment the prayers which Jerahmeel had offered time and time again for Apollos were answered. Apollos in his state of misery and penitence decided he would no longer live life for self, but from now on his life would be dedicated to serve the Christ who died on his behalf. Apollos knew that this would please Jerahmeel. He almost had a sense of Jerahmeel being there with him, approving this fundamental change of outlook and attitude, and this sense mollified Apollos' grief, and he was able to fall into a peaceful sleep.

The following day, Apollos returned to the house in Sidon at which the church met, where Jerahmeel's body had been laid out ready for burial. He found Philip was waiting there, kneeling by Jerahmeel's body. Philip spent a large part of the rest of that day in Apollos' company, and Apollos found it a great relief to unburden himself to Philip, and let him know what had transpired in his mind over the past twenty-four hours. Philip played very much the role of listener, but had just the right words of comfort and reassurance at those times when Apollos paused to regather his thoughts as he finished narrating some aspect of his life's history, or describing his relationship with Jerahmeel, or recounting his inner mental conflicts, not just of the last twenty-four hours, but from the time he had been challenged to change his faith in Jerusalem. Apollos spoke too of his concerns for his parents in Alexandria in view of the news of the Alexandrian riots.

Philip asked Apollos about his immediate plans. Arrangements were already in hand for Jerahmeel to be buried the following day. Philip undertook to conduct the ceremony in a way which was consistent with the practice of the Sidonian Church, whenever one of their members was laid to rest. He asked Apollos if he felt he would be able to say anything on that occasion, but did not press Apollos, knowing that in his state of grief, he would perhaps feel unable to speak at what would be for him, a time which would be highly charged with emotion. However, Apollos very much wanted to speak. He wanted to publicly tell the Sidonian Church what manner of man was Jerahmeel, and how much he was indebted to his friend. Although Apollos felt very emotional about his bereavement, a strange sense of peace had come upon him since the mental battle he had waged the previous night, and to speak on the occasion that his special friend was laid to rest, was the least that he could do. The day after the morrow, the *Trojan Hero* would leave Sidon for Caesarea, and Apollos would continue on the next stage of his return to Alexandria. Philip was obviously pleased that Apollos was prepared to speak at the sombre ceremony which would take place the following day. He told Apollos that his own home was in Caesarea, and although he had been preparing to make the return journey on foot, he wondered if Apollos would like his company on the boat. Philip could take the berth which had been booked for Jerahmeel. Apollos was delighted with the prospect of company for the next few days which he knew would be difficult for him, especially the company of someone like Philip, and he gladly took up Philip's suggestion.

Jerahmeel was laid to rest in a small cemetery on the outskirts of Sidon which the Christians used for such occasions. About thirty members of the Sidonian Church gathered to pay their last respects to someone who had created a very positive impression on them in the very short time that they had known him. The ceremony was not sad or morbid. Philip spoke words of great comfort, and the positive assurance that all present had of Jerahmeel's entry into the better life beyond, provided an uplifting, even exhilarating, sense of joy and triumph. Apollos spoke in a way that only he could, of the many wonderful qualities and virtues of Jerahmeel. The warmth of the gratitude he felt for Jerahmeel's sacrifice of his own life to save him from a terrible fate, overflowed to enthral all present, but Apollos expressed another dimension of gratitude as he explained how the witness of Jerahmeel in showing the greatest love that one human could have for another, had brought him to a living and personal faith in the one Jerahmeel described as his saviour, the Jesus in whom they all believed and who enabled them to celebrate at that moment, not a disaster, but the ending of Jerahmeel's life in victory.

The following day, the Sidonian Christians came to the harbour of Lessor Sidon to wish Philip and Apollos bon voyage. The *Trojan Hero* caught the breeze which took her to the harbour mouth, and her master then steered a southwards course, making for Caesarea.

231

34

The Debriefing

Apollos had no idea that the black ship was commanded by his former rival in love. No sooner were the unfortunate Sidonian youths aboard the ship than the new sail was hoisted and caught the wind which took the ship rapidly out to sea, before any pursuit could be organized. Indeed, pursuit of a well armed war galley would have been a futile and dangerous gesture.

The protesting youths were chained to the oars and soon silenced under the cruel lash of the soldier who had become the new slave master to replace the one suffocated in the smoke, along with his slaves, on the night of sea battle. Most of the youths were ethnic Greeks rather than Phoenicians, but this was an academic point of no great concern to Claurinius. Even with the few surviving slaves and captured pirates, there was not a full complement of rowers. The rowers were therefore deployed two to an oar, rather than the customary three. In this way, the ship would at least look from the outside as if fully manned, even though the rowers would not be efficiently used. Appearance and outward impression were all important to Claurinius who wanted to make his return to Ostia in as noble a looking ship as possible. No military training took place on the return journey. The soldiers were employed in renovating the ships timbers as best they could with the wood picked up at Sidon. *The Jupiter's* name was repainted and a soldier with an aptitude for carving was suspended over the bows to restore some shape to the figure head. Of course, the vessel would need a total overhaul when back in port, but after a few days work at sea, *The Jupiter* began to look a proud ship again, her battle scars adding to, rather than detracting from her pride.

There were no more sea battles and *The Jupiter* arrived back at Ostia, about a fortnight later. The new team of galley slaves had by then, been disciplined to row tolerably well in time, so that the ship that docked at Rome's nearest sea port had every appearance of making a triumphant return. Claurinius knew that there would be a debriefing when he might face some difficult questions, and he prepared for this as best he could.

The debriefing took place two days later. Some concern had been expressed that only two, rather than three, vessels had survived the sea battle, and of these, only one had returned safely to port. A team of very senior officers was assembled to conduct the enquiry. The panel consisted of Marcus Asianus, Commander of the Fifteenth Legion, Caius Intripio, the Praetorian Guard Commander, and two retired officers who had held the rank of colonel during distinguished military careers. This was equivalent to the rank held by Claurinius. Marcus Asianus and Caius Intripio held the rank of General, and Claurinius knew that these would ask most of the questions. Claurinius arranged to have a captured pirate brought along to the enquiry. Claurinius picked the one whom he deemed would be the most accommodating in giving information to provide any corroboration that might be needed if his story was challenged. This pirate had been briefed to say that there were seven rather than only three ships in the flotilla which had attacked the vessels under Claurinius' command. Reward was on offer if he complied, dire threats if not.

Caesar himself insisted on being present at the inquiry. This was most unusual, but there was method in his madness. Caligula calculated that if it was established that this naval mission had successfully achieved its objective and cleared the seas of pirates, then he might derive some mileage from this success.

Caius Intripio suggested that they should start by going through Claurinius' log. Claurinius had not considered the log to be important and had neglected to keep records of the mission but he could not tell the committee of inquiry this. Claurinius therefore claimed that it had been destroyed in the fire which broke out on *The Jupiter* during the battle. The panel expressed surprise at this as the ship's log would normally be kept in a secured box, and would have been one of the items most likely to have been salvaged from any ship which was not actually sunk. The enquiry had started badly for Claurinius.

Marcus Asianus then asked Claurinius to describe in as much detail as possible, the course of the battle from the time the pirate ships were first sighted. When Claurinius told them that the first indication that the pirate ships were there, was the red hot rock projected on to his deck from an enemy ship, it was obvious that it was a night engagement in which the pirates were aware of the Roman galleys while undetected themselves. They therefore had the advantage of surprise. Questions were raised about the lookouts on the Roman ships. Claurinius truthfully stated that four look-outs were posted on each ship to keep watch, and were relieved every hour. Claurinius had to admit that his ships were lit whereas the pirate vessels were not, and claimed that he displayed a minimal amount of light out of responsibility to other shipping which had legitimate reason to be at sea, night fishing vessels and the like.

Claurinius stated that there were seven ships in the fleet which attacked them. He described how *The Vulcan* had been rammed by a pirate vessel and stated that both vessels had foundered as the impact had holed them below the water line. Claurinius stated that red hot missiles from the enemy ships had set both *The Jupiter* and *The Minerva* on fire, but they had been able to contain the fires and had replied with their own ballista. Claurinius claimed *The Minerva* had sunk one vessel and damaged another. He claimed three ships sunk for *The Jupiter* and one damaged. He stated that the engagement ended when the damaged enemy ships fled into the night.

Caius Intripio asked Claurinius why *The Minerva* had not returned with him to Ostia. Claurinius had expected this awkward question. He answered by explaining that *The Minerva* had sustained worse damage than *The Jupiter*, and that he had therefore ordered *The Minerva* to make the nearest port to carry out repairs. As two pirate ships had escaped, Claurinius claimed that he considered it his duty to return to Rome to warn the city as soon as possible. This would enable a force to be sent to the pirates' lair to clear them once and for all from the seas, before they harassed any more Roman shipping.

Claurinius considered this to be a clever answer.

Marcus Asianus enquired where this pirates' lair might be, and on being told it was near Carthage, he asked how Claurinius knew this. Claurinius explained that they had interrogated the pirates whom they had captured. He volunteered the information that he had a captured pirate under guard outside who could furnish them with further information.

The pirate was brought in and maps were fetched. The pirate was questioned and Claurinius felt relieved when he stated as Claurinius had instructed him to, that there were seven ships in his fleet. It soon became evident that this pirate was no more than an ordinary seaman and could not read a map to give any indication of the geographical location of his harbour. However, the information that it was within twenty kilometres of Carthage would be sufficient to enable the Romans to seek out and destroy this menace to their shipping. The Roman governor of Carthage had obviously been very slack in his coastal surveillance.

Claurinius hoped that at this point, the captured pirate would be sent out, but he was further questioned as to how their fleet was able to find and surprise the Roman war galleys. The pirate told them that they had learnt of the Roman presence in the eastern Mediterranean from other shipping, and the galleys had been easy to find at night because they were so well lit. Claurinius felt most uneasy as the pirate gave a graphic description of the lighting on the war ships. The questioning reverted to Claurinius who was challenged as to why he displayed such excessive illuminations when on a mission in which he was expected to encounter hostile ships at any time of day or night.

Claurinius fidgeted uncomfortable under the glare of this committee, acutely conscious that his reaction was being scrutinized by his own Commanding Officer and the General who had lost nearly one hundred (he did not yet know the worst) of his most seasoned troops in this encounter. Claurinius could think of no clever explanation. He then looked at Caligula Caesar who so far had taken no part in the interrogation. Claurinius had what he considered to be a brainwave.

'Pullusodon told me to keep my ships well lit at night!' Claurinius suddenly blurted out.

'Who the blazes is Pullusodon?' demanded Marcus Asianus, a puzzled frown creeping across his brow.

Caesar then spoke for the first time.

'Pullusodon is the God to whose protection I committed this young man. I thought that Pullusodon was only a cockerel, but I discovered he was a God like myself. Pullusodon obviously gave this young man good advice, for the pirate boats were decoyed by our noble Roman ships and lured to their destruction. Well done young man.'

Marcus Asianus and Caius Intripio exchanged glances. It was useless to continue to conduct a serious enquiry if Caesar's madness was going to interfere with the outcome, and they declined to ask further questions.

Caesar continued.

'I think that this young man is to be congratulated for the service he has performed for Rome.' Caesar kept referring to Claurinius as 'young man' because he had forgotten his name. 'I think we should arrange to hold a triumph in honour of his clearing the seas of Rome's enemies.'

Marcus Asianus nearly exploded.

'Hold a triumph to celebrate a minor sea battle!' Marcus remembered the grudging recognition he had been afforded on his return from the fierce and difficult campaign he had fought against the Dacians. 'The job has not been finished yet. We have the pirates to clear from Carthage first.'

Only a full general would dare to dispute a suggestion made by Caesar, but what Marcus had stated, needed to be said.

Caesar, mad though he was, was aware of his growing unpopularity. He had an inward conviction that something like a triumph would do much to restore his popularity and make the people think of him as a Caesar who brought glory to Rome.

'We must consult another God,' said Caesar, and he called out to an attendant to bring in Equinodon.

The gathering was subjected to seeing the charade of this horse being brought in, Caligula pretending to consult with it, holding his ear to his mouth to hear his pronouncement, and then declaring the result of this deliberation.

'Equinodon says we must hold a triumph. Have a triumph prepared for Wednesday!' he ordered Marcus Asianus and Caius Intripio. 'After that, this young man can take a powerful fleet to clear the remainder of the pirates from Carthage. Now leave us!'

Caesar swept out of the room. The enquiry had come to an abrupt end and was suddenly over. Claurinius was the only one satisfied with the outcome. His wildest dream had been realized. He left the palace in a state of euphoria to tell Demeter and his parents of the honour about to be bestowed on him. The others left in a less contented frame of mind.

35

Claurinius' Triumph

The triumph which Claurinius had secured by duplicity rather than earning through valour, was the greatest day in Claurinius' life. He first paraded with Julius Messana, Valerian and the men who had survived the mission, outside the great Temple of Jupiter. The High Priest of Jupiter and his attendants appeared at the top of the great flight of steps leading to the portal of this magnificent edifice, containing the huge statue of the god, reputed to be one of the wonders of the ancient world. This god, Jupiter, was invoked, prayers of thanksgiving were said for the protection he had given the ship which bore his name, and a sacrifice was offered to the deity, regarded by the Romans as the chief of the gods.

Claurinius then led his men along a processional way, lined with members of the Praetorian Guard holding back the crowds who always gathered to see such spectacles for which Rome was famous. The triumphal procession had been easy to organize because so few men were involved, and the limited scale of this event was probably a disappointment to the crowd who had been used to much greater and spectacular triumphant processions. However, they cheered in recognition of the men whom, they had been told, had survived a hazardous mission to rid the seas of the pirates which threatened Rome's prosperity. But for the valour of the men they now cheered, these pirates could, in time, have become a threat to the very safety of the City.

As the small procession reached the foot of the Palatine Hill, it stopped before Caesar's Palace, and Claurinius mounted the steps to be embraced by Caesar, and have a crown of laurel leaves placed on his head. He turned to face the cheering crowds, waved to them, savouring the adulation, and then rejoined his men and continued the march to the Circus of Maximus, located in the valley between the Palatine and Aventine Hills. In those days before the Colosseum had been built, such events reached their climax at the Circus of Maximus.

At this point, the dozen or so Carthaginian pirates were brought out and led in chains behind Claurinius' men who made a double circuit of the huge arena designed for the chariot racing. Although he could have augmented the captives in his train with the Sidonian youths, Claurinius deemed it prudent to keep them incommunicado, chained to their oars in *The Jupiter*. The small body of men and the meagre number of captives displayed on this occasion, would have seemed paltry in comparison with the monumental triumphs the Romans had witnessed when Julius Caesar or Pompey returned from their campaigns. However, heralds announcing the names of personalities and describing the groups parading or being paraded, made exaggerated claims to vaunt the significance of the spectacle, making frequent mention of Caligula Caesar who was claimed to have specially upheld the venture with an effulgence of his divine power.

During Claurinius' second circuit of the arena, Caesar appeared, clothed in imperial purple, and took his place on his throne, prominently located at the end of the circus. Claurinius mounted the steps which climbed to the throne to have his arm held aloft by Caligula. The two of them turned from side to side to face the cheering crowds. Demeter and Claurinius' parents, occupying seats of honour near Caesar, looked proudly on.

The whole of this barely gave more than half an hour's entertainment to the crowd. The organizers of the event, aware that public relations would sour at so short a spectacle, had arranged gladiatorial combats to provide further entertainment until it was nearly evening. Everybody seemed to return home happy at the end of the afternoon's diversion.

When back with his family, thoughts turned to more serious things. The news of the Alexandrian riots had reached Rome and Demeter pleaded with Claurinius for them to return to Alexandria as soon as possible to verify the safety of her parents. Claurinius was very off-hand about this, assuring Demeter that such accounts were always exaggerated, and that people of her parents' social class, invariably escaped unscathed when the plebeian masses became involved in street fighting. He explained that he was unable to go in the immediate future as he had been ordered by Caesar to finish the job he had started, and destroy the pirates in their lair at Carthage. Until this was done, no one was safe at sea, and it would be unwise to cross the Mediterranean, even in a war galley if this was unescorted. However, Claurinius promised Demeter that they would go to Alexandria as soon as he returned from Carthage so that she could reassure herself that her parents were safe.

A few days later, Claurinius returned to the camp of the Fifteenth Legion with six new officers who would command ships on the expedition to Carthage. They came to inspect the men who would be placed under their command in the fleet of war galleys which would sail on this mission. While Claurinius had been away, ships from Rhegium and Puteoli had been concentrated at Ostia. *The Jupiter* had now been sufficiently well repaired to continue to operate as Claurinius' flag ship. His new fleet would consist of *The Jupiter* and six other vessels of a similar size.

Claurinius arrived at Marcus Asianus' tent and sensed a certain hostility from this General. When they reached the parade and drill area, the legionaries who were to accompany Claurinius were assembled as before, but as he walked between their ranks, Claurinius realized that these were not men of the same calibre as those he had had under his command on the previous mission. He spoke to some of the men and was not impressed with their bearing or the way they answered him. He quickly formed the impression that these were the dregs of the Fifteenth Legion, men of whom Marcus Asianus would gladly be rid. On asking the General if he had any better men available, he received a curt reply which conveyed the message that Marcus took offence at a suggestion that any men from the Fifteenth Legion were not satisfactory for any mission to which they were assigned. Claurinius deemed it wise to say nothing more that Marcus

240

might regard as impugning the honour of his men, and thanked the General for having organized the men who would serve on his additional six ships, so promptly. Claurinius left the camp with misgivings about the men he was to command.

The day came for the ships to set sail. Claurinius bade his farewells to Demeter and his parents, and joined his ships which were to make the fairly short crossing from Rome to Carthage, on the African shore of the Tyrrhenian Sea at the narrowest part of the Mediterranean.

Claurinius' worst fears were realized. His new men were difficult to manage and control. Although there was no real difficulty on *The Jupiter* which was still manned by the soldiers he had had on the first mission, the captains of the other ships complained of laziness and indiscipline among their men. At night time, Claurinius sailed under subdued lights. He had learnt his lesson from the engagement in the eastern Mediterranean, which although projected as a triumph, had in reality been a naval disaster. In the evenings, only the men on *The Jupiter* occupied their time in singing. On the other ships, gambling seemed to be the men's main pastime, and this gave rise to ill-feeling between men who should have been building up camaraderie as comrades-in-arms.

In the event, the whole mission proved a great anticlimax. They reached the other side of the Mediterranean and berthed at Carthage. Claurinius called to see the Roman Governor to inform him of his mission and to obtain as much information as he could on the geography of the coast near Carthage. A message must have been sent to this governor by a friend from Rome, ahead of Claurinius' task force. The Governor had been informed that it appeared that pirates were operating from under his very nose. The Governor had investigated and discovered the pirates' lair in a well concealed cove. The cove was about thirty kilometres from Carthage, not quite as close to the city as the captured pirate had claimed. The Governor had mounted a successful operation from the land, destroying the pirates' headquarters and burning their ships. Claurinius sailed down the coast to investigate and he found the cove where the hulks of the burnt out pirate vessels lay ignominiously on the beach. There was nothing left for Claurinius to do. He had no alternative but to return to Rome. Claurinius could at least report that the pirate menace had been suppressed, although he would not be able to claim credit as by now, the Governor would have undoubtedly sent despatches back to Rome, reporting his own action.

In the short time that Claurinius had been away, momentous events had taken place in Rome. The people could tolerate their mad Caesar no longer. Caligula had been assassinated. The Praetorian Guard had made Claudius, a nephew of Tiberius, Caesar in his place. The Guard had been reorganized and Claurinius' post no longer existed.

News had got back to Rome of what appeared to be a great crime, committed by Sextus Sindinion, captain of *The Minerva*, when at Sidon, but the ship had not yet returned to Ostia when the charges could be investigated. The pride which Sextus' family had felt at the news of their son being involved in a great naval victory, had turned to shame, and now they were experiencing acute concern at the unaccountable delay of *The Minerva's* return.

Nothing was known by those in power to associate Claurinius with this shameful deed. Although Claurinius was regarded as a favourite of Caligula, this in itself was not a crime, but the new Caesar felt happier with such favourites away from Rome. Claurinius was therefore appointed procurator of a province in Gaul. Before taking up this post, he was given leave to return to Alexandria with Demeter so that they could reassure themselves of the safety of Demeter's parents. Such reassurance was not forthcoming. On their return to Alexandria, they discovered the dreadful truth that Parmenion and Camporina had perished in the riots. They heard that Diana had survived but were quite unable to trace her whereabouts. None of their friends, who were preoccupied in the process of rebuilding their lives after the riots, seemed to know where Diana had gone.

Claurinius and Demeter returned to Rome in an unhappy state of mind. The sadness, arising from the tragic way in which Demeter had lost her parents, was compounded by the fact that neither of them wanted to leave their comfortable and luxurious life in Rome. A short while earlier, destiny appeared to have great things in store for Claurinius and Demeter. Claurinius now knew that he had no alternative but to accept the post in Gaul offered by the new Caesar, but even though this appeared to be a promotion, it was not really to Claurinius' liking.

36

Philip's Daughters

As Apollos and Philip sailed from Sidon along the eastern coast of the Mediterranean, they had many things to talk about. Philip had adopted the role of listener at Sidon when Apollos had to unburden himself of so much after the death of Jerahmeel, but now, Philip took the initiative in their conversations. He gave to Apollos, the possessions which had been found on Jerahmeel by those who prepared his body for burial. These amounted to the pen which Jerahmeel used for writing letters, some money, and a special item, the copy of John Mark's biography of Jesus. The cover showed unmistakable blood stains, and this book with its special link with Apollos' two saviours, became his most treasured possession.

Philip spoke warmly of the Jerusalem Church, and recounted the story Apollos had already heard of the martyrdom of Stephen, but as Stephen's special friend, Philip's account was coloured with the warmth and affection he felt for his fellow deacon of the Jerusalem Church.

Philip explained to Apollos how he came to be working in Samaria and the surrounding districts. He started by recalling Jesus' final commission to the disciples before he was taken up into heaven. Jesus had told his disciples that they should proclaim to everyone, all they knew of him, the things they had learnt from his teaching, and the deeds and miracles they had witnessed him perform. Their objective was to make new disciples. Jesus instructed his disciples to start in Jerusalem and Judaea, and then move outwards to Samaria, and continue with this work to the farthest points on earth.[148] As Philip spoke, he referred to the story of Jesus, and the significance of his life and sacrificial death,

244

as the gospel. This word, meaning good news was not a word which Apollos had previously encountered at the many churches he had visited since leaving Jerusalem with Jerahmeel. The gospel was an appropriate name for it was indeed good news that eternal life was assured for all who responded to this message by committing their lives to Jesus' control. Philip explained how the task of really spreading the gospel beyond Jerusalem, started as the Church of Jerusalem was dispersed through persecutions. As the disciples moved outwards, Philip said that he could see the gospel being taken to the farthest parts of the earth, while Samaria was being overlooked.[149] As Jesus had specially mentioned Samaria in his great commission to the disciples, Philip decided that he himself would take the gospel to Samaria.

Philip considered that Jesus had a special regard for the Samaritans whose religion was essentially the same as that of the Jews. The Samaritans, whose Jewish ancestors escaped being exiled, were disdained by the exiles who had returned from Babylon a few hundred years earlier, because their Jewish ancestors had intermarried with the surrounding tribes. The Samaritans were therefore, no longer of pure Jewish racial stock.[150] Philip explained to Apollos that this accident of history was obviously of no great importance to Jesus, and Philip used an example from the medium in which Jesus gave much of his teaching to confirm this point. He explained that the stories Jesus told to illustrate spiritual truths were called parables. Philip told Apollos that in one of these parables, Jesus had unfavourably compared a Jewish priest and a Levite with a Samaritan. This Samaritan had helped a man, left for dead by thieves, while the priest and the Levite had just passed him by on their journey.[151]

'When Jesus first told this story,' said Philip, 'it was to answer the question with which a lawyer had challenged Jesus, and to explain to him, just who is our real neighbour, but in some ways, Jesus himself could be likened to the Good Samaritan. This is something we have only realized since we have come to recognize the full significance of Jesus' life and death, and to discover deeper meanings in some of his stories. Until Jesus came, the Jews had always relied on following the teachings of the Law and the Prophets to make themselves right with God. We now know that no one can make themselves right with God by these means.'

This point registered with Apollos because it had been a misconception he held himself. His recent conversion, which had come about through the death of Jerahmeel, had caused Apollos to rethink his faith, and he no longer trusted in the moral quality of his life for salvation.

'The man who had fallen among thieves,' continued Philip, 'represents each one of us humans, who, in our sinful state, are quite unable to help ourselves to real and fulfilling life. The Levite and the Priest represent the teaching of the Law and the Prophets, but they were unable to rescue the man, and they would have left him for dead. The Good Samaritan, who was able to give the man succour and who paid the innkeeper the price needed for the man to be looked after and restored to fitness and health, represents Jesus himself. Jesus was able to help fallen mankind in a way the Law and the Prophets could not, and he paid the price required to heal us from our sin.'

Apollos realized that he was learning a great deal from Philip. Listening to Philip was profitable for Apollos, not just because he was becoming enlightened to new spiritual truths. The teaching he was receiving was helping to take Apollos' mind off the death of Jerahmeel and the painful thoughts evoked by this memory.

Philip described with enthusiasm, the way the Samaritans had responded to his preaching and spoke with joyful satisfaction rather than pride, of the many churches he had been able to found in Samaria.[152] Philip's base was now Caesaraea, the principal town of Samaria.[154] Caesarea had been built relatively recently by Herod the Great, and so named, to ingratiate Herod with Augustus Caesar. Philip told Apollos that although he operated from Caesarea, the church in Caesarea had not been founded by himself, but owed its existence to the first gentile to become a Christian, a Roman centurion called Cornelius.[153] With the Caesarean Church under the safe leadership of Cornelius, Philip felt free to use this church as the base from which he could travel to oversee the other churches he had founded. These were not all in Samaria, but some, like the Church of Sidon, were in Phoenicia to the north, and others were in Philistia to the south.

Philip had noticed that Apollos shuddered as Philip mentioned that Cornelius was a Roman centurion, and guessed the thoughts that were passing through Apollos' mind.

'I know that you have had a very unfortunate experience at the hands of Roman soldiers,' continued Philip, 'but we must not judge men on the basis of their following a profession whose practitioners often perform actions we hate and despise. This attitude is as bad as racism. Jesus had a wonderful ministry among prostitutes and tax-gatherers, and these social outcasts responded to his teaching in a way that the people who had a reputation for being religious, did not. On one occasion, Jesus met a Roman centurion who knew that Jesus could heal his sick servant without even coming into the house where he lay. Jesus healed this centurion's servant and commended the centurion as one who had greater faith than any person Jesus had met among the people of Israel. When you meet Cornelius, you will find he is different from any soldier you ever met before.'[155]

They soon arrived at Caesarea where the *Trojan Hero* was putting into port for a couple of days. Philip took Apollos to stay with him in his house until the boat was ready to continue the journey. Philip was a widower and his home was run by his four vivacious and attractive daughters, Anna, Miriam, Deborah and Abigail. They had obviously inherited the jollity and sense of fun of their father, but they had a serious side to their nature to balance their jovial bearing. They greeted their father with warm hugs and peals of girlish laughter, teasing him that returning by boat instead of his customary route by road, showed that he was getting lazy in his old age. Philip introduced Apollos, and when he had explained the rather sad circumstance which had brought them together, they immediately became quiet and displayed genuine sympathy for this new friend of their father's.

After a good meal, Philip suggested that they should go to Cornelius' house to meet this rather special elder who led the Church of Caesarea. Philip expected that this encounter would dispel from Apollos the misconception bred from his recent experience, that all soldiers were unprincipled men of violence. In the event, Apollos never met Cornelius because he was away from home, but the reason for his absence did as much as a personal encounter, to assure Apollos that here was a soldier of great generosity and compassion. The servant who answered the door of Cornelius' house told Philip that the master would be away for a week on his food round. Philip explained to Apollos that several times a year, when various fruits ripened or the grain was harvested, Cornelius would buy up a large quantity of food, and travel with a group of his servants to the poorest villages in Samaria where he distributed it among the most needy peasants.

'Cornelius was known for his charitable acts, long before he became a Christian,' Philip told Apollos, 'and that led to one of the most remarkable conversion stories that had been encountered, even in the early church which was winning vast numbers of converts as it exploded with missionary zeal and fervour. Although he was a Roman, Cornelius recognized the futility of the Roman Gods and prayed to one God whom Cornelius acknowledged as the creator of the universe and to whom he ascribed all power and might.'

'To all intents and purposes,' explained Philip, 'Cornelius worshipped Jehovah, and Jehovah rewarded Cornelius' devotion and acts of charity by giving him a vision that he should send for a man called Peter who was staying at Joppa with one called Simon the Tanner. At the same time, Peter was given a vision which he correctly interpreted as meaning that he should not withhold his company from a person, just because that person was a gentile. The two visions were complementary, and Peter, the most prominent of Jesus' disciples, came and explained the gospel of Jesus Christ to Cornelius and his family. And so started the Church of Caesarea!' concluded Philip.[156]

Had Cornelius been there to recount the story himself to Apollos, he would undoubtedly have told Apollos of the great outpouring of the Holy Spirit of God which had accompanied his conversion. A rather strange aspect of

Philip's ministry, was that he taught very little about the Holy Spirit of God. This was unusual for a man who himself, was so obviously filled with spiritual power. Philip had few equals as an evangelist. When he preached, crowds would listen spellbound at the eloquence and conviction with which he spoke, and large numbers were converted through his ministry. In the very early days when Philip first went to Samaria, he made spectacular numbers of converts, but it was not until Peter and John came from Jerusalem and prayed for the Samaritan Christians, that they might receive the Holy Spirit of God, that the newly converted Samaritans received this special power, available to Christians.[152] Apollos had learned so much about Jesus from the many great Christian teachers whom he had met on his travels, including Philip. Apollos had witnessed the power of the Holy Spirit in the lives of these Christians, but he had been given no formal teaching about the Holy Spirit, and was therefore, not explicitly aware of the Spirit's existence. When Sandas-cum-Barama had spoken of the Spirit at Apollos' synagogue in Alexandria, Apollos did not know enough about the Christian faith for the mention of the Spirit to register with him as significant.

Apollos returned home with Philip. That evening, he was to experience another aspect of the power of the Holy Spirit without being aware of its source, for the Holy Spirit had given each of Philip's daughters, the gift of prophecy. Apollos was not to learn about the nature and source of this power for some weeks.

After the evening meal, Philip, his daughters and Apollos spoke together of many things. They spoke of the Church in Samaria. Apollos recounted his experiences in the churches he had visited on his journey with Jerahmeel. Their thoughts dwelt on some he had met who were now common acquaintances of both Philip and Apollos. Apollos spoke with great affection and tenderness of Jerahmeel and of all this remarkable man had been to him. Apollos explained the reason for his having to break off his journey through Greece, and the anxiety he now felt as he returned home to Alexandria. After talking for perhaps a couple of hours, the six of them turned to prayer. During the time of prayer, each of the daughters prophesied in the power of the Holy Spirit.[157]

249

Anna prophesied first. She spoke of the sadness that Apollos would experience on his return to Alexandria, but her prophecy was not specific as to the source of this sadness.

Then Miriam spoke. She prophesied that Apollos would pass on to others the wonderful things he had learnt of Jesus, and that many would come to know and trust in Jesus as their Saviour through his words.

The Spirit of prophecy then came upon Deborah who proclaimed that Apollos would start his preaching ministry in Alexandria, but would return to Greece to bring great blessings to the Greek churches, and in turn, Apollos would experience the most joyful event of his life while in Greece.

Finally, Abigail prophesied. Hers was a strange prophecy. She stated that Apollos would meet three people in his life who had actually been present at the crucifixion of Jesus. She prophesied that soon after he had met the third of these people, Apollos would enter into great glory.

The prayers and prophecies ended, and the company retired to sleep. Many thoughts, which had arisen from all Apollos had heard that day, churned in his mind, but he was drowsy and dropped into a deep and peaceful sleep.

37

Barabbas

The prophecy of Abigail came to Apollos mind as he rose that morning. He had met one person who was certainly at Jesus' crucifixion. That was Simon of Cyrene, the Presiding Elder of the Church of Antioch. This strange prophecy of his youngest daughter was also in Philip's thoughts.

After breakfast, Philip made the suggestion that they should go to visit a Christian living in the outskirts of Caesarea who had rather an interesting tale to tell.

'This man has a first name which is Jesus,'[158] said Philip. 'and has a surname which could be interpreted to mean, Son of the Father!'

Philip led Apollos away from the sea-front of Caesarea, and they walked inland, almost to the boundary of the city. In fact, the house they stopped at, was the last but one before the dwelling places gave way to open country. They knocked at the door which was opened by a stocky man whose face seemed to bear the scars of deep cuts, perhaps sword wounds he had received in some battle, long ago. The stocky man smiled warmly when he saw who it was who had called and invited Philip and his companion in. Philip introduced Apollos and told the man a little of Apollos' circumstances. He then asked the man if he would recount his tale. The man knew exactly what Philip was referring to, and led them into his main room where he gestured for them to sit down. When they were all comfortable, the man began his tale.

'My friends tell me I am the luckiest man to be alive,' he started. 'I know what they mean, but sadly, not all of them understand me when I tell them that they could be equally lucky.

'My name is Jesus Barabbas. I used to be a Jewish revolutionary. We were known in those days as Zealots. Our objective was to drive out the Roman troops who were occupying our lands and imposing crippling taxes on our people. Sadly, our plans went wrong. We had organized a little guerilla troop and had planned to attack the fortress of Antonia, which was the key to the control of Jerusalem. From there, we could have rallied Israel and defeated the Romans. Unfortunately, our intelligence was wrong. The fortress was more strongly garrisoned than we expected, and most of our band were killed in the attack. I was captured and I knew what to expect. The Romans have a cruel way of dealing with those who oppose their rule.

'The night before I was due to be crucified, I sat in my cell, reflecting on my past life. It had all gone wrong. Not just the revolt, no, but the time before when I was hiding in the hills with my band of Zealots. We had to get food to survive, and the Arabian camel caravans, which passed by each week on their way to Jerusalem, were easy pickings. I had not felt too happy about killing the camel drivers, fat Arabs though they were, but secrecy was essential to the success of our revolt, and dead men tell no tales. It was my part in killing these innocent men which worried me then, much more than the revolt which I felt was fully justified, failure though it was.

'As I was feeling at my lowest, I heard the jailer's iron clad feet, clanking along the corridor, and could see his shadowy shape by the bars of my cell as he turned the giant key in its lock. Had my execution been brought forward a few hours?

'"You're free!" he said, and led me out to the dazzling sunlight of the square at the back of the Governor's house. "Whatever has happened," I wondered.

'"The mob must love you." said the jailer bitterly. He had lost a brother in the fight in the Antonia fortress, and was looking forward to seeing the dreadful vengeance that Roman Law had reserved for me.

'"They found another man who seems prepared to die in your place, and Pilate, damn him, is obeying the demands of the mob out front."

'I could hear the cries of "Crucify him!"[159] coming from the front of the house, and I rushed round, expecting to be acclaimed by the crowd who had won my release. However, as I reached the front of Pilate's house, I was completely ignored. The crowd's attention was fixed on the balcony of the house where Pilate seemed to be making a great display of washing his hands. A bearded man in chains, flanked by two soldiers, was also out there on the balcony. This was the man who was going to die in my place, so that I, the great Zionist patriot, could gather together the remnants of my Zealot band and start from scratch, brave fellow that I was. But no, I must have read the situation wrong. The crowd were ignoring me, and shouting abuse at this condemned man, standing on the balcony by Pilate. He was clearly disliked by the crowd.

'As I looked at this man, who remained calm and dignified, although he must have been under considerable stress, and then surveyed the screaming mob, howling for blood, the people I was attempting to serve by liberating them from the Romans, I felt strangely sick. My life up to that point, suddenly seemed a worthless thing, a lot of effort directed to futile ends. Then I looked to this man who was going to die in my place, and strangely, peace returned to my mind. As I kept my eyes fixed on him, he seemed calm and confident, as if he was fulfilling a destiny which was rushing on apace. I owed this man my life, and yet there was nothing I could do to repay him.

'Pilate turned his back on the crowd and walked into the house, followed by this man and the two soldiers. Later that day, I saw that man crucified. I winced as I saw the nails driven into his hand, and saw his whole body shake as the cross was hoisted into an upright position, and dropped with a thud into its socket. "That could have been happening to me," I thought. I waited as the man met his end. Although many in the crowd were jeering, he met his death with great dignity. He spoke words of comfort and reassurance to those around him who were his friends and even prayed for forgiveness for those who were inflicting this terrible pain on him.[160] I walked away from the din of the crowd, this man's face imprinted on my mind's eye. While my mind felt at peace, it also felt confused. I asked myself,

What cause did this man serve?
Why was he prepared to die in my place?
Why was the crowd so hostile?

'I didn't get the answer to these questions for six weeks until the next big Jewish festival, the Feast of Pentecost. Then the followers of this man, whom I found out was called Jesus, burst out of hiding and declared that this man had risen from the dead, that he was the Messiah who had come to conquer death, that he died in the place of sinful man.[75]

'I knew that what they said was true, not just because he had died in my place and saved this sinful man from death, but because of the impact that his appearance outside Pilate's house, had on my mind. I suddenly realized that the destiny he knew he was fulfilling, was that of the suffering servant, written of by the prophet Isaiah. The words had flashed across my mind, "The Lord had laid on him the iniquity of us all."[162]

'Yes, I was lucky that he first died in my place, but I tell my friends, if they will but understand the meaning of my words, Jesus died in their place too!'

Apollos had read of Barabbas in the book he had called John Mark's biography of Jesus.[161] (From now on, he would use Philip's terminology and refer to the biography as John Mark's gospel.) Apollos had always regarded Barabbas as one of the villains of the events, leading to the crucifixion of Jesus, but as he looked at the scarred but peaceful, and yes, gentle face of this former revolutionary who had just shared his testimony, Apollos revised his opinion.

Apollos thanked Barabbas warmly for telling him of this unique experience, and assured Barabbas that he shared his good fortune, by outlining the totally different set of experiences which had brought himself to the same state of faith.

Barabbas explained that he had left Judaea because, although reprieved from execution, many Roman soldiers in that province nursed a grudge against him for assassinations carried out by his Zealot band, and in time, one of the soldiers would have found a means to despatch him. He had therefore come to Samaria, and had the joy of expressing the release that Jesus had won for him, by identifying himself with the followers of Jesus, and worshipping with Christian friends he had made at the Church of Caesarea.

'Of those friends, there is none in whom I hold in greater

esteem,' concluded Barabbas, 'than Philip here, and one who is a Roman soldier, the centurion, Cornelius.'

The following day, Barabbas joined with Philip and his daughters to wish Apollos farewell as he continued on the final stage of his journey, home to Alexandria. Philip was still concerned as to whether Apollos should travel alone in view of his recent sad experience and the uncertainty of what news awaited him at Alexandria. Philip offered to accompany him, but Apollos reassured Philip that he now felt strong and composed. The memory of the two refreshing days that he had spent at Caesarea, often returned to Apollos' mind. He always retained the fondest recollections of Philip, his vivacious daughters with the gift of prophecy, and Barabbas, the converted Zealot.

38

Apollos' Return to Alexandria

At last the *Trojan Hero* reached Alexandria. Apollos paid the master his dues and immediately made his way home, or to what had been his home. The prophecy of Anna, that Apollos' home-coming would be a sad event for him, had prepared Apollos for some sort of shock. In the event, things were worse, much worse, then Apollos feared in his most downcast moments. Although many of the Greek homes in the area where Apollos' family lived were tolerably well repaired since the riots, those where the occupants had been killed in the worst outbreak of violence, were still in total ruin. They were in an even worse state now than they had been immediately after the riots, for they had been looted, and building materials cannibalized to restore neighbours' properties. Apollos gazed sadly at the remains of what had once been his home. He philosophically accepted the loss of his house, and immediately set about finding where his parents were now staying. He was soon to make a sad discovery which was much harder to accept than the destruction of the house where he had lived most of his life. He went round to the home of friends of the family which appeared to have escaped serious damage in the riots.

Memnon and Hera were at first surprised to see Apollos. They had almost forgotten his existence, as the Greek community of Alexandria had come out of its trauma and struggled back to a state of normality after the devastation of the riots. They invited Apollos in and broke the news of his parents' violent death to him as gently as such news can be broken. They talked for some time about all that had happened. Apollos felt alarm as the names of other friends of the family, who had lost their lives in the riots, were mentioned. Parmenion and Camporina perished! What of Diana? It was with some relief that Apollos heard that she had been away from home when the riots struck, and in his sadness, Apollos felt a tinge of joy on hearing that the reason Diana survived, was due to the fact that they occurred on the first day of the week when Diana was in the Jewish quarter of the City. She was meeting with a group for whom the first day of the week was special, called Christians. Apollos told Memnon and Hera that he too had become a Christian during his travels. He shared with them his experiences, including the sad news of the death of Jerahmeel as the result of an act of violence. Memnon and Hera expressed further sadness at this news, for they too knew Jerahmeel well. He was a man held in high esteem by all who knew him.

Memnon took Apollos to the necropolis, as the Greek burial ground was called, located just outside the city wall to the south-west, and showed him the last resting place of his parents, a pair of simple wooden posts bearing the names, Cambiades and Aspasia, identifying the two graves. Apollos stood for some time in silence, contemplating those graves. He felt specially sad that his parents had been suddenly taken from him as it were, in his absence, giving him no opportunity to begin to repay the fond devotion they had bestowed on their only son. Apollos then returned to the city with Memnon and was invited to share the meal that Hera had prepared.

On leaving Memnon and Hera after eating, Apollos immediately made his way to the Jewish quarter of the city, and came across the home used as the Christian meeting house, without needing to ask for directions. The familiar cross was painted prominently on the wall above the door. Apollos called and was admitted. He introduced himself as a Christian who had just returned home to Alexandria after a visit to Greece. He told them of the sad discoveries he had made, and that he had heard news of a Greek friend of his called Diana, whom, he was told, had joined the Christian Church in Alexandria. Jedidiah, the owner of the house confirmed Apollos' news.

'Diana was introduced to our church by Anaxagoras,

another Greek,' began Jedidiah.

Apollos nodded at the mention of Anaxagoras to indicate that he too was known to Apollos.

'Diana was a wonderful young lady,' continued Jedidiah, eulogising over this Greek damsel who had become such a favourite with the Alexandrian Church. 'Sadly, her parents suffered the same fate as yours in the riots, and she and Anaxagoras left soon after that sad night. I am not sure where they were finally heading for, but Barnabas will know. Barnabas is the presiding elder of our Church. He gave Diana a lot of comfort after that tragedy, and they would have discussed the future together.'

Apollos started at the mention of the name, Barnabas. This was a name he had heard before. Yes, the Christians at Antioch had prayed for him and John Mark when the Cypriot Christian gave news of their mission to Alexandria. This must be the same person. Jedidiah arranged to take Apollos to the house where Barnabas was staying, and Barnabas and Apollos spent some time talking together.

Apollos was anxious, first for news of Diana. Barnabas told Apollos that Diana had considered her best option was to go to stay with her sister in Rome. Barnabas explained that her sister was married into a wealthy and aristocratic family there, but this was a fact of which Apollos was only too well aware. Barnabas had not realized that Diana had changed her plans since he had spoken to her, and Apollos accepted without question that Diana had gone to Rome as this is what he would have expected her to do in these circumstances. Barnabas did not mention to Apollos that Diana was pregnant as he saw no reason why this fact should be of any importance to Apollos. He told Apollos that Diana would have been well protected on her journey as she travelled in the company of Anaxagoras. Although sad that he would not meet Diana again, Apollos was relieved to learn that Diana's future appeared to be secure.

Apollos then told Barnabas of his own mixed experiences during the past months, making particular mention of the time he had spent at Antioch, where Apollos had first heard Barnabas' name. Apollos sensed that Barnabas experienced a peaceful satisfaction as Apollos spoke of the Church at Antioch, and the prayers which were being offered for him there. Barnabas also knew Philip well and was pleased to hear news of the flourishing church in Samaria. Apollos spoke of his triple bereavement, the death of his friend and mentor, Jerahmeel, and the loss of both his parents, all the deaths occurring as a result of acts of violence. Barnabas spoke words of great comfort to Apollos, as he had to Diana. How apt and appropriate was the name Barnabas, Son of Consolation.[144] Barnabas was specially interested in the way that the things Apollos had learnt and experienced on his journey, had led to his becoming a Christian, and he asked if Apollos would be able to tell the Church of Alexandria this remarkable story. Although Barnabas had expected Apollos to need some time to recover from the shock of his recent bereavements and the loss of his home, Apollos was anxious to give his testimony on the earliest possible occasion. It was arranged that Apollos should speak to the Church the coming Sunday.

Thoughts then turned to where Apollos should stay until he could make arrangements for permanent accommodation. Barnabas mentioned that his assistant, John Mark, was being put up at a very large house and would be glad of someone of his own age to share the accommodation. Apollos took from his pocket the blood stained and well thumbed copy of John Mark's gospel, and showed it to Barnabas. He explained that this had been a gift to Jerahmeel by James, the presiding elder of the Church of Jerusalem.

Barnabas took Apollos to meet John Mark, and the two young men experienced instant rapport. They both had so much to tell each other. Barnabas left Apollos and his nephew, well pleased at having met Apollos. He felt a conviction that Apollos would make a great contribution to the development of the Church of Alexandria.

A particular question which Apollos asked John Mark, was whether he had actually been present as Jesus was crucified. John Mark had described the events of the crucifixion so clearly in his gospel that Apollos felt sure that he must have been an eye-witness, and Apollos still had in mind the strange prophecy of Abigail. John Mark would have been the third witness of Jesus' death and passion that Apollos had met. John Mark told him that he had had to write his account of the crucifixion on the basis of information he had received, from eye-witnesses who where there. He drew Apollos' attention to something he had written in his gospel about the arrest of Jesus in the Garden of Gethsemane.

> Then the disciples left Jesus and ran away. A certain young man, dressed only in a linen cloth was following Jesus. They tried to arrest him, but he ran away naked, leaving the cloth behind.[163]

'I was that young man,' confessed John Mark. 'The apostle, John, was the only male disciple who remained with Jesus, right through to the end. He was commissioned to take special care of Jesus' mother, Mary, by Jesus as he spoke his dying words from the cross.[164] The rest of us disciples went into hiding, and we didn't show our faces until three days later when we began to receive news that Jesus had risen from the dead. Then, over the next six weeks, we all saw Jesus many times until he was taken up into heaven.

'I am afraid that in those days, I was not a particularly courageous person,' continued John Mark. 'Indeed, on the first missionary journey in which I accompanied my Uncle Barnabas, and Paul, I am afraid that I rather let them down. We met considerable hostility in Cyprus, and when we came to Pamphylia, I decided that I had had enough. We sailed from Paphos in Cyprus to Perga, and there I left Uncle Barnabas and Paul, and returned to Jerusalem.'

John Mark looked very shame-faced as he told Apollos this. Apollos felt a great affection for this young man who had written the most wonderful book he had ever read and who had so much to be proud of in the support he had been to his uncle in founding the Church of Alexandria. Yet here he was, not trying to project himself as someone very special, but admitting his faults and weaknesses to a new acquaintance.

'I was the cause of my uncle and Paul splitting up. After I had deserted them at Perga, Paul did not want me to accompany him on another missionary journey. However, my Uncle Barnabas still had faith in me, and we returned to Cyprus, while Paul went back to the provinces of Asia and Galatia on the mainland in the company of Silas.[165] I have learnt a lot since those days, and I am now prepared to trust in the protective power of God to work out things for the best. My uncle and I faced some difficult situations in Cyprus, and I don't think my uncle has any complaints now, that I have not displayed courage on occasions when we were threatened by mobs who were disturbed by the challenge conveyed by the message we brought to them.'

Apollos soon felt comfortable in the company of John Mark. On the Sunday, they met the Alexandrian Christians in a room, set out just like the many church meeting rooms in which Apollos had now shared sabbath worship. John Mark introduced Apollos to the Christians there, and Apollos found there were one or two Greeks and one or two Jews whom he had known before setting out on his journey. Barnabas presided at the service and Apollos was invited to speak and tell the gathering of the experiences he had had on his journey, with special emphasis on the impact it had had on his spiritual outlook. The congregation were enthralled as Apollos used his gift of oratory to give a concise but graphic account of all that had happened, up to the time that Jerahmeel's death at Sidon had resulted in his finally being prepared to commit his life to Jesus. At the end of the service, the congregation left in an animated and excited state, and Barnabas was clearly delighted at the impact of Apollos' words.

Over the next few days, Apollos made a point of making contact with the members of the Hebron synagogue, where he had worshipped before leaving Alexandria. In particular, he spent the best part of a day with Dathan Barjoseph, the synagogue's president. Dathan told Apollos that they were aware of the Church in Alexandria. This was after all, in the Jewish quarter of the city and not too far from the Hebron district. The members of the synagogue knew that the Church proclaimed the Jesus of whom they had first heard from Sandas-cum-Barama. However, they were awaiting the return of Jerahmeel and Apollos, whose objective had been to investigate the claims of Jesus, before making any commitment themselves. Dathan was naturally saddened to hear of Jerahmeel's untimely death, but was encouraged that he had not died in vain and that their mission had had a positive outcome. Dathan invited Apollos to speak at the

261

synagogue the following sabbath, which was Saturday for the Jews rather than Sunday.

Apollos went to the synagogue in the company of John Mark whom he was able to introduce as an eye-witness of many of the events of Jesus' life. Apollos then described in a way which was similar to the address he had given the previous Sunday, the significant things which Jerahmeel and himself had experienced on their journey. The Jews at the Hebron Synagogue were saddened, as Dathan had been, at the news of Jerahmeel's death, for nowhere was Jerahmeel so highly honoured and respected as in that Synagogue. Indeed, the love and respect that Jerahmeel commanded was posthumous in its effect. The whole congregation unanimously decided that they would adopt the Christian faith. The following day, the Alexandrian Church was filled to beyond its normal capacity as the members of the Hebron Synagogue came to meet Barnabas and the Christian people who worshipped in their city, and whom they hoped to join.

Barnabas, John Mark and Apollos spent much time over the next few weeks, teaching the members of the Hebron Synagogue about the significance of Jesus' life, but as Jews, well steeped in the religious traditions of their nation, they had the necessary foundation to recognize the significance of that instruction. Barnabas spent rather more time with Dathan, and was soon satisfied that Dathan was the right man to continue as the presiding elder, but this time, of the Hebron Church in Alexandria, rather than the Hebron Synagogue. Thus two strong and flourishing churches, able to provide mutual support and encouragement, were established to grow side by side in the principal city of Egypt.

Then one day, Barnabas arranged a meeting with John Mark and Apollos. Even before he spoke, his relaxed and happy face conveyed to them that he was very pleased about something.

'I have received a letter from our brother, Paul,' he began. 'He has written to us in the most warm and encouraging terms,' Barnabas continued, 'and obviously news has reached him of the way our Church is growing here in Alexandria. Paul is at Ephesus where there is more opportunity for building and expanding the church there than he and Silas can manage by themselves, and he is appealing for helpers. He wants only Christians of the highest calibre to share in this work with him, and he has specifically asked if I could spare John Mark for this task.'

John Mark could not prevent a delightful smile spreading across his face. Barnabas and Paul had been reconciled. He had been reinstated as a worthy missionary. There was nothing that John Mark would rather do at that time. Yes, of course he would go to Ephesus.

Barnabas then explained why he had invited Apollos as well as John Mark in to share this news.

'It is contrary to our normal practice to send a missionary to travel alone,' Barnabas told them. 'As I have noticed how well you two work together, and have observed your complementary gifts, I thought that the two of you might consider pairing up to help Paul in his work. I have prayed hard about this, and the answer I am receiving is that this would be right.'

The three of them spent further time in prayer together, and then John Mark and Apollos left, both in a state of euphoria.

Apollos and John Mark needed only a few days to pack. A passage was booked on a ship, bound for Ephesus, and stopping only at Salmone in Crete en route. A week later, a goodly gathering of Christians from the two Alexandrian churches, lined the quay to wave their farewells to Apollos and John Mark as they left Alexandria for this new adventure.

39

The Mission at Ephesus

Apollos and John Mark reached Ephesus after a pleasant and uneventful crossing of the Mediterranean. Although a much travelled young man, John Mark had not been to Ephesus before, and Apollos felt a very experienced traveller in being able to conduct John Mark through Ephesus, straight to the Christian Church. They were expected and warmly welcomed by the reception committee who were staying at the house where the Ephesian Christians worshipped, and looking after those assembling to work with Paul and Silas on their great mission to Ephesus. John Mark and Apollos joined a group of Christians whom Paul had invited from various churches which he had either founded, or with which he had special connections. Every one had some particular gift or ability or specialized knowledge which would contribute to the work to be undertaken.

Most of those present were young men, of about the same age as Apollos and John Mark. There was one married couple in the group who had travelled from Corinth to Ephesus with Paul. This couple were residing at a house near the Church. The rest of the group had been staying in rooms in the Church building itself. None of these had been there for much more than a fortnight. Apollos and John Mark were the last of the members of the team being formed, who had been expected to arrive at the Ephesian Church. Strictly, speaking, John Mark was the last expected arrival, for Apollos was not known to Paul and Silas, and had not been specifically invited. However, anybody commended by one as respected in Christian circles as was Barnabas, had an assured welcome in that gathering.

About mid-afternoon, Paul and Silas themselves returned to the Church from their business in town and were pleased to learn that their team was complete. Apollos was the only stranger to these much travelled missionaries, and John Mark introduced his new friend to them. Paul and Silas shook Apollos warmly by the hand, and enquired about the state of the Church of Alexandria. Paul was particularly concerned to hear how his old friend Barnabas was faring. John Mark briefly outlined how well the Alexandrian Church which Barnabas had planted, was flourishing under his vigorous leadership. He then gave what Apollos considered to be a flattering account of how Apollos had won a complete synagogue to Christianity, so that there were now, two flourishing churches in Alexandria. Paul and Silas beamed at Apollos as John Mark gave this account. They knew that anyone who came, bearing Barnabas's recomendation as credentials, would be a valuable addition to the team, and John Mark's words confirmed this expectation.

Apollos paid great attention to Paul and Silas about whom he had heard so much but whom he had only just met. Paul's head was shaved. Apollos discovered that this was an indication that Paul had recently taken a special vow[166]. Both Paul and Silas seemed to convey a great power, a personal magnetism which Apollos had encountered in few others. Apollos wondered what the source of this special power might be. Although both possessing this power and magnetic quality, Paul and Silas were different from each other in other respects, and made up a complementary pair. Silas was relaxed and cheerful, while Paul was intense and very serious. They were obviously, both highly respected by the company present at the Ephesian Church.

They went into another room where a meal had been prepared for them, and after Paul had said grace, conversation began to flow freely. Everybody present seemed to have had a very adventurous life. Apollos noticed that a young Greek showed particular interest in John Mark and the fact he had written a biography of Jesus.

After the meal, the company adjourned to another room. Paul and Silas explained that they had been invited to join them at Ephesus because the openings for doing effective

265

missionary work were so great and varied, that they needed help to take full advantage of the opportunities available. After saying a little about the work in which they themselves had recently been engaged, Paul and Silas suggested it would be a good idea if all present said a little about themselves.

The young married couple spoke first. Their names were Priscilla and Aquila. Aquila was a leather worker who originated from Pontus, but their permanent home was in Corinth, where they had met Paul who had lodged with them when he was preaching in that city. They had recently been to Rome where they reported that the Christians were having a hard time. The new emperor, Claudius Caesar, had expelled all Jews and Christians from the city[167], and that is why they had returned to Corinth earlier than intended. Apollos' mind turned to Diana. He had reason to believe that she was in Rome. How was she faring as a Christian?

The Greek who had shown such interest in the fact that John Mark had written a biography of Jesus, was a young doctor, called Luke. His interest in John Mark's work arose from the fact that he too was researching to write a biography of Jesus. Luke had travelled with Paul and Silas on many of their missionary journeys[168].

A rather delicate and frail young man called Timothy spoke next and described his family background. He had a Greek father and a Jewish mother[169]. His mother had become a Christian[170], but his father had resisted the attempts of himself and his mother to bring him to share their faith. Apollos sensed that Timothy would be specially sensitive in his dealings with other people. Although not an extrovert or domineering in the mould usually associated with people of leadership potential, Timothy undoubtedly had leadership qualities, and Apollos formed the opinion that he would be much loved by any whose care was his responsibility. Timothy had come to Ephesus with Silas, shortly after Paul had arrived from Corinth with Priscilla and Aquila.

The fourth young man to introduce himself was Titus, a Roman citizen who had been converted on hearing Paul speak on one of his earlier missionary journeys. He had quickly learned the fundamentals of the Christian faith, and Paul had recognized that Titus had considerable organizational and administrative skills. He had a responsible position in the Corinthian Church where he had the special task of organizing the collection of money from this relatively affluent church to help support the Church in Jerusalem[171]. Apollos knew that the members of the Jerusalem Church included many poor and elderly widows.

Apollos and John Mark introduced themselves in turn.

When all the introductions were over, Silas led the group in a time of prayer during which they remembered the churches from which each of those present had come, and they prayed that God would help them proclaim the good news of salvation in Ephesus in a way which would be effective and bring many into the fold of the church.

After the time of prayer, Paul and Silas asked Apollos to join them as they withdrew to another room. They invited Apollos to tell them more about himself and of how he had become a Christian. Apollos was the one person in that group, not already well known to Paul and Silas. Apollos started by explaining how he had first adopted the Jewish faith, and described how he had been accepted as a teacher at the Hebron Synagogue. Apollos then described the details of his journey with Jerahmeel as a commission from the Hebron Synagogue to investigate the claims made on behalf of Jesus by the Ethiopian, Sandas-cum-Barama. He explained how the eye-witnesses who had met the risen Jesus, had left him in no doubt that Jesus was indeed the promised Messiah, but that he had resisted the notion that Jesus had died on the cross to pay for his sins. Apollos described the events which occurred on the sea-shore at Sidon, and how it had taken the death of Jerahmeel to save him from being taken as a galley slave, to lead him at last to realize how one person's life can be bought by the blood, shed by another on their behalf. Jerahmeel acknowledged that Jesus had bought his life, and as Jerahmeel had bought Apollos' life, so Apollos had accepted that ultimately he owed his life to Jesus. Apollos now accepted that Jesus had first claim on his life and he knew that this dedication was in line with Jerahmeel's dying wish. Apollos spoke of the peace that this had given him, and the strength to bear, not only the loss of Jerahmeel his dearest friend, but to cope with the discovery that his Alexandrian home had been destroyed and his parents killed. He acknowledged the help he had received from both Philip and Barnabas over his recent bereavements. Apollos finally described how he had completed the commission of the Hebron Synaogue, and that his report to those Alexandrian Jews whom he knew and loved so well, had resulted in that Synagogue becoming the Hebron Church in Alexandria. This Church would work closely with Barnabas's Church which occupied a neighbouring suburb of the Jewish quarter of Alexandria.

Apollos' account clearly pleased Paul and Silas, and helped them see how Apollos would fit into the team they had assembled.

Good sleeping accommodation had been provided at the Ephesian Church for the mission team. They reassembled the following morning, having slept and breakfasted well. Paul and Silas had risen early that morning to pray for guidance in planning the mission, and they joined the team to explain their strategy. Silas spoke first.

'We see three categories of people to whom we are called to proclaim the gospel,' he started, 'and the different gifts and abilities we contribute as the different individuals we are, will suit each of us to work specially effectively with one or other of these groups.

'First, there are those who are actually attending the Ephesian Church. The Church here has grown considerably since we founded it, but we know from the elders of the Ephesian Church, that although many of the members attend regularly, not all of them have fully understood the gospel being proclaimed. Their allegiance to the Church is half-hearted and lukewarm. They have not seen in Jesus, the Saviour to whom they must fully commit their lives. This is a very common problem in churches. Great tact and diplomacy is needed in ministering to such people, for offence can so easily be taken if they feel they are being judged and found wanting. We would seek to judge no man, but the fruits of men's lives are often revealing symptoms that all may not be well, and such symptoms are evident here in the Ephesian Church. We therefore have a mission to conduct which is internal to the Church here at Ephesus.

As both Titus and Timothy have had the oversight of churches themselves, and have the skills to complete the understanding of those with only partial faith, we will assign to them the responsibility of working alongside the elders of the Ephesian Church to deepen the faith and commitment of all its members.

'Secondly, our most fruitful mission fields have always been the Jewish Synagogues, for their faith is incomplete, and the message we bring puts all they have learned in a meaningful and satisfactory context. Those who are not more concerned with their own status than with discovering the truth, see in Jesus, the long awaited Messiah and the completion of their faith. The Jews can only be convinced by someone who already has a firm understanding of their faith, and they will test that understanding with arguments based on their reading of the Scriptures. However, for those who are genuinely seeking, truth prevails. Jesus came first of all to save the lost sheep of Israel, and the well instructed Jewish convert has a firmly based and sound faith. Presidents of Synagogues will allow those with the right credentials to speak at their meetings. Priscilla and Aquila have a sound knowledge of the teachings of the Law and the Prophets, and Apollos is an accredited Synagogue Teacher. Their part in this mission is therefore to take the gospel to the synagogues of Ephesus.

'Thirdly, there are the pagans, the people in this city who worship Diana, or who acknowledge no god at all. We cannot proclaim the gospel in Diana's Temple, but we can reach these people by speaking in the market squares and on the street corners. Many of the intellectual Greeks like to meet at the Lecture Hall of Tyrannus and these people will welcome discussions on matters of religion[172]. Ministry to the pagans will largely be the job of Paul and myself, but we need help. As Luke and John Mark have already been with Paul or with myself in this open air work, we have chosen them to support us in this task.'

Apollos looked across at John Mark and could see that this arrangement pleased him. He would now have the opportunity to prove to Paul and Silas, as he had already proved to his Uncle Barnabas, that he had the stomach to boldly proclaim the gospel, even when confronted by a hostile mob.

Paul then spoke briefly.

'It is not our intention for you to feel that you are being restricted to exercise your ministry in just the particular areas that Silas has outlined. It is our hope that all of us will be able to contribute to each other's work, counselling the members of the Ephesian Church, explaining the relevance of the gospel to the Jews, and preaching the gospel outside in the streets of Ephesus.'

An opportunity was given to raise questions, but Paul and Silas had so aptly allocated responsibilities to their team in line with their gifts, that few points were raised, and the team spent an hour in prayer for the work which lay ahead.

The mission started the following day. It was the Jewish sabbath, and Priscilla, Aquila and Apollos made their way to a synagogue to arrive well before the time of scheduled worship. Priscilla was an eloquent and outspoken woman, but as a woman, it was not considered appropriate for her to seek to speak at the synagogue. Aquila was a quiet man with only limited experience at public speaking, but he was powerful in the way he used Scripture in religious discussions. Apollos was the obvious spokesman on this occasion. They introduced themselves to the President, and Apollos presented his credentials in the form of the letter of introduction he had received from Barjoseph of Alexandria before he had departed with Jerahmeel on his grand tour. The President invited Apollos to speak at the meeting.

The Synagogue filled as the time for worship approached and the service followed its normal form. At the appropriate time, the President introduced Apollos as a learned Jew from Alexandria. Apollos based his message on words from the prophet, Zechariah, and showed how these words applied to Jesus.

'Rejoice greatly, O daughter of Zion, shout, O daughter of Jerusalem. Behold, thy King cometh unto thee. He is just and having salvation, lowly, riding upon an ass, and upon a colt, the foal of an ass.'[173]

Apollos explained that these words obviously referred to

the Messiah, for he is described as the King of Zion, but unlike the popular misconception of what the Messiah would be like, he came, not on a victorious war-horse, but on the humblest of beasts, a donkey. Apollos then described how this prophecy had been fulfilled in the way one called Jesus had entered Jerusalem. He outlined the work and teaching of Jesus in his life-time, and then quoted from another part of the prophecy of Zechariah.

'And I will pour upon the house of David, and upon the inhabitants of Jerusalem, the Spirit of grace and supplications, and they shall look upon me whom they have pierced, and they shall mourn for him, as one mourneth for his only son, and shall be in bitterness for him, as one that is in bitterness for his firstborn.'[174]

Apollos used this passage to launch into the story of Jesus's passion which followed soon after his trumphal entry into Jerusalem on the donkey. He told the people present at that Synagogue, that this prophecy, alluding to the people of Jerusalem looking on 'me whom they have pierced,' was a prophecy with three strands which were incomprehensible, apart from them being realized in Jesus. All these words applied to Jesus, first because the people of Jerusalem looked on Jesus as he was pierced by a spear while he hung on the cross, secondly, because he was the first born Son of God, and thirdly, because he was divine in his own right, and in a special way, he was one with his Father, God, who had channelled these special words he had to speak to the Jews through his prophet Zechariah, hundreds of years earlier.

Apollos then explained the nature of the salvation that Jesus had brought. He asked Aquila to join him, and invited the congregation to ask any questions that arose from what he had said.

This teaching had been a very different challenge for a congregation whose usual diet of sabbath instruction was an exposition on the Law of Moses. However, they were aware that many Ephesian Jews had been turning from conventional Judaism to follow this Jesus of whom Apollos had just spoken. Paul had not been to that particular synagogue on previous occasions when he had visited Ephesus, and this was their first opportunity to debate this teaching in public. As Apollos and Aquila had anticipated, many were hostile, and some very challenging questions were thrown at Apollos and Aquila. They were more than adequate to cope with these, and everyone present must have been impressed with Apollos' knowledge and understanding of the Jewish faith, for his answers were embedded in Scriptures, familiar to the Jews to whom he spoke, and showed in every case, how they clearly pointed to the Messiahship beging fulfilled in Jesus. Many were influenced, but not immediately prepared to commit themselves, and they invited Apollos, Priscilla and Aquila to return the following day.

That evening they returned to the Church and the mission team shared their experiences of the day. There was a common feeling of exhilaration and excitement among them, and Paul and Silas anticipated a rich harvest from their work. The evening closed with a time of prayer.

When the team reassembled the following day, Paul led them again in prayers. A lesson that Apollos was learning from Paul, was the great emphasis this man of God placed on prayer in everything he undertook. After breakfast, Apollos returned to the Synagogue with Priscilla and Aquila, and although it was not the Jewish sabbath, many had come to continue the debate which Apollos had started the previous day. It was a matter of considerable importance to these Jews of Ephesus that they properly sorted out their faith and discovered the truth. Theirs was no nominal adherence to the religion of their parents, but a faith which affected every aspect of their lives. Apollos and Aquila prevailed in the discussions, but some of the Jews were stubborn, and although lost for further arguments with which to challenge Apollos' assertions, left mumbling that they would consider the matter further before they met Apollos again. Many however were won over by the power of Apollos' eloquence and clarity of thought, and arrangements were made for them to have further instruction from the elders of the Ephesian church.

The mission continued for a month. During that time,

Apollos spoke with considerable success at a number of synagogues in Ephesus. As Paul had suggested at the beginning, the team interchanged roles, giving Apollos a chance to teach new members of the Ephesian Church, and to try his hand at speaking in the market place. John Mark had excelled in open-air preaching when on this mission, and Apollos rejoiced that his new friend had proved himself so valuable a member of the team by doing what Apollos considered to be the most difficult job of all. Paul and Silas followed up the work that Apollos, Priscilla and Aquila had started at the synagogues, by paying further visits themselves and continuing the discussions with those who were the hardest to convince.

After their visits to the synagogues, Priscilla and Aquila used to invite Apollos to the house they occupied near the Church, and they would discuss the events of the day, critically examining the way they had presented the gospel and dealt with the questions. Although a woman, and not able to speak at the gatherings, Priscilla was a shrewd observer of all that transpired. She was very perceptive and had noticed that in his answers to the questions raised, Apollos had said nothing about the Holy Spirit. The second passage Apollos had used from the prophet Zechariah, spoke of the pouring out of the Spirit, and seemed to present an ideal base for letting the Jews at the Ephesian Synagogue know, not only how God was experienced in the person of His Son, Jesus, but also, through the power of His Holy Spirit. Apollos had to admit that he did not know about the Holy Spirit. He had met so many Christians, including some great Christian teachers in recent months, and had come to a firm grasp and understanding of the work and nature of Jesus Christ, but somehow, no one had taught Apollos about the Holy Spirit. This was a gap in Apollos' understanding that Priscilla and Aquila were well able to fill.

Priscilla asked Apollos if he had been baptized, and he described the baptism conducted by Caleb of Jezreel at Beersheba. They explained to Apollos that this was the baptism of John that signified repentance, but that Christian baptism was for the washing away and forgiveness of sins, and was carried out in the name of the three aspects of God, first the Father, who was the creator and controller of the universe, secondly Jesus, the Son, who, besides dying to purchase our forgiveness, showed us in his human form, the perfectly good and loving nature of God, and thirdly, the Holy Spirit of God, who was indeed, God himself, not geographically restricted to work at one place on earth, but the source of strength and power for any who sought to serve him.[175]

They described to Apollos how the first disciples had received this great power on the day of Pentecost, and how it was available now. They explained that this was often conferred by baptism or by the laying on of hands to commission a Christian for some special service. Apollos realized that Paul and Silas had the gift of the Holy Spirit in good measure and this was the source of power which their very presence conveyed. Apollos remembered that Sandascum-Barama had spoken of the Spirit of God when he visited the Hebron Synagogue in Alexandria. The power of the Holy Spirit was clearly a gift that Apollos needed to make his ministry fully effective.

A baptism was arranged for Apollos. The ceremony was conducted by Paul. It took place in the River Cayster which flowed through Ephesus and was attended by the full mission team and many senior members of the Ephesian Church. John Mark and Aquila stood as joint sponsors for Apollos, and after the baptism, Apollos knelt before Paul who laid his hands upon the young man and commissioned him in the name of the Father, Son and Holy Spirit, to proclaim the gospel with authority and power. Apollos sensed a great exhilaration, and spontaneously spoke of the dramatic change he had experienced in his life and outlook since becoming a Christian. Apollos was naturally eloquent, but he now spoke with an assurance and power which had considerable impact on all his hearers. Apollos was conscious of this power at work in him as he spoke at the remaining synagogue meetings which were arranged for this mission. It was not a matter of mere chance that many more were swayed by his words after his baptism and the laying on of hands, than had been at the beginning, when he had relied entirely on his own natural eloquence and quickness of mind to harangue the devout Jews in their synagogues.

Paul accompanied Apollos on one of these visits to the synagogue, and afterwards, he spoke to Apollos of a church that was very close to his heart, the church he had left at Corinth. Paul was about to send a letter to this Church, and he asked Apollos if he would consider visiting Corinth to help that Church[176]. Apollos was flattered by this suggestion and prayed about the matter. Being very new to this sort of missionary work, Apollos felt that he needed a clear answer from God. He told Paul that at that moment in time, he felt no clear direction that this was what God wanted him to do. Apollos was soon to receive a clearer answer to his prayer.

40

The Church of Corinth

The intensive phase of the mission was scheduled to last for a month, and at the end of the month, the team met to review the exercise. The results were encouraging in every phase. Many members of the Ephesian Church who had been lukewarm in their faith, had made very positive commitments, and had undertaken extra responsibilities to make it as easy as possible for those who were totally new to Christianity to be absorbed into the Church. Worshippers of Diana and others who were classified as total pagans, had been influenced by the preaching carried on outdoors and in the Lecture Hall of Tyrannus. A significant number had recognized that Christianity was credible and gave meaning to their lives in a way that the Greek and Roman idolatory could not. A number of Jews from each of the synagogues where Apollos, Priscilla and Aquila had debated the claims of Christ, had been won over and rejoiced in discovering that their ancient faith had at last been fulfilled in the person of Jesus. Paul considered that seeds had been sown in the synagogue which were yet to bear fruit. He knew from his own experience, that a firmly held faith is not lightly discarded and changed for something new. Apollos had shared with Paul this reluctance to recognize that the Jewish faith they so dearly held, had been superceded by a new faith, which although based on the old, was fundamentally different in its teaching. Paul expressed an intention of returning to Ephesus when the seeds that had been sown had, as he put it, germinated.

Now that the mission was over and the euphoria of seeing new converts flooding into the church was an experience behind the team, there was a danger of an anti-climax setting in. Paul was aware of this danger and spoke of follow-up work to be done to consolidate their gains. He and Silas withdrew to pray about the ways in which this follow-up might be conducted.

Paul and Silas spent the rest of the day in prayer and it was not until the following morning that Paul re-assembled the mission team with the elders of the Ephesian Church to work out future plans. Something had obviously upset Paul since the previous day. The team all detected that Paul had some preoccupation which was disturbing his mind, and they wondered what the cause of the trouble might be. They knew from the previous day's meeting that he had been more than satisfied with the outcome of the mission, and as far as the company knew, he had spent the rest of the day praying with Silas. This activity did not usually adversely affect Paul's humour. It was not until the end of the meeting that the source of Paul's concern became apparent.

Paul had only been in Ephesus for a very short time. It was barely two months earlier that he had arrived from Corinth with Priscilla and Aquila. The Ephesian elders therefore pressed Paul to stay with them longer. However, Paul felt moved to return to pay a visit to the churches in Berea, Philippi and Thessalonica[177], and when the Spirit guided Paul in a particular direction, Paul would allow no human agency to divert him from the way he knew that God wanted him to go. Paul suggested that Priscilla, Aquila and Titus should remain at Ephesus to consolidate the gains which had been made during the mission and to counsel the new converts. Timothy and Silas had come to Ephesus via Corinth, but had unfinished business in Mysia where the churches had particular need of their help, and it was obviously right that they should return to the churches around Troas, Mitylene and Assos[178]. Paul had asked John Mark and Luke to accompany him to Macedonia and this they were glad to do.

Then the matter which was worrying Paul came into the open. He had just received a letter from the elders of the Church at Corinth, and it was clear that in the short time he had been away, a number of things were going wrong with the Church and some long term malpractices had suddenly been discovered. Paul was not entirely surprised at the

277

contents of the letter because he knew the Corinthian Church well. He had founded the Church there, and in many ways, the response of the lively minded Corinthians made that Church one of the most exciting in the young Christian world. They were intelligent, they had received spiritual gifts, they were generous, but they were so prone to using their intellectual gifts to distort the Christian message. Paul shared with his special Christian friends some of the things he had learned from the communication he had received that day. The love feasts of that Church were degenerating into meals where some took too much and others were left with nothing to eat[179], there was a suspicion that at least one member of the Church was involved in an incestuous relationship[180], they had few qualms about taking one another to pagan courts when differences arose between them[181], and there were numerous misunderstandings of fundamental doctrines[182].

After hearing Paul's outpourings, Silas suggested that they should pray together for the Church of Corinth. As they prayed, Apollos' mind returned to his earlier conversation with Paul when Paul had suggested that he might go to Corinth. At that time, Apollos had not received a conclusive answer to his prayer, but now, Apollos experienced an irresistable urge to go to Corinth. He would have gone to Corinth with Jerahmeel from Athens, had not the news from Alexandria cut short their tour of Greece, but his urge now was not to go sight-seeing but to serve the Church. Prayers were being made for someone to be found who could put the affairs of that Church in order.

'Lord, here am I,' prayed Apollos, 'send me!'[183]

When they finished praying, Apollos spoke of the urge he had felt to be available to serve the Corinthian Church. Others in that gathering also mentioned that Apollos had come to mind as they prayed for that Church. Paul had had the conviction that Apollos should go to Corinth, even before receiving the letter from the Corinthian Church elders. Apollos had special gifts and understanding of the Christian faith, he was the only one of the mission team whose immediate sphere of work and activity had not been decided on, and he was not known to the Corinthian Church as were most of the others in that team. Sometimes,

278

an authoritative stranger can be more effective in disciplining a wayward church than a teacher who is also a familiar friend.

Further prayers were said for Apollos, and the whole group acknowledged that Apollos was the right choice to go to Corinth. They therefore immediately set about writing a suitable letter of introduction. Aquila penned the letter and addressed it particularly to Titius Justus, Crispus and Sosthenes who were reliable elders of the Corinthian Church. Paul said that he too would write another letter to the Corinthian Church, but this letter would be concerned with the adverse report he had received and would require much thought and prayer. It would be some little while before he would have composed such a letter to his satisfaction.

A few days later, Apollos left for Corinth. Priscilla and Aquila gave him detailed directions of where to find the people and places that mattered, including their own house. This was being used for Church meetings, but had ample room for Apollos to be able to make his home there while in Corinth. Paul, Silas and his fellow workers at the Ephesian Church gathered by the quay as Apollos' ship pulled out, to wish him God-speed on his way. They remained on the quay until the ship was out of sight, and then they too dispersed to do the various types of work to which God was calling them in Ephesus.

On arrival at Corinth, Apollos made his way first of all to the house of Titius Justus, which was the principal building used by the Corinthian Christians for their meetings[184]. He presented his letter of introduction and was warmly welcomed by Titius Justus who took him round to meet Crispus and Sosthenes. Crispus[185] and Sosthenes had formerly been presidents of Jewish synagogues, but were now elders of the Christian Church.

All three of them were composed, phlegmatic people, but a great peace and joy shone through their calm appearance. Unlike Crispus and Sosthenes who had been converted from the Jewish faith, Titius Justus was a Greek who had rejected the idolatory of his nation, knowing that there could be only one true God. He worshipped this unknown God in spirit until Paul had arrived in Corinth to declare to

279

him the nature of this God revealed in Jesus. Crispus and Sosthenes read Aquila's letter of introduction[186] which Titius Justus handed to them and were delighted that someone, specially commended by Paul, had come so promptly to help them deal with the difficulties which had arisen in their churches. Christianity had spread rapidly in Corinth, and the Corinthian Christians met at more than one worship centre.

They gave Apollos a full account of the conditions existing within the Corinthian Church, and in the wider community in the city. They told him that the new Governor of Achaia was a cynical Roman called Gallio who had no religious convictions whatever. He gave the Christian Church no support, but on the other hand, he ridiculed the Jews who had tried to get Gallio to persecute the Christians because they taught doctrines which the Jews considered to be contrary to their Law. Roman Law was the only law that Gallio was concerned with upholding, and religious arguments were of no concern to him whatever. The Jews in Corinth felt particularly threatened because many of their most prominent members, including Crispus and Sosthenes, had become Christians, and taken many fellow Jews with them. The problem for the Jews was aggravated by the fact that Titius Justus's house, which was one of the buildings used for church meetings, was right next to the main Synagogue of Corinth. Thus the Jews had this constant reminder that their faith was being challenged, and that some of their former leaders were worshipping God in the new way, in the building next door.

Sosthenes told Apollos of how the Jews had beaten him up in front of the court, perhaps to impress upon Gallio the intensity of their feelings, or perhaps, to provoke the Christians into some sort of retaliatory reaction which would have forced Gallio to intervene. Crispus added to this by explaining to Apollos that Sosthenes had shown great dignity in publicly proclaiming that he forgave the Jews for this outrage, and the Christians accepted their leader's guidance and restrained themselves from responding to this provocation. Gallio remained indifferent to what he called, mere religious squabbles[187]. Some of the more moderate Jews on the other hand, disgusted by this unwarranted display of violence by the more fanatical members of their faith, and impressed at Sosthenes's dignity of bearing, left the Synagogue and joined the Church. The net result therefore, was that the Jews gained nothing, but on the contrary, saw a further movement of members of this Synagogue into Christianity.

Apollos was aware of the problems within the Church of Corinth from the letter that the three of them had recently sent to Paul, and they gave Apollos more details of the things which appeared to be going wrong. Apollos spent some time in prayer with Titius Justus, Crispus and Sosthenes. They then showed him round the city, and took him to the house of Priscilla and Aquila which was to become his home. The house was as Priscilla and Aquila had described. It had plenty of accommodation, including a particularly large room which was ideally suited for one of the Corinthian Churches to meet for worship[195].

Two days later when the Christians who met at the house of Priscilla and Aquila had gathered for their Sunday worship, Sosthenes introduced Apollos to them. Apollos delivered his first address to the Corinthians and so began his ministry in Corinth. Apollos certainly found ministering to the Corinthian Church, a very challenging experience. The Church members were a much more lively and extrovert fellowship than any of the Christians he had met at the other churches he had visited on his travels. They were also rather full of themselves and the spiritual gifts they claimed to possess. They took to Apollos very well. He was a Greek with a Greek mind, and was more than equal in debate to any who might have sought to challenge his authority. They particularly admired the eloquence with which Apollos could present his well organized thoughts, and recognized that Apollos spoke in the power of the Holy Spirit. Apollos travelled round the half dozen or so churches in Corinth. There were four churches in the centre of the city, and one each at Corinth's two seaports, Lechaeum on the west, and Cenchreae to the east. The churches not only admired the oratory of Apollos, they respected his teaching. Through Apollos' patient teaching and guidance, the love feasts again adopted the decorum fitting for an occasion which had the remembrance of

Jesus's death and passion as its focus. Christians in dispute with one another agreed to have their differences sorted out by a committee of Church elders, rather than washing their dirty linen in public in a pagan court. Apollos clearly showed the Christians how such acrimonious public, legal squabbles brought discredit on the Church. Apollos passionately declared to the Corinthians that the love reciprocated between its members had to be the prominent hallmark by which Christians were recognized as different.

Some of the instances that Apollos had to deal with were almost amusing. One of the poorer Christians used to pray at the prayer meetings, that he might have one of the purple cloaks which were becoming a fashionable item of clothing among the wealthy Corinthians at the time. When he appeared one Sunday, wearing such a cloak, Apollos commented that his prayer appeared to have been answered. The man shamefacedly explained that as God had not actually given him a cloak, he had stolen one and then prayed for forgiveness. Apollos was able to gently correct this man in his misinterpretation of the doctrine of divine forgiveness, and arranged to have the cloak returned to its rightful owner.

Apollos derived great satisfaction from exercising his gifts of oratory and teaching in the Corinthian Church, but he found he was able to give of himself in many other ways. He was frequently called out to visit the sick or comfort a bereaved member of the Church. On some days, there was so much pressure on his time that Apollos scarcely had time to eat or sleep as he made the service of God's people the first priority of his life. Apollos continuously reminded himself that his life was not his own, but had been bought at a great price, and he continually sought to honour the memory of Jerahmeel by living his life in the way he knew Jesus would want him to.

One day, Apollos reflected on his life, and he was amazed as he realized how he had changed from the rather selfish and spoilt, proud and arrogant youth that he had been in Alexandria, to a person who lived for the service he could give others. Apollos now felt a happiness and a peace he had never experienced in his younger days, and he certainly radiated joy as he went about his work with the Corinthian Church.

Six months after Apollos arrived at Corinth, Priscilla and Aquila returned from Ephesus, their work there completed. They were delighted to see all that Apollos had achieved for the Church in so short a time, but were anxious that he was neglecting himself in the time and energy he was devoting to the Corinthian Christians. Life became much easier for Apollos as he was mothered by Priscilla who made sure he ate well and took enough rest.

During the two years that Priscilla and Aquila were with Apollos, the three of them made a missionary excursion to Athens. The Church at Corinth was now fairly straight-forward to manage and Apollos had no qualms about leaving the Church in the capable hands of Titius, Crispus and Sosthenes. Although the intellectual Athenians were pleased to listen to Apollos, Priscilla and Aquila, and to debate the claims they presented, the threesome felt that they achieved very little in Athens and returned to Corinth with a sense of some disappointment. They had won arguments and prevailed in discussions they had entered into with the keenest minds in Athens, but somehow, the Athenians had not taken the gospel to their hearts. They seemed to be merely interested in philosophizing, and they did not seem to recognize that Christianity was not just another philosophy, but that Jesus was one who had first claim on their lives.

A year later, Apollos was invited to join Titus who was working in Crete. Although the Cretans were uncouth[188] in comparison to the cultured Athenians, the mission that Apollos shared with Titus on this island was most fruitful. When the time came for Apollos to return to Corinth[189], Titus and Apollos contemplated with some satisfaction the three flourishing churches they had planted in Crete. During their mission, they had been encouraged by a letter they received from Paul.

After four years, Paul himself returned to Corinth and was delighted, as Aquila and Priscilla had been, at the way Apollos was fulfilling his mission. At that time, Peter, of whom Apollos had heard so much, came to Corinth, and for a few months, Apollos, Paul and Peter used to meet regularly at one of the churches in Corinth to share experiences, and review the way the Church was faring. A

283

very special bond grew between them, because each of them shared memories of the very unsatisfactory people they had been before they had received the forgiveness which had purchased their lives, and had then been commissioned to serve Jesus in a special way. Apollos remembered the arrogant, promiscuous youth he had been, whose wayward pride had been responsible for his best friend meeting a violent death. Peter carried memories of how he had denied knowing Jesus at the time when Jesus' need of friends was greatest[190]. Paul had perhaps the hardest memories to bear, for he had deliberately persecuted Christians to death in his fanatic attempt to resist the challenge Christianity posed to his orthodox Jewish faith[191]. However, all three had the peace of knowing that the price of these sins had been paid.

On Sundays, Apollos, Peter and Paul used to preach at different churches in Corinth. In the history of the world, no city could have had three such preachers, operating simultaneously within its boundaries. Of these three, who could perhaps be regarded as the three greatest preachers the world has known after Jesus, Apollos with his natural eloquence was the greatest orator. Peter and Paul had other unique and special gifts, but even they were not able to expound Scripture as could Apollos. Sadly, this surfeit of excellent preaching caused another aberration to manifest itself in the Corinthian Church. A partisan spirit of rivalry began to grow up. The Christians who worshipped where Apollos taught, claimed some superiority because they followed Apollos, the greatest preacher, while similar claims of superiority were made by those who attended the Church led by Peter, because he was Jesus's foremost disciple. Those at Paul's Church based their claims to be the greatest, on the grounds that they were led by the one who was undoubtedly the most outstanding founder of new churches. Paul was certainly the most effective Christian missionary working at the time.

Apollos, Peter and Paul raised this matter of concern at one of their meetings. This partisan spirit which had grown up around their names and reputations, caused them both concern and sadness, for it indicated they were failing in the important matter of proclaiming Jesus Christ as the only name that mattered. Apollos, Peter and Paul regarded themselves as no more than worthless vessels who had the great privilege of conveying in the power of the Holy Spirit, the message which led to new life in this world, and an assurance of eternal life in the next. This matter again made Apollos aware of how much he had changed since becoming a Christian, for in his youth, he would have gloried in being acknowledged as the head of a faction.[192]

They decided that on the following Sunday, they would each read a joint communique, deploring this party spirit which was growing in the Corinthian Church, and insisting that the only person that Christians should claim to follow was Jesus Christ.

Wayward as the Corinthian Church was in so many ways, their hearts were in the right place. Their intentions were good and they paid heed to what they were taught by their acknowledged spiritual leaders. Nothing could have been more compelling than a joint communique from Apollos, Peter and Paul, expressing sadness at the attitudes which were developing in the churches. As a consequence of receiving this communique, the churches decided that they would mix up the congregations, so that the same Christians did not become exclusively associated with one worship centre, with the ensuing temptations to rivalry and one-upmanship which had reached unhealthy proportions. Apollos, Peter and Paul were relieved at the way this problem resolved itself in answer to their prayers. As this source of church division receded to be remembered as just one of the growing pains the church had overcome, Apollos, Peter and Paul had the pleasure of seeing the Corinthian Church experience real growth in numbers, in spiritual strength, and in the great love the members bore to one another.

After a few months, Peter and Paul felt called to leave the Corinthian Church, which was obviously in good hands, to continue on their missionary travels. Peter left first to go to Rome where the Christian Church was still growing, despite Claudius Caesar's attempt to expel the Christians, but it was experiencing a hard time and was in need of apostolic support. Shortly afterwards, Paul left for Macedonia whence he intended to retrace his missionary journeys as he returned to Jerusalem[193]. Both Peter and Paul warmly commended Apollos for the work he was doing for the Church they both loved so well before each departed on their separate ways from Corinth.

41

A Journey from Ephesus to Corinth

Diana was a person with a very positive frame of mind. She had made a good decision in coming to Ephesus, for her uncle, Diomedes, and her aunt, Calliope, were among the kindest of people. They had no children of their own, and although elderly, they were glad for Diana to come and share their home, after the ordeal she had experienced at Alexandria. They were naturally distressed at the news of the violent deaths of Parmenion and Camporina. They had fond memories of Alexandria as such a peaceful place, and found it hard to believe that this city could degenerate into violence.

Diana was able to put the thoughts of the tragic death of her parents out of her mind as she was taken up with caring for Selenece. Selenece was a lovely child, and motherhood fulfilled for Diana, all that Parmenion had told her when she first confided her pregnancy to her parents. Diomedes and Calliope were fascinated with the child, and the company of Diana and Selenece brought a brightness to the evening of their lives.

Anaxagoras found suitable accommodation near by. Because of his great strength, Anaxagoras had no difficulty in finding work in the docks of Ephesus. It was a busy port, and the services of Anaxagoras were much sought after by the masters of the larger vessels who often had bulky cargoes to unload. Because of his good humour, Anaxagoras soon became very popular with the other dock workers. In spite of his clumsiness, Anaxagoras had considerable manual skills, and these were often put to good effect in helping his friends.

Anaxagoras had a great regard for Diana, and gave

287

generously from the money he earned at the docks to ensure that neither she and Selenece, nor the aunt and uncle who had allowed her to share their home, lacked for anything they needed. One might have wondered whether there was any romantic attachment between Anaxagoras and Diana, but Anaxagoras was aware of his clumsiness and under-rated his attractions. He had the qualities of loyalty, kindness, generosity and considerateness which were worth far more than the superficial charm, the pose, the dash of the young Greeks in that society who were considered to be very attractive. However, Anaxagoras was some fifteen years older than Diana. He set her on a pedestal as someone indescribably cleverer and more beautiful than himself, and his joy was derived entirely from being of help and service to Diana.

Anaxagoras and Diana soon settled at the Church of Ephesus. Diomedes and Calliope were nominal adherents to the cult of Diana, as were most Greeks living in Ephesus. However, Diana was not seriously regarded as a deity by them, and Anaxagoras and Diana persuaded them to come to the Ephesian Church with them. Diomedes and Calliope both accepted the Christian faith and were baptized. This faith gave an added meaning to their remaining years, and they counted this as a great blessing which had come through Diana staying with them.

During the mission that Paul's team conducted at Ephesus, it was rather surprising that neither Anaxagoras nor Diana ever met with Apollos or John Mark. There was more than one building in Ephesus where the Church met, and on occasions when John Mark or Apollos were speaking at one of these buildings, Diana and Anaxagoras were at another. Over the two months of the mission, Apollos did not often speak in the Church buildings, as his work was concerned mainly with the synagogues, and as Selenece was still very young, Diana did not often take her into the busy thoroughfares of Ephesus, where she might have seen John Mark preaching. Had anyone been wanting them to meet, it would have been tantalizing to see one or other of the four go out of view into a shop or down a side street, just as another of the four passed by. Just a glimpse could have initiated the meetings which would have led to a reunion of four people for whom Alexandria provided a special link. Who knows what may have come from Apollos meeting up again with Diana? However, no one in Ephesus was aware of this special connection. No one was praying for a meeting to take place.

On one occasion when Diana had remained at home to look after Selenece, and Anaxagoras was attending a meeting at another Church building at Ephesus, Diomedes and Calliope returned with glowing accounts of the address which had been given by a learned Jewish rabbi from Alexandria called Apollos. However, Apollos was a common enough name, and Diana never imagined there could be any connection with the Apollos she knew. Diana regarded the Apollos she remembered as a Greek, and an Apollos described as a learned Jewish rabbi sounded like someone totally different from the Apollos with whom she had shared a fleeting moment of love.

Anaxagoras and Diana did hear both Paul and Silas preach during the mission, and their words left a lasting impression on them. The messages proclaimed by Paul and Silas led to them both renewing the faith which had helped them cope with the tragic events in Alexandria and the upheaval that had caused in both their lives.

The intensive phase of the mission ended. Apollos left for Corinth. John Mark departed a short while later with Paul and with Luke who was able to draw on John Mark's knowledge as he prepared to write a parallel gospel. Anaxagoras and Diana remained oblivious to the fact that special contacts from Alexandria had been in their city, and had even preached in their churches.

The next few years passed happily for this new family grouping. Diana had the delight of seeing Selenece develop and grow into a most lovely child. Diomedes and Calliope were spared the loneliness that can sometimes overtake an old couple with no immediate family. Diana and Selenece extended the lives of Diomedes and Calliope in one dimension, while their new faith and the contacts this brought with other Christians, including some of their own age, brought yet another dimension to their lives. Anaxagoras's joy arose largely out of his knowledge that he was able to provide for all the financial needs of Diana as she brought up Selenece while she was sharing her uncle and aunt's home.

The Church at Ephesus continued to flourish. After a couple of years, Paul returned to Ephesus where he was able to reap the harvest which had been sown in the synagogues by the words of Apollos and Aquila during the earlier mission. Many Jews who had wavered on that occasion had had sufficient time to weigh up in their minds the claims of Jesus, and a large number responded to Paul's preaching and became Christians. During his time at Ephesus, Paul performed a number of miracles which added to his credibility and helped convince some of the pagans that here was a genuine man of a genuine God. Thus, Paul's preaching was successful among the Greeks as well, and many left the Diana cult to join the Church. This caused serious alarm among those who made and sold statues of the goddess and saw their trade diminish. Demetrius, leader of the silversmiths guild, led a riot against Paul, supported by many who considered their livelihood threatened, but the riot was calmed by the chief Roman official of the city before any serious damage was done.[137]

Paul left Ephesus soon after the riots, but not without saying some parting words of encouragement to the Ephesian Church. From Ephesus, Paul travelled via Troas to Macedonia, and then down to Achaia where he shared a ministry with Apollos and Peter in the Corinthian Church of which we have written[193].

For a while Timothy returned to Ephesus to lead the Church. Timothy was only there for a few months before returning to Macedonia, but during those months, the Church at Ephesus really consolidated all the gains which had been made during Paul's missionary enterprises.

Then a rather special leader moved into Ephesus to look after the affairs of this Church, and to give some supervision to the six other flourishing churches in the cities near Ephesus. This was none other than John who was reputed to be the most loved of all Jesus's special disciples. John was accompanied by Jesus's mother, Mary, who was now quite old and beginning to go blind. However, her mind was perfectly clear, and she was able to give the Ephesians a number of special insights into Jesus's life when he was a young man living at home. Diana felt privileged to have met this very special lady.

When Selenece was about five years old, a combination of events caused another upheaval in the lives of Diana and those close to her. Diomedes died. He was already elderly, and caught a cough from which he never recovered. His final illness was not a long drawn out affair and he passed away peacefully. The special contentment which had come upon him from the time that Diana arrived at his home, never left him. John, the new leader of the Ephesian Church, had ministered to Diomedes during the last days of his life, and had come to respect the old man. He spoke warmly of Diomedes as the Church gathered to pay their last respects to this kindly and gentle man. This was not a sad but a triumphant occasion.

A financial problem then began to arise for the family as a result of a geographical phenomenon. The mouth of the Cayster river started to silt up, and the harbour, which had made Ephesus a popular sea-port, became no longer usable for the larger ships on which Anaxagoras relied for the majority of his work. Anaxagoras, Diana and Calliope took stock of their situation. Calliope had relatives in Greece, cousins who lived in Athens and Thebes, and a widowed sister who lived at Cenchreae, the westerly sea-port of Corinth. (This sister was no relation of Diana. Diomedes had been Parmenion's brother.) Calliope knew that they could stay with her sister, and as Cenchreae was a particularly busy sea-port, Anaxagoras would find no difficulty in getting work there. Calliope wrote to her sister and received a positive reply within two months.

So it was, Calliope sold up her home, and Anaxagoras arranged a passage for Calliope, Diana, Selenece and himself on a small vessel bound for Piraeus, Athens's sea-port. They found the home of Calliope's cousin where they stayed for nearly a week. Cenchreae was barely eighty kilometres west of Athens, and connected by a good road along the Isthmus. They decided that if they bought a couple of mules and broke the journey half-way at Eleusis, they could complete the journey in a couple of days. They bought two mules in Athens and set out. Calliope rode one mule while Selenece rode with her mother on the other. Anaxagoras led the party on foot. They made Eleusis without incident and stayed overnight there at an inn. The following day they started the second lap of their journey. There was plenty of traffic on the Athens-Corinth highway and with so many travellers in sight, they felt quite safe. By late afternoon, the Acropolis of Corinth could just be seen. The road had reached a point where it passed quite close to the sea-shore, and it was suggested that the journey could be continued along the beach.

They made their way by the shore, expecting that there would be another point nearer Cenchreae where the road was again accessible so that they could complete the remaining few kilometres on the highway. A pleasant breeze was blowing in from the sea, and Selenece delighted in watching the waves gently breaking on the beach. The business of the road soon became remote and the foursome were beginning to enjoy the tranquillity and peace of what seemed to be an isolated stretch of shoreline.

Suddenly, they heard a shout and an arrow landed just ahead of them. They turned to see four men coming at them. The men were about a hundred metres away, down the beach. Three were running and one was on horse back. The arrow clearly indicated that these were hostile, and Anaxagoras ordered the women to ride on ahead as fast as they could and make for the main road. They set off but were inexperienced riders and moved at no more than a trot. Anaxagoras, his staff firmly gripped in his hand, turned to face the approaching brigands. The horseman, who was also the archer, was ahead of the others and he made to pass a few yards to the seaward side of Anaxagoras to cut off the women. They were only making slow progress on mules, unaccustomed to being required to move at speed.

Anaxagoras picked up a rock and hurled it with tremendous force at the rider. His aim was good and he struck the rider on the head. He fell stunned from his horse. By this time, the other freebooters were on Anaxagoras. The first one slashed at Anaxagoras's head with his sword. Anaxagoras ducked the sword blow and brought up his stout staff to strike his assailant a tremendous blow on the

292

side of his head which probably cracked his skull. Before the next man could even raise his sword, he received a blow across the shoulders from Anaxagoras's staff which was swiftly struck as if it had immediately rebounded from the head of the first man. The second man reeled and fell at this blow. Anaxagoras's reflexes were quick enough to raise his staff to parry the sword of the third man whom he had seen just in time, coming at him from the side. The sword embedded itself deeply into the staff and the man who wielded it could not immediately withdraw it to strike another blow. Anaxagoras brought his fist crashing into the man's face with mighty force. As he fell, the second assailant struggled to his feet, but Anaxagoras despatched him with another blow from his trusty staff, before the man had properly regained his balance. The third man was lying unconscious, but Anaxagoras struck him another hefty blow for good measure.

The immediate danger apparently past, Anaxagoras looked down the beach and saw with some relief, the two mules, struggling up a slope where the women had obviously seen a point at which they could regain the road. This lapse of concentration from the fight in hand proved fatal. The horseman who had been earlier felled from his mount by Anaxagoras's well aimed rock, had recovered his bow and loosed a bolt aimed at Anaxagoras. The arrow entered his neck, killing Anaxagoras instantly. So passed Anaxagoras, a man loved by those who knew him much more than he realized. The giving of service and pleasure to others had been the main motivating force of his life, and he had spent his last breath in the way he would have most wanted to, in saving those he loved dearest in this world.

Having made the highway, Calliope and Diana with Selenece mounted in front of her, made for the city as fast as they could. They were not accustomed to riding, but they had not far to go. They made the outskirts of Cenchreae twenty minutes later. They immediately reported the incident to the authorities, not knowing at that time what had befallen Anaxagoras, but fearing the worst. They were told that there had been a number of attacks on travellers in that area over the past year but the robbers had never been found. The Isthmus was too narrow to afford a hiding place for a band of thieves, and the theory was, that they operated from the sea, escaping by a boat, which must have been large enough to take a horse, each time they committed a robbery. A party of soldiers was sent to investigate and returned somewhile later, bearing three bodies which they had discovered on the beach. Diana identified Anaxagoras.

They found the home of Calliope's sister, Euphrosyne, who had been expecting them since she extended the invitation to her sister on hearing of the death of Diomedes. Euphrosyne was a wealthy woman with a lovely home, but had suffered loneliness since she had been widowed some five years earlier, and was looking forward to the arrival of her sister and two generations of nieces to provide her with company. It was a very sad party who made their way into that home. They recounted their experience on the last phase of their journey to Cenchreae, and Euphrosyne realized that their sadness was borne of more than the passing of Diomedes. Euphrosyne was a warm hearted person and did her best to comfort Calliope and Diana. Selenece was too young to understand what had happened and was merely told that her uncle had had an accident.

They made contact with the Church at Cenchrea and Fortunatus[194], the elder of that satellite of the Corinthian Church, made arrangements for the funeral of Anaxagoras. Although he was unknown to the Church at Cenchrea, several of the Church members came to support Diana and Calliope at the funeral. Fortunatus gave a most uplifting valedictory address, based on all that Diana had told Fortunatas of Anaxagoras. All who stood by the graveside were in no doubt that they laid to rest a hero, whose only obvious fault was genuine and excessive modesty.

42

Selenece is Lost and Found

As the days passed, the intense sadness that Diana and Calliope had felt at Anaxagoras's death which had come about to ensure their safety, mollified into a softer grief. The memories of this strong but gentle man were sweet. No one had anything they could hold against Anaxagoras and the world was poorer at his passing. Diana and Calliope soon became acclimatized to the comfort of Euphrosyne's ample home. Euphrosyne took almost as much pleasure and pride in Selenece as did Calliope. Fortunatus, the elder of the Church of Cenchreae, paid several visits to the home, and Diana and Calliope soon became absorbed into the warm fellowship of that Church.

When they had been at Cenchreae for a few months, they decided that they would pay a visit to Corinth itself, to buy some clothes and to visit the Acropolis. By a strange juxtaposition of names, Diana was specially interested to see the great Temple of Apollo, the principal place of Greek worship in Corinth, just as Apollos had shown great interest in visiting the Temple of Diana while in Ephesus. The rush of the bustling city had left Calliope feeling weary, and she decided that she could not face the steep climb to the Acropolis. Calliope was therefore left looking after Selenece, while Euphrosyne conducted Diana to see the sights for which Corinth was famous.

There was plenty going on to keep Selenece amused. A group of entertainers passed by with acrobats and puppets. Those with children crowded round to see the tumblers and puppetry. Calliope had to hold Selenece aloft for the child to get a view but her old arms could not hold the child for long. She therefore arranged for the child to stand at the front with the other small children where she could see the antics while Calliope waited in the crowd behind. Everything was so fast moving. After a while the puppet operators started to move in one direction and the acrobats in another. Calliope was not good at negotiating crowds. She suddenly realized that she did not know where Selenece was. Which group had she followed? Calliope went after the puppeteers. Selenece was nowhere to be seen. Calliope frantically ran in the other direction to see if the child was following the acrobats, but where had they gone? Calliope was not used to the bustle of Corinth and soon realized her search was hopeless. She asked passers-by if they had seen a small child, but all to no avail. In some distress, Calliope made her tearful way to the point where she had arranged to rendezvous with Diana and Euphrosyne. What would she say to Diana?

Apollos was conducting some visitors who were staying in Corinth around the city. They had recently left Rome to escape persecutions which were continually harrying Christians in that city, and relishing the freedom which Christians experienced in Greece. They stopped as a group of acrobats passed by, enjoying the laughter of the children who were excitedly following their antics. The acrobats moved on, followed by the children whose parents were in attendance close behind. One little girl stumbled and fell in the rush. She looked up, initially shocked, and then her face puckered as she burst into tears. Apollos rushed forward to pick up the child lest she should be trampled by the crowd. He held the sobbing child in his arms. He scanned the crowd for her parents but no one came forward to claim the child. He looked back at the little girl. There was a muddy mark on her tunic where she had fallen, but otherwise, the immaculate garment made of the finest of cloths, spoke volumes for the love and care that had been bestowed on that child. Apollos felt a great affection for this distressed child who nestled into his arms. Where were her parents? As he looked again at the child, he noticed the fish symbol embroidered into the collar of her tunic. This was obviously a Christian's child.

Apollos realized that the parents of this girl could be located by sending messages round the network of Corinthian churches, and he made his way back to the home of Priscilla and Aquila with the visitors from Rome. The child had now stopped crying but said she wanted her Mummy and her Granny. She could not give their names but told Apollos that her name was Selenece. Apollos pacified the child by telling her that someone had gone to find them. As soon as he arrived at the house, Apollos arranged for messages to be sent around the churches concerning this child, and then set about washing her grazed knees. A visitor from Rome who had not been with Apollos in town that morning, came into the room where a calmer Selenece was talking in her charmingly childish way to Apollos. Seeing the remarkable facial similarity between Apollos and the child, the visitor from Rome remarked to Apollos that he had not realized that he had a daughter. Apollos sadly shook his head and assured the visitor that this child was not his, for he was not married and had no children.

It took only two hours for the news to reach Diana that Selenece had been found and was being looked after in the Church building in the middle of Corinth. Fortunately, a member of the Cenchreae Church called Phoebe[196] was in Corinth as messages were being conveyed between the churches, and immediately recognized the name Selenece as the name of the child of Diana who had recently joined their Church from Ephesus. Phoebe had met Diana, Calliope and Euphrosyne earlier that morning and knew of their plans to visit the Acropolis. She found the three anxious women, soon after Calliope had met Diana at the rendezvous near the Acropolis to break the worrying news. Phoebe brought good tidings, and conducted Diana and her aunts to the home of Priscilla and Aquila.

As Diana came into the room where Apollos was waiting with the visitors from Rome who were doing their best to keep Selenece amused, her strained face relaxed into the most wonderful smile as she discovered her precious Selenece, safe and well. Apollos recognized Diana immediately, and was quite taken back at her remarkable beauty. In recent years, Diana had experienced hardships and great sadnesses, but she had conquered these without any bitterness entering her mind. Her beauty was not that of a young girl, but the loveliness of a mature woman which radiated the inner beauty of character and personality within Diana. This was not a beauty which would fade with time, but the sort of beauty which grows as the inner woman enriches it with the warmth and love such women have to share with the world. For Apollos, it was as if the summer shone with a thousand suns, and every bird combined to herald the dawning of earth's brightest day. He stood spellbound, scarcely able to assess the implication of what he saw.

After cuddling for a while her precious daughter who had been lost and found, as if to make sure that this was really Selenece and not some illusion to be snatched from her, Diana at last felt able to take her attention from the child and survey the assembled company. Her eyes came to rest upon Apollos, and her recognition too, was instant. Apollos and Diana regarded each other for a full ten seconds, both stunned by this unexpected meeting in unexpected circumstances, neither being able to speak, until at last, Apollos asked Diana if she would come into the Church meeting room with him where they could give thanks. They had more to give thanks for than Diana's reunion with her lost child, which was all that the onlookers thought that Apollos had meant by his invitation.

When alone with each other and Selenece, they had so much to share of their experiences since they had parted some six years earlier when Apollos had set out on his trip with Jerahmeel. Yes, Selenece was his child! There were some great similarities in what had befallen both Apollos and Diana since that parting. They had both lost their loving parents in the Alexandrian riots. They had both become Christians. They had both been saved from a terrible fate by a devoted friend giving his life on their behalf. Apollos told Diana what had happened to Jerahmeel and Diana recounted the way Anaxagoras had recently met his death. They had independently made common friends since their parting, and they spoke of John Mark and Barnabas whom they had both first met at the Alexandrian Church at different times but in similar circumstances. They must have spoken for over an hour, and still they had not shared all their news.

The next day they met again, and the next. Their waking

hours were filled with a certain euphoria, and sweet dreams accompanied their sleeping hours at night. Their conversation soon turned to marriage. Apollos had doubts that Diana who had been shamefully and irresponsibly deserted by him to face the social isolation of bringing a child into the world alone, could now trust him with her future happiness. Diana firmly believed that Apollos could not have had the slightest notion of her condition as he departed with Jerahmeel, for neither had she, on the day he had left Alexandria. Apollos had all the physical attractiveness that he had six years ago, and more besides. He had grown in maturity and had special magnetism and power in his bearing. He was loved by the members of the Church which he had done so much to build up. He had also lost some things too, the arrogance and selfishness which Diana had observed six years ago, not as congenital defects, but the result of being over-indulged by doting parents. Diana had speculated then as to whether these traits might be erased from the young Apollos when he lived in different circumstances. Her speculation was now confirmed. Apollos was indeed a new person, but still the old Apollos who had been her secret love. His good qualities had been enhanced, his poor qualities eradicated, and new qualities had grown in him. He was considerate, gentle, and yes, even humble, but he had so much to be proud of, things to be proud of that mattered far more than his youthful wit and charm. He had depth and stability. He was acknowledged to be the greatest preacher and teacher to be found in any of the young churches which were growing up at that time. This was a specially remarkable distinction, because the Church was not short of really prodigious preachers in that first generation of Christianity, when the Church had exploded with missionary zeal from its cradle in Judaea. Would such an eminent man really want to marry her? But of course he did.

Apollos and Diana were married at the Church in the centre of Corinth. Titius Justus conducted the ceremony. Such an event was an occasion of undiluted joy for the Corinthian Greeks who certainly knew how to enjoy life. Selenece too realized that something was happening which made her mother extremely happy, and that she herself would now have a very special father to replace the beloved uncle who had had that accident. Strangely, no one questioned why Apollos should so readily accept Selenece as his daughter, but no, this was not strange, for in the world outside the Church, the moral standards of the Corinthian Greeks who clung to their pagan Gods, was a backcloth against which a Christian marriage which subscribed to the very finest ideals of man and woman relationship, was like a brightly shining star in a dark sky. A child embraced by parents in that special relationship, only cemented it and made it more wonderful, more precious. The actual time at which the child arrived was for those Greeks, merely an insignificant matter of chronology.

43

A Visit from Timothy

The next years were truly happy ones for Apollos and Diana. They bought a house of their own, not too far from the large house of Aquila and Priscilla which functioned as the Church building for that part of Corinth. Living away from the Church building afforded Apollos and Diana the privacy to develop their family life without in any way detracting from Apollos' ministry among the Corinthians. Marriage in fact, considerably helped Apollos in his ministry, as Apollos and Diana developed what was very much a shared ministry. Aquila and Priscilla had provided a model of an effective shared ministry, but whereas Aquila and Priscilla were called to itinerant work, visiting new churches in Greece, Italy and Asia Minor, and planting churches in towns where a sufficient number of the population were receptive to the gospel, the ministry of Apollos and Diana for some years was anchored in Corinth. Apollos and Diana really got to know the established members of the Churches in Corinth in depth, and had the challenge of ministering to ever growing congregations. Many Greeks joined the brotherhood as they recognized the futility of idolatory and saw the attractive love and joy exhibited by the adherents to this new religion.

Apollos found that being married gave him greater confidence in his ministry among married couples. His teaching also had a powerful influence on the single people of Corinth. The licentiousness of his own youth enabled Apollos to speak with special authority of a better way of life to the promiscuous young Greeks of that society, who had been reluctant to turn their back on what they had found a pleasurable but unsatisfying existence. They could identify with Apollos as a Greek who had lived his young life as they themselves were living. His testimony was therefore effective in convincing many young Greeks of the deeper joy and satisfaction which came from living a disciplined life of service to others and commitment to one spouse, rather than a dissolute life of self-seeking pleasure.

The conventions of the times did not allow Diana to speak publicly at Church meetings, but the experiences of grief she had come through in life gave her a special ministry, not just among the women, but among many who had experienced bereavement.

Selenece was a source of great joy to both her parents. She was very much her mother's daughter, manifesting all the qualities of gentleness, compassion and enthusiasm which had radiated from her mother from a very young age. The settled life at Corinth enabled Selenece to experience the stability and security which can contribute so much to a young person's emotional development in their formative years. As well as what might be described as the religious ministry of Apollos and Diana, they started a little school for Church members. By and large, the Greek children were bright, but Selenece shone, even among this peer group. By the time she was ten, it was clear too, that Selenece was going to be a great beauty.

In the evenings, when they had time alone together, Apollos and Diana often used to wonder at what they had done to deserve such a blissful existence, where every need, spiritual, material and emotional, seemed to be satisfied. They speculated on why it was, they had never met when they were both in Ephesus, where some strange fate had seemed to prevent their paths from crossing. Apollos called to mind the prophecies which had been made by the daughters of Philip in Caesaraea, and realised that he was experiencing their fulfilment. Anna had prepared him for the sadness he was to suffer on his return to Alexandria where he had learned of the violent death of his parents. Miriam had spoke of the effectiveness of his ministry among others to whom he would communicate his faith. Deborah had been specific that his would be a preaching ministry which would start in Alexandria, but would continue in Greece. This was exactly what was happening now. Deborah had added that the most joyful event of Apollos' life would occur in Greece, and surely, this could be none other than his meeting up with Diana again and marrying this treasure among women. It was almost as if this prophesy had constrained them not to meet in Ephesus, for Deborah had identified Greece as the land where this joyful event was to occur.

Then there was Abigail's prophecy which had so far, been only partially fulfilled, for Apollos had met in Simon of Cyrene and Barabbas, only two eyewitnesses of the crucifixion. Diana too, had met in Ephesus, Jesus' mother, Mary, and the beloved apostle, John, who had stood at the foot of the cross on that fateful day, but no opportunity arose when it would have seemed right for Apollos and Diana to leave their work in Corinth and return to Ephesus where Apollos could meet Mary and John.

The worst crisis that Apollos and Diana had to contend with during the time they were in Corinth was a severe food shortage which occured about five years after their marriage. This was not a local catastrophe. Harvests had failed throughout the empire and bread was in very short supply. Apollos realized that this was the fulfilment of another prophecy, that which Agabus had made many years earlier at Antioch[119]. The Christian community came through this famine rather better than most. This was partly due to the readiness of the Christians to pool whatever food they had and no one was greedy in claiming more than their fair share of provisions. In a miraculous way, the pool of Christian food always seemed to be sufficient for the needs of the community, while individual hoards were soon exhausted.

During the years that Apollos was presiding elder at the Church of Corinth, the Church was stimulated by frequent visits by Christian missionaries who kept the Corinthians up to date with developments of the Church in other lands within the empire. Aquila and Priscilla regarded Corinth as their mother Church and were the most frequent visitors. The Corinthian Church supported them generously with their prayers and giving. Sometimes, Aquila and Priscilla brought exciting news of a new church being started or an established church experiencing sudden growth, and at other times, they reported the great fortitude with which Christians were holding out in cities where they faced open persecution. Of these, the church in Rome seemed to be in most need of support and prayer, for inspite of the edict of Claudius Caesar, expelling Christians, the church had continued to grow, but it was forced to carry out clandestine worship in the catacombs, the caves beneath the city where the dead were buried. Here, the Christians were free from molestation from the superstitious Romans who feared to enter the chambers where their ancestors lay at rest.

The Corinthian Church was also visited on separate occasions by Timothy, Titus, Luke and John Mark. Apollos was able to introduce Timothy, Titus and Luke to Diana as fellow workers in his missionary days in Ephesus. John Mark needed no introduction to Diana, for they had already met at Alexandria. John Mark was both surprised and delighted that two Christian friends whom he had met in Alexandria, and between whom he was aware of no connection, should have come to be married in Corinth. Luke brought with him a specially welcome gift. It was a copy of his own gospel, his autobiography of Jesus. Several copies of John Mark's gospel had been made for use at the Corinthian Church, and Apollos arranged for Luke's work to be made similarly available. It was a wonderful and scholarly account. As Apollos read it through, he could see that Luke had made much use of the facts in John Mark's biography, but had done considerable research to add important additional material. He had met Mary, Jesus' mother, when he was passing through Ephesus, and she had provided Luke with information concerning the birth and early childhood of Jesus. Luke reported that he was in the middle of writing another book which described the way the good new of Jesus was being spread and the exciting story of the growth of the early church. As someone directly involved in this adventure, Luke could write much of this from first hand experience.

Then one day, a missionary friend visited Corinth and brought news that set up a train of events which was to have a considerable impact on the settled life-style of Apollos and Diana. Timothy arrived at Corinth from Troas. On reaching Corinth, he followed his usual custom of calling first on the home of Apollos and Diana. They always had a warm welcome for him, and there was something particularly soothing and relaxing about the atmosphere of domestic bliss generated in that household. Timothy had never enjoyed particularly good health[197], and Apollos and Diana were disturbed to see how tired and drawn he looked. They sent Selenece to warm some milk and prepare some hot food for Timothy while they anxiously sat with him to hear his news. Timothy sat for some moments, breathing heavily before he felt adequately composed to start talking. He had nothing but good news to bring of the churches he had recently visited in Asia Minor, but the main burden of his message concerned Paul.

Timothy told them that some years earlier, against the advice of the prophet, Agabus[198], Paul had returned to Jerusalem and his presence had caused a disturbance among the orthodox Jews who feared the impact of Paul's ministry. Agabus' forebodings were fulfilled and Paul was arrested[199]. Indeed, it seemed that as he journeyed back to Jerusalem, Paul was independently aware that he would be arrested. He had had this premonition, long before Agabus had made his prophecy at the house of Philip in Caesaraea[200], where Paul and his friends stayed for a few days as they broke their fateful journey to Jerusalem. Timothy explained that Paul's arrest by the Roman authorities was the best thing that could have happened to Paul in the circumstances for he would otherwise have been lynched by the Jewish mob. Even when he was in Roman custody, Paul was in danger, because a Jewish assassination squad had sworn to kill Paul[201]. Paul's nephew had found out about this plot and warned the Roman commander responsible for Paul's safe custody. This Roman had discovered that Paul was a Roman citizen, an honour which the commander respected greatly, as he himself had purchased Roman citizenship at great expense[202]. He therefore took great care of Paul, and arranged for him to be secretly transferred to Caesaraea before any harm befell him[203].

Timothy explained that Paul had the support of a number of trusted Christian friends, including Luke whom

Apollos and Diana knew well. It was from Luke, that Timothy had learned of all that had befallen Paul. The friends who had access to Paul, were able to travel with Paul who, as a Roman citizen, was treated as a privileged and even, respected prisoner. He had done nothing to offend the Romans, and the Romans were no great friends of his Jewish accusers. Timothy told Apollos and Diana that Paul was far from dismayed at his imprisonment which he saw as a fulfilment of prophecy. Paul had told Luke that while in prison, he had a vision of Jesus who had encouraged Paul by telling him that this was to be the means by which his powerful testimony to the truth of the gospel, would be transferred from Jerusalem to Rome itself![204]

Timothy told Apollos and Diana that there was some delay in this coming about. The Roman Governor, Marcus Felix, mistakenly expected that he would be bribed by the Christians to release Paul,[205] whom he must have realized, was innocent of any serious crime. When the bribe did not materialize, Marcus Felix left Paul in prison, knowing that this would curry favour with the Jews.[206] Because of his privileged status as a Roman citizen, Paul was allowed frequent visits from his friends, and Paul made sure that his time in Caesaraea was quite productive.[207] He wrote letters of encouragement to the churches and influenced a number of important officials in the Governor's household.

Timothy was now approaching the crux of his account and started to speak with greater intensity.

'A crisis point came after two years,' continued Timothy, 'when Felix completed his term as governor and was succeeded by Porcius Festus. Festus wanted to commence his period of office in a way which would commend himself to the Jewish people who were known to be notoriously difficult to govern. He suggested sending Paul back to Jerusalem, knowing that this would be a popular move among the Jews. Paul knew his destiny lay in Rome, and he used his prerogative as a Roman citizen to appeal to Caesar.[208]

'Festus did not really understand the charges Paul was facing and he had no idea how he would explain the pretext under which he was arranging for Paul to be tried in Rome under Caesar's jurisdiction. Festus used the opportunity afforded by a visit from King Herod Agrippa to learn exactly why the point of contention between Paul and the Jews was deemed to be so serious, and he arranged for Paul to speak before Herod Agrippa and himself.

'Porcius Festus made the occasion of Paul's address to Agrippa, his queen, Bernice and the nobility they had brought in their train, an opportunity to impress his guests with a display of Roman pomp and pageantry. Festus imagined the actual appearance of Paul would be relatively insignificant, but Festus had not reckoned with Paul's eloquence. As Paul spoke of Jesus, of his own life, of his spectacular conversion, and his commission to preach the gospel, Festus felt the power of God's Spirit working in his heart and mind. He was in danger of being converted by Paul's words himself, and he interrupted Paul, accusing him of madness. King Herod Agrippa too, was on the point of accepting the claims of Christ and said as much to Paul. The Jewish King and the Roman Governor abruptly closed the proceedings and privately deliberated on what they had heard. Even though they were not prepared to admit publicly that Paul had won them over, they were prepared to acknowledge that Paul had committed no crime whatever, and they were on the point of releasing him. However, the convolutions of Roman Law restricted their freedom to do this. Because Paul had appealed to Caesar, they had no alternative, but to send him to Rome, and this was what Paul wanted, as the Holy Spirit had revealed to him that this was his destiny.'[209]

Timothy paused at this point to eat some of the food that Selenece had placed before him. Apollos and Diana were glad to see that, although not as well as they would have hoped, Timothy had a good appetite. At one point, they feared that Timothy was becoming so embroiled with the burden of relating this narrative to them, that he would allow his food to get cold.

After eating a significant proportion of the food on his plate, Timothy wiped his mouth and continued with his account.

'Paul travelled to Rome in the custody of a very responsible and perceptive centurion who recognized in Paul, a man of complete integrity. He allowed Luke and the

307

others to accompany Paul on this journey, and permitted Paul more latitude than a soldier would normally allow a prisoner,[210] for the fate of a soldier who allows a prisoner to escape, is normally worse than the prisoner's might have been. However, as you will be well aware, the centurion's confidence was not misplaced, and in spite of the journey being beset with hazards, a severe storm,[211] shipwreck,[212] and Paul being bitten by a venomous snake,[213] Paul and his party arrived safely in Rome.[214]

'Although both Jews and Christians have been officially expelled from Rome, it is well known that many remain in the capital, worshipping in secret. The Romans cannot abide the Jews in particular, for the arrogant way in which they insist on their infallibility in religious matters. Although a prisoner, Paul's reputation of making even the Jews uncertain about their religious standing, has made him quite a celebrity among the Romans. Being a Roman citizen, he has been treated as a very special prisoner. As he seems to have done nothing wrong, except to challenge the Jews in a way which has obviously discomfited them on their claim to the monopoly on religious truth, Paul has even earned the admiration of Romans of high office.

'Paul's imprisonment has been no more than house arrest, and he has exercised a very effective ministry from that house. Indeed, now that he is getting older, the open fields and bustling markets are no longer the environments where Paul should be working in all weathers, sometimes facing the aggressive hostility of the crowds being harangued. I am sure Paul is as prepared now as he was in his younger days, to confront crowds who are all too ready to resort to stoning a speaker who can touch them on a raw nerve by exposing the follies of their societies. However, this is not something an old man should face. The fairly comfortable house from which Paul now operates, is probably as effective a mission platform, as the street corners were, in his days of youth and vigour. Some of the most elevated in Roman society have visited him to enjoy his eloquence, and have found his words have challenged them about the present order and given them considerable food for thought.[215] Paul has also used the opportunity of his imprisonment in relatively congenial circumstances, to write some wonderful letters to the churches and his Christian friends. Both Titus and I have received letters which have not only given us encouragement, but which contain such timeless advice and good teaching that they will be of inestimable value to other Christians like yourselves who have leadership roles in churches.'

Timothy paused at this point to finish the remainder of the food. Apollos and Diana looked at each other with expressions of troubled puzzlement. Although they had initially felt concern as Timothy had started to recount the circumstances of the threat to lynch Paul and of his arrest and imprisonment, the continuation of the narrative of Paul's adventure had been most reassuring. Everything which was happening to Paul seemed to be under divine control. He was in fact, experiencing protection rather than persecution from the authorities, and was now in a state of relative comfort, doing what he would most want to do, exercising a powerful ministry at the heart of the Roman Empire. Why then did Timothy seem so upset and agitated at Paul's predicament? Apollos and Diana were soon to receive their answer. Having completed his repast, Timothy resumed his account.

'Sadly, things have changed for the worse for Paul,' continued Timothy. 'Although Claudius Caesar was no friend to Christians, or to Jews for that matter, his administration was sound. Roman society was fairly well structured and ordered, and people knew where they stood in relation to recognized authority.

'Claudius is now dead. It is believed that he may have been poisoned. Be that as it may, his decease has meant there is a new order in Rome. His successor is his stepson, Nero. Nero does not really seem to have a grasp of government, and Romans in elevated social positions are taking advantage of the fact that they can manipulate the instruments of administration to suit their own interests. Some influential Romans are becoming disturbed by the effect that Paul's teaching is having on those who spend time in his company. These Romans have seen to it that visits to Paul are now severely restricted. The soldiers who had the responsibility of guarding Paul have been replaced by a singularly uncouth and insensitive band of elderly legionaries. New charges are being drawn up against Paul, not the old accusations of the Jews which carry no weight in Rome, but charges that he is undermining Imperial authority by his seditious teaching. These charges will not be difficult to press home, because Paul will not mince his words in proclaiming the unique claim to divinity of Jesus, if he is challenged in court to assert the divinity of the Emperor. Paul anticipates that he will be executed before the year is out. While we, his friends, are naturally upset, because Paul's forebodings are invariably fulfilled, Paul himself is quite cheerful and reconciled to his fate. I think he has always hoped for a martyr's death. Being a Roman citizen, his execution will be by beheading, rather than by one of the barbarous means which the Romans use to despatch an offending slave. Paul's remaining wish is to see as many of his old friends and fellow workers as possible before he leaves this world. I have been travelling around the churches, bearing this news to any whom Paul has said he would particularly like to see. Among these, Paul has specially mentioned your name, Apollos!'

44

The Church in Rome

The suggestion that Apollos should go to Rome left Apollos and Diana momentarily speechless as they thought of the implications of such a journey. Rome was a city which Apollos had always wanted to visit. The demands of running the Church at Corinth had left Apollos with little time to go sight-seeing abroad, but he still had nostalgic memories of his tour with Jerahmeel when he had seen sights and experienced the atmosphere of places of which he had previously only book knowledge. Apollos fondly recalled the missionary journeys he had made from Corinth in his early days in that city, in particular, his excursion to Athens and the time he had spent with Titus in Crete. However, he was no longer a bachelor. He now had a wife and daughter to consider. The domestic bliss that he had enjoyed over the years he had spent with Diana and Selenece since his marriage some eight years earlier, was such that he could scarcely contemplate being parted from them for more than a few days. But Paul was someone very special. From the time of his conversion, Paul had unselfishly served the needs of others. Now that he was in prison, and under imminent threat of execution, Paul needed and deserved any comfort and support his Christian friends could give him. Apollos felt inwardly honoured that Paul had identified him by name as someone he specially wanted to see during his remaining days on earth. However, Rome was a dangerous place for Christians. If Paul faced execution for denying the divinity of the Emperor, would not he, Apollos, be no less in jeopardy if challenged to acknowledge Caesar as a God? Would it be fair to Diana and Selenece to expose himself to such risk?

311

Timothy did not expect an immediate answer, and it was clear that Timothy would have to stay with them for several days to renew his strength before he would be fit enough to travel. Timothy responded well to the care and nursing he received from Diana. Selenece immediately took to the kindly man with gentle countenance, and spent much time in Timothy's company, marvelling at his stories of the places he had visited and the adventures that had befallen him. When he had been with Apollos and Diana for a little more than a week, Timothy's vigour returned. He now had the energy to visit the churches in Corinth to keep them up to date with news of the other churches from which he had recently returned and to bring them tidings of their old friend, Paul.

Paul was the subject of fervent prayer offered from the Corinthian churches. The intercessions of Apollos and Diana for Paul had another dimension. They needed God to guide them in solving the dilemma of how they should respond to Paul's request for Apollos to visit him in prison. Apollos and Diana talked through the situation together and their deliberations seemed to be guided by a further consideration to which they had previously given no thought. Diana had completely lost touch with Demeter. To the best of Diana's knowledge, Demeter was living in Rome, but she had no address to which she could send letters with any confidence of their reaching her sister. The tragic events which had occurred at Alexandria some thirteen years earlier had effectively severed any chance of contact between the two sisters. If Apollos went to Rome to visit Paul, he might be able to trace Claurinius and Demeter. Although Rome was a big city, Claurinius came from a family of some prominence, and it would not therefore be too difficult to obtain a lead from which Apollos could locate Claurinius and Demeter. Claurinius's family were among the patrician class and an association with such a family could well prove valuable to Apollos, should he encounter any particular difficulty in his quest to see Paul in a city which was hostile to Christians. As they prayed further, Apollos and Diana became convinced that it would be right for Apollos to accompany Timothy to Rome. They felt an assurance that God's protection would guarantee

312

safe passage for Apollos and Timothy.

The next three weeks were spent in busy preparation for the journey, and leaving everything in good order in the Corinthian Church. Apollos arranged for Titius Justus to take responsibility for the oversight of the Church while he was away and Apollos had every confidence that the Church would continue to grow and prosper under the guidance of this wise leader. Apollos and Timothy booked a passage on a ship leaving for Ostia from Lechaeum, the western sea-port of Corinth. A large crowd from the Corinthian churches gathered to wish the pair bon voyage on their day of departure. Apollos bade farewell to Diana and Selenece, and then boarded the waiting ship.

The ship pulled out into the Gulf of Corinth and sailed slowly through these sheltered waters until it passed Patrae where the gulf issued through a narrow neck into the Ionian Sea. In the stronger winds of the open sea, the vessel made good headway and soon reached Italy. The ship called at Rhegium on the toe of Italy before turning northwards for Rome, arriving a few days later at Ostia. Apollos and Timothy made their way on foot from the sea-port to the capital of the Empire.

Timothy was good company for the journey. He was both wise and well educated. His travels had left him with a wealth of experience and he could talk freely on most subjects without dominating conversation, which can be a shortcoming of individuals who seem to know everthing and who seem to have been everywhere.

Apollos was profoundly impressed with the grand city of Rome, with its triumphal arches, its broad streets and splendid buildings. The city was busy, but not congested or crowded as Jerusalem had been. Off-duty soldiers strutted by, carrying richly plumed helmets, the sun catching their brightly polished cuirasses. Patricians in their white togas walked by in pairs, or gathered in small groups in the city squares, intense in conversation and perhaps hatching political intrigue. The plebeian masses hustled to and fro, carrying their wares to market or returning with the goods they had bought.

Timothy knew his way around Rome well. After pointing out to Apollos some of the principal sights, Timothy

313

conducted him through the quieter sidestreets to the house where he knew they would be able to stay while in Rome. Timothy tapped on the door with a special rhythm which reminded Apollos of the coded knocks which were used to gain admittance to the church building in Jerusalem. The door opened cautiously, but as soon as the one inside recognized that it was Timothy who had knocked, the portal was flung open wide and a tall balding man stepped out into the street and warmly embraced Timothy. He was followed by a pleasant looking plump woman who similarly embraced Timothy and kissed him. They beckoned Timothy and Apollos to come in, and Timothy made the introductions. The man was Philologus, a Greek weaver who had worked in Rome for some years. He had married a Roman woman, Julia, who was the lady who had followed him out of the house. Apollos was flattered to find that his name was already well known to Philologus and Julia[216] who had heard of his work for the gospel in Alexandria, Ephesus and Corinth. Apollos was surprised to discover how detailed and up to date was their knowledge of the Church of Corinth, and found that the source of their information was a common acquaintance, Phoebe, who was a prominent worker in the Church at Cenchreae.[196] Phoebe had left Corinth a year or so earlier to stay with her brother in Rome, but maintained contact with her friends in Cenchreae with regular correspondence. In fact, Phoebe was none other than the lady who had brought news to Diana that Selenece had been found on that momentous day when Diana had been reunited, not only with her child, but the lost love of her youth.

Conversation soon turned to Paul. Timothy and Apollos were reassured to hear that Paul was in good spirits, but sad to discover that he was beginning to experience some of the privations of old age. His sight was failing and he suffered from rheumatism. However, his mind was as sharp and active as ever. His prison was a fairly comfortable room and he was not short of good food. A major cause for concern was that it was much more difficult now to visit Paul. During the reign of Claudius Caesar, everthing had become very bureaucratic. Forms had to be completed before one could do many normal things or enter some public buildings. The prison service was no exception but, provided one had completed the irksome paperwork, necessary before visiting a privileged prisoner like Paul, there was no restriction to access. The new Caesar, Nero, seemed to have no understanding or interest in bureaucratic procedures, and these had been largely swept aside. However, the new condition was worse than the former. Petty officials were arbitrary in their administration, and people who had travelled quite a long way to visit Paul were often curtly turned away by the quite junior ranking soldiers who guarded prison establishments, with no reason being given. Although it was contrary to the way the Roman Church would have liked to conduct things, bribery was often the only way to get past the guards to see Paul. Another restriction which hindered visiting, was the guards' insistence that Paul could only receive one visitor at a time. Thus Paul was now no longer able to see the small groups of people who used to gather to listen to the profound teaching which Paul imparted to his spiritually hungry guests.

Timothy asked Philologus and Julia how the Church in Rome was faring and whether it was experiencing harassment from the authorities. Philologus reassured Timothy that while the Church kept a low profile, the authorities had too many other distractions for them to concern themselves over the Church which was causing harm to no one.

'We can witness discreetly,' explained Philologus, 'and each week we win new converts. We worship in the evenings in the catacombs. I am sure the authorities are aware of this, but as we are giving them no trouble, no one disturbs us. In any case, the Romans are a superstitious people, and will not lightly enter the places where they believe the spirits of their ancestors lurk.'

Two days later, on the first day of the week, Apollos had the opportunity of experiencing worship in the catacombs. The catacombs were entered through caves, located around the perimeter of the city. The Christians made their way to these caves, soon after dusk. Philologus and Julia explained to Apollos that there were half-a-dozen or so large caverns in the catacombs where different Christian congregations met to worship. Apollos found himself conducted through

315

the caves to a cavern where about a hundred and fifty people could comfortably sit on crude benches which were lifted down from where they were stacked against the cavern wall. Light was provided from a number of torches which were supported by brackets, fixed round the walls of the cavern, and these burned brightly away. There were a number of entrances to the cavern into which Apollos had been conducted, and pairs of Church members stood at each opening to welcome the worshippers. Timothy explained that these men had the further duty of keeping a look-out, lest the authorities might choose to raid the catacombs.

'The catacombs form a complex which is a vast maze of underground tunnels,' Timothy explained to Apollos. 'Should the men on entrance duty sense danger, they will give a signal, and we can quickly evacuate the cavern through the caves where no unwelcome intruders have been detected. When Claudius Caesar first issued his decree, expelling Christians from Rome, the Authorities used to come into the catacombs fairly frequently, but they did not manage to apprehend many of the brotherhood. The catacombs have not been raided for some years now, but precautions against getting arrested are maintained, just the same.'

Worshipping underground in this slightly claustro-phobic environment with the latent threat of the procedings being interrupted by the intrusion of law-enforcement officers, vested with authority from a regime hostile to Christianity, was a new and somewhat eerie experience for Apollos. However, once the worship started, and Apollos recognized that many of the hymns were the same as the ones being sung in Corinth, Apollos found he was able to relax and enter into the spirit of worship.

The meeting was presided over by a Christian called Aristobulus.[217] At an appropriate point, he welcomed Timothy back to the assembly after his recent travels, and extended a very special welcome to Apollos whom, it seemed, was already well known by reputation to that gathering. Timothy spoke of the churches he had recently visited. Apollos brought greetings to the Christians of Rome from the Church of Corinth, and gave the Roman Christians news of how that Church was flourishing. After the service, many gathered round to shake Timothy and Apollos by the hand, and plied them with further enquiries about the churches in Greece and Asia Minor.

It was quite late when Apollos and Timothy were finally able to return home with Philologus and Julia. That night, Apollos fell asleep, musing on the rather special atmosphere he had experienced through worshipping with Christians in a persecuted church, so different from the freedom of religious expression to which he was accustomed at his Church in Corinth.

45

A Visit to Paul

The following day, Apollos and Timothy went to visit Paul. Timothy conducted Apollos along a straight road running northwards called the Flaminian Way. They passed an impressive looking monument, which Timothy identified as the Mausoleum of Augustus Caesar, and continued another hundred metres or so until they arrived at an area surrounded by a fortified wall. When they reached the entrance to this enclosure, Apollos could see, through the gate, that behind the wall was a complex of tents and small houses. These occupied the land between the wall, which ran by the road, and the River Tiber, which flowed southwards towards the city centre, forming a natural boundary along the opposite side of the enclosed area. Beyond the river, stretched beautiful gardens and magnificent villas. These were obviously the homes of wealthy patricians.

The military were very much in evidence within the enclosure which Apollos now surveyed. At least one soldier stood outside each house, while others sat around their tents, sharpening their swords and burnishing their breastplates. Timothy explained to Apollos that this was where political prisoners were held, men of wealth and status who had not committed the usual crimes of robbery or violence, but who were regarded as being potentially dangerous to the state if left at liberty. Paul was regarded as such a prisoner.

Timothy stated to the guard on the gate that they had come to visit the prisoner, Paul. The guard looked them up and down and then called to another soldier who appeared from a hut near the gate. This soldier came over and beckoned Timothy and Apollos to follow him into the hut. When in the hut which obviously functioned as the guard house, the soldier made a token body search of Timothy and Apollos for concealed weapons, and then asked for five denarius. This was apparently the standard bribe for being allowed to see Paul. On receiving the coins, he barked at the couple,

'Well, what are you waiting for? You know the way!'

Apollos did not know the way, but Timothy did. The couple went out of the guard hut and Timothy identified the house which was Paul's prison. The pair walked up to the house where the guard outside told them that they could only go in one at a time, and demanded a further five denarius.

'You go in first,' said Timothy.

Apollos paid the coins and entered the house. There, sitting at the table in a sparsely furnished room, writing in very large letters was Paul.[225] Paul looked up but did not immediately recognize his visitor until Apollos spoke. Paul left his chair and warmly embraced Apollos, exclaiming how good it was to see him. First, Paul wanted to hear all about the Corinthian Church, and Apollos filled Paul in with as much detail as he could, continuing his narrative up to the point where he left Lechaeum in company with Timothy. Paul was delighted with what he heard. He was particularly pleased to hear that the party spirit which had split the Church into factions when he had been in Corinth with Peter, had never recurred at the Church.

Paul then spoke of his own predicament, but made light of being in prison. He spoke of the wonderful support he had received from the Church in Rome which seemed to be in the ambiguous position of being outlawed, but tolerated by authorities who had to contend with really dangerous sources of subversion, and saw no great threat from the significant proportion of Rome's population who had become Christians. These were for the most part, poor plebians with no political influence, but Paul knew that some of senatorial rank had joined the brotherhood.

Paul spoke warmly of those who had come to visit him, and these included the names of everyone who had been in the team who had worked together in the mission at

Ephesus. It seemed that John Mark and Luke were currently in Rome, although Apollos had not yet met up with these in the short time he had been in the City. Paul explained that he spent much of his time in writing, but lamented the fact that he had to write in such large characters, now that his eyesight was failing, and commended John Mark and Luke for the time they had spent with him, acting as his amanuenses. He passed over to Apollos a rolled up scroll which he explained was a letter to the Church at Colossae. He explained to Apollos that two Christian friends called Tychicus and Onesimus, who worshipped in the catacombs at the Church led by Aristobolus, were soon to depart for Colossae. They were expecting this letter which Paul had asked them to convey to the Church there.[220] Paul was anxious that they should have this letter as soon as possible, so that their departure should not be unnecessarily delayed. The letter was not sealed and Paul invited Apollos to read the letter before he passed it over to Tychicus and Onesimus.

'Although the letter contains matters which I wished to specially impart to the Colossians,' explained Paul, 'there is nothing of a particularly private nature in the letter, and I think it contains many matters which will be of general interest to anyone like yourself, who has the responsibility of running a church.'

Paul then broached another matter which, it transpired, was the particular reason why he had wished to see Apollos.

'I know that I have not much time left in this world,' he explained, and Paul sounded strangely cheerful, even elated as he spoke. 'I have not courted a martyr's death, but I will welcome that when it comes, for that will bring me into the glorious presence of my Lord whom I have seen in visions, and whom I have heard speaking to me. When his presence with me is unseen, it is still real, and he has always been a source of strength and comfort. In times of danger and difficulty, his presence and support has been of inestimable value. He has given me the power, when needed, to perform miracles and even restore men to life. When stoned by crowds, he has diverted any stone which could have caused me serious harm,[218] and when bitten by venomous snakes, he has neutralized the poison.[213]

'However, there is much work to be done. We have scarcely spread the gospel within the Empire, and there is a world beyond the Empire, still waiting to hear of Jesus. Indeed, the Empire almost seems to be growing faster than we can spread the good news. North Africa, Spain and Gaul lie on our doorstep, and the Emperor Claudius has expanded the empire to a cold land in the far north called Britannia. I have been told that an apostle called James is taking the gospel to Spain, and a disciple from Arimathea called Joseph, whom I once knew many years ago when he was a member of the Sanhedrin,[219] has gone to Britannia.'

Paul then looked straight at Apollos.

'Who will take the gospel to Gaul?'

Apollos felt challenged as Paul asked this question. Paul continued.

'Several months ago I had a vision. The Lord appeared to me and asked the same question. "Who will take the gospel to Gaul?" I replied that because of my imprisonment, I could not go, although it was a commission I would dearly like to fulfil. The Lord then said to me, "Seek out Apollos and send him!" I had particularly wanted to see you, Apollos, before the time came for me to leave this world, but this vision has increased the intensity with which I have longed for this meeting when I could speak to you, face to face.'

This challenge came out of the blue to Apollos, although he had felt over the past few months as he had prayed, that he was being urged to leave Corinth and plant a church in a land which had not yet been reached by the gospel. Then Apollos had thought of Diana and Selenece, and considered that it would not be right to disrupt their settled life-style. Apollos told Paul of his family commitments and the constraints this put on his adopting an itinerant ministry. Apollos found that Paul had had news of his marriage from Priscilla and Aquila, who had crossed his path in their travels within weeks of the marriage taking place.

'You are right to consider your family in this way,' continued Paul. 'You are a fortunate man, for your marriage was clearly fore-ordained and made in heaven. In cases like this, the Lord will not call a person to serve him in a way which will cause undue stress to his marriage.

Speak to Diana of what I have said to you. You will find that she has a reason for wishing to go to Gaul which may seem even more pressing than your own.'

Paul and Apollos then spent some time in prayer together.

As they finished praying, Apollos remembered that Timothy was waiting outside and left Paul, with promises that he would be back to see him several times before leaving Rome. Apollos went into the open air to find Timothy patiently sitting outside on a bench. Timothy went in to spend some time with Paul while Apollos sat down and passed the time of waiting in reading through the letter Paul had given him to be delivered to the Church at Colossae by the hand of Tychicus and Onesimus. As he read the letter, Apollos realized that this letter contained profound truths which would be of inestimable value to future generations of Christians. Apollos had read other letters which Paul had sent to the churches, and in particular, the letters he had sent to his own Church in Corinth. Apollos had arranged for copies to be made of these, and had carefully stored the originals. He realized at that moment, that if Paul's letters could be preserved for posterity, Paul would have a ministry which would continue long after his death. Apollos had not travelled in his ministry as Paul had done and had not therefore had the same cause to write letters. However, there was much that Apollos wanted to impart to Christians beyond his immediate Church at Corinth. If the Lord showed him clearly that he should go to Gaul, then this would be an opportunity for expanding his ministry. However, the spoken word is ephemeral, and from that time, Apollos thought of writing a letter himself which could provide teaching, not just to the immediate recipients, but to future generations of Christians.

After an hour had elapsed, Timothy left Paul, and Timothy and Apollos returned to the home of Philologus and Julia where they were staying, pleased to bring news that Paul was in good spirits.

46

Quintus Albinian

During those weeks that Apollos stayed in Rome, he wrote several short letters to Diana and to the Church of Corinth, keeping them informed of all that was happening in the Church of Rome and reassuring them of his own well-being. Apollos also set about writing a much longer letter in which he concentrated so much of his scholarship and understanding of Jewish scripture and his appreciation of the new light and relevance which Christianity threw upon those scriptures. In his letter, Apollos showed too, how the Jewish scriptures threw special light on the role and nature of Christ. This letter was a theological treatise and took Apollos many weeks to write, so that several letters had been sent to Corinth before this special letter was ready for despatch. Apollos put so much of himself into that letter, and he hoped that it would be used beyond the immediate circle of the Corinthian Church. Indeed, he had hopes that this letter, together with those he knew that Paul had written, might be preserved for posterity. Apollos felt sure that they would find a place alongside those splendid gospels which had been written by John Mark and Luke.

While in Rome, Apollos visited Paul several times. He often went with Timothy, but sometimes he went alone and sometimes, in the company of one of the other members of the Roman Church. Apollos soon made many new friends at that Church and met up with some old ones. Mark and Luke were in Rome at the time, sharing a special bond in their both having written biographies of Jesus, and serving Paul as his amanuenses. Mark and Luke worshipped at a church which met in another part of the catacombs from the church led by Aristobulus, but they found many occasions when they could meet up with Apollos and Timothy with whom they had so much in common and so much to talk about.

It was an education for Apollos to see how the Church of Rome prospered, even under the cloud of threatened persecution. However, in those early days of the new Emperor, the authorities in Rome had so much adjustment to make in the new ways of running the state under Nero, who did not possess the statesman-like qualities of his stepfather, Claudius Caesar, that they had little time to concern themselves with harassing a benign sect in their community whose only crime seemed to be their refusal to acknowledge Imperial divinity. Nobody in Rome really believed the Emperor was divine, anyway, although it was politically expedient for those building their careers to pay at least lip service to this precept.

Among the new acquaintances that Apollos made at Rome were Tychicus and Onesimus who were to deliver Paul's letter to the Church at Colossae.[220] Tychicus and Onesimus had other letters of Paul in their possession which they had undertaken to deliver on their travels. Tychicus had a letter, specially addressed to the Church of Ephesus,[221] and Onesimus was taking a letter home to one called Philemon, Onesimus's master in Colossae.[222] Tychicus and Onesimus were surprised that Paul had finished the letter to the Colossians so quickly. Although frequent visitors to Paul, preparations for their journey had left them too busy to go and see Paul for a few days. As Tychicus and Onesimus had not expected Paul to finish the letter for another week or so, they had delayed making final arrangements for catching a ship to Ephesus, from which port they would procede to Colossae. They knew that a ship would be leaving from Ostia in five days and they could now book a passage on this to make their journey before the season when Mediterranean storms were likely to break. Although they now had Paul's precious letter which they were to deliver to the Church of Colossae, Tychicus and Onesimus told Apollos that they would visit Paul again before finally leaving Rome.

Apollos' other mission of importance when in Rome, was to trace Claurinius and Demeter. A lead came with

324

surprising facility. On making his initial enquiries among the members of the Church led by Aristobolus, Apollos was directed to a member of that Church called Narcissus[223] who had contacts with the patrician classes. Narcissus was a wealthy merchant who had been led to Christianity by three men who had formerly been slaves in his household, and who had continued to work for Narcissus as servants, after he had granted them their freedom. Narcissus knew of Claurinius Albinian and remembered the celebration that had been held some years earlier when he had returned from a successful naval engagement. Narcissus did not know of the present whereabouts of Claurinius but he knew where Claurinius' father, Quintus Albinian lived. Narcissus explained to Apollos that Quintus was a retired senator who had been widowed some two years earlier, and he explained to Apollos just how to find Quintus' splendid villa on the other side of the Tiber.

Apollos made his visit to the home of Claurinius' father in the company of Timothy. They crossed the river and made their way through the fashionable quarter of Rome where the wealthy classes lived in magnificent villas. Narcissus' directions had been good, and they found the home of Quintus Albinian with no difficulty. Apollos described himself to the servant, who answered the door, as the brother-in-law of the Senator's son, Claurinius. Apollos and Timothy were conducted through a splendid atrium, where fountains sparkled and danced as they cascaded clear water into a rectangular pool where fish swam lazily beneath the lily pads, and they were finally led into a spacious reception room. The servant motioned them to sit on one of the couches, and went off in search of the master. A short while later, a distinguished looking elderly gentleman, wearing an immaculate white toga, edged with purple, entered the room and introduced himself as Quintus Albinian.

Quintus looked curiously from Apollos to Timothy, and asked which of them claimed to be his son's brother-in-law. Apollos then recounted the rather involved story of how he knew Claurinius and Demeter when he was a young man in Alexandria, of how Demeter's sister, Diana had left Alexandria after the riots, going first to Ephesus and then to Corinth where Apollos had met Diana again and married her, and of how he now came to be in Rome to visit a political prisoner called Paul. It was a long story, but Apollos was a good raconteur and held Quintus' interest. Quintus nodded each time something was mentioned, like the Alexandrian riots, of which he had independent reference. He nodded too at the name of Paul of whom he had obviously heard.

Quintus told Apollos that he knew from his most recent letter from them, that Claurinius and Demeter were both well. He explained that they no longer lived in Rome as Claurinius was now Procurator of Narbonensia, a province in southern Gaul, and was seldom able to return to the capital. Quintus had not seen his son or daughter-in-law for two years when they had last paid a fleeting visit to Rome on the sad occasion of Claurinius' mother's funeral. He told Apollos that Claurinius and Demeter had returned to Alexandria after the riots to ascertain that Demeter's family were safe, only to discover that Demeter's parents had both been killed. As they had been unable to trace Diana, they had assumed that she too had perished. Quintus was clearly delighted that he would be able to pass on good news of Demeter's sister when he next wrote. Quintus invited Apollos and Timothy to stay for a meal so that they could continue to talk about the many things in which they had a mutual interest.

Quintus went out to give his servants instructions and returned to talk further with Apollos and Timothy. As the discussion continued, a table was laid and the servants brought in tender meats, freshly baked bread and sumptuous fruits for Quintus and his guests to eat. An atmosphere of luxury pervaded the home of Quintus Albinian and purveyed a sense of opulence which went far beyond anything Apollos had experienced before, even in the days when he was a member of the affluent Greek classes in Alexandria. The standard of life which Quintus enjoyed was not unusual for households of the upper classes living in Rome, for wealth poured into the city as it received tribute from its conquests in southern Europe, Asia Minor and north Africa.

Conversation turned to Paul of whom Quintus had heard

through his reputation of being so persuasive in speech and argument, that even dyed-in-the-wool Romans who heard him speak, were prepared to completely rethink their approach and attitude to life. Timothy and Apollos explained to Quintus that Paul's great gifts of argument and persuasion were a special gift from God, and declared that they too were Christians. Introduction of Paul into the conversation gave Apollos and Timothy the opportunity to profess to Quintus the dramatic change that becoming Christians had made to each of their lives. Quintus was clearly impressed by the fact that Apollos and Timothy were so freely prepared to acknowledge that they were Christians when they were in a society which manifestly disapproved of Christianity and its adherents.

Quintus explained that he was not a religious man, but that he had gone along with traditional Roman religion because it was expected of him, indeed, necessary for him, to hold his position in society. However, now that he was in retirement and had time to think, he had to admit that Roman religion was neither credible or satisfying. The futility of Roman religion had particularly come home to Quintus when the mad emperor, Caligula, had not only declared himself a god, but also, ascribed deity to his domestic animals.

Apollos and Timothy used the opportunity provided by Quintus revealing his own inner conflicts, to speak more fully of their own faith and to describe Jesus to whom they ascribed divinity for reasons which contrasted in every way with the grounds on which a Roman emperor might claim divinity for himself.

Quintus was impressed with these young men. (Although they were both in their late forties, to one of Quintus' age and status, they were young men.) Since his wife had died, life had become very lonely for Quintus. He had a lot of time to think, and as his life was drawing to its final stages, he had thought carefully about the meaning of life, and whether there was anything beyond. Apollos and Timothy had done much to dispel what could be described as Quintus' state of inner mental despair, not so much by what they said, but by the way they said it, with such sincerity and conviction. Quintus had not enjoyed an afternoon for

327

years in the way he was enjoying the time he was spending with Apollos and Timothy. Although elderly, Quintus had prided himself that his mind remained alert and fresh, and Quintus' pride was not misplaced, but these young men displayed a mental agility, the like of which he had never before experienced. After a couple of hours discussion, Quintus realized he could absorb no more that day. Quintus wanted to learn more from these new acquaintances who had brightened his day, one of whom it seemed, was related to him in a distant sort of way. Quintus told Apollos and Timothy that he wished for time to think on what they had said to him, and he suggested another day when they might come and visit him. Apollos and Timothy readily accepted this invitation.

As they left the home of Quintus, Apollos felt inwardly glad that this duty call had provided an opportunity to proclaim the gospel where it was clearly being thoughtfully received.

47

A Rewarding Personal Ministry

Apollos and Timothy kept their appointment and called on Quintus again when they had a further opportunity to speak to the Senator on spiritual matters. After they had explained in very clear terms the essentials of the gospel message, Quintus took advantage of the company of these very persuasive speakers to unburden himself of many matters which troubled his mind.

'Now that I am in the autumn of my years,' began Quintus, 'I can survey the passage of my life and see in perspective the way I used the time when I had vigour and influence. I don't really like what I see from my present vantage point. Throughout those years, I was preoccupied with advancing my career, gaining influence and power, becoming involved in subterfuge if I saw that I might benefit by the outcome, and to what end? I have lain awake at night, fretting and cursing when I saw another receive honours and promotion when I considered myself to be more deserving. I have seen that elevation to positions of influence and power was more a matter of having friends in high places than of merit. I have been party to unjust laws being passed by the Senate which have benefited a privileged few at the expense of the well-being of thousands of the poorer classes. I have not enjoyed many good things like the warmth of my family to the full, because I have been so busily involved in political chicanery. I feel ashamed now of the wealth and luxury I enjoy, and know that we rich Romans have achieved our wealth by bleeding our empire. Until recent years, I have not concerned myself seriously with religious matters or given much thought to what lies beyond this life, being content to go along with the puerile notions which pass as Roman religion, purely out of expediency.

'What is worse, I fear that I have instilled my restless ambition into my son, Claurinius, who is discontented with the position he holds in the system by which Rome governs the world. When Claurinius returned from his prefectship in Alexandria to marry Demeter, he was confident and happy with a zest for living. Once he started to taste success, his personality started to change. After he had returned from his great naval victory, he seemed to become nervous and distracted. This was particularly noticable when we were in the company of other officers who had shared that expedition with Claurinius. Claurinius found favour with Caligula Caesar, and had Caligula remained emperor, Claurinius would have gone far. This was not to be. The lottery of state appointments fell badly for Claurinius when Claudius succeeded his nephew, and Claurinius was sent to a corner of the empire to which he had no wish to go.

'As I speak with you young men, I see a joy and a vision, a sense of purpose which sees beyond this life. This is missing from even my acquaintances who have been successful in the promotion stakes, for in their quieter moments, they must wonder what lies beyond this life. They, no less than I, have lived selfishly, ruthlessly grasping what they wanted for themselves, regardless of the loss, or even pain, it inflicted on others. I have always recognized that the Jews had something sound and solid in their religion, but I have not been attracted to their faith because I find distasteful their exclusive belief in themselves as the only chosen ones of God. What you have told me of your faith, on the other hand, is attractive, for it has all the spiritual wisdom of the Jewish faith without its arrogant exclusiveness. You young men have clearly worked hard to share this faith with others and I can see the joy and fulfilment it has obviously brought you. You deserve the treasure stored up for you in the next world. I see that Paul is not alone in your sect of being of persuasive speech, for you would almost have me become a Christian. However, it is too late for me. At my stage in life, I cannot do enough to right the wrongs of my youth and earn myself the blessings that you both confidently expect to enjoy.'

At this point, Timothy took up the conversation.

'We thank you for sharing your innermost thoughts with us in this way,' said Timothy, smiling warmly as he spoke, 'for this has shown us that you are not far from the Kingdom. The benefits of the Kingdom of God are available for believers to enjoy in part, here and now, and this is the secret of the joy you say you have detected in Apollos and myself. There is an important precept of our faith, however, which you have not yet grasped. This is not surprising, for both Apollos and myself took a long time to come to terms with this crucial point. The benefits of this faith are not to be thought of as a prize to be earned. They come as a free gift. Neither I, nor Apollos, nor even Paul, would claim to have earned the benefits of the faith we have in Jesus which are both for this life and the life beyond. These all come as a free gift, and were bought for us as Jesus suffered on the cross to cancel out the shortcomings, serious shortcomings, that we all have which separate us from the love of God. I can demonstrate the truth of what I say from the ministry Jesus extended to a helpless creature, during the final moments of his earthly life.

'We have told you that Jesus was crucified in the company of two criminals who had committed many serious acts of theft. Now that they were nailed to crosses, it would have appeared that it was too late for them to make amends in any way for their past misdeeds. They were surely destined for hell. They even compounded their crimes by casting scorn upon Jesus who shared in their final hours of suffering. Then one of those thieves saw in Jesus, the divinity to which he had previously been blind. He rebuked the other thief who continued to rile Jesus, pointing out to him that they deserved their punishment, while Jesus had done nothing wrong. This thief saw in Jesus, a King whose Kingdom transcended anything we know in this world, who was shortly to come into his own. This thief realized that he himself had done nothing to deserve entry into this Kingdom, but he acknowledged Jesus' kingship in a simple request. He asked Jesus to remember him when he came into his Kingdom.

'Jesus did not answer as many might have expected him

to, that it was too late now for the dying thief to seek his place in heaven. Jesus knew that no one can enter heaven, except by repentance and making an act of faith in himself. In the words that thief had just spoken to the other crucified thief, and to Jesus, the dying thief had done just this. In his final words to the repentant thief, Jesus told him that that night, he would be with him in paradise.'

Timothy stopped speaking at that point. His words had clearly affected Quintus, who remained silent, musing on what Timothy had said. After a while, Quintus broke the silence and suggested that they should eat. He called a servant, and a sumptuous meal was set as before. Little was said during that repast. Quintus was clearly ruminating on all he had heard that morning and Apollos and Timothy had the sensitivity, not to force conversation at that time.

As they left, Quintus arranged for Apollos and Timothy to call and visit him yet again. Over the next month, Apollos and Timothy called many times on Quintus, and were impressed to see how seriously and carefully he was thinking out the implications for himself of what he had learnt from Apollos and Timothy. Apollos and Timothy told other members of their Church and Paul of these meetings with Quintus, and they became a focus for prayer.

After a month, Quintus expressed a wish to come to a meeting of the Roman Church. Apollos and Timothy were delighted to see how their prayers had been heard and answered. They suggested that Quintus might like to attend in the company of Narcissus who was already known to him. Narcissus was pleased to make the arrangements to call upon his old friend, and Quintus sat among the family and household servants of Narcissus when the Church next met in the catacombs. Apollos and Timothy continued to pay their visits to Quintus.

48

Timothy Imprisoned

After a few weeks in Rome, Apollos considered his mission
to be completed and he began to think about making
preparations to return to Corinth. He had received letters
from Diana which were, for the most part, reassuring. Diana
and Selenece were both well and his letters were getting
through to Corinth. However, the Corinthian Church was
beginning to face some problems they had not faced for
some time. The Jewish merchants, who controlled many of
the business interests, were using new tactics to harrass the
Church. They were exploiting their commercial power to
prevent traders who were dependent on their patronage,
from having dealings with those known to be Christian.
This was restricting the market in which some of the
Christian traders and merchants could sell their goods, and
was denying employment to those who earned their keep by
services they were able to render to the managers of
business. Sadly, this persecution was actually causing some
of the weaker Church members to renounce their faith.
Diana also informed Apollos of strains of false teaching
which were entering the Church. These heresies did not
come through the accepted leaders, but through vociferous
hangers-on to the community. These people sought to use
the Church as a platform on which they could expound
weird and wonderful theories of their own, which had no
basis in either the Jewish scriptures or the teachings of
Jesus. These problems were matters which Apollos decided
he should address in the major epistle he was writing to the
Church.

Then a disturbing event occurred which caused Apollos
to delay his preparations for returning home. Timothy had

gone to visit Paul and had not returned to the home of Philologus and Julia where he and Apollos were lodging. Apollos went the following day to visit Paul, only to discover that Paul had seen no sign of Timothy the previous day. The Christians made further enquiries of those who had seen Timothy on 'his way to visit Paul, and these enquiries left the Christians in no doubt that Timothy had actually reached the prison compound where political prisoners like Paul were held. Two Christians went to make further enquiries at the prison and an uncouth guard revealed that Timothy himself had been thrown into prison for, as the guard put it, 'failing to show proper respect and deference to his betters.' The guard refused to allow the two men access to Timothy. Apollos and some other Christians went to make their representations to the guards but to no avail. The guard at the gate of the compound discouraged Apollos and those with him from taking their complaints to higher authority, by scoffing at them as Christians who would themselves end up in prison like Paul and Timothy if they were brought before the magistrates.

The Church led by Aristobolus grew increasingly concerned for the well-being of Timothy, and met frequently to pray for him. Apollos went to visit Quintus who was initially surprised to see Apollos arrive alone, until Apollos told him of the predicament in which Timothy was placed. Quintus' brow puckered with anger as Apollos explained the situation, and he immediately suggested to Apollos that they should set out for the prison. He called a servant to prepare his chariot and as soon as this was ready, they drove at speed to the prison compound.

The guard at the gate came to attention as the chariot drew up at the prison gate, the senatorial rank of Quintus being clear from his toga. Quintus dismounted from the chariot with Apollos, and told the driver to pasture the horse in the meadows by the river as his visit to the prison might be protracted.

'We have come to see the prisoner, Timothy,' thundered Quintus, as one who was used to instant obedience from a mere legionary.

The guards were used to senators coming to visit important political prisoners in that place, but why would one of such importance want to see a Greek who obviously belonged to the poorer classes.

'We have orders to allow no one to see the Greek,' stammered the guard.

'Then take me to the one who issued this order!' roared Quintus. Old man as he was, he certainly had a loud voice.

The guard signalled to another soldier to take his place, and let Quintus and Apollos to the guard room. A slovenly looking corporal slouched at a desk. He suddenly sprung to his feet as the Senator entered. Before the soldier had a chance to say anything to the corporal, Quintus made his demands known in an authoritive tone.

'We have come to see one called Timothy who is held in prison here. We want to know by what authority he has been put in prison, and what the charges are. We want to know why he is being held here, which is a place for convicted political prisoners, without a trial. If I do not receive satisfactory answers to these questions, I will demand that he is released immediately or I will take up the matter with higher authority.'

'I ordered him to b'be put in p'prison,' said the corporal 'because he was g'giving a bit of trouble to the guard on the g'gate.' Under the fixed scruting of Quintus' penetrating gaze, the corporal's stammer was worse that the guard's, 'I didn't think he was very important, sir. I suspected he might be a Christian. I think most of those who visit the prisoner Paul are likely to be Christian.'

'I would like to visit the prisoner, Paul,' said Quintus. 'Are you going to throw me into prison on suspicion of being a Christian?'

'Certainly not sir,' the corporal replied respectfully.

Apollos looked intently at the corporal. He had a moon-shaped scar on his cheek. Apollos had learned from Jerahmeel on the night they had escaped from the Amalekites at the inn near Beer-sheba, the importance of making unequivocal identification of malefactors. Apollos looked down at the corporal's left hand. It had been mutilated in some battle and had only three fingers.

'You were among the soldiers who landed from the black ship at Sidon and took the young men prisoner to become galley slaves. You were the soldier who killed my friend!'

335

declared Apollos, his voice rising to a crescendo.

The corporal looked even more uncomfortable. Disturbing thoughts passed through his mind. Who were these men? Why should a senator be interested in a poor Greek? How did they come to know what had happened at Sidon?

'N'no, we only gathered stones for the b'ballista at Sidon,' answered the corporal to this accusation, his stammer becoming more pronounced. 'I was on *The Jupiter*. It was *The Vulcan* who captured the galley slaves.'

Quintus became strangely pensive, and fixed the corporal with an even more penetrating stare. There was something about Quintus' posture that caused both Apollos and the corporal to remain silent. After thinking for a while about what he had just heard the corporal say, Quintus spoke again, this time in a quiet subdued voice.

'I thought that it was *The Minerva* which went to Sidon for repairs and that *The Vulcan* had sunk in the battle,' queried Quintus.

'Oh, yes, sir, that's right,' replied the corporal. '*The Jupiter*'s crew only went there to gather stones.'

'I thought that *The Jupiter* returned straight to Rome, after the sea battle,' said Quintus.

The corporal looked even more uncomfortable. Worried thoughts continued to pass through his head. However do these men know so much about that expedition? The Senator seems to be well informed about the ships. The young Greek speaks as if he were an eye-witness. But it all happened so long ago. Why is it being dragged up now? Is that Greek we locked in the shed in someway involved with the incident? Whoever are these men? How can I get them to leave me alone?

Quintus and Apollos waited for the corporal to answer this question. Apollos was bemused by the names of the ships which Quintus was mentioning which seemed to be in some way connected with the Sidon incident. What was the battle to which he referred, about which, this corporal seemed to have special knowledge?

At last, the corporal suddenly spoke.

'I will release the prisoner, Timothy, for you straight away,' he said, not bothering to reply to Quintus' final query. 'If you like, the three of you can visit Paul. You may stay as long as you like. I will get some food brought round for you.'

Without waiting for the pair to say anything more, the corporal grabbed a huge key from a hook on the wall and hurriedly left the guard-room. Quintus and Apollos followed him out. The corporal went across to a shed and opened the door. There, sitting on the floor, was Timothy. He blinked as his eyes adjusted to the unaccustomed light. Timothy rose stiffly to his feet, and as his pupils contracted and he was able to see clearly in the bright daylight, he recognized Apollos and Quintus. He rushed out of his prison and embraced them, relieved to be out of that dark and uncomfortable place. He had lost count of how many days he had been in there. Apollos wondered why Timothy had been confined in a shed and not in a proper room like Paul. Apollos had not fully appreciated that Timothy was not an important political prisoner, and his imprisonment in this way was quite irregular. However, the bully-boy soldiers had not reckoned on this poor Christian Greek, whom they counted as being of no importance, having a friend as influential as a Senator to intercede on his behalf.

'I will enquire of you further, about the deployment of *The Jupiter*, *The Vulcan* and *The Minerva* during and after the sea battle,' said Quintus to the corporal.

The corporal nodded with a now bland expression on his face, inwardly thinking that he had better prepare a story in line with the official annals, before this nosey Senator started to interrogate him on his involvement in what he knew to be a shameful affair.

For years, Quintus had been puzzled about certain rumours which had come to his ears about the events occurring during Claurinius' naval mission, which seemed to contradict the account his son had given. As Claurinius had gained great honour in this engagement, Quintus naturally believed his son's account. This after all was the version entered in the annals as the official record of events. The corporal, who had obviously been a member of *The Jupiter*'s company on that fateful mission, had unwittingly let it slip that he had called in at Sidon. This made Quintus rethink the authenticity of what he had accepted for years as the true account of the events surrounding the naval engagement. Only one ship had returned to Rome. It was known that *The Vulcan* had been sunk in the action, but the disappearance of *The Minerva* remained an unexplained mystery. The corporal had been positively identified by Apollos, who somehow must have been at Sidon when it was claimed the crew of *The Minerva* took some Sidonian youths as galley slaves. But Claurinius' account of *The Jupiter's* movements explicitly stated that the ship returned straight to Ostia after the sea battle and had not accompanied *The Minerva* to Sidon where it had been sent for repairs. The identification of *The Minerva* by the officer commanding the Roman garrison at Sidon, was based purely on the information he had been given by an officer from the ship.

As these thoughts turned over in Quintus' mind, he mentally reconstructed the events as they really must have taken place after the battle. Quintus' reconstruction was nearer the truth than the official version. It was not necessary to be a great detective to make this deduction from the new evidence which the corporal's unwitting remark about being in Sidon afforded, coupled with the corroboration of Apollos' positive identification of the man. But how was Apollos involved in this affair? This was something he would have to learn from Apollos.

Quintus was awakened from his preoccupation as he suddenly became aware that they had reached the house in the compound where Paul was kept. The trio were shown into Paul's room without any attempt being made to extract a bribe. After looking hard at his visitors, Paul recognized Apollos and Timothy, and warmly embraced them, glad to see that his fellow worker on so many missionary enterprises was apparently free and well. Quintus was introduced as the father of Apollos' brother-in-law, and the one who had been responsible for securing Timothy's release. Quintus had heard so much about Paul, and was intrigued to have this personal encounter with one whose influence, even from a prison cell, was so far reaching.

There was now so much to talk about. Timothy's release had induced a state of some euphoria in Apollos and Timothy. Quintus was strangely quiet. Paul was anxious to know the circumstances of Timothy's imprisonment. Timothy explained that when he had last come to visit Paul, he had been admitted to the compound on paying the usual bribe of five denarius, but the soldier outside Paul's cell had demanded fifty denarius. Timothy had refused to pay. He argued with the soldier. The corporal was called and Timothy had found himself unceremoniously bundled into the dark hut, from which he had just been released. He had been kept there for the last few days and supplied with just about enough food and water. Paul and Apollos inwardly realized that because of his frail appearance, the soldiers had imagined that Timothy could be easily bullied into paying a bribe above the going rate. Having thrown him into the shed, only to discover that Timothy had sufficient fortitude to withstand this ordeal, they faced a dilemma. If they released Timothy, he would undoubtedly complain, and the soldiers knew full well that they had broken a code of conduct which their senior officers would expect them to uphold.

'We must make an offical complaint, and see those ruffians brought to book,' muttered Quintus, angrily.

Timothy expressed no such desire himself. He was happy to be released. In true Christian manner, he was not set on revenge.

'If I make a fuss,' he said, 'it could make life more difficult for Paul. If any retribution is called for, then I leave that to my Father in Heaven.'

Apollos looked across at Timothy. Although nearly fifty and of frail appearance, Timothy looked much younger than his years. His face was hardly lined. Apollos suspected that it was the complete lack of malice in Timothy's nature which was the secret of his evergreen countenance.

Quintus referred to the exchange which had taken place earlier between Apollos and the corporal, and asked Apollos to tell him what had happeded at Sidon. Apollos described the black ship which they had seen come to anchor near Sidon. He recounted the train of events which led to the death of Jerahmeel at the hands of the soldier whom he had today recognized as the corporal in charge of the party of soldiers on guard at the prison compound. Quintus listened sadly as he obtained an even fuller picture of events. Claurinius had committed a great crime, but

Quintus felt inwardly, very much to blame himself, for he knew that he was largely responsible for instilling in Claurinius, the attitude that in any venture where one's personal prestige was at stake, it was necessary to succeed at all costs.

Apollos in turn asked Quintus about the ships which had been mentioned by the corporal and himself. Quintus told Apollos the official version of what had happened during that naval campaign, but added that he believed there were other important facts that had not been properly accounted for by those who returned safely to Rome from that mission. Quintus could not bring himself to describe his worst suspicions to Apollos. How could he tell this young man that it was on the orders of his brother-in-law, that his best friend had been killed and he had almost been taken into service as a galley slave?

As the four of them spoke together, an obsequious soldier came in with bread and wine and a basket of fruit. Paul raised his eyebrows. To what did they owe this unprecedented hospitality?

The afternoon wore on and the visitors prepared to take their leave of Paul. Quintus' chariot was somewhere outside the compound, but it could only accommodate two passengers with the driver. Quintus insisted that the chariot should be used, first to take Apollos and Timothy back to the middle of Rome, and then return to collect himself. He let it be understood that there were personal matters he wanted to bring before Paul for his consideration and advice. Quintus left the compound with Apollos and Timothy, gave his instructions to the driver whom he found resting under a tree, watching the Tiber flow by, and then, Quintus returned to spend some further time with Paul as the younger men were driven to Rome.

Quintus' short acquaintance with Paul was sufficient to confirm in Quintus' mind that Paul's reputation as a man of great spirituality was fully justified. Quintus unburdened himself to Paul of the discovery he had made that day of his son's sin. This, Quintus acknowledged to be his own sin which he had transplanted into the next generation by the ambitious attitudes he had instilled into his son. Quintus was intellectually honest enough to recognize this as being his own displaced ambition. A realization of the human misery and suffering caused by that ambition had come home to Quintus that day. Although he had learnt of the scope of divine forgiveness from Apollos and Timothy, Quintus wanted the chance to talk over the matter with Paul, whose riper years, coupled with his spirituality, made him an acceptable mentor for Quintus. The two men talked and prayed for nearly an hour. When Quintus finally took his leave of Paul, he found his chariot ready and waiting outside the compound. Although Quintus now carried a sense of sadness and disappointment about his son's duplicity and the way he realized Claurinius had conducted his command of the small fleet which he had been commissioned to lead, Quintus returned home with the sense of inner peace which comes with the knowledge of forgiveness of personal sins.

The following day, the Church met in the catacombs to discover with joy that Timothy had been released and was with them. It was made clear that the Lord had used Quintus as the means by which their prayers for Timothy were answered. The old man was sitting with Narcissus and his family and was really quite overcome with the credit which was attributed to him for acting in a way which he felt was the only natural way he could have behaved.

Apollos completed his epistle to his Church in Corinth. As he had already sent a short letter, informing them of Timothy's imprisonment, he concluded his letter by telling them the good news that Timothy had been released, and that they should expect them both back in Corinth in the very near future.[224] Apollos despatched this letter which he expected to arrive in Corinth a short time before he and Timothy would reach that city themselves. Apollos and Timothy spent the next few days, bidding their adieux to both their old friends and the many wonderful new friends they had made during their short but eventful stay in Rome. As Apollos and Timothy boarded the ship docked at Ostia on which they had booked their passage, they gazed eastwards to catch their last glimpse of that great city, built on seven hills. Their hearts were filled with a strange mixture of both hope and apprehension, as they contemplated what the future might hold for those wonderful Roman Christians.

49

Departure from Corinth

Apollos and Timothy enjoyed an uneventful and therefore, relaxing journey home to Corinth. No one knew the actual day that they would arrive, so there was no reception committee waiting for them on the quay at Lechaeum, their port of disembarkation. Apollos and Timothy proceeded on foot to Corinth and made their way to Apollos' house. It was the middle of the afternoon and the house was not unsurprisingly empty, as that was the time of day when Diana and Selenece often visited town. The travellers washed and Apollos warmed up some soup which the pair drank with relish. After a little more than an hour, Diana and Selenece returned to enjoy the delightful surprise of finding Apollos, safely at home after his trip to Rome, and Timothy with him too. Apollos and Timothy had so much to tell of their visit to Rome that the foursome sat up until the small hours of the morning, sharing their news. Selenece was fascinated by the description of the catacombs in which the Roman Christians worshipped, and Diana took great interest in all they had to tell her of Quintus Albinian, her sister's father-in-law.

'He sounds a lovely gentleman,' she mused. 'I would like to meet him.'

Timothy recounted the way he had been put in prison, and then released as a result of the efforts of Apollos and Quintus. He described this episode in the way he figured would most appeal to Selenece. Although the memories of that ordeal in solitary confinement in what was no more than a shed, not knowing when he would be released, must have been among the most worrying and uncomfortable experiences of Timothy's life, he caricatured the soldiers who were his guards on that occasion with such humour that Selenece laughed until the tears ran down her face. Apollos mentioned some of the Roman Christians who had been particularly helpful to them while away, particularly Philologus and Julia whose hospitality they had enjoyed, and Phoebe whom Diana remembered well. Apollos, Diana and Selenece owed a particular debt of gratitude to Phoebe for the part she had paid in their reunification when she had lived at Cenchreae.[196] It was Phoebe who had expeditiously brought news that Selenece was safe, when Diana was beside herself with anxiety at the discovery that her infant daughter was lost in the busy city of Corinth. Timothy and Apollos brought reassuring news of the continued good health of John Mark and Luke who were known to Diana and Selenece from the occasions they had called at Corinth on their missionary travels. They described how useful these scribes were to Paul who made much use of them in preparing the letters which were such an inspiration to the churches and individuals who received them.

They then spent some time talking about Paul. Visiting Paul had, after all, been the objective of their journey. Although he was ageing and going blind, they could report that Paul was nonetheless, in good spirits and happy and comfortable in prison. Timothy, who knew Paul better than most, explained that the very worst that could happen to Paul was martyrdom and that Paul would welcome ending his life in this dramatic way, which would be totally paradoxical to the Roman authorities. Paul desired martyrdom on two counts. His absolute faith and assurance of an after life would encourage others, and he continually longed for the time he would be in the perpetual company of his Lord. Apollos said nothing of Paul's suggestion that he should go to Gaul. He deemed it better to broach this at a later time when he was alone with Diana.

Diana thanked Apollos for writing such reassuring letters and sending these regularly to Corinth. It appeared that none had been lost in transit. In particular, she thanked him for his last very long letter which had been read to the Church, and had provided so much instruction and encouragement to the brotherhood. She said that the Church would be surprised to find that Apollos and Timothy had arrived so soon after receiving this letter. Apollos realized that they might wonder why he should have gone to the trouble of compiling a letter which contained such concentrated teaching, if he knew he would be returning so soon and be able to deliver the teaching first-hand. However, Apollos inwardly hoped that the thoughts he had committed to paper might be a legacy to leave to posterity in a way he could not bequeath the ephemeral spoken word.

Diana also had hopes that this letter would be read by future generations of Christians and she drew Apollos' attention to the fact that he had not signed the letter or provided an indication in its contents that he was author. In fact, the only living Christian mentioned in the letter was Timothy, for Apollos had alluded to his release from prison. Apollos explained that in his youth, he would have wanted to receive credit and plaudits for anything he had successfully accomplished, but that now, his priorities were different. His sole purpose in life was to serve his Lord. If the letter Apollos had written proved to be of value to this and future generations of Christians, then this was the only thing which mattered. The anonymity of the letter was itself of no importance.

News soon spread around Corinth, Cenchreae and Lechaeum that Apollos and Timothy were back, and the home of Priscilla and Aquila, where the Church still met, was packed on the first day of the week at the time the Christians gathered for worship. Timothy and Apollos were held in very special and genuine affection by the Corinthians who hung on every word the pair had to tell them, as they described the state of the Church in Rome, and spoke of individual Christians of whom the Corinthians had knowledge. In particular, Titius Justus was relieved to see Apollos back, as the Church had gone through a difficult time while Apollos had been away. They were facing a form of economic persecution, there had been some apostasy, and false teachers were attempting to steal the minds of the faithful. Apollos was aware of these problems from the letters he had received from Diana, and they continued to provide a focus for Apollos' fervent prayer.

A few days later when he was beginning to feel settled back into the routine of life at home in Corinth, Apollos decided on an occasion when he was alone with Diana, that the time was right to tell her of Paul's suggestion concerning his going to Gaul. However, before he had broached the matter, Diana made mention of her sister, Demeter, saying how much she would like to see her again, and suggested herself, that they could visit Gaul. Apollos remembered Paul's words when the implications for his family had been mentioned and smiled. Diana was initially puzzled and perhaps a little annoyed, misinterpreting this smile as a sign that Apollos was treating her suggestion lightly. Apollos then recounted the commission that Paul had challenged him to fulfill on an occasion when he had visited Paul alone. Paul had suggested that Apollos' family might have a pressing reason to visit Gaul which was quite independent of Paul's challenge. Apollos and Diana immediately recognized that Paul had pointed them to a sign, and that this sign had just materialized in Diana's expression of a deep desire to go to the land where she would again meet her sister.

Apollos and Diana discussed this in great depth. They realized that if the journey to Gaul was not going to be just a visit to Demeter and Claurinius, but was to involve Apollos in missionary activity to the Gauls, then they would not be away from Corinth for just a few months, as was the case with Apollos' visit to Rome, but could be away for many months, or indeed, years. This would mean that special provision would have to be made for running the Church of Corinth for the foreseeable future. Diana's aunt, Calliope, and Calliope's cousin Euphrosyne, had died two years earlier in Cenchreae, and Diana felt released from the responsibility of caring for her relatives in their old age. Apollos and Diana prayed long and hard about embarking on this mission, and the more they prayed, the more it seemed right that they should go to Gaul.

Apollos shared this prognosis with the Church elders and very specially with Titius Justus and Timothy. Although Titius Justus had done a marvellous job in running the Church while Apollos had been away, it had been a great strain on him and his family. He had some trepidation about resuming this responsibility, expecially to cover the long term absence that Apollos predicted his trip to Gaul would involve. However, Timothy was not anxious to resume his travels at that point, and volunteered his services to stay and help Titius. That clinched the matter. Titius had no qualms about running the Church with the support of one as able and erudite as Timothy. Apollos told Timothy that he could have the titles to their house, where Timothy had been staying as a guest since returning from Rome with Apollos.

It took several weeks before Apollos and Diana had fully put their affairs in order and were ready to depart the city which held such happy, happy memories for them. Any misgivings they may have had that Selenece, who was now in her early teens, might resent being uprooted from her environment where she was clearly happy and had many friends, proved quite unfounded. Over the years, Selenece had thrilled at the stories she had heard of lands beyond Greece which the many missionary visitors to the Corinthian Church had told. She probably had something of her father's wanderlust in her anyway. Selenece received the news that her parents were considering going to work in another country where they hoped to meet her long lost aunt and uncle, with rapturous enthusiasm. Had Apollos and Diana sought to change their mind about this enterprise after that, they would have been put under considerable pressure by Selenece to adhere to their original intentions. However, no such thoughts crossed the minds of Apollos and Diana. As the date on which they were due to sail approached, preparations for their departure accelerated, and the family were carried along by the momentum, generated by the frantic activities involved in leaving everything straight for Titius and Timothy to continue their work, and saying goodbye to their many friends.

At last the day dawned when the family would leave Corinth. As their ship gently slipped away from the quayside at Lechaeum, a large crowd had gathered to wave farewell and wish bon voyage to a family who had done more than can be expressed in words for the Church at Corinth. There were few dry eyes as the ship slowly made its way down the Gulf of Corinth and finally disappeared from view.

50

Massilia

The ship carrying Apollos, Diana and Selenece made slow headway through the Gulf of Corinth, but once past Patrae and through the Ionian Islands, the ship picked up a good easterly breeze in the Ionian Sea which carried them briskly westwards. Their first port of call was Syracuse in Sicily, whence they turned northwards for Puteoli. The ship stayed for two days at Puteoli, unloading one cargo and taking on board another, before continuing its journey westwards. It took two days to cross the Tyrrhenian sea to Corsica where the ship pulled in to Ajaccio. Three days later, the ship completed the next phase of its journey, which had taken it to Massilia in the Roman province of Narbonensia to the south of Gaul. This was the port of disembarkation for Apollos, Diana and Selenece.

Having reached Gaul, the family had no immediate notion of how they were to trace the whereabouts of Claurinius and Demeter. However, this was not the only objective of their journey. Paul had commissioned Apollos to bring the gospel to Gaul, and there were a number of reasons why Massilia was a good place to get acclimatized to life in Gaul. Although not part of the Greek empire which had spread eastwards, rather than west from Greece, this section of the Mediterranean coast had come within the sphere of Greek influence when Greece was at its zenith. Massilia itself had been founded by the Phocaeans some six hundred years earlier, and there was enough evidence of Greek culture for Apollos and his family to feel at home. Greek was still spoken in some quarters, although Latin was the language of officialdom. The family soon discovered that the language spoken by the ordinary people was a Gallic patois. While Greek and Latin were sufficient to get them round Massilia, Apollos realized that to communicate effectively with the Narbonensians in a way which would overcome him being regarded as an alien, it would be important for him to acquire a working knowledge of this language.

The first thing the family did on disembarking was to seek out a suitable inn to be their temporary accommodation. They soon found suitable hostelry and put up in a small but clean inn, some distance from the busy sea-front and harbour. Apollos and Diana were pleased to see how delighted was Selenece at the exciting experience of exploring a new place to be home, on her first major excursion from Corinth. After a few days, they found a suitable house to become their permanent residence, which would be not only large enough to acommodate the family, but would allow scope for work that could be developed to establish links with the community and eventually provide means of securing an income. This latter need was not immediately pressing however, as they had been given ample funds by the generous Corinthian Church to support them in their missionary venture.

Once settled in their new home, they set about starting up a school. This was immediately well patronized as their charges for tuition were modest, and there were few other facilities in Massilia where parents could get their children off their hands during the day, let alone educated. The school proved successful on a number of counts. As well as providing tuition in Greek, Latin and mathematics, Apollos and Diana were able to impart the not inconsiderable knowledge they possessed of Mediterranean geography and the cultural heritage of the peoples who inhabited its coasts. Also, Apollos and Diana were able to use this school as a medium for learning the Gallic patois spoken in Narbonensia themselves. Apollos and Diana continued in the evenings to cater for the education of Selenece who proved a rewarding pupil as her father had been before her. Also, Selenece was of an age and maturity which enabled her to contribute to the running of the school and to teach the younger children.

After about six months, Apollos and Diana felt confident

enough in the new language they had acquired, to start work among the adults. The children they taught provided a natural bridge to the adult community, most of whom had time on their hands. The members of this community welcomed the opportunity of expanding their horizons of knowledge and understanding of the world beyond Massilia, provided by this erudite and charming family who had come to live in their midst. The only religion these people knew was the puerile idolatory which was the legacy of the Greeks and Romans who had colonized the city. The Massilians gave this religion about as much credence as that afforded by perceptive Greeks and Romans themselves to this aberration of their otherwise magnificient cultures. There were Jewish traders in the city, but the Jews have no missionary zeal to spread their faith, and the Massilians had only vague notions of what the Jewish belief system involved.

Apollos and Diana were therefore working in a virgin mission field, and had the gifts to first interest, and to then convince those who came to hear them, of the truth of the gospel and its relevance for their lives. A flourishing little church soon started to meet at Apollos and Diana's new home. The close proximity of the sea provided the location for conducting public baptism of the new converts, and these aroused great interest among citizens of Massilia who lived well beyond the immediate environment of Apollos and Diana's home. For Apollos, a particularly encouraging aspect of the work, was the rapid emergence of new Christians with intellectual and leadership qualities, who showed a genuine desire for taking on responsibility in the Church. Copies were made of the gospels of John Mark and Luke, along with copies of two of Paul's letters which Apollos always regarded as his most treasured possessions. Apollos was so busy with his teaching and missionary work in Massilia, that he found no time to translate these documents into the domestic language of the Gauls, but many of them had a smattering of Greek, and Apollos provided Greek classes for the Massilians, hungry for knowledge. While the initial attempts at verbal communication in Gallic patois were hesitant and laboured, the family soon became fluent speakers of this new language for them, into which many familiar Latin words had beeen absorbed. After about two years, Apollos began to speak with the eloquence, approaching the quality with which he could harangue a meeting in Greek. While in Massilia, Apollos and Diana made enquiries about the Roman Procurator. People knew of the Procurator, but no one could remember his coming to Massilia. As Gaul was a very large country, the procurators of the various provinces did a great deal of travelling, seldom staying at one administrative centre for more than a few weeks at a time. Although Roman government had obviously established a good framework for maintaining law and order, and provided good communications, taxation was heavy, and Apollos and Diana realized that the imposition of alien government was unpopular among the proud Gauls who resented living in the knowledge that they were a conquered race. Diana discovered that the main centre of Roman administration in that part of Narbonensia was the city of Nîmes, a few kilometres inland to the northwest of Massilia. It appeared that the Procurator sometimes stayed there for a few months at a time, but he kept a low profile, and often, the people in Massilia were unaware of his proximity until some weeks after he had left Nîmes to oversee business at some other centre of Roman administration in Narbonensia.

Diana and Apollos came to the conclusion that the strategy they should adopt, to give them the best chance of meeting up again with Claurinus and Demeter, was to actually transfer their centre of operation from Massilia to Nîmes. Besides giving them the best opportunity to meet their long lost sister and brother-in-law, there were good reasons of spiritual practicality for making this move. The Church at Massilia was now strong enough to survive independently of Apollos' leadership, and indeed, Apollos' translation to Nîmes would give the much needed opportunity for the aspiring elders in the Massilian Church to develop as fully-fledged Church leaders themselves. After a year or so, Claurinius' circuit of duty would bring him to Nîmes where Apollos and Diana would be able to make contact with this branch of the family. Also, Nîmes was sufficiently close to Massilia, that Apollos would easily be able to return to provide any help or support needed by the Church in its early years of indigenous leadership.

Thus, after a stay of a little over two years in Massilia, Apollos called together the Church elders and informed them of his future plans. At first they protested, being reluctant to lose a family whose contribution to every aspect of the life of their community had been so beneficial, but they accepted that the Church could grow to become strong and independent in a special way if Apollos were to move. Nîmes was, after all, no more than a few kilometres from Massilia, and close contact with the family could be maintained. Apollos and the elders prayed hard about the choice of successor, and the Holy Spirit moved them to recognize an elder called Asvendix as the one with all the gifts and grace to prove a worthy successor to Apollos. He was commissioned for this task, and the family moved to Nîmes. The move was very straightforward. Apollos had reconnoitred that city in the company of a Massilian elder who knew Nîmes well, and a house had been identified and purchased. This house was large enough to be suitable for community use and for Apollos and Diana to carry out teaching work as they had done in Massilia.

51

Nîmes

The winter and early spring had been unusually wet and cold for Narbonensia where the hot dry summers were usually followed by mild winters which would normally be described as moist, rather than wet. Apollos and Diana stayed at Massilia until they had celebrated Easter with the Church they had founded and built up from nothing to a vigorous and flourishing body representing a complete cross-section of Massilian society. Two days after Easter, Apollos, Diana and Selenece moved to Nîmes. The day had dawned dull, but the clouds soon dispersed to welcome the finest day that that spring had yielded to date. They watched the white clouds scudding across the sky, and breathed the spring air as they sensed the refreshing breezes caress their faces. They looked forward to the next phase of their work with a confident expectancy. The favourable turn in the weather seemed to augur well for their future ministry.

Nîmes was a lovely city which had been developed by the Romans to become a metropolis of some distinction. It had a good supply of fresh water from an impressive aqueduct which was a masterpiece of Roman civil engineering. A number of temples had been built on prominent sites within the city. Although no more than shrines to impotent idols, these temples were architecturally superb. Apollos teased Diana that her pagan cult had spread too far when the first temple they encountered was found to be dedicated to Diana, but it was not long before Diana was able to counter this jibe when they discovered another temple, dedicated to Apollo. Most of the principal Roman deities were represented among temples which punctuated the rows of shops and commercial buildings. To the north of the town was a Roman fort and a rather grim looking building called the Citadel. This was neither house nor fortress, but combined aspects of both types of building without aspiring to resemble anything grand enough to justify the appellation of palace. The Citadel was the main administrative building of the city. Two sentries guarded the main portal through which there was a fairly continuous stream of traffic as officials, tax-collectors and Roman soldiers passed to and fro on their business. This was where the Roman Procurator would stay when in residence in Nîmes, but enquiry revealed that he was not expected to be there for some months. By far the most impressive building in the city was a huge Roman Circus, right in the centre of the town. Here, the Romans indulged their love of gladiatorial combats, a taste for which was all too readily acquired by the indigenous population of the City.

Apollos and Diana started their work in Nîmes as they had done so successfully at Massilia, by founding a small school. As before, this provided a bridge to the adult community, and having already surmounted the language problem in their initial enterprise in Massilia, Apollos and Diana soon established the nucleus of a Church. Apollos reckoned that if the rate of growth experienced during the first few months, was maintained for two years, they would have to split into two communities, and this left him with the challenge of identifying and training those who might be called on to lead any such daughter Churches which might be formed.

Of those who joined the Church at Nîmes in its early days, special mention must be made of a young Roman called Solarus. Solarus had been a soldier in the Imperial legions for two years, but had paid the necessary sum of money to secure an honourable discharge. Solarus had been attracted to the army by the pomp and pageantry of the parades he had witnessed when a boy in Rome. The army was highly esteemed in ancient Rome as the populace there knew that they relied on the army more than anything else, not just for their security, but for the wealth and affluence which an ever expanding empire allowed that city to enjoy. Solarus' parents had died when he was quite young, and the army seemed an obvious career for him. He enlisted when he was eighteen and had enjoyed most aspects of army life, the comradeship of the other soldiers, the framework of discipline which made much of daily life predictable, and the opportunity to travel and experience what Solarus regarded as great adventures. While Solarus had found the excitement of battle stimulating, he found some of the tasks the army had to perform disturbing. He took no pleasure in turning villagers out of their houses after their tribe had been defeated by a Roman legion, and then witnessing the looting and burning of what these poor people had regarded as their homes. Solarus had an aversion to the enslavement of fit and strong men whose only crime was to attempt to defend land, on which their tribe had dwelt for generations, against the aggressive expansion of the Roman Empire. As a Roman soldier, Solarus had no alternative but to obey the orders issued by his commanders to perform these tasks. However, Solarus was a thinking man who considered carefully the meaning and responsibility of life, and realized that for him, it was a mistake to abdicate his freedom to make moral choices, and render unquestioning obedience to an army which clearly had few, if any, moral scruples. Thus, after acquitting himself well in a campaign fought in Germania, Solarus took the steps necessary to secure his discharge from the army when his regiment returned from that campaign.

Solarus now worked as a Roman government official. He was a good organizer and understood well the Roman systems of record keeping. He was therefore able to efficiently schedule the work of those who served the administration, and he kept the records needed for official purposes, meticulously up to date.

The nature of his work in Roman administration led Solarus to become aware of the activities of Apollos and Diana among the community which occupied the district where they had set up their home in Nîmes. Solarus made a point of attending one of the meetings led by Apollos and was deeply impressed by what he heard. Apollos' words and teaching seemed to provide Solarus with the meaning for life which he had long sought but which, until that time, continually evaded him. Solarus was not just impressed by the eloquent style of Apollos' oratory, which was sufficient to sway many whose ability to think and analyse was less developed than Solarus'. The whole tenor of Apollos' teaching supported a framework of irrefutable logic. Solarus attended further sabbath meetings at the Church and soon got to know Apollos and Diana personally. They were impressed with the intelligence and integrity of this young man. As he continued to absorb instruction, and to debate with Apollos on the deeper significance of some of the doctrinal issues which arose, Apollos inwardly identified Solarus as a potential Church leader of the future. As Solarus became increasingly absorbed into the Christian fellowship, Apollos and Diana noticed with some pleasure, that a romantic attachment began to develop between Solarus and Selenece. Selenece was seventeen years old.

52

A Family Reunion

Some months after Apollos and Diana had arrived in Nîmes and were beginning to feel well settled into their new environment, they discovered by the usual channels that news quickly spreads in cities such as Nîmes, that the Procurator's duty tour of the province had brought him back to the city. They learned that he and his wife were now in residence in the Citadel. At last they would have the opportunity to renew acquaintance and restore family ties.

Apollos and Diana made their way to the Citadel which was the Roman administrative centre, and also served as the Governor's residence when he was in the city. They announced to the sentry on duty that they were related to the Governor, that Diana was in fact, the Governor's wife's sister whom she had not seen for many years. The sentry looked incredulously at this family who were not dressed in a style which would mark them out as Roman nobilty. He did not believe them and decided that they were just townsfolk, trying to exploit what they imagined to be the naivety of an ordinary soldier to gain unauthorized entry into a Roman official building. The soldier decided that it was not worth bothering a senior officer to deal with such an unlikely tale and used his own initiative. He told them that if they wanted to see the Governor, they would have to apply by sending a letter, explaining the pretext for which an audience was requested. The family felt frustrated, but went home and returned with the letter.

A different sentry was on duty, and they again explained who they were as they gave him the letter. He called the guard commander who looked as incredulous as the first sentry, but he allowed them into the vestibule, furnished with crude benches on which they could sit, while the letter was taken to the Governor. After they had waited for nearly an hour, a soldier appeared and asked the family to follow him. They were conducted through yards of drab corridors and up a couple of flights of stairs, at last emerging into a lighter more airy part of the building which contrasted strongly with the claustrophobic atmosphere of the maze of passages which linked the military messes and administrative offices located in the lower storeys. They had reached the living quarters of the Governor and his household.

Apollos, Diana and Selenece were shown into a room where Claurinius and Demeter were waiting to meet them. It is hard to describe the impact of that meeting on the individuals involved who had known each other so well in the heady days of their youth, but who had been separated for nearly eighteen years as a result of a situation in which three of them had shared the tragic loss of their parents.

The shock was greatest for Claurinius and Demeter who had believed for so long, that Diana had perished with her parents in the violence of the Alexandrian riots. They had received a letter from Claurinius' father, Quintus, informing them that Diana was alive, but they did not really expect ever to see her again. Apollos and Diana had at least the advantage of the initiative in arranging this meeting, and had therefore braced themselves for any surprises this encounter might bring. The course of their lives had been so different and the effect of such contrasting life-styles on their appearances and personalities had been so profound, that all the parties to this reunion experienced a greater degree of astonishment than they had expected.

Diana and Demeter embraced and Apollos and Claurinius grasped each other's right wrist which was the conventional Roman handshake. Apollos and Diana introduced their daughter to her long lost uncle and aunt. Claurinius and Demeter had no children. They all sat down. There were now the momentous events of nearly two decades to share. Where should they begin? The conversation which followed was somewhat one-sided. Claurinius and Demeter did not seem to be particularly forthcoming, but Diana and Apollos had so much to recount of those eventful eighteen years. More interesting even than the

357

exciting tales of travels and tribulations, of trials and triumphs, which Diana in particular was pouring forth, were the inward thoughts of these people as they surveyed with bemused bewilderment, former acquaintances and relations who were so very, very different from anything they could have imagined, prior to this reunion.

Claurinius and Demeter surveyed Diana with amazement as she spoke in animated tones of the blessings which had come to her in the wake of the devastating upheaval in Alexandria. Diana was now so much more outgoing than the quiet, reserved young lady they remembered from Alexandrian days, and her beauty was now quite breathtaking. As Apollos had realized when he had first seen Diana when they made their surprise meeting in Corinth, Diana's was a feminine beauty which increased and deepened with the advancing years, as all the inner beauty of her character and personality became imprinted in that lovely face. Diana had responded with grace and forebearance to every adverse situation she had met in life, and had poured love and compassion from within herself on all those whose fortune had been to encounter Diana when they were experiencing need or despairing over some apparently hopeless situation. All this loveliness was carved in Diana's face which was a wonder for all to behold.

Apollos regarded Demeter's countenance which had been the object of his infatuation in the days of his immaturity. Although she must have been approaching fifty, in some ways, her face had not changed at all. The perfect Greek features were there, just as Apollos had remembered them all those years ago. Amazingly, there was not a blemish, not a wrinkle on that face. However, in another profound and disturbing way, the face was totally different. It was no longer a face which would invoke the beholder to inward fantasies of love and adoration. Demeter's face was completely white and expressionless. The secret of her apparently unchanging features lay in the layers of paste and cream with which she daily made up her countenance to maintain the contours and smoothness of her youthful beauty. However, what people now beheld was not the face of Demeter, but in effect, a mask of what Demeter had looked like twenty years earlier. That face might still have looked beautiful in a photograph, had such technology existed then, but in the reality of the living and moving world, it was dull and lifeless. Demeter did not dare to change her expression, lest that mask should crack. In that day and age, when photography was unavailable, the likenesses of the rich and famous were preserved for posterity in busts of stone and marble, and such a medium would have ideally portrayed Demeter, for though living, she projected all the coldness and chill of polished marble.

The appearance of Claurinius on the other hand had totally changed. Here was no longer the dashing soldier whose swagger might have led one to believe that he was the pride of the Roman army. Here was a prematurely aged Imperial administrator, whose brow had become wrinkled and shoulders bowed under the pressures of trying to raise the tribute demanded by his superiors in Rome. Claurinius had to arrange the collection of taxes from the hostile Gauls whose resentment of Roman authority was second only to that displayed by the Jews at the other extreme of the empire. Beneath his balding temples, Claurinius' face looked haggard, and there was something unsettled and furtive in his expression. One felt that here was a man who did not sleep well at nights and expected the dawn of each day to be the harbinger of bad news.

Demeter studied Apollos, the amorous swain whose suit she had rejected when she held sway as the belle of Alexandrian society. Although good looking, he had been such a talkative young man and too much study had made him boring. Demeter had had no understanding of most of the controversies on which Apollos used to philosophize. Apollos' youthful good looks had now given way to handsome maturity, and although he was still talkative, the manner of his speech was different. He spoke with an arresting animation and held the interest of all who listened, with the colourful descriptions and vivid figures of speech which he used to aptly illustrate everything he talked about. As the meeting continued, Demeter first started to mentally contrast Claurinius unfavourably with Apollos, and then, to experience inward envy of her sister, Diana, who was obviously enjoying to the full all the good things life had to offer her. Demeter's expressionless face gave no hint of what was passing in her mind.

It was not possible in one meeting for the foursome to exchange all the exciting news that had transpired over half a lifetime which had been filled with very eventful years. Apollos and Diana invited Claurinius and Demeter to visit them in their home, but this was declined. It seemed it was neither safe nor proper for a Roman proconsul to be entertained in an ordinary dwelling house. However, arrangements were made for Apollos, Diana and Selenece to visit the Citadel again. Over the next six weeks, before Claurinius had to move on to the next centre of administration where he had duties to perform, Apollos and Diana attended the Citadel several times in the process of renewing the family tie, broken by the adverse circumstances which had occurred in Alexandria at the end of the reign of Caligula Caesar.

During the meetings at the Citadel, the conversation was still very one-sided. Apollos and Diana found ample opportunity to speak of their faith and the wonderful difference that had made to their lives, but received little response from Demeter and Claurinius. Diana considered that Demeter had not experienced many events of great happiness in her life that would have provided her with things to talk about and which she would have wanted to share. Apart from the first year in Rome, when it seemed Demeter had acclimatised herself well to the Roman social scene, very little had happened to afford Demeter a natural source of conversational material. She detested Gaul. The hostility of the native population severely limited her opportunities for social outlets, even with other families of Roman nobility. All journeys had to be undertaken in the company of a small troop of soldiers to provide an armed escort.

Apollos formed the impression that Claurinius' reserve and reluctance to contribute much to conversation arose from the fact that there were things he wished to hide, and was wary about speaking too much, lest some chance remark should let slip something which he would rather remained concealed. Apollos naturally told Claurinius that he had met his father, Quintus Albinian, in Rome, and that Quintus had become a Christian. There was no obvious response from Claurinius to this news. Apollos ventured to tell Claurinius of what had happened in Sidon, when Jerahmeel, whom Claurinius would have known from his days in Alexandria, had been killed. Apollos mentioned that Quintus had told him that the offending ship was from a flotilla that Claurinius had commanded, but that it had never returned to port. Apollos sensed that Claurinius looked uneasy as this matter was raised. He asked Claurinius if he could tell him any more of the circumstances surrounding this event, as Quintus had indicated that he suspected that the official version recorded in the Roman archives may not have been a completely accurate account. Claurinius became very evasive and claimed that all this had happened so long ago that he no longer had a detailed memory of the deployment of the ships in his flotilla. Claurinius then quickly changed the subject and Apollos increasingly sensed that Claurinius was withholding something which would clear up some of the mystery which surrounded the black ship.

On completing his official duties in Nîmes, Claurinius and Demeter had to travel to another part of Gaul, but they told Apollos and Diana that they would be returning to Nîmes within the year, and that next time, their stay in Nîmes would be longer. Claurinius and Demeter duly departed, leaving Apollos and Diana with some sense of anticlimax.

53

The Arverni Community

An episode which illustrates the quality of the ministry of Apollos and Diana in Nîmes, occurred when they had been in the city for just over a year. In the early months of their time in Nîmes, most of the people who attended the Church lived very near the house of Apollos and Diana which, besides being their home, doubled up as a school and as the building where the Christians met for worship. As they became more firmly established, and as the news of what they were doing for those living in their quarter of Nîmes spread, people started to come from further afield. Among these was a woman called Astaveldi who came from a community of weavers and dyers. The members of this community originated from the Arverni tribe which lived in central Gaul. They now dwelt on the southernmost out-skirts of Nîmes. These Arverni had come to the city some years earlier. It was rumoured that they were fleeing from some trouble that they had had with the Roman authorities when in the settlement they had occupied previously. Whatever the trouble may have been, no Roman official ever came to Nîmes to demand reparations for the things they were supposed to have done to earn Roman displeasure.

One day, Astaveldi arrived at the Church in a state of some distress. As Apollos and Diana spoke to her to discover the source of this distress, they learned that the infant son of her sister had recently died. Astaveldi spoke of her community as one that was doomed because of the crimes it had committed in the past. She cited many instances of young children in the community, and even babies, becoming ill, developing a fever and dying soon afterwards. Astaveldi had tried to persuade others from her community to come to the Church, for Astaveldi had formed the impression from the stories of Jesus and the miracles that he performed, that Christianity was a source of wonderful healing and miracles, but she herself felt unable to channel this healing to her community. The men of Astaveldi's community were generally sceptical, and although Astaveldi felt that some of the women might have accompanied her to Church, their husbands had usually objected. Like many of the societies of the day, Astaveldi's community was very male dominated.

Apollos and Diana agreed to go with Astaveldi to visit her family. They were to discover a fairly tattered little community, living in crudely constructed huts, scattered among the tanks and vats which were used for their dyeing activities. Astaveldi introduced Apollos and Diana to her sister and to others who had lost infant children in recent years. As they walked round the settlement which was generally untidy and unkempt, Apollos and Diana realized that hygiene standards were poor. Then Diana's attention became drawn to the plumbing, and with some horror, she realized that this community was polluting the water which was not only used for making dyes, but also for domestic washing, drinking and cooking purposes. Diana could not fail to recall the situation which had occurred in Alexandria, so many years earlier, where many child deaths in the Egyptian community had resulted from their water supply being polluted by effluent from the Greek tanneries. How could she ever forget? The tragic consequence of that situation had been the riots in which the parents of both Apollos and herself had perished. A big difference between the situation which had led to rioting in Alexandria and this situation, was that these Gallic weavers were not the victims of inconsiderate behaviour of some other community but were polluting their own water. She pointed this out to Astaveldi who arranged to take her to the leader of their community.

The community was led by an arrogant young Gaul called Kervanindrax. Kervanindrax owed his position to the fact that he was the grandson of Vercingetorix, a Gallic chieftain. Vercingetorix, the leader of the Arverni tribe, had succeeded in establishing some form of hegemony among the competing Gaulish tribes, and had the distinction of being one of the very few men to defeat the redoubtable Julius Caesar in pitched battle. Vercingetorix had won his victory at Gergovia. His grandson lived on the glory and prestige the Arverni ascribed to this one success, and Kervanindrax had almost absolute autocratic authority in that community.

When Diana explained to Kervanindrax her recognition that the infant mortality his tribe was suffering was due to their polluting their own water supply, Kervanindrax was disdainful. He was not going to take advice from a woman. Similarly, Diana was not going to be ignored by an arrogant ignoramus when the lives of children were at stake. Her eyes flashed as she persisted in her argument. Kervanindrax disdainfully picked up a tankard from the table, filled it at a nearby vat, downed the contents and contemptuously claimed that he anticipated no ill effects.

Diana explained that through long exposure to the source of disease in the water, he and the adult members of their society had developed an immunity to the harmful effects of that water, but that infants had not the advantage of this protection. Kervanindrax could not deny that the harmful effects of the water were only experienced by children. Diana declared that she had no such immunity and would not therefore contemplate drinking a single drop of that foul liquid.

By this time, several more of the community had gathered round, wondering what all this fuss was about. Some of the women timidly ventured to suggest that perhaps they might try out changing the system by which waste was drained from their settlement, just in case this made things better. The concept of acquiring immunity to a disease as a result of exposure over many years to the source of the disease was not appreciated or understood by Kervanindrax, but in any case, Kervanindrax was not going to be guided by any woman. It appeared that an impasse had been reached.

Diana then suggested an alternative way of deciding the issue. She reminded Kervanindrax that she had just stated that she would not drink one drop of that water, because of the effect she knew it would have on her. She told

Kervanindrax that she was prepared to drink this water, if she could do so in a way which proved that it was disease ridden to one like herself who had built up no immunity to whatever source of infection lay in that water. Kervanindrax did not immediately reject this suggestion, and some of the men standing round persuaded Kervanindrax that he could lose nothing from such a demonstration. At this point, Apollos objected. He agreed that this would be a good test, but insisted that it should be himself, rather than Diana, who would drink from the water supply under test conditions that would irrefutably prove the water to be the source of disease. There followed the only serious argument between Apollos and Diana in their married life. Diana insisted that as leader of their Christian community, it was unfair to that community for Apollos to expose himself to an unnecessary risk on behalf of another community when someone else had already volunteered to take the risk. After further argument, Apollos suggested that if Diana insisted on drinking this water, then he too would drink it. Diana countered this by saying that it was foolish for two to take a risk that need only be taken by one, and she pointed out to Apollos that she was relying on him being fit and well to pray for her safety whilst conducting this test. In the end, Diana had her way.

Apollos and Diana returned home and called a meeting of Church elders to explain what had been undertaken. Arrangements were immediately made to form prayer groups. Apollos and Diana then went back to Astaveldi's settlement where a hut had been made available for Apollos and Diana to stay during the course of this test. Apollos drank only water that was brought to him by members of the Christian community in Nîmes, but all the water Diana drank and all the food she ate, was brought to her by the community led by Kervanindrax. For two days, Diana showed no ill effects, and she started to suspect that she was being given water from a different source. Then, on the third day, Diana began to feel ill, and by the evening she had developed a high fever. This fever continued into the fourth and fifth days. Perspiration poured from Diana. She became delirious and completely unaware of what was going on around her as she tossed and turned on her bed.

To those who came to visit her, there was no doubt that she was desperately ill. This was no feigned fever. The water which Diana had been given to drink was replaced by water brought daily for Apollos by the elders from their Church. Apollos remained by Diana's side, almost beside himself with worry and anxiety, but he availed himself of the opportunity to pray earnestly and fervently that Diana would recover. On the sixth day, the fever started to subside, and that night, she fell into a deep sleep. When she woke on the morning of the seventh day, Diana sat up, feeling well but weak. She had no memory of the previous three days.

Diana had made her point. When she appeared from the hut that morning, leaning on Apollos' arm, pale but smiling, the whole of that community of weavers and dyers came out to cheer and applaud this brave woman who had so effectively proved the validity of her case at such great risk to herself, so that they would know what steps to take to safeguard their children's health. In fact, the remedy had already been taken. At the first sign of Diana's fever, Kervanindrax himself had demolished the offending drainage system and organized the digging of new drains and channels to clear the community's waste in a way which would not jeopardize the cleanliness of their water supply. Kervanindrax stepped from the crowd that had gathered to greet Diana and warmly hugged her. He shook Apollos by the hand and continued to lead the people in their applause for Diana.

Apollos and Diana returned to their home to receive a rapturous welcome. It is difficult to know who had experienced the greatest ordeal. While it cannot be denied that Diana had to cope with the extreme physical discomfort and danger of the fever, Apollos had the anguish of sitting by her bedside, witnessing his wife undergoing discomfort he would have gladly suffered on her behalf as she risked death. Selenece on the other hand, had the added anguish of empathizing with her mother's danger at a distance, uncertain of what was happening between the daily visits when she brought fresh food and water from the community for her parents.

The Church insisted that the family should take a

holiday, and they returned to Massilia for a fortnight where they found that that Church was flourishing under the leadership of Asvendix. After relaxing for two weeks, they returned to Nîmes. Over the following weeks, many from Astaveldi's community of dyers and weavers, including some of the men, travelled across the city on the sabbath to learn of this faith which manifested itself in such love and sacrifice, and came to worship the God of the Christians. Thus, the Church of Nîmes experienced a significant further growth.

54

Valerian

Over a year elapsed before Claurinius and Demeter returned to Nîmes. During that time, life passed smoothly for the Church. A special event which took place on the eighteenth birthday of Selenece was her betrothal to Solarus, an occasion of great rejoicing and excitement for the Church, and very specially for Apollos and Diana who could not have wished to see a better match for their daughter.

The involvement of the Arverni people from Astaveldi's community of weavers and dyers with the Church had an unexpected profit for that community. Apart from essential trade which was carried out in the Nîmes market, the dyers and weavers had previously kept themselves very isolated from the affairs of the city. However, as links were established between the Arverni people and members of the Church, great improvements took place in the weavers' settlement. Those in the Church with building skills established contracts with their new Arverni friends to build good houses in place of the primitive huts which were the dwelling places of that fringe community. Infant mortality in that settlement became an increasingly rare calamity. The Arverni began to learn new skills and diversified their activities from the cloth trades which had been the sole metier of that whole community for generations. Apollos found too that they were quick to understand and learn the spiritual message that they received when they attended the Church for instruction.

The elders of the Church felt some concern that these Arverni had to travel so far across the city to attend Church meetings and to bring their children to the school. It soon became abundantly clear that a daughter Church which provided schooling and community services should be set up in the Arverni settlement. After much prayer, an elder was identified to lead that development, and a second Church was established in Nîmes.

While such positive developments were occurring for the Church at Nîmes, disturbing news from the world outside was coming in to the city. The excesses of Nero Caesar had drained the vast wealth held in the coffers of the city of Rome, and Nero had alienated the ruling classes. He was seeking to make the Christians the scapegoat for his own follies, and reports were being received that the Christians in Rome were being savagely persecuted. Meanwhile, the Empire itself was being shaken by really serious revolts among the peoples it held in subjugation. The Jews had revolted in Judaea. In Africa, Macer led another rebellion, and to the east, Volgases, King of the Parthians, inflicted a disastrous defeat on the Romans. To the north, Boadicea, Queen of the Iceni, was leading an uprising in Brittania, while in Gaul itself, the chieftain, Vindex, had re-established a Gallic hegemony. The Sequani and the Suevi, the Aquitani and the Helvetti, the Cimbri and the Teutoni, were rallying to Vindex's call to expel the Romans from their lands.

When Claurinius and Demeter returned to Nîmes, their entourage was a much larger contingent of soldiers than that needed for the protection of Roman officials in times of peace and stability. Soon after his arrival in Nîmes, Claurinius commissioned extensive building work within the Roman Circus. Considerable interest was aroused by this. It appeared that preparations were in hand for some very spectacular event.

That Sunday, Solarus attended the Church in the company of a Roman centurion who had arrived at Nîmes with the military entourage which had recently escorted Claurinius and Demeter. It appeared that Solarus had served under this centurion and had great respect for him. He had led Solarus' company in Germania during the time that Solarus was serving with the Roman legions. They had renewed acquaintance when Solarus discovered that this centurion was part of the increased garrison of Nîmes and was billeted in the Citadel where Solarus worked. At the end of the Church meeting, Solarus introduced the centurion to Apollos. His name was Valerian. Solarus had discovered that Valerian was wrestling with the same conscience problems that had troubled himself and had led Solarus to leave the army. Apollos invited them into a quiet room in the part of the house which was set aside as the dwelling quarters for the family. Diana prepared a light meal, and she and Selenece joined the men to listen to Valerian whom Solarus had described as a valiant soldier with many interesting tales to relate.

Valerian quickly came to the point. The army had been a rewarding career for him in many ways. Most of the time he was performing duties and marching on campaigns which he considered to be honourable and proper for a soldier seeking to render loyal service to his nation. However, he had also had to obey orders to do things which he found most distasteful, and he was now on the point of seriously considering quitting the army which had been his life for twenty-five years. Things had come to a head when he had recently been ordered to burn a village because the villagers were suspected of harbouring spies of the rebel chieftain, Vindex. The villagers had protested that they had not even heard of Vindex, but to no avail, Valerian was ordered to raze the village to the ground and scatter its livestock.

Apollos then asked Valerian to cite some other examples of orders which he had had to obey against the dictates of his conscience, and among the incidents Valerian mentioned were some of particular interest to Apollos. Valerian told Apollos that this was his second tour of service under Claurinius who was now Proconsul of Narbonensia. Valerian was now commanding part of the extra guard which had been sent to reinforce the garrison at Nîmes. Valerian explained that many years earlier, Claurinius had been in command of a fleet which the Romans had sent out to clear the sea of pirates. He described the disastrous sea battle in which the ship on which he was sailing, *The Jupiter*, had been the only surviving vessel, but had lost most of its galley slaves in the fire which had all but gutted the ship. Valerian described how they had put in to Sidon for repairs and of how he had been ordered to lead the soldiers to take captive a group of innocent Sidonian youths to make up a working contingent of galley slaves. Diana and Apollos looked across at one another in horrified amazement. Momentarily, Apollos was stunned by this revelation, and he paused to consider his words before saying anything of his own involvement in the incident which Valerian had just described. However, before Apollos could say anything, Valerian had resumed his narration of what he regarded to be particularly unpalatable activities in which he had been ordered to take part. The next incident which Valerian described had an even greater emotional impact on Apollos than the revelation he had just received of the truth behind the Sidonian incident.

Valerian gave an account of an event which occurred soon after he had been made a centurion, and was serving with the troops garrisoned at Jerusalem. The incident he described was so special that the remains of the food and the dishes from the meal they had just shared, were completely forgotten as everyone's attention was focused on Valerian while he narrated a graphic account of an experience he would never forget.

'Many years ago, I was posted to Judaea,' began Valerian. 'I had just been made up to centurion and was proud of achieving this rank at so young an age, but I was uneasy about this particular posting. I had been told that the land of Judaea was the most insalubrious corner of the Roman Empire, a state, populated by religious fanatics and fervent patriots. My regiment was responsible for maintaining law and order in Jerusalem, a hell hole of seething revolution. My particular responsibility was to command the platoon whose job was to administer punishment to law breakers. Barely a month went by, but some Zealot had to be crucified for leading a rebellion. I and my men had to be specially watchful on such occasions that some demagogue in the mob did not use the Jewish patriotism, aroused by the execution of a Zealot, to stir the mob to violence.

'There was one such occasion which I will always remember because it was so different from the usual execution. It was just before one of the Jews' big religious

371

festivals, and Jerusalem was the most crowded I had ever known it. Three men were due for execution on the Friday. Two were ordinary robbers and the other was a typical Zealot, a man called Barabbas, the sort who usually meant trouble. However, some strange intrigue went on before the execution and those crafty schemers, the Jewish priests, must have master-minded some cunning political trick. They presented to Pontius Pilate, the Governor, a man they claimed was the worst revolutionary of them all, a man claiming to be King of the Jews, called Jesus of Nazareth. I knew that something underhand was going on when they claimed that they were revealing this man's plottings because of the loyalty they felt for Caesar. I knew full well that the priests hated us Romans, even more than the merchants and the peasants, so I realized that they were up to no good. Rumour in the centurions' mess had it that Pilate wanted nothing to do with executing this Jesus of Nazareth, but that the priests had used their rabble rousers to scare Pilate into thinking that the mob would revolt and get him replaced as Governor. We soldiers knew that Pilate wasn't much of a Roman, easily scared, and specially afraid of getting into Caesar's bad books. We were not surprised when we were told that because the mob had shouted for the release of Barabbas, Pilate was going to execute this Jesus instead.[226]

'When I went out next day to take the prisoners to be executed, I had expected some difficulty from Jesus. I thought he was just a pawn in the priests' cunning scheme to get Barabbas released. As I went to his cell, I had expected to meet a scared little man, a man protesting his innocence, a man without the understanding or influence to get off what was clearly a trumped up case, a man demanding a fair hearing to escape this monstrous frame-up. However, I was surprised. Although he had been flogged the night before,[227] and was obviously still in pain and very tired, he had great dignity and an air of authority. Had he given me an order, even told me to release him, I somehow know that I would have obeyed. However, he calmly went out to his cross and raised it on to his shoulders without being told what to do. Right up till the time he was nailed to the cross, he preserved his dignity, even though he had collapsed on the way through the streets under the cross's great load. He was quite different from the other two being crucified with him, who were crying and screaming and yelling abuse, behaving the way criminals usually behave when confronted with Golgotha.

'Yes, somehow this Jesus was different, and I got the strange feeling that, condemned man though he was, he was in control of all the events. This feeling grew increasingly upon me, even after my soldiers had nailed him to the cross. In spite of the fact that he must have been in extreme agony, the words he spoke were definite and deliberate, and in a strange way, comforting. The words he spoke to his mother, conferring her to the charge of a man I found was his favourite disciple, and even the words he spoke to those who were being crucified with him, were calming and consoling. He also spoke to his God, whom he addressed as Father, so definitely and confidently, that I knew that his God really was there, except for a time when the sky strangely darkened, and this Jesus momentarily spoke in anguish as he seemed to sense that his Father had left him.

'However, he finally declared in a loud voice that he had completed the task his Father had sent him to do, and then he died. No, he didn't die, that would be the wrong way of describing what I saw. It was more that he yielded up his life to his Father. I realized as I watched all this that the claim to be God's son which this Jesus had made at his trial, a claim which my men had laughed about, was indeed a valid claim. Why then had he ended like this? What was the task he declared in a loud voice to his Father that he had finished? As I thought back on the words he spoke on the cross, I remember his saying, "Father, forgive them, for they know not what they do."[228]

'I think many thought he was referring to the group of Jewish leaders and priests who were jeering at him,[229] and perhaps he was, but somehow, I felt that I was included too. Even though I was acting under orders and wouldn't reproach myself for doing my duty, I wasn't happy about executing this man. Indeed, I wasn't really happy about a lot of things in my life, but at that moment as Jesus spoke to his Father, I felt that all these things were forgiven. I don't think this relief could have come upon me at that time when

373

I was feeling particularly down and depressed, had not this Jesus spoken and died the way he did. Somehow, I feel, although I cannot explain why, that this was the very reason that Jesus died as he did. I remember remarking to the young soldier whom I had posted to guard those crosses that surely, this was the Son of God.

'Many things have happened to me since that day, but the memory of that execution has never been totally forgotten. So much of what I have told you today I described the other day to my young friend, Solarus, here. He became most excited and told me that that Jesus was indeed the Son of God, that three days after his crucifixion, he had arisen from the dead, and after proving that he was alive by appearing to his disciples over a period of six weeks, he went up into heaven in full view of his disciples. Solarus tells me that this Jesus is now worshipped as the God of Forgiveness by your sect whom we call Christians, and that Solarus has received this forgiveness for himself. I felt the great relief of sins forgiven on that day, but I have done much wrong since. Again I feel in great need of that forgiveness now. Solarus has said that this is still available for me and that is why he has brought me along to meet you tonight!'

Apollos and Diana, Solarus and Selenece, listened in great awe while Valerian spoke. Valerian's account of his part in the crucifixion had put any thoughts Apollos may have harboured of the incident at Sidon, completely out of his mind. For the next two hours, Apollos spoke of the life and ministry of Jesus, and the effect that Jesus had had on his own life. Valerian listened intently, occasionally asking a question, but for the most part, absorbing all that Apollos said. When it was nearly midnight, Apollos said a prayer and an arrangement was made for Valerian to come again the following evening. Valerian and Solarus bade their farewells and returned to the Citadel.

Valerian made many visits to Apollos over the next three weeks and attended every Sunday worship meeting. The teaching he received made complete sense to Valerian and explained the significance of what Valerian had seen and heard that Friday when he had supervised the crucifixion of two thieves, and Jesus. Valerian became a believer. The following Sunday, the Church gathered to witness the baptism of the one who had commanded the soldiers on the occasion that Apollos' friend, Jerahmeel, had been killed, and who had also been in charge of men who crucified Jesus.

Valerian made inquiries of his commanding officer regarding the steps he would need to take to leave the army, but was curtly told that while there was unrest among the Gauls, the army would not be prepared to relinquish the services of a centurion with his experience.

55

Claurinius Reveals His Plan to Demeter

It was seven o'clock in the morning. Claurinius was sitting in the room in his living quarters in the Citadel, where breakfast would be shortly served. He fidgeted nervously. After quarter of an hour, he was joined by Demeter. Five minutes later, two servants came in bearing trays on which sparse breakfasts had been prepared and placed them before Claurinius and Demeter. There was nothing unusual in any of this. Claurinius did not sleep well and always rose early. He always fidgeted nervously while waiting for his wife to join him, although today, his fidgeting displayed more nervousness than usual. The servants always brought the breakfast in about five minutes after Demeter had taken her place.

Claurinius spoke. This was unusual. Breakfast was usually eaten in silence. Most meals were eaten in silence. Claurinius and Demeter did not have much to say to each other.

'I have had news that three legions are being sent from Rome to face Vindex. Caesar will not be pleased that I have been unable to prevent the Gauls from rising. I will have to do something which Caesar will recognize as an extravagant display of support and loyalty.'

'I know you will do what you think best, Claurinius,' replied Demeter. 'You always do. There is no need to tell me. You know I am not interested in affairs of state.'

'What I have decided to do will affect Diana, Apollos and their daughter. You may wish me to modify my plans.'

'I don't think so,' replied Demeter in a bored lanquid manner, 'but tell me just the same.'

Claurinius paused, bracing himself before he disclosed

his plan to Demeter.

'Nero has identified the Christians to be the source of all the trouble in Rome. He has rounded them up and put them to death. They were fed to the lions in the Circus Maximus as a public spectacle.'

Claurinius looked across at Demeter to gauge her reaction but she carried on eating as if the statement Claurinius had just made had no relevance. Claurinius continued.

'If Caesar regards the Christians as the source of trouble in Rome, he will no doubt regard them as the source of trouble in other parts of the Empire. He will expect his representatives to deal as firmly with them in their provinces as he has in Rome. I am therefore making arrangements to dispose of the Christians in the Circus here at Nîmes, but I have kept my plans secret. No one yet knows why I have commissioned the works which are being undertaken at the Circus or what spectacle will be laid on at the games which I have proclaimed will take place on Monday.'

Demeter continued to eat without showing any noticeable reaction to this disclosure. Claurinius had expected her to say something at this point. He added,

'Your sister, Diana, and Apollos are leaders of the Christian community!'

Demeter put her spoon down as she sat, turning things over in her mind. At last she spoke.

'Diana is my sister. Is it not possible for her to be spared this fate? We did grow up together. She was always good to me when we were young.'

'What of Apollos and Selenece?' asked Claurinius.

From the time she had seen Apollos at the surprise reunion a year earlier, Demeter had inwardly rued and lamented that she had spurned Apollos in her youth, for he had clearly become everything that it really mattered for a man to be. The knowledge that not only was this paragon still around but espoused to her sister, no less, was a continuous source of inward reproach for Demeter. This reproach would vanish if Apollos were done away.

'Apollos is nothing to me and I hardly know Selenece,' answered Demeter. 'Let them perish with the rest of their vile sect!'

'I shall let no one know of my plans until Sunday when the Christians can be rounded up at the home of Apollos and Diana where they all meet on that day,' confided Claurinius. 'Can you make arrangements to get your sister to safety in a way which arouses no suspicion? I think unnecessary problems may arise if we try to separate Diana from her family after they have been taken in and are aware of what is going on.'

Demeter nodded. The rest of the meal was completed in silence. Each had much to think about. Claurinius was glad that Demeter had made no special plea for Apollos. From conversations that had taken place when Apollos and Diana had visited the Citadel last year, Claurinius realized that by some strange coincidence, Apollos was involved in the incident at Sidon, and that he had met one of *The Jupiter*'s complement when in Rome. What had he learnt there? Claurinius did not know that Valerian had become a Christian and that Apollos had only recently discovered the whole truth from this highly respected centurion. Claurinius had even forgotten that Valerian was the centurion in charge of the soldiers on *The Jupiter*. Although unaware of the source of Apollos' information, Claurinius was convinced that Apollos had discovered what had really happened at Sidon.

'He must surely know the truth,' thought Claurinius to himself. 'It is as well that he will soon be done away.'

56

An Exhibition of Great Resourcefulness

Apollos and Diana were aware that Claurinius and Demeter
had been in residence in Nîmes for several weeks and were
surprised that they had not been contacted. As Claurinius
and Demeter had insisted that meetings should always take
place at the Citadel, it had always been left to them to take
the initiative in making arrangements. Therefore, it was
with some satisfaction that they at last received a note from
the Citadel, arranging a meeting. To be more precise, the
note was sent from Demeter and just addressed to Diana. It
invited Diana to come early on the Sunday morning and
spend the day with Demeter. She was specifically requested
to come alone.

'I shall return in time for the evening service,' Diana
promised Apollos.

When Diana arrived at the Citadel and was conducted to
the suite set aside as Claurinius and Demeter's residential
quarters, Diana felt that Demeter looked somewhat strange
and uneasy.

'I have never taken you on a tour of the Citadel, have I?'
said Demeter. 'Would you like me to show you around?'

Diana assented and Demeter conducted her first round
the Governor's residential suite. After this, Demeter took
Diana into the working part of the building. They seemed to
be walking for miles along corridors and up and down stairs
before Demeter showed her another room. On the way to
this room, they had at first passed many people in the
corridors of that busy building, all scurrying about on some
errand or matter of state importance. For some little time
however, they had seen no one. They seemed to be in a
deserted unused part of the Citadel. The room into which

Diana was shown was a small room with only a few benches as furniture. It was dingy and dusty. The plaster on the wall was crumbling. There was only one small window, placed high in the wall, and that was barred. As Diana stood and looked around the room, she heard the door slam behind her and a key turn in the lock. Demeter had gone out and locked her in.

'What are you doing?' cried Diana, shouting to be heard through the thick, studded door.

'I have locked you in there for your own safety!' shouted Demeter in reply. 'You Christians have done great harm to the stability of our Empire and must be done away. The Christians in Rome have already been killed. Tomorrow, the Christians in Nîmes will be taken to the Circus to suffer the same fate as those in Rome, but I have interceded for you, that your life may be spared. While you remain here, you will be safe. When you come out, you will have to renounce your silly Christian ways and pay Caesar the respect due to him.'

Could Diana believe what she was hearing?

'Let me out, let me out!' she yelled, banging on the door, but she received no reply. Demeter had obviously gone away. What should she do? It was obviously no use calling out, she was in a deserted part of the building, and in any case, anyone around would be Roman servants or soldiers, obeying Demeter or Claurinius. What danger was being faced by Apollos and Selenece? The whole Christian community in Nîmes was in peril. What could she do? How could she warn them from this prison cell?

Diana was a very dynamic person and not one to sit and mope in a desperate situation. She tried the door. It was firm and solid. There was no easy way out there. She piled the benches against the wall under the window and reached up to try the bars. She shook them in turn. One gave a little. She saw that the mortar had not only cracked where this bar was set into wall, but was beginning to crumble. Diana looked around the floor, which was thick with dust and woodshavings. The room must have been used for carpentry at some time. Diana found a large nail among the shavings and set to work to scrape away at the mortar. She shook the bar again. It was looser. After about half an hour of diligent work, Diana managed to completely dislodge the bar. Could she squeeze through the space she had opened up? Diana piled more benches against the wall and managed to wriggle her way through the opening. It was not until she stood on the ledge outside that she realized how high up she was. The courtyard was about forty feet below her. Diana did not have a good head for heights but she now faced an extreme emergency. Diana closed her eyes, still holding on tightly to the window bars and started to breathe deeply. The panic she had felt when she first discovered her plight and realized the dangers faced by her loved onces began to subside.

She started to take stock of the situation. Although she had overcome one barrier, she was still in a desperate predicament. As the pulsating beat of Diana's heart slowed to a calmer pace, Diana did something which she realized she would have done well to do earlier. She prayed. As she prayed, she felt a great calmness and confidence come over her. She looked down again to the courtyard below, but the height no longer worried her. Roman soldiers strutted to and fro. This was some sort of exercise yard. No one looked up. People seldom take notice of anything much above eye-level unless their attention is specificaly directed upwards. Diana realized that she could not go up. She could not go down. She therefore started to make her way along the ledge which was broad enough to give her quite a good foothold. She made her way past a number of barred windows like the one from which she had just emerged. She peered through to see similar, empty, dingy rooms. Diana looked down. She was now above another courtyard, much smaller than the one below the window where she had made her exit. This courtyard was empty most of the time, but every now and then a soldier walked from one side to the other. She could tell by the plumes in the helmets that these were centurions. She deduced that this courtyard must open on to their quarters. A centurion came into view whom she recognized. It was Valerian. Diana picked up the crumblings from a piece of derelict masonary and threw them down. Valerian looked up.

'It's Diana,' she called out to the surprised face gazing up at her. 'Can you help me!'

Diana deemed it wise not to shout too loudly. Valerian stood still, momentarily dumbstruck at this unexpected apparition. He then assessed the situation and sprang into action.

'Stay where you are!' he called back. Like Diana, Valerian did not shout too loudly. 'I will be with you in a minute.'

Valerian disappeared through a door immediately below the point where Diana was hanging. A few moments later, Diana felt a rope pass before her face and looked up to see Valerian leaning out of the open window above her.

'Catch hold of the rope,' he called, again, not too loudly, 'and I will haul you in.'

In a few moments, Diana was standing next to Valerian in a room at the top of the Citadel, trembling a little after the ordeal that the unaccustomed activity of clambering across a building at great height had been for her. She told Valerian the situation. Valerian bade her sit down. He sat down beside her, deep in thought, assessing what was going to happen and what action would need to be taken to save the Christians. After several moments reflection he turned to Diana.

'I know how the Romans will set about capturing a group who are known to meet at a certain place at a certain time. They will place soldiers to stand as unobtrusively as possible at the ends of any roads and streets leading to the target building. They will allow people to pass them who are going towards the building, but any who attempt to come the other way, they will direct back to their homes on the pretext that there is some danger afoot and it is not safe for them to be out of their houses. When they think that all who are likely to meet at the target house are assembled, they will move in and arrest them.'

'How are we going to save them?' asked Diana.

'We know of the danger early enough to warn the Christians not to go to Church today.' answered Valerian.

'What of Apollos and Selenece who are already at the house?' pleaded Diana. 'What of the elders and their families who meet early to discuss business and arrange the final details of the service? Some of these will already be there!'

Valerian thought again. His face suddenly lightened. 'I

could go as the officer with the duty to conduct the Christians to the cells at the Circus where it appears they will be held until whatever Claurinius has planned for them on Monday becomes clear. When well away from the Church where the main body of soldiers will be sealing off the area, I can allow them to escape,' said Valerian, but then his face clouded again. 'One officer would never take a group of prisoners that sort of distance by himself,' said Valerian. 'If I arrived at the Church by myself and told the soldiers that I would escort the prisoners to the Circus unaided, it would arouse immediate suspicion. Even with a legionary to help him, a dozen prisoners is the maximum number that a single officer would be entrusted to supervise. With a legionary, I could arrange some way of getting the Christians out without arousing suspicion, but where can I find a legionary to do such a thing which is obviously contrary to the orders of the Governor? There are no Christian legionaries in the Citadel.'

Valerian and Diana spent another few moments in thought. Diana said nothing to interrupt Valerian's train of thought. She had every confidence in his knowledge of the way the Roman army worked, and waited for him to come up with a solution. At last, Valerian's face brightened again.

'Solarus was once a Roman soldier,' Valerian suddenly declared. 'I can get him a uniform and armour which fits. He can accompany me on this venture. At this moment, Solarus will be working in the records office. I will fetch him and we can explain to him the situation and the action we are considering to save our brothers and sisters. You wait here, Diana. No one comes up to these rooms at the top of the Citadel. I have no idea why they built the place to be this big.'

With that, Valerian left Diana to find Solarus. The first day of the week was not a holiday for Romans but a normal working day. That was why most churches in the Empire had to hold their main time of Sunday worship in the early evening. Diana was still very worried about the perilous situation being faced, but Valerian's resourcefulness gave her a real feeling of hope. It was this quality that had enabled Valerian to reach the rank of centurion so early in

383

his army career, the maximum rank to which someone of Valerian's class could have hoped to aspire, regardless of ability.

Valerian was not gone for more than a quarter of an hour, but with such urgent business to attend to, it seemed like an age to Diana. Diana's mind was racing as she thought of other action which needed to be taken to protect the members of their Church from the sudden danger which was looming on them unawares. Diana realized that only the elders and their families would be at the Church. Most of the members would not set out for Church until the men folk had returned from work. If she could get a message to a few of them, they could spread the news and prevent others from going to Church that evening and falling into the trap laid for them.

At last Valerian returned with Solarus, both of them somewhat breathless from their rapid ascent of the stairs. Valerian was carrying some Roman armour which he asked Solarus to slip on while Diana told him of the situation. Valerian explained the plan. Diana would return to the Church to warn them of the danger and tell them the part that he and Solarus were to play. A short time later, Valerian and Solarus would arrive with the chains and take the Christians away, releasing them to make their escape when out of sight of the soldiers sealing off the roads which led from the Church. They would return to the Church for as many times as necessary to remove the Christians in groups of a dozen, the maximum batch of prisoners which could leave under the escort of only two soldiers. Solarus looked grave but resolute, glad that he would be involved in rescuing his fellow Christians from this monstrous stratagem to have them exterminated, specially pleased that he would have a part in rescuing his beloved Selenece.

'Are we all clear what we have to do?' said Valerian.

Diana and Solarus nodded. Both of them, no all three, had feelings of considerable trepidation at the hazardous mission ahead.

Diana turned to Solarus.

'If any difficulty arises, if anything starts to go wrong with our plans, you will make Selenece's safety your first priority?' she implored.

384

Solarus nodded.

'Well, let's get going then,' said Valerian, always the man of action.

The three of them left the room and Valerian guided them downstairs and along the corridors, taking a route which would enable them to leave the military quarters in the Citadel without meeting any soldiers who would have wondered how a woman came to be in that strictly enforced male enclave. When they got near enough to the entrance so that Diana could find her way out unaided, Valerian told Diana to go on ahead, saying that he would follow with Solarus in half an hour. Valerian and Solarus followed Diana, maintaining a discreet distance to ensure that she got out of the building safely. Valerian then went into the armoury where he knew he could pick up the standard chain for shackling a dozen prisoners. He rejoined Solarus and they walked at a measured but not too brisk a pace to the entrance and out into the open air. The two of them made their way from the Citadel and ambled round the streets as they made their way slowly towards the home of Apollos and Diana. Solarus could barely disguise his impatience to get there as soon as possible but Valerian restrained his young friend's impetuosity. He explained that the whole plan would be wrecked if Diana did not have a clear half hour to get home and explain what was going on, especially as on her way back to her home which was also the Church building, she would have to contact others to spread the warning not to go to Church.

At last they reached the road leading to the Church. A group of soldiers was posted there as Valerian had expected. They were dealing with the remonstrations of townsfolk who were not members of the Church, but who lived in the same road as Apollos and Diana and were protesting at the soldiers refusal to allow them passage. The soldiers returned them to their homes, telling them that this was for their own safety as Gallic terrorists were believed to be in the city that day.

Valerian and Solarus marched to the corporal in charge who came to attention as the centurion approached.

'We have come to collect the Christians. Which house are they in and how many do I have to deal with?' asked

Valerian imperiously, pretending not to know the identity of the building where the Church met.

The corporal pointed out the house of Apollos and Diana. 'There are only about twenty in there at present,' he told Valerian. 'We were told to expect about seventy to be there by early evening.'

He looked at the chains Solarus was carrying.

'Will the two of you be able to manage by yourselves?' he queried.

'If there's only twenty, we will have no trouble,' said Valerian with genuine confidence.

'That's as well,' replied the corporal. 'I can't spare any men and guarantee to keep the street sealed.'

Valerian and Solarus made their way to the house and went through the door which had been left ajar. Diana had already arrived. The assembled company had not suspected anything to be amiss until Diana had come in about twenty minutes earlier. They were all looking very grave and obviously appreciated their vulnerability. They had prayed for help and guidance over the perilous situation in which they now found themselves. Apollos had already reached an important decision. Of the twenty-four Christians who were met there, ten were elders and all in their late fifties or older. He and Diana were both forty-nine. The remaining twelve were sons and daughters of the elders gathered there, all in their late teens or early twenties.

'Those who leave with Valerian and Solarus first will have the best chance of escaping this trap,' Apollos advised those present. 'Therefore, the young people should go with the first batch and the rest of us will take our chance with the second.'

The elders had all agreed that this was sound advice. After quickly hugging their parents, the girls weeping as they made these embraces, the young people held out their wrists upon which Valerian and Solarus quickly fastened the shackles. The young people had been advised by their parents to leave Nîmes as soon as possible. They all had friends in other nearby towns and cities where they could take refuge. Selenece had been told to make her way to Massilia where, hopefully, Apollos and Diana would be able to join her when they made their escape. This was considered safer than hanging about to rendezvous in Nîmes where they would be sought out by the authorities.

The corporal at the end of the street was surprised to see how soon Valerian and Solarus returned with their band of woeful youths and weeping maidens as they led the shackled group out of the trap, and he remarked as much to one of his soldiers.

'Ah, yes,' replied the soldier, 'that centurion is Valerian who came to Nîmes with the Governor when he returned a couple of months ago. He is known to be just about the most efficient officer in the army. The men under him say he's one of the best!'

As they left the soldiers who guarded the street leading to the church, Valerian and Solarus encountered the first hitch to their plans. The streets were extremely busy and there seemed to be a large number of military personnel abroad. There was nowhere that Valerian and Solarus could unshackle the Christians without those around becoming immediately aware that something irregular was happening. As a consequence of this, the bewildered little party had to go the whole way to the Circus. Once inside the Circus, things were more straightforward. Although there were guards waiting in the cells below, Valerian did not conduct his band straight to the cells. He knew that there were many parts of that vast building which were completely deserted as it was not due to be opened to the public for the entertainment that Claurinius had promised them until the following day. Once in one of the empty cavernous spaces beneath the terraces, Valerian and Solarus quickly removed the young people's chains and Valerian conducted them to a little used door onto the street where they left in ones and twos at ten second intervals. Selenece was last to leave. She hugged Solarus and told him that she would wait at the house of a friend whom Solarus knew well for one hour before obeying her parents and making her way to Massilia. Solarus warned her of the dangers of travelling alone, but realized that Selenece would have no alternative if he could not be there with her parents within the hour.

Valerian and Solarus had lost precious time in having to go the whole way to the Circus and they hurried back

387

towards the Church. Before they reached the Church they were conscious of hearing voices singing a familiar tune. It was a popular hymn. As they turned the corner, they realized with dismay that they had not made it to the Church in time. Apollos, Diana and the elders of their Church were being escorted by about twenty soldiers, a chain connecting their shackled wrists. They all looked in surprisingly good spirits, and sounded almost joyful as they sang. Valerian and Solarus stopped and watched with the amazed townsfolk as this party passed them by. The Christians obviously noticed Solarus and Valerian and felt thankful that they at least had succeeded in their mission to get the young ones to safety, but gave no incriminating glances at this pair of soldiers as they continued on their way. Their other cause of thankfulness was that the message Diana had left with a Christian family on her way from the Citadel to her home, had obviously got round. No more Christians had come to the Church to find themselves enmeshed in the Roman trap.

Solarus looked with despair at Valerian.

'What now?' he asked.

'Now you must obey Diana's instructions and see to the safety of your betrothed,' he replied calmly.

'But what of Apollos and Diana and the rest?'

'You heard the way they were singing,' answered Valerian. 'I think they know they have a divinely ordained destiny to fulfill. However, they can only do this with a quiet mind if you obey your orders. While you are in that uniform, I am your superior officer, so my order underlines the instruction that Diana gave you. Take Selenece to safety at once!'

As a serving soldier, Solarus had obeyed centurions' orders when they had instructed him to perform unpalatable tasks. He was now being ordered to do the thing he most wanted to do. Valerian held out his arms and Solarus threw down the shackles he still carried and warmly embraced this hardened veteran of many well fought campaigns. He then stood back, saluted Valerian, turned and quickly made his way to the house where he knew Selenece was waiting. By noon, the following day, Solarus and Selenece were safely with friends in Massilia.

57

The Spectacle in the Arena

The soldiers entered the Church to take Apollos, Diana and the elders into custody about ten minutes after the time that their worship would have started in normal circumstances. Army intelligence sources had furnished the time when the Church was most likely to be full. The centurion who arrived with the platoon to escort the prisoners to the Circus was surprised to find that one batch of prisoners had already been collected. He was even more surprised to find only a dozen Christians waiting placidly in the house. He had been given to expect that there would be upwards of seventy people to be escorted to the Circus and he made a caustic comment about the pathetic state of Roman military intelligence services in Gaul.

The elders who had remained in the Church after Valerian and Solarus had left with the young people had spent the time in prayer, praying first and foremost that their sons and daughters would reach safety, praying that Valerian and Solarus would return in time so that they themselves would also escape from this trap, and praying that whatever happened, they would conduct themselves in a way which displayed to the world that they knew that their eternal destiny was secure. Most of them were well over the age of fifty, which was the normal life expectancy for people living in those times. They were all looking forward to meeting their Saviour face to face with expectant faith, but felt natural trepidation in the realization that that time was nearer than they had expected when they rose that morning. As they prayed, they became acutely conscious of the closeness of God as he made his presence felt in response to the desperate situation in which his people now found themselves, and their initial reaction of shock and horror at the alarming news Diana had brought them, gave way to an inner peace and confidence. They experienced a spontaneous desire to sing, and they sung hymns as they were taken from the Church and conducted along the streets of Nîmes, not dull and mournful dirges, but bright hymns which anticipated joy and triumph. Their hearts felt uplifted as they met with Valerian and Solarus who had obviously discharged their errand. The prayer they had uttered most fervently as they waited in the Church had been answered. When the elders reached the Circus, they were taken to a large chamber which could have held many times their number. The fact that the young people were nowhere to be seen and the jailer who locked the door on them confirmed that they were the only prisoners who had been committed to his charge, reassured them that their prayer for the young people's safe escape had indeed been answered.

Apollos, as leader of the group, was very conscious of his need to maintain this morale among his flock. A glance round the chamber into which they had been herded confirmed his fear that there was no means of escape from that place. He therefore suggested that they should conduct the service of sabbath worship which they had been unable to perform earlier that evening in their house where the Church usually met. They prayed and sung hymns well into the night, and then a great drowsiness came over them and they lay down to sleep on the straw mattresses which were scattered about that communal cell. They were well aware that death awaited them on the morrow, but they had no idea of how this death was to come. Notwithstanding, they fell into deep and dreamless sleep as if they were tired children who had stayed up late after an exhausting day. Each hour of the night the jailer checked the security of the cell in which the Christians were confined and was amazed to find them in such a state of peaceful slumber.

When they awoke with the cock-crow the following morning, they needed a few moments to reorientate themselves to their new situation, but the pervading atmosphere of confidence and calm was sustained as they came to terms with the fact that this would probably be their last day in the world.

Breakfast was brought in to them and then the Officer in charge of the Circus entered the chamber with his assistant and spoke. He told them that they had been brought there because they were Christians, a sect which was known to threaten the security of the Empire in many ways and, in particular, by failing to render to Caesar the honour due to this divine person. He looked around at the group gathered there. There were only twelve men and women, and most of these were elderly. He had been given to expect seventy people between the ages of twenty and sixty. Normally, the Officer would have offered an amnesty to any who were prepared to come forward and acknowledge the error of Christian beliefs and publicly uphold the divinity of the Emperor. However, he realized that if that meagre number were depleted further, the games scheduled for that afternoon would not be accepted as a worthwhile spectacle by the thousands who would have paid to fill the terraces of the Circus. He therefore made no such offer of amnesty, but even had he done so, there would have been no response.

The Officer told them that that afternoon, they would face execution by the archers of the Governor's bodyguard but added that the Romans were fair people and would give the Christians every chance to protect themselves. The Officer then ordered the Christians to follow him. They filed through the door of their prison chamber and found that a troop of about twenty soldiers was waiting to escort them to the arena. They went up through a tunnel into the bright daylight which flooded the oval shaped arena at the centre of the Circus.

As their eyes became accustomed to the light, they could see that the arena was enclosed by vast terraces which could probably accommodate upwards of fifty thousand people. In the centre of the arena, a strange wooden structure had been erected. It consisted of low screens, short flights of steps, and narrow platforms. The officer explained that twenty archers would be deployed around the edge of the arena, some forty metres from this structure. The Christians would be able to use the erection in the middle of the arena to provide shelter for themselves against the arrows. As the Christians surveyed this structure, they

391

realized that substantial though it appeared, the construction would afford very meagre protection. Wherever the Christians went within the structure, the archers moving around the edge of the arena would be able to find some position from which they could shoot directly at them. Apollos, Diana and the others realized that the spectacle that would be presented to the crowds would be a battle of wits between the Christians and the archers, the Christians having to continually clamber around this structure to keep out of a direct line of sight of the archers. They realized that the odds were heavily stacked in the archers' favour, and that it was unlikely that anyone could survive in that structure for more than quarter of an hour under a hail of hostile arrows from archers who were free to continually move to favourable vantage points from which to loose their bolts.

The Officer asked the Christians if they had any questions and was surprised to be met with a reaction of apparent total disinterest. This after all, was a matter of life and death for them! He took them back to the chamber beneath the terraces where they were being confined. Once the door had been closed and locked behind them, Apollos led the Christians in a time of prayer and then they talked calmly among themselves, discussing the strategy they would adopt that afternoon to outmanoeuvre those who had devised this fiendish method of turning a mass execution into an entertaining spectacle. At midday, food was brought in to the Christians. Apollos blessed the bread and the meat and they settled down to eat. As the meal progressed, they were conscious of the terraces above them becoming noisy as they filled with people who had come to see the special spectacle which had been devised for their entertainment. Had they been out in the open, the Christians would have discovered that the crowds were first being told that the Christians were responsible for the instability and rebellion which was currently threatening Gaul. They were then being given the same explanation that the Christians had received that morning, of the purpose of the wooden structure in the centre of the arena. Booths had been set up in the ambulatories around the stadium and bets were being taken on how long it would take the archers to draw first blood, and on the time expected to elapse before all the Christians in the arena were killed. Very high odds were offered against any Christian surviving for more than half an hour. Anyone betting on three Christians still being alive after half an hour, stood to net a small fortune. Vast sand glasses had been placed on a platform at one end of the arena to measure intervals of time. Placards bearing huge numbers were ready to place by the sand glasses to indicate the number of victims who had fallen as each glass emptied to meter the passage of a unit of time.

As they waited in that gloomy chamber, the Christians heard a trumpet sound. This marked the arrival of the Governor and his lady. A moment later, the cell was opened and the Officer in charge of the Circus informed the Christians that it was time to move into the arena. He was surprised that he did not have to send soldiers in to drive them from that chamber. They calmly made their way through the door to the waiting troop of soldiers who escorted them up the tunnel which led to the arena.

A momentary hush fell on the crowd as the party came into view at the end of the tunnel. The soldiers waited round the edge and the Christians continued into the middle of the arena to the wooden construction. There were only twelve of them! The wooden construction partly hid them from the view of those sitting at the end where the Governor and his lady had taken their places on the thrones in their special box. Another figure came to join them from a different point on the edge of the arena. He seemed to have come from the crowd, for he was not escorted by any soldiers. This man was obviously known to the Christians already in the arena, for handshakes and embraces took place as he reached that little band.

The Commander of the Archers walked up and down his line of bowmen, giving them their orders in a harsh military manner.

'When the trumpet fanfare finishes, you can start shooting and not before,' he barked. 'You can move to any point around the edge of the arena, outside the rope. This rope makes a forty metre circle around the refuge where the Christians are taking their cover. You'd all better remain behind the rope or I'll draw my bow and shoot any one of you who crosses it myself! You have thirty minutes to finish them off. If you can't do it in that time, you can take their places and become the targets yourselves for the second company of archers!'

The noise from the crowd was beginning to swell again. The archers were dashing round to find good vantage points behind the ropes. The Christians seemed strangely inactive.

The trumpeters took their position below the Governor's box. The fanfare started to sound. What was happening? The Christians were moving out in a sort of procession into the open! They were singing. The Governor's wife seemed to recognize someone among the Christians and was on her feet yelling 'Stop!' but she could hardly be heard above the noise of the crowd, the trumpet fanfare and the lusty song which came from the band of Christians. The fanfare suddenly ended. The whine of twenty arrows could be heard as the archers immediately loosed their bolts. A second wave of arrows was released in quick succession. No more arrows were needed. The sound of singing had stopped. The Christians lay lifeless in the sand. The Governor and his wife abruptly left their box. A hush fell on the crowd. Silently they filed out of that vast stadium. The afternoon had been an anti-climax on which they had spent a lot of money. But no, many in that crowd realized that in a few seconds, they had witnessed something rather awesome, something special. The way those Christians walked into the open, with joy on their faces and a triumphal song on their lips was something which they would not forget. It was purposeful. It had meaning. This was something about which inquiries would need to be made.

The Officer in charge of the Circus felt disorientated and bewildered. He did not issue the order for his men to clear the bodies like so much dead meat. They were left lying in the sun, the silently moving crowds gazing awestruck on those lifeless corpses. The Circus orderlies who usually cleared the arena, were first deployed in cleaning the rubbish from the terraces as the crowds left that vast stadium.

Two hours later, the corpses were still lying where they had fallen. A message reached the Officer in charge of the Circus, that the leader of the community of weavers and dyers had heard of what had happened that day and had requested to take the bodies for burial. The Officer assented. Kervanindrax arrived with six men from his community and gently lifted the bodies on to the wagons he had brought. The corpses of the youngest Christians were readily recognized. They were clasped in a final, loving embrace, and their faces projected peace and calm. They were not separated as they were reverently lifted on to the wagon. The leather wrist strap on one of the other corpses was the badge of rank of a centurion in the Roman army.

The wagons made their way slowly to the settlement at the south of the City and the bodies were interred. Kervanindrax defiantly erected a large cross above their last resting place. Had he put his own community in jeopardy by so strongly identifying themselves with the Christians who had just met their end? No. The impact of the spectacle Claurinius had witnessed that afternoon had left him with no stomach to persecute Christians further.

Demeter and Claurinius were silent in each other's company for several days. Why had Demeter not discovered that her sister had escaped? The soldier who had been sent up by a member of the Governor's household staff with food for a prisoner in one of the upper rooms, had not been able to find an occupied cell. He reported the matter to the officer in charge of prisoners held at the Citadel. The officer assured the soldier that there were no prisoners, and certainly no woman, confined in the cells at the top of the Citadel. The soldier wondered what aberration had caused the household servant to prepare this food for a non-existent prisoner and he ate the meal himself.

The wave thundered against the rock and the showering spray obliterated everything from view. A second wave, and then a third crashed, throwing myriads of sparkling droplets into the air. Apollos felt the cool water run down his body as the foaming surf settled round him but somehow, he was not getting wet. No more waves struck and as the mist of white droplets cleared from the air, Apollos could see that others stood with him on that shore.

There next to him was Diana, looking more lovely than she had ever looked before, and there were the elders who had entered the arena with him but they were not old. Their faces were young and bright as he had never seen them before. There too was Valerian, but his face was smooth and showed none of his battle scars.

As the mist cleared further, they could see a shining sea in front of them. As they peered across the sea, a small island could be seen in the distance, but as they watched it was no longer a small island. It was rapidly getting larger. A wind was rushing by their faces. They seemed to be moving towards this distant shore at great speed. The wind then dropped to a gentle breeze which carried the sound of sweet music from the land which they were fast approaching. As the land loomed nearer, they could see a great City, the like of which they had never seen before. Its bricks and stones did not seem to reflect light, but appeared like luminescent jewels, radiating glorious colours of their own. Every hue could be seen, but there was no visual clash, for every shade and tint blended in harmony.[230] The gentle music that wafted over the sea came from the voices of thousands who lined the shore to watch the rocks on which Apollos, Diana and their company stood, approach their land.[231] The City rose in splendour behind the singing company of its citizens whose voices rose to a crescendo as the breeze dropped and the rocks slowed to a halt before they reached the land.

Apollos and his company were now near enough the City to recognize many of those who stood at the front of that vast crowd. Aristobolus who led the Church in the catacombs of Rome was standing there. There were Philologus and Julia with whom Apollos had stayed when he went to Rome with Timothy. Surely, those two wearing dazzling crowns were Peter and Paul, but they were not quite as Apollos remembered them. Both appeared full of youthful vigour. Peter no longer had his stoop and Paul's eyes gleamed clear and bright as he gazed across the water. Standing side by side were Anaxagoras and Jerahmeel, smiling a welcome which seemed specially directed at Apollos and Diana. Although unmistakably Anaxagoras and Jerahmeel, these too were not quite as Apollos and Diana had remembered them on earth, but stood as young men in the prime of life. So many, many others lined that shore with whom Apollos and Diana longed to renew acquaintance, Priscilla and Aquila, Diomedes and Calliope, Phoebe and Euphrosyne, a myriad of faces from their past whom they had loved and lost awhile. The narrow band of sea, separating the rocks on which Apollos and Diana were standing from the mainland, started to ebb away across golden sands, exposing a marble causeway which led from the City to the rocks. Along this causeway came the one who would be first to greet those who were soon to be admitted into his Kingdom. Of those standing on the rocks, only Valerian had seen his face before, but everyone knew him and crowded along the causeway to be received by their King.

We are not permitted to glimpse any more of the new land into which Apollos and Diana were going to continue the lives which had started for them when they were young people, Apollos returning to his native Alexandria after experiencing the trauma of seeing his friend, Jerahmeel, dying from wounds received in rescuing him from capture by the crew of the black ship, and Diana in Alexandria, just before her life had been apparently shattered by the tragic loss of her parents in the violence of the Alexandrian riots. Sufficient to know that a future of bliss lay in store for Apollos and Diana which would not be marred by sad and tragic partings.

And so it was, Apollos and Diana, the Sun and Moon of Alexandria, departed the world, but they left in their wake, a legacy from which the world still benefits. From their new vantage point, Apollos and Diana were to see that in Solarus, a new Sun would rise, in Selenece, another Moon would wax, to shed a light illuminating the way to be followed by any whose privilege it would be to come to love and know them.

58

Conclusions

The triumphal entry of Diana and Apollos into glory in fulfilment of the prophecy of Philip's daughter, Abigail, would be a fitting point to end this tale, but the reader might wonder what became of Claurinius and Demeter. Were they dealt a savage retribution as the misdeeds of their lives were exposed? They certainly experienced some turmoil in the turbulent months that followed the spectacle in the great Circus of Nîmes.

The Empire was in a state of disarray. In Rome, Nero was abandoned by the Praetorian Guard and forced to flee the city by the exasperated people who were alarmed at the perilous state to which his neglect of duty and extravagant excesses had brought the Empire. Vindex's rebellion in Gaul was put down by the legions sent from Rome. Galba, the Roman Governor of the Spanish province of Tarragona marched on Rome and was proclaimed, Caesar. Nero committed suicide. Claurinius decided it would be politically expedient to declare for Galba, but Galba's hold on the Empire was not secure. Months of civil war followed. Galba was ousted by Otho who in turn was quickly replaced as Caesar by Vitellius, General of the Roman army in Germania. The armies in the east decided that the highest office in the Empire should be held by their General, Vespasian, rather than Vitellius. They marched on Rome, defeating Vitellius at Cremona and installing their own candidate, Vespasian, as the new Caesar. No further claimants attempted to secure this title for themselves and thus, Vespasian became undisputed Emperor. However, the Gauls took advantage of the temporarily weakened state of the Empire caused by the civil wars which had been promoted by personal power struggles. The Gauls rose in revolt under Civilis, Prince of the Batavi clan. Had not rivalry existed among the Gaulish tribes, they might have prevailed, but they could not work together and the Roman legions defeated them at Trèves. Claurinius' position was now precarious. He had backed the wrong Imperial candidate and had failed to prevent the Gauls staging two serious uprisings. Claurinius was recalled to Rome.

Claurinius' father, Quintus, had mysteriously disappeared towards the end of Nero's reign. Claurinius and Demeter were allowed to move into Quintus' villa which had become derelict from two year's neglect. One might have expected Demeter to delight in the opportunity to again take her part in the social life of aristocratic Rome. However, they had been many years away from Rome and they had neither the contacts in that city to gain entry into the Roman social scene, nor the funds to restore Quintus' villa to a state which would make it an acceptable centre for high class Roman soirées. They had been less than a year in Rome when Demeter was quite suddenly taken ill and died. Claurinius increasingly lived in social isolation, tortured by his memories and the fears of what others knew of his ill conceived schemes and stratagems. The plebian masses may have dutifully bowed as Claurinius made an occasional excursion in his chariot, wearing the toga which seemed to mark him out as a man of some importance, but those who really knew him, found little in Claurinius' personality to enamour him to them. To his servants, he was unpredictable and irritable, often spending days in dark moods of depression. In the absence of close friends, Claurinius became almost a recluse and died three years after Demeter, looking much older than his fifty-five years.

Although a large number of great and prominent Christians, including both Peter and Paul, were among those who met martyrs' deaths during Nero's reign, his persecutions failed to eliminate Christianity from Rome. The remains of many of the Christians who fell in the arenas during Nero's savage persecution, were interred in land by the Pincian Hill, which stands to the north of the old city wall. For years, the site where they were reputed to be buried, was lovingly tended by a very old man who had the speech and bearing of a Roman aristocrat. It was believed that he lived with a Christian family who still worshipped in the catacombs. The only name he answered to was Timotheus. However, many said that was not his original name, but a name he adopted when he himself was baptized as a Christian in the Tiber during the reign of Nero Caesar. This old man, at any rate, must have been among the remnants who survived the persecutions of Nero. Although advanced in years, this hoary sage was credited with sustaining the Church of Rome when it was being decimated by savage persecution, by steadfastly exercising his own resolute and enduring faith.

APPENDIX 1

A Letter to the Church

Having spent some hours in the company of Apollos and Diana while following their biographies, the reader may feel sad at parting from two such individuals who brought light and hope to so many. Of course, Apollos and Diana are part of the great communion of saints which, although unseen, perpetually surround us. But Apollos left another legacy which enables us to share his thoughts and enjoy his scholarship, almost as if he were alive and with us today. The letter he wrote to the Corinthian Church was preserved for posterity as Apollos had hoped, and I know that many readers will be familiar with that epistle. The version which you, my readers, will be familiar with, has been painstakingly translated from the earliest available text, but this has been through the hands of many scholars. They may have amended some of the text and put their own slant on some of the teaching contained, to leave future generations with a modified form of Apollos' letter. The author has neither the knowledge of Greek nor access to the original text to be able to provide the reader with any better version than the many excellent translations currently available. However, on the following pages, the author has attempted to paraphrase the standard translations in modern use in an attempt to provide an alternative version of Apollos' communication to his Church.

To my dear fellow Christians,

God's Word through his Son.

In the past, God spoke to our ancestors many times and in many ways. The medium through which he spoke were the men we call the prophets. God has now spoken to us through none other than his Son. God's Son was there at the beginning of all things, for God created the Universe through his Son. God's Son will also be there at the end, for he has been chosen to possess all things at the end of time. God's Son is indeed, no less than an alternative revelation of God himself, for as we look upon the Son, we see all the wonderful attributes of God, His wonderful nature, His power which sustains the Universe, and His great glory. After purging the sins of mankind and achieving the means by which men might receive forgiveness, the Son took his place in the most honoured position of all, that is, seated at the right hand of Almighty God.

The superiority of the Son over the Angels

Man has always recognized that the immensely powerful and wonderful creatures that we call angels, have played a very special part as mediators of God's revelation to mankind. However, our message concerns the Messiah, the Son of God. As we study the Scriptures to find the way God refers to his Son, we cannot avoid reaching the conclusion that the Son is inestimably greater than the angels. The very title, Son of God, is one which indicates precedence over an angel. An angel is never addressed as God's Son, yet we find verses in Scripture which refer to the Messiah in just these terms.

Psalm 2 v 7: You are my son; today I have become your father.

2 Samuel 7 v 14 & 1 Chronicles 17 v 13: I will be his father and he will be my son.

402

The status of God's Son above the angels is emphasized in the book of *Psalms* in a verse which describes the second coming of God's Son.

Psalm 97 v 7: All the angels bow down before him.

As God spoke through the ancient psalmists, they described the angels, who are God's messengers and servants, in terms which leave one in no doubt of their great power.

Psalm 104 v 4: You use the winds as your messengers and flashes of lightning as your servants.

However, in a psalm which addresses God's Son, much greater power and authority is ascribed to the Messiah than to the angels.

Psalm 45 v 6,7: The kingdom that God has given you will last for ever and ever. You rule over your people with justice; you love what is right and hate what is evil. That is why God, your God has chosen you and has poured out more happiness on you than on any other king.

The psalmists also declare the eternal nature of the Messiah, that is, as one who was in creation, who will outlast heaven and earth and who will be there at the end.

Psalm 102 v 25–27: O Lord, you live for ever; long ago you created the earth, and with your own hands you made the heavens. They will disappear, but you will remain; they will all wear out like clothes, and they will vanish. But you are always the same, and your life never ends.

Again, in the *Psalms*, God awards his Son of the position of honour at His right hand while He subdues his enemies, speaking in a way that God never used to address an angel.

Psalm 110 v 1: Sit here at my right until I put your enemies under your feet.

The Message of Salvation

Am I then suggesting that angels are not to be highly esteemed? Indeed, no. The angels are the spirit beings who serve God in a number of most important ways. One of the tasks he sends them to perform is to help those who are to receive salvation. If we are convinced of the truth by the agency of angels, then we must firmly hold on to that truth and not allow others to divert us into false ways. The messages given to our ancestors by the angels turned out to be true and reliable. If those of our ancestors who disregarded the truths revealed by angels were punished, how much more do we deserve to be punished if we ignore the even greater revelation of salvation which has been given to us? This salvation was first announced to us by none other than the Lord himself, and those who first heard the Lord have demonstrated the truth of his teaching. God reinforced the evidence of their witness by performing miracles and giving the gift of the Holy Spirit to those whom he chose to receive it.

The Humanity of Jesus

In the present order, men are inferior to angels, but man will rule over the world to come. The fulfilment of the salvation of which we speak will be life in this new world. The change in authority which will be the order in this new world is anticipated in the book of *Psalms*.

> *Psalm 8 v 4–6*: What is man, that you think of him;
> mere man, that you care for him?
> Yet you made him inferior only to the angels; you
> crowned him with glory and honour.
> You appointed him ruler over everything you
> made; you placed him over all creation:

Now while it is true that man has dominion over much of God's creation now, we do not see man ruling over all things. These verses therefore cannot apply to man in general, but in the case of Jesus, we do see a man to whom these words apply. In becoming a man like us, he did take on a status for a while which was lower than the angels. This was necessary so that he should be able to die on behalf of everyone as an act of divine grace. Because of the death he suffered, he has now been crowned with glory and sits in the place of honour from where he rules over all creation.

It was characteristic of God, who creates and preserves all things, that he should provide us with a Saviour like Jesus, who demonstrated his perfect nature by suffering on behalf of men in the way he did. He suffered to bring many people to share his glory. The response that people have made, in recognition of the suffering that Jesus bore on their behalf, has led them to salvation, for Jesus has been able to purify these people from their sins. These individuals have become children of God just as Jesus was the Son of God, and Jesus calls them his brothers and sisters. This is something we discover from the *22nd Psalm*. The significance of the *22nd Psalm* was hidden from us until Jesus suffered his passion. Then we discovered that this is a prophetic psalm, written as words spoken by Jesus to his Father, God, describing the emotions he experiences during his passion. As this psalm turns from despair to triumph, he declares,

> *Psalm 22 v 22*: I will tell my brothers and sisters what you have done, I will praise you in their assembly.

The Messianic prophecies in *Isaiah* also speak of God being given children through the Messiah.

> *Isaiah ch 8 v 17, 18*: The Lord had hidden himself from his people, but I trust him and place my hope in him. Here I am with the children the Lord has given me.

These children are human beings just like ourselves. Jesus himself shared this human nature so that he would be just like us. He did this so that he would be able to suffer death, and in suffering death the way he did, he destroyed the special power that the devil has over death. Death was no longer an experience to be feared, and thus, men have been released from a form of slavery which is represented by life, overshadowed by the fear of the death which will end life. It is clear from Scripture that he did not come to bring salvation to angels, but to those who were descended from Abraham in a physical, or more importantly, a spiritual sense. In order to do this, he had to become like them in every way. Having taken on human nature and conducted himself in a way that no one could fault, he was able to become a rather special High Priest. He was a High Priest who could effectively intercede with God for the forgiveness of his people, because he was tempted and exposed to great suffering himself, but he never succumbed to temptation or committed sin.

The Superiority of Jesus to Moses

You, my Christian brothers and sisters, have been called to have this faith, just as I have. It is instructive to make a comparison between the work of Jesus, who was sent to be our special High Priest, and the work of Moses. Both Moses and Jesus were faithful in the work they did for God. As a special servant in God's household who was able to prophesy the future, Moses may be regarded as part of God's house. However, the man who builds a house is worthy of more honour than the house itself. The house has been built by God himself, for God has built all things. Christ has authority over that house, whereas Moses is a household servant. We can have a share in this authority if we courageously and confidently sustain our hope and faith to the end.

The Rest that God has promised his people

The Holy Spirit speaks to us through *Psalm 95* which warns us of the danger of relating to God in the same way as the Israelites whom Moses led through the desert.

Psalm 95 v 7–11: Listen today to what he says.
'Don't be stubborn, as your ancestors were at
Meribah, as they were that day in the desert at
Massah. There they put me to the test and tried
me, although they had seen what I did for them.
For forty years I was disgusted with those people.
I said, "How disloyal they are! They refuse to
obey my commands." I was angry and made a
solemn promise: "You will never enter the land
where I would have given you rest."'

Fellow believers, take care not to become stubborn and
unbelieving so that you are deceived by sin and turn away
from the living God, as the Israelites did in the desert.
Those words of warning in the Psalm apply to us now, for
they start, 'Listen today to what he says.' We must uphold
and support one another in our faith and, in this way, work
confidently in partnership with Christ with a faith which is
as fresh and vigorous as it was when we first became
believers.

Who were the people who heard God's voice, yet still
rebelled against Him? They were the Israelites whom
Moses led out of Egypt.

With whom was God angry for forty years? Those same
people who rebelled against him and died in the desert.

Of whom was God speaking when he solemnly promised
that they would never enter the land where He would have
given them rest? Those same rebellious Israelites. They
were disqualified from receiving God's promise because
they did not believe.

That episode in the desert was a prophetic representation
of our current situation. God has promised us that we may
enter a land of rest. We must take great care then, not to fall
into the same pitfall as the ancient Israelites and become
disqualified from benefiting from God's promise. In the
same way that they were given the good news that they were
journeying to a wonderful promised land, so too, we have
heard the Good News that our journey through life will lead
us to a promised land where we may rest from our labours.

That rest from our labours, spoken of in the psalm, must
not be regarded as a time of idleness and inactivity, but

rather a time of fulfilling refreshment. This is the sort of rest that God experienced on the seventh day when he had completed his work of creation.

> *Genesis Ch 2 v 2,3*: By the seventh day, God had finished the work he had been doing, so on the seventh day He rested from all his work. God blessed the seventh day and made it holy because on that day he rested from his work of creation.

This does not mean to imply that God has been idle from the time he completed creation but that he has entered into a new phase of fulfilling activity. Entry into the promised land would not have meant idleness for the nomadic Israelites, but they would have been released from the privations and hardships of desert life to enter a more fulfilled existence as a nation. Those who first received the news of this fulfilment did not experience this promised rest because they disbelieved. The promise was received by others.

Now if that promise had been completely fulfilled when Joshua led the next generation of Israelites into the promised land, that would have been an end of the matter. The time of resting would have been achieved and no further mention of it would have been made in Scripture. However, this was not the case. We see from the *95th Psalm* that many years later, King David says,

> *Psalm 95 v 7*: Listen today to what he says.

This promise of rest, the type of rest that God experienced when he completed creation, is offered as a promise then to us today. However, we must take care to remain faithful and avoid being disqualified from that rest as were the early Israelites because of their lack of faith.

The quality of our faith will be scrutinized by God at Judgement. The Word of God provides us with the means of assessing that faith for ourselves, for Scripture probes our thoughts and motives more keenly than a sharp two-edged sword can dissect bones and marrow. Careful study of Scripture can expose many unworthy thoughts and dubious motives which we may conceal from the world, and could almost conceal from ourselves. However, nothing can be hidden from God, and ultimately, we are accountable to Him.

Jesus, our great High Priest

It is therefore essential that we hold firmly to our faith, reassured that where we have weaknesses and our faith falls short, the High Priest who mediates to God on our behalf is fully aware of those weaknesses and is sympathetic to them. That High Priest is none other than Jesus who was able to experience first hand, all the problems and temptations that we face ourselves. However, in his case, he coped with temptation without falling into sin. The fact that Jesus is our mediating High Priest should give us every confidence that we can approach God's throne, where we will find all the grace and forgiveness we need.

Let us think of what the office of High Priest entails.

Every High Priest is selected from his fellow men to serve God on their behalf and to make sacrifices and offerings for the sins of his fellow men. Indeed, because he himself has human failings and weaknesses, the sacrifices he offers cover his own sins as well as those on behalf of whom he serves. The fact that he himself is fallible and weak in many ways helps the High Priest to deal gently with those who sin and make mistakes because of their ignorance. The honour of being High Priest is not one which a man bestows on himself. Entry to the priesthood is a matter of divine vocation. Aaron, who is our prototype High Priest, was called to this office.

In the same way, Christ's role as our High Priest is not an honour which he seized for himself. The status of Christ, both as the Son of God and as High Priest, is declared through the Messianic psalms.

In *Psalm 2*, we hear,

Psalm 2 v 7: He said to me: 'You are my son, today, I have become your father.'

and in *Psalm 110*, it is written,

> *Psalm 110 v 4*: You will be a priest for ever in the priestly order of Melchizedek.

Melchizedek was the rather special High Priest who blessed Abraham.

When he was on earth, Jesus prayed earnestly, and with tears to God who could have saved him from death. Even though he was the Son of God, he was obedient and accepted the way of suffering he had to follow. Because he was humble and obedient, God heard his prayers, and when he had come through his sufferings in a way which clearly demonstrated that he was perfect, God declared him to be High Priest in the order of Melchizedek.

Exhortation to persist in faith

There is so much we would wish to teach you on this, but it is hard to explain these mysteries to you because you are spiritually immature and do not readily grasp these divine secrets. You have been Christians long enough to become teachers of the faith yourselves, yet you still need to have someone to teach you the fundamentals of the faith. You are like children who should be eating solid food, but are still drinking milk. A child who has not been weaned off milk does not have a clear understanding of right and wrong. Solid food, on the other hand, is for adults who can distinguish between good and evil.

We want to take you forward to the deeper lessons of Christianity, and give you teaching which is appropriate for those who are spiritually mature. We should be able to move on from teaching the fundamentals of Christianity,

> belief in God,
> the futility of reliance on good works to earn salvation,
> teaching on the significance of baptism,
> the benefits bestowed by the laying on of hands,
> the resurrection of the dead,
> and the certainty of eternal judgement.

410

We want to move forward with our teaching, and, God permitting, so we will. The sin of apostasy, that is abandoning the faith once firmly held, is one for which repentance, necessary for forgiveness, is almost impossible. Those committing this sin have, for a time, lived in God's light and experienced all the good things of Christianity. These good things include a share of the gift of the Holy Spirit, an appreciation of God's word, and an anticipation of the wonder and power of the world to come. If these people now abandon their faith, they are publicly denigrating God, and this is just like crucifying the Son of God all over again. Such sin is almost beyond repentance.

Soil which absorbs the rain God sends and grows plants which are useful to feed and sustain men, is blessed by God, but soil which only produces thorns and weeds is worthless and in danger of being destroyed by fire. We say this to warn those among you who are not producing spiritually good fruits but are harming those in God's family.

These words sound harsh, but we are confident that you will receive the blessing of salvation. God is not unfair and will remember all the work you have done in the past and are still doing for your fellow Christians. We earnestly desire that you will all sustain your faith, continue to work hard in the cause of the gospel and exercise patience, so that your hopes may be fulfilled and you will receive God's promises.

The certainty that God's promise will be fulfilled

When men make solemn promises to one another, they will often make a solemn vow in God's name, signifying to each other that they expect divine retribution should they go back on their word. In the book of *Genesis*, we read of God's solemn promise to Abraham.

> *Genesis ch 22 v 16–18*: I make a vow by my own name – the Lord is speaking – that I will richly bless you. Because you did this and did not keep back your only son from me, I promise that I will

give you as many descendants as there are stars in the sky or grains of sand along the seashore. Your descendants will conquer their enemies. All the nations will ask me to bless them as I have blessed your descendants – all because you obeyed my command.

Notice how God emphasises the solemn nature of this promise by making the vow in his own name. Abraham waited patiently, and this vow was fulfilled. Things turned out as we would have expected because we know that God cannot lie and that he would not go back on His word. This greatly encourages us to firmly trust in the promises God has made to us. Our expectation of God's promise to us of eternal life is something on which we may anchor our lives. This promise is something which connects us to God through the curtain which now separates us from heaven. The imagery of a curtain separating us from God is based on the model God provided for us when he ordained the way the Temple was to be designed. The Holy of Holies was separated from the rest of the Temple by a curtain through which only the High Priest could pass. Jesus is the High Priest who intercedes on our behalf, and he has passed through the curtain which separates us from heaven, ahead of us.

The characteristics of Jesus' priesthood

Jewish thought focuses its ideas of the priesthood on the Levitical model. Aaron was the first High Priest of this order, and subsequent High Priests have been descended from Aaron and have held this office for the duration of their lifetime only.

The priesthood of Jesus is significantly different. Jesus was not from the tribe of Levi but from the tribe of Judah, a tribe not associated with the priesthood by Moses. Jesus' tenure of the office of High Priest is not limited to a human life span but lasts for ever. Jesus is a High Priest of an order which is encountered in Scripture, long before the Levitical priesthood was instituted, that is, the priestly order of

412

Melchizedek.

Let me remind you of the features of Melchizedek's priesthood which correspond to the type of priesthood we recognize in Jesus. Omissions from Scripture sometimes have as much significance as things which are specifically mentioned! First, Melchizedek is presented in Scripture as one without beginning or end. There is no record of his parents or ancestors, neither is mention made of his death. Like Jesus, his priesthood is of an eternal nature. Secondly, his name and titles have meanings which correspond to the attributes we recognize in Jesus.

The name, Melchizedek means, 'King of Righteousness'.
He was also King of Salem, and this title means 'King of Peace'.

Thirdly, he was greater than Abraham. This is clear on two counts. When Abraham returned from his victory over the four kings, it was Melchizedek who blessed Abraham rather than the other way round. Then, Abraham donated to Melchizedek one tenth of the spoils he had won in battle. This example of tithing predates the practice of tithing instituted by Moses.

Fourthly, Melchizedek was greater than the Levitical priesthood which was to be established later, in the time of Moses and Aaron. The Levitical priests not only collected tithes but also paid them. As Abraham was their ancestor, their seed was within Abraham as he presented his tithe to Melchizedek. Thus, in a sense, at that moment, the whole of the Levitical priesthood was involved in the act of giving Melchizedek a tithe.

The work of the Levitical priesthood was intractably associated with the Law. Had the role of the Levitical Priesthood and the function of the Law adequately served the divine purpose, there would have been no need for the priestly order of Aaron to be superseded by the priestly order of Melchizedek.

A number of important consequences follow from this change to a new order of priesthood.

First, the Law is required to completely change, because the operation of law is dependant on the role and function of the priesthood in the system within which it operates. Secondly, the office and role of High Priest are concentrated in one person, the person of Jesus, for ever, and do not have to be passed on to another individual at the end of each human lifespan. This eternal dimension of Jesus' High Priestly role was prophesied in the Psalm which I have already quoted.

Psalm 110 v 4: The Lord made a solemn promise and will not take it back:
'You will be a priest for ever in the priestly order of Melchizedek.'

Thirdly, the old imperfect Law of Moses which was totally inadequate and could bring nothing to perfection, has been replaced by a completely new framework within which we can approach God. We can now approach God directly through Jesus. He is always able to save those who come through him, because he is continually there with his Father, pleading our case with Him.

What more can I teach you about the special priesthood which is exercised by Jesus now?

Jesus serves from the Most Holy place in heaven, that is from the throne at the right hand side of the Divine Majesty. The Holy of Holies which was made, first in the Tabernacle and then in the Jerusalem Temple, was only an earthly representation of this heavenly reality.

Jesus is Holy and has no fault or sin. He has been set apart from the domain inhabited by sinners to be enthroned in the most honourable position in heaven.

Jesus does not have to offer sacrifices daily to cover both his own sins and the sins of the people. Unlike the Levitical priests, Jesus is perfect and has no sin, and the sacrifice which he offered of himself was a perfect sacrifice, more than adequate to cover the sins of the people for once and for all.

The instructions Moses was given, when God told him on the mountain to construct the Tabernacle, were very precise. The Tabernacle and the work of the Levitical priests, who offered sacrifices there to conform to the Law given as part of the Old Covenant, was a copy of the heavenly realities, but it was only a shallow model. However, it was important that such an earthly model should be set up to educate the people. This would enable them to understand the heavenly counterpart, provided by the New Covenant.

The Old and the New Covenants

If the Old Covenant had been adequate to establish a satisfactory relationship between God and man, there would have been no need for another covenant. However, God saw that his people did not faithfully abide by the provisions of his first covenant, and he told the people of Israel through his prophet, Jeremiah, that he would make a New Covenant with his people.

> *Jeremiah ch 31 v 31–34*: The Lord says, 'The time is coming when I will make a New Covenant with the people of Israel and the People of Judah. It will not be like the Old Covenant that I made with their ancestors when I took them by the hand and led them out of Egypt. Although I was like a husband to them, they did not keep that covenant. The New Covenant that I will make with the people of Israel will be this: I will put my law within them and write it on their hearts. I will be their God, and they will be my people. None of them will have to teach his fellow countryman to know the Lord, because all will know me, from the least to the greatest. I will forgive their sins and I will no longer remember their wrongs. I, the Lord, have spoken.'

The fact that God speaks of a New Covenant implies that God regards the original covenant as old. Things which are old and worn out, and for which a replacement has been found, are soon discarded.

The teaching that can be derived from the Old Covenant

It is instructive to examine worship ritual associated with the Old Covenant, and the artefacts and environment associated with this ritual, because they all provide illustrations which explain the realities of the new order which governs our worship at the present time.

The place set aside for worship was called the Tabernacle. The Tabernacle was a tent structure. The large outer tent was called the Holy Place. In the Holy Place stood the lampstand and the table on which was placed the bread, offered to God. Behind a curtain in the Holy Place was another tent called the Holy of Holies. In the Holy of Holies were the gold altar where incense was burnt, and the Covenant Box, often referred to as the Ark. This was covered with gold and contained a gold jar of manna, Aaron's rod that had sprouted leaves and the two stone tablets on which the Ten Commandments had been inscribed. Statues of angels with wings spread out were placed above the Ark to represent the presence of God in the place where sins were forgiven. There is no need now to go into further detail.

Priests enter the outer tent, that is the Holy Place, to perform their duties every day, but only the High Priest enters the inner tent, the Holy of Holies. He enters the Holy of Holies only once a year bearing sacrificial blood. He offers this to God on behalf of himself and the people for all the sins they have committed, both knowingly and unwittingly.

The Holy Spirit guided Moses into making these arrangements which clearly teach that entry into the Holy of Holies, where God's presence can be most keenly appreciated, is restricted. The prescribed offerings and sacrifices and purification ceremonies are all to do with material things like food and drink and external show. These cannot therefore make the inner worship of the heart perfect. However, this was the way things had to be done until God arranged something better.

The Way in which the New Covenant supersedes the Old

We now have the better way. We now have Christ as our High Priest, and he serves in the Holy of Holies in heaven, rather than in a man-made tent on earth. The blood which the priests sprinkled on the people to ritually cleanse them, was merely the blood of bulls and goats which have been sacrificed. However, Christ, our High Priest, purifies us by his own blood, shed when he offered himself as a perfect sacrifice, and this will achieve much more than a mere ritual cleansing. The New Covenant has thus been established by Christ, whose death frees people from the sins they committed under the Old Covenant, and enables those who have been called by God, to receive the eternal blessings he has in store for them.

A worldly analogy which enables us to see why a death is necessary for people to obtain benefits is provided by the example of a will. While the testator is alive, the beneficiaries can receive nothing from that will. The will only comes into effect with the death of the testator. The importance of a death having taken place for the people to receive the divine benefits of purification and forgiveness was indicated by the way Moses used blood under the first covenant. After reading the provisions of God's Law to the people, he mixed the blood of bulls and goats which had been sacrificed with water. Then, using a sprig of hyssop and some red wool, he sprinkled the blood over all the things associated with worship, including the Book of Law, the Tabernacle and the people. All this was to impress that purification and forgiveness of sins can only take place if blood has been shed.

All these were pointers to the divinely foreordained way that men may receive real purification and forgiveness in the fullness of time. That time has now been fulfilled and the new way of becoming reconciled to God has now been made available to us. The earthly pointer or model of what was to come, was provided by the Jewish High Priest entering the Holy of Holies each year with the blood of a sacrificed animal, but the heavenly reality requires a much better sacrifice. Now, as we approach the end of time, Christ has appeared to finally remove sin through the blood

417

of his own perfect sacrifice. This was not a sacrifice which Christ had to make many times, undergoing intense suffering on each occasion. Christ's sacrifice was sufficient and perfect when made on just one occasion.

As Christ died once, when he offered himself as a sacrifice to cover men's sins, so each of us must die once. Then we will be judged by God, but Christ will appear a second time. He will not appear to deal with sin all over again, but to save from judgement, all those who have put their trust in his sacrifice and expectantly await his coming.

I have described the Law and the ancient Jewish ritual of the High Priest scattering the blood of sacrificed animals to effect purification and forgiveness, as a model of the real thing which has now been provided by Christ. However, this is a very poor and imperfect model. If it had really fulfilled its purpose, the people who came to worship God would have been purified and would no longer have felt guilty of their sins, but it did not work like that. Had it done so, there would have been no need for further sacrifices, but the blood of bulls and goats can never adequately cover sin, and the ritual had to be repeated annually.

We can now recognize that *Psalm 40* is a prophetic psalm. It is written as words spoken by Christ before he actually entered the world. Christ declares to God through the psalmist, the part he would take in his own body to replace the sacrifices which could never properly satisfy God.

> *Psalm 40 v 6–8*: You do not want sacrifices and offerings; you do not ask for animals burnt whole on the altar or for sacrifices to take away sins. Instead, you have prepared a body for me, and so I answered, 'Here I am; your instructions for me are in the book of the Law. How I love to do your will my God! I keep your teaching in my heart.'

Even though animal sacrifices are prescribed in the Law, Christ declared that God neither wanted nor was pleased with animal sacrifices to take away sins. He then offered himself to perform God's will. Thus, God has done away with the old system of animal sacrifices and has accepted the sacrifice of Christ in their place. Because Jesus

418

faithfully fulfilled God's will for him, we are all purified by the offering he made of himself, once and for all on our behalf.

The Jewish priests go through the same daily rituals and repeatedly offer sacrifices to God, but these can never take away sins. Jesus, on the other hand, offered once, a sacrifice which was effective for ever, and then he took his place in the position of honour in heaven at the right hand of God. There he will remain until everything has been brought in subjugation to him.

The Holy Spirit testified to the inward, rather than superficial effect that the New Covenant will have on the people, when he spoke through the prophet, Jeremiah.

> *Jeremiah ch 31 v 33,34*: The New Covenant that I will make with the people of Israel will be this: I will put my Law within them and write it on their hearts. I will be their God, and they will be my people. None of them will have to teach his fellow countryman to know the Lord, because all will know me from the least to the greatest. I will forgive their sins and I will no longer remember their wrong. I, the Lord, have spoken.

Thus, if sins have been forgiven and forgotten, there is no further need for an offering to be made to take away those sins.

An exhortation and encouragement to be steadfast in faith

What then is the significance of all this for us? It means that the death of Jesus allows us to enter the Holy of Holies. The curtain that symbolically separated us from God is no longer there. Jesus has opened up for us a new way to God, a living means of access which is made through his body. He is our great High Priest in charge of God's House, so let us confidently approach God with pure hearts, sincere minds, sure faith and clear consciences as people who have been thoroughly washed and cleansed with pure water. Let us be confident in the hope we hold and profess to others, because anything promised by God is certain to come about. We must continue to show concern for one another, and to live loving, good and helpful lives. We must continue to meet regularly together and not withdraw from the fellowship as some are doing. Rather, we should meet frequently to give one another encouragement, as the Day of the Lord will soon be here.

If we continue to sin after we have been taught the truth, there is no sacrifice that will purge those sins. We will have no alternative but to await the coming Judgement and the unquenchable fire which will destroy all God's enemies. If anyone who disobeyed the Law of Moses was put to death on being found guilty on the evidence of two or more witnesses, how much more deserving of even worse punishment is one who disregards the Son of God. What a terrible thing it is to behave as if the blood, Jesus shed to establish this New Covenant, was of no account. This is about the worst insult a person can pay to God. Let us pay due heed to the warning God gives his people in the book of *Deuteronomy.*

> *Deuteronomy ch 32 v 34*: It is mine to avenge; I will repay. In due time their foot will slip; their day of disaster is near and their doom rushes upon them.

In the following verse, we are reminded that God will come in judgement.

> *Deuteronomy ch 32 v 35*: The Lord will judge his people.

Take heed then, for the consequences of being judged by the living God and found wanting will be absolutely terrible.

However, you may take encouragmenet from the experiences you have undergone from the time you first came into God's light. You were exposed to many persecutions, publicly insulted, treated badly and forfeited your belongings. Yet you endured all these with the utmost fortitude, even with joy. You were prepared to go further and identify with those who were being imprisoned for this cause. The source of your joy was the sure knowledge that you had something better to look forward to in the world to come, which would last for ever. Do not falter in your courage and fortitude at this point then. Sustain your patience just a little longer and continue to faithfully do God's will. The words of the prophet, Habakkuk, should be of great encouragement to you.

> *Habakkuk ch 2 v 3,4*: The time is coming quickly, and what I show you will come true. It may seem slow in coming, but wait for it; it will certainly take place and it will not be delayed. And this is the message: 'Those who are evil will not survive, but those who are righteous will live because they are faithful to God.'

Having come this far, we are not people who will turn from the righteous way and so be eternally lost. Rather, we have a faith which is strong and will sustain us in the way which leads to salvation.

The ways in which men's faith have brought them to triumph

What does it mean, to have faith? Faith is being sure of the things which are hoped for, being certain of things which cannot yet be seen. We see faith clearly in operation in the ancient Scriptures, and those who exercised faith won God's approval.

Faith was in operation right at the beginning in the act of creation. It was the means by which the Universe was created at God's word and the visible brought into existence out of the invisible.

It was by faith that Abel made an offering which, unlike Cain's, was acceptable to God and Abel won God's approval as a righteous man. Even though he is dead, we are aware that through a righteousness, borne of his faith, Abel pleased God with his offering, and in that sense, Abel's faith still speaks to us now.

Another of the ancient patriarchs who pleased God was Enoch who was taken up to God without actually dying. Scripture records that Enoch was taken up to God without dying because he had pleased God. No one can please God unless they have faith, because without faith, a person will not believe that God exists and seek after him to earn the rewards he has to give.

Noah could not see the future, but by faith, he heeded God's warnings and built the Ark in which he and his family were saved. The rest of the world was condemned, but Noah was reckoned by God as a righteous man because of his faith.

It was an act of faith in God which caused Abraham to leave his comfortable home to journey to an unknown land which God had promised he would give him. Abraham lived as a nomadic herdsman in that country where he was regarded as a foreigner. The same promise was given to his son, Isaac and his grandson, Jacob who continued to live nomadic existences in that land. Abraham, Isaac and Jacob were prepared to live there as foreigners because they looked forward to the same hope that we share, the coming of God's City which will last for ever.

Through an act of faith, Abraham trusted in the promise that God had made him that he would become a great father, even though he and his wife, Sarah, were humanly speaking, too old to have children. Abraham's faith was well founded for he became the ancestor of descendants, more numerous than the stars in the sky and the grains of sand on the sea-shore.

All these people died in faith. They did not actually receive in their life-times the ultimate blessing of life in a new world which God had promised, but they knew this was to come. They readily described themselves as foreigners and refugees as they lived on earth, for the land they awaited as their own was yet to come. They clearly lived with their hopes centred on this heavenly kingdom and did not concern themselves too much about the land they would ultimately leave behind. Thus, God was glad for them to acknowledge Himself as their God, for it was for people like them that He had prepared the Heavenly City.

It was a very spectacular act of faith which brought

422

Abraham to the point of offering his son Isaac as a sacrifice to God, for God had already promised Abraham that his progeny would be descended through Isaac. Abraham had faith enough to believe that God could raise Isaac from death, and in a sense, Abraham did receive back Isaac when he was on the point of death.

It was through an act of faith that Issac blessed his younger son, Jacob, rather than his elder son, Esau.

It was an act of faith which led Jacob to give the double blessing to Joseph rather than to his eldest son. Just before he died, he leaned on his stick and gave each of Joseph's sons a blessing which put these grandsons on a par with his sons. This was done as an act of worship to his God.

Joseph's declaration on the point of death, that the Israelites would leave Egypt, was an act of faith. He then left instructions on the way his body should be buried.

Moses' parents displayed their faith by disobeying the king's order. They saw what a wonderful child Moses was, and did not kill him as ordered but hid him for three months.

Moses displayed his faith by refusing to identify himself with the Egyptian royal family. Instead, he accepted the suffering of his own people and the ridicule that went with it. Although life in the Egyptian royal household would have been enjoyable, Moses had faith in the future of his own people as the nation who would in the course of time, bear the Messiah. He considered that this event, which he knew would happen a long time in the future, was a far more worthwhile focal point for the way he should chart his life, than all the transient pleasures of the Egyptian court.

Although he incurred the king's wrath, Moses' faith found him steadfast in his task of leading his people out of Egypt. Nothing could induce him to turn back. His faith was vindicated when he instituted the Passover and ordered blood to be sprinkled on the doors of Israelite households. The Angel of death did not kill the eldest children in households which bore this sign but destroyed the first-born sons of the Egyptians.

The Israelites demonstrated their faith by entering the Red Sea which opened up, enabling them to cross on dry land. The pursuing Egyptians were engulfed in its waters.

The Israelites won their first victory in the promised land as a result of exercising their faith. Instead of attacking the city of Jericho, they simply marched round as commanded by God, and after seven days, the city's walls collapsed.

Rahab survived the conquest of Jericho as the result of an act of faith, for she recognized that the Israelites were God's people and gave their spies shelter when they came to reconnoitre Jericho. Rahab was therefore spared while the rest of the citizens were killed.

I could go on indefinitely citing examples from the Scriptures of those who demonstrated the power of their faith. There were the Judges, Gideon, Barak, Samson and Jephthah. There was King David, and Samuel and the prophets. Through faith, some of these defeated whole nations, single handed. Because they were obedient to God, he afforded them his protection against the great dangers they encountered from raging lions, fierce fires and great battles. Although, humanly speaking, they were weak, they achieved great things. Men defeated armies of nations, hostile to God, and women received back relatives who were raised from death.

In many cases, the exercise of faith did not have a triumphal outcome. People bravely displayed their faith when it would have been easier to accept the offer of freedom. Instead, they withstood torture, mockery, imprisonment, stoning, or being subjected to a cruel death. They experienced poverty, having no more than animal skins to wear and having nowhere better to live than caves. They put up with persecution and bad treatment, because they realized that they were only passing through this world as a temporary dwelling place, until they entered the permanent home that God had prepared for them.

They were really too good for this world. What an example they have set by their faith. They have not yet received the fullness of God's promises to them because God has decided on an even better plan which will include both them and ourselves. His purpose is that all of us should enter into perfection together.

Although we cannot see them, the faithful who have departed this life await in paradise the fulfilment which God has prepared for both them and ourselves. We are surrounded by their spirits who see all that we are now doing with our lives. Let us therefore get rid of the sins which cling to us and stand in the way of the service we would wish to offer. We are entered in a race and we must exercise all our will power and determination to complete the course. As we run, we must keep our eyes fixed on Jesus in whom our faith has its roots and in whom it will have its fulfilment. He ran a tougher course than we do, before us, but he did not give up because he had to endure the cross. On the contrary, he made light of the suffering and shame of crucifixion because he knew the prize which lay in store, and now he is seated in the position of honour in heaven on God's right hand.

The Fatherly nature of God

Consider the suffering that the hatred of sinners caused to be heaped on Jesus, and do not become discouraged yourselves. You have not had to face death in your struggles against the forces of evil which confront you. As you endure suffering, keep in mind the encouraging words that God spoke to his servants who faced suffering in the past and who were taught to regard suffering as a means by which they could learn from God. Job was advised by his counsellor, Eliphaz,

> *Job ch 5 v 17*: Happy is the person whom God corrects! Do not resent it when he rebukes you.

Again, we find this same wisdom expressed in the book of *Proverbs*.

> *Proverbs ch 3 v 11.12*: When the Lord corrects you, my Son, pay close attention and take it as a warning. The Lord corrects those he loves as a father corrects a son of whom he is proud.

You will find suffering easier to endure if you regard it as God's means of teaching you as his children. Are not all children disciplined by their parents as part of their

425

upbringing? If you do not experience the same discipline that God uses to instruct all his children, you might do well to question whether or not, you really are a true child of God. Since we recognized that the disciplining we received from our own parents was for our own good, we respected them for exercising this discipline. In the case of our earthly parents, the discipline they imposed during the short period of time we lived at home and were subject to them, was directed by their view of what was good for us. God's discipline, on the other hand, is directed to absolute standards of goodness and will lead us to share his holiness. We should therefore accept the discipline God imposes on us with joy rather than resentment, and in due course, the reward will be the peace that comes from being able to live a righteous life.

Things to avoid in living the Christian life

Do not become despondent then, but renew your efforts and combat the fatigue and listlessness which can easily overtake you, as you become weary of the continual spiritual strife in which you are engaged. If you falter, then weaker members of your body may fall away altogether. On the other hand, if you strive manfully, weaker brethren will be encouraged by your fortitude and will derive strength themselves.

As far as is possible, remain at peace with those around you and strive to live a holy life. You cannot hope to see God if your lives are not holy. Take care not to regress in your spiritual lives and reject the message of God's grace which you once so enthusiastically accepted. In particular, do not live among the brethren as a discontented trouble maker. Such a person can poison a whole fellowship by his bitter and vindictive words. In the person of Esau, Scripture provides us with an object lesson we would do well to heed. Esau had a wrong sense of priorities and placed material things above spiritual matters in his set of values. He despised the blessing of his father which was his right as the elder son, exchanging this for a mere meal. He later realized his folly, and he tried to regain his birth-right in great contrition. However, his father had already bestowed the blessing on another, and there was no way that blessing could be recalled.

The contrast between the Old and New Covenants

Just consider the vast difference between the Covenant which has been established for you, and the Old Covenant, made with the Israelites who journeyed from Egypt. The Old Covenant was established on Mount Sinai, and was associated with many fearsome signs. As Moses led the Israelites to the foot of the mountain to meet God, there was thunder and lightning. Thick cloud appeared over the mountain and the sound of a very loud trumpet blast was heard. Then the Lord came down on the mountain with fire, and thick smoke covered the mountain. God gave the order that anyone touching Sinai, even an animal straying on to that mountain, should be stoned to death. The people trembled at the sound of the voice of God, and even Moses, who went up to the mountain to meet God face to face, was afraid at the sight of God.

In contrast, you have come to Mount Zion where Jesus has arranged the New Covenant in heavenly Jerusalem, the city of the living God. You have come to a place of joy, guarded by vast numbers of angels, where all the children of God, whose names are recorded as citizens of Zion, have gathered together. You have come to God, who is the judge of all mankind. You stand with the spirits of all the good people who have been made perfect by the blood of Christ, shed for them. Unlike the shed blood of Abel which cried for vengeance, the sprinkled blood of Jesus promises nothing but good things.

A warning to be heeded

Take care then, to listen to and heed the divine message. If those who rejected the message brought to them on earth by the prophets did not escape retribution, how much less will we escape punishment if we disregard the divine

427

messenger who speaks from heaven. On Sinai, his voice shook the earth, and speaking through his prophet, Haggai, he has declared that the earth will be shaken again.

Haggai ch 2 v 6: Before long I will shake heaven and earth, land and sea.

These words warn us that everything superficial and without firm foundation will be shaken away, leaving only the things which are inviolable, because they are firmly rooted in God.

Let us then thank God, and worship him with reverence and awe in a way that he will find pleasing, thanking him that although he has the power to wreak great destruction, he has prepared for us an eternal kingdom which cannot be shaken or destroyed.

Final words of advice

What final advice can I give you then on how to live in a way which pleases God? First and foremost, we must love one another as Christian brothers and sisters. We must also exercise hospitality and welcome strangers. In welcoming strangers, some have actually entertained angels, unaware of the status of their guests. Empathize with those who are experiencing any kind of suffering, whether it be sickness, bereavement or even imprisonment. Enter into their sufferings as if they were your own.

The institution of marriage is to be respected and husbands and wives must remain faithful to one another. The immoral and adulterous will come under God's judgement.

Avoid materialism. Be satisfied with whatever possessions you have, for God will make sure that you always have sufficient. He has made this promise more than once in the Scriptures.

Deuteronomy ch 31 v 6: Your God, the Lord himself, will be with you. He will not fail you or abandon you.

428

Deuteronomy ch 31 v 8: The Lord himself will lead you and be with you. He will not fail you or abandon you, so do not lose courage and be afraid.

Joshua ch 1 v 5: I will always be with you; I will never abandon you.

Cherish the memories of your former leaders who first brought you God's message. Think of the way they lived and died, and try to match their faith in your own lives.

Hold fast to the knowledge, that Jesus never changes. Yesterday, today, for ever, he is always the same, completely consistent in all his dealings with mankind.

Be careful not to be influenced by the many strange teachings which are being circulated and are conflicting with the true message of the Gospel. Such teachings can divert you from following the way that leads to truth. Do not set too much store by ritual, obeying special rules about food, and the like. Those who have paid great heed to such rules have derived very little help from them. You should rely on God's grace as the source of inner strength rather than the observance of rules and rituals.

An example of ritual which finds no place in Christian teaching, is provided by the practice followed by the priests serving in the Jewish Temple, in dealing with sacrifices. The High Priest brought the blood of sacrificed animals to the Holy of Holies as an offering to cover the people's sins. The bodies of the animals may not be eaten and were burnt outside the city. The implication was that everything inside the city was now put right, and the city's wrongs had been disposed of outside the city. However, Jesus would not endorse a system which implied that all was well within the man-made institutions of the city. Jesus died outside the city. His cross is our altar and we identify ourselves with the shame Jesus experienced outside the city, for we do not regard worldly cities and all they stand for, as providing us with a permanent home. The city we look forward to is not of this world and is yet to come. Let us demonstrate our reliance on the sacrifice of Jesus by the praise we offer with our lips and the acknowledgement we make that Jesus is our Lord.

Obey your spiritual leaders and be guided by their instructions, because your souls are a responsibility for which they must one day be accountable to God. If you cooperate with your spiritual leaders, they will enjoy the service they exercise on you behalf. If you oppose them, their work becomes a sad and burdensome duty, and that is of no benefit to you.

Continue to pray for us so that our consciences may remain clear. This is important to us because we really want to feel assured that our motives are pure and that we are doing the right things at all times. My most earnest request of you is that you will pray to God to send me back to you soon.

Final Benediction and messages

Finally, I commit you to God's safe keeping with my own prayer. May the God of peace provide you with all the gifts you need to serve Him, and may He do all the things he wishes in both your lives and in our lives also. I pray this through the name of our Lord Jesus Christ, the Great Shepherd of the sheep, who sealed the Eternal Covenant by his sacrificial death, and whom God raised up from death. To Christ be the glory for ever and ever, Amen.

I entreat you, my brothers and sisters to listen carefully and patiently to this letter which I have sent to encourage you, for it is not unduly long. I am pleased to be able to tell you that our brother Timothy has been released from prison and I hope to have him with me when I return to you.

Give our greetings to all your leaders and to all the members of your churches. The Christians in Italy send you their greetings too.

May God's grace be with you all.

APPENDIX 2

Genealogies and Family Trees

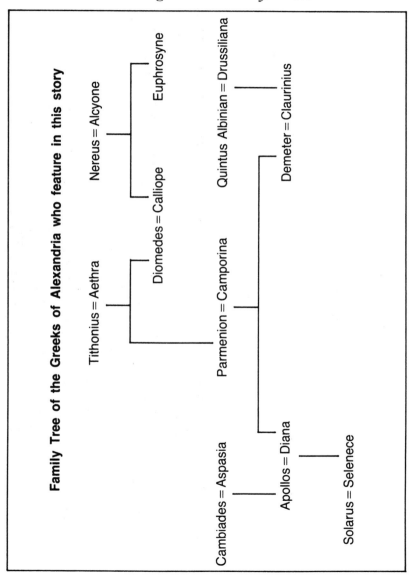

Family Tree of the Greeks of Alexandria who feature in this story

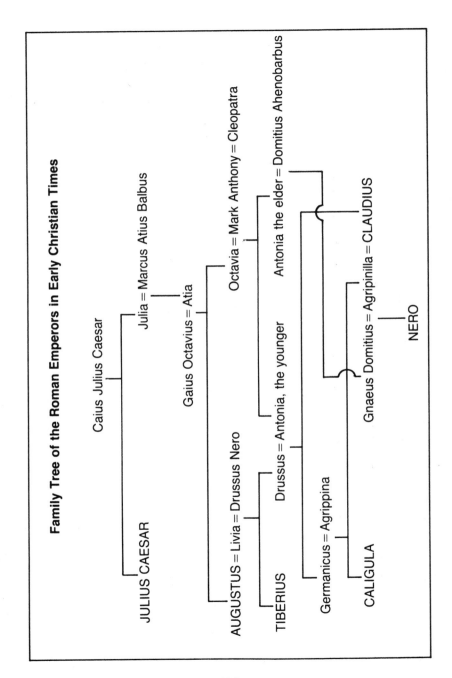

Family Tree of the Roman Emperors in Early Christian Times

Caius Julius Caesar

Julia = Marcus Atius Balbus

Gaius Octavius = Atia

Octavia = Mark Anthony = Cleopatra

Antonia the elder = Domitius Ahenobarbus

JULIUS CAESAR

AUGUSTUS = Livia = Drussus Nero

Drussus = Antonia, the younger

Gnaeus Domitius = Agripinilla = CLAUDIUS

TIBERIUS

Germanicus = Agrippina

NERO

CALIGULA

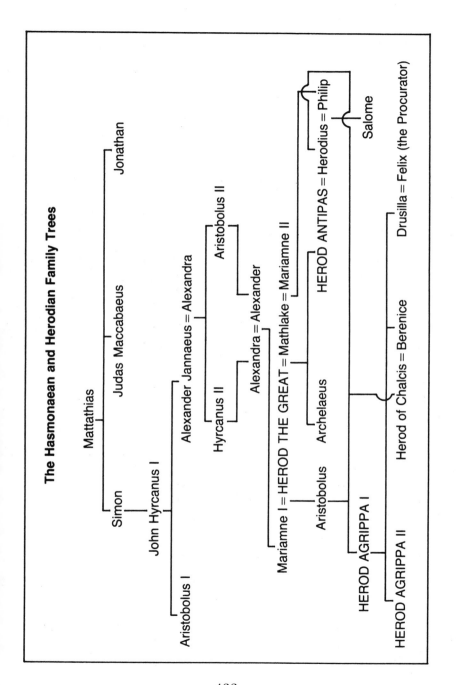

The Hasmonaean and Herodian Family Trees

APPENDIX 3

Maps and Plans

Key to The Eastern Mediterranean:

1. Cyrene
2. Alexandria
3. Jerusalem
4. Antioch
5. Ephesus
6. Philippi
7. Athens
8. Corinth
9. Giza
10. Memphis
11. Gaza
12. Gerar
13. Beersheba
14. Hebron
15. Bethlehem
16. Dead Sea
17. Sea of Galilee
18. Caesaraea Philippi
19. Tyre
20. Sidon
21. Tarsus
22. Derbe
23. Lystra
24. Antioch (in Pisidia)
25. Colossae
26. Laodicea
27. Philadelphia
28. Sardis
29. Smyrna
30. Pergamum
31. Adramyttium
32. Assos
33. Troas
34. The Hellespont
35. Doriscus
36. Neapolis
37. Amphipolis
38. Apollonia
39. Thessalonica
40. Beroea
41. Mount Olympus
42. Larissa
43. Pharsalus
44. Thermopylae
45. Thebes
46. Marathon
47. Delphi
48. Sparta
49. Salamis
50. Gulf of Corinth
51. Rhodes
52. Caesaraea
53. Crete
54. Cyprus
55. Byzantium
56. Apollonia (on the Adriatic)
57. Mytilene

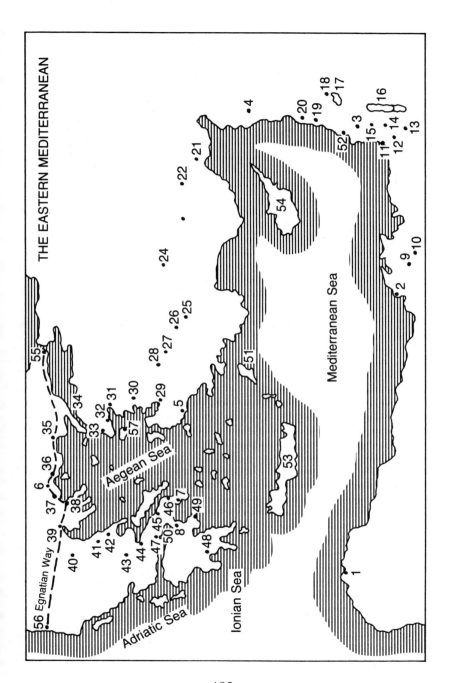

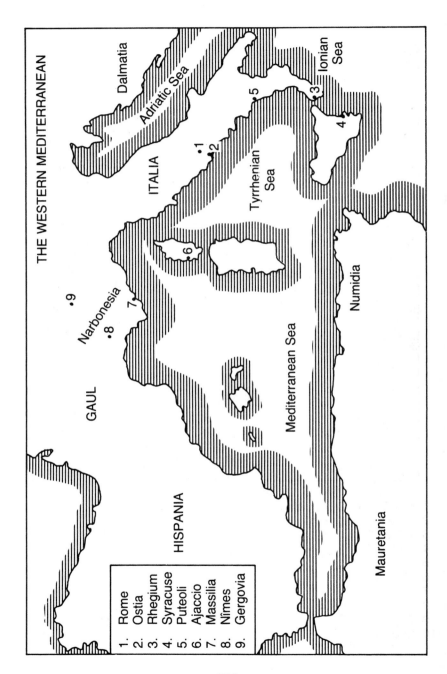

THE WESTERN MEDITERRANEAN

Dalmatia
Adriatic Sea
Ionian Sea
ITALIA
•1
•2
•5
•3
4
Tyrrhenian Sea
•6
Narbonesia
•7
•9
•8
GAUL
Mediterranean Sea
Numidia
HISPANIA
Mauretania

1. Rome
2. Ostia
3. Rhegium
4. Syracuse
5. Puteoli
6. Ajaccio
7. Massilia
8. Nîmes
9. Gergovia

ROME

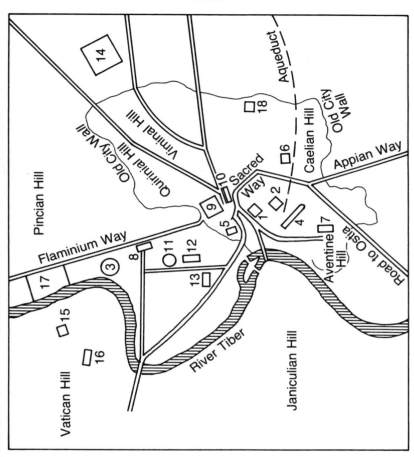

1. Palace of Tiberius and Caligula
2. Palace of Augustus
3. Mausoleum of Augustus
4. Circus Maximus
5. Temple of Jupiter
6. Temple of Claudius
7. Temple of Diana
8. Arch of Claudius
9. Forum
10. Senate
11. Pantheon
12. Baths
13. Theatre of Pompey
14. Camp of Praetorian Guard
15. Villa of Quintus Albinian
16. Villa of Claurinius and Demeter
17. Compound where Paul was imprisoned
18. Home of Philologus and Julia

Key to Alexandria:

1. Library
2. Roman Administrative Centre
3. Hall of Justice
4. Temple of Poseidon
5. Stadium
6. Theatre
7. Temple of Sarapis
8. Greek Tannery
9. Temple of Ganymede
10. Home of Cambiades, Aspasia and Apollos
11. Home of Parmenion and Camporina, Diana and Demeter
12. Anaxagoras's Shop
13. Hebron Synagogue
14. Church of Alexandria
15. Gate of the Sun
16. Gate of the Moon

ALEXANDRIA

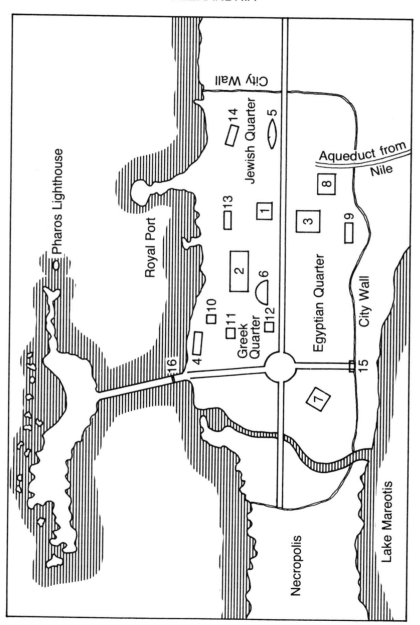

Pharos Lighthouse

Royal Port

Greek Quarter

Jewish Quarter

City Wall

Egyptian Quarter

City Wall

Aqueduct from Nile

Necropolis

Lake Mareotis

Key to Antioch:

1. Palace
2. Circus
3. Forum
4. Museum
5. Theatre
6. Basilica of Caesar
7. Baths
8. Daphne Gate
9. Aleppo Gate
10. Church of Antioch
11. Apollos and Jerahmeel's lodging place

ANTIOCH

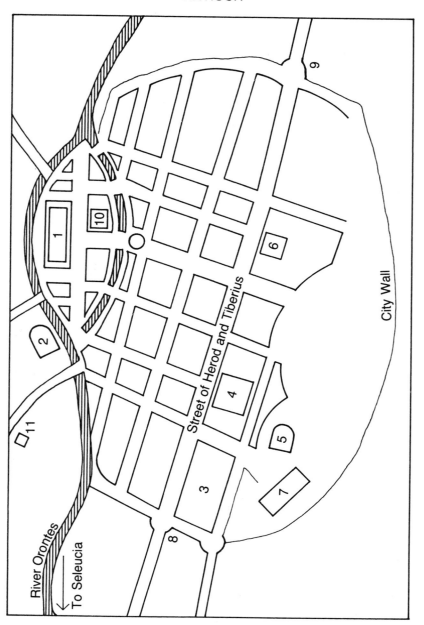

PHILIPPI

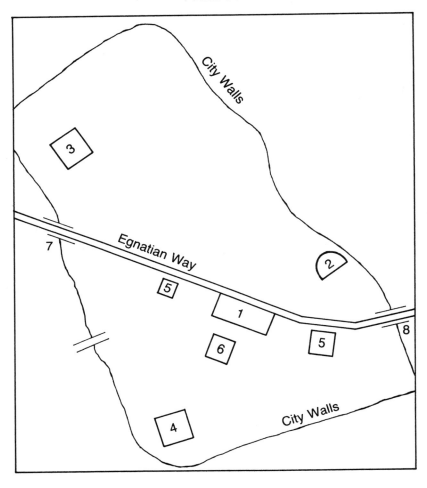

1. Forum
2. Theatre
3. Jail
4. Baths
5. Temples
6. Lydia's House
7. Krenides Gate
8. Neapolis Gate

442

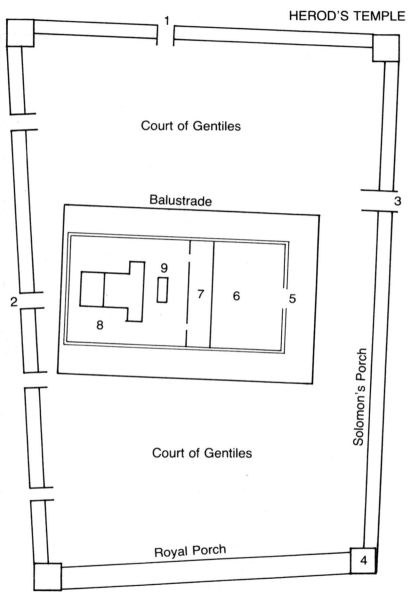

HEROD'S TEMPLE

Court of Gentiles

Balustrade

Court of Gentiles

Royal Porch

Solomon's Porch

1. Sheep Gate
2. Warren's Gate
3. Shushan Gate
4. Pinnacle of the Temple
5. Beautiful Gate
6. Court of the Women
7. Court of Israel
8. Court of Priests
9. Altar

CORINTH

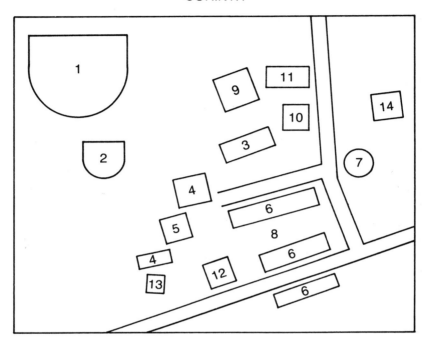

1. Theatre
2. Odeon
3. Temple of Apollo
4. Temples
5. Museum
6. Shops
7. Fountain
8. Market Area
9. North Market
10. Synagogue
11. Home of Titius Justus
12. Home of Aquila and Priscilla
13. Home of Apollos, Diana and Selenece
14. Law Courts

NIMES

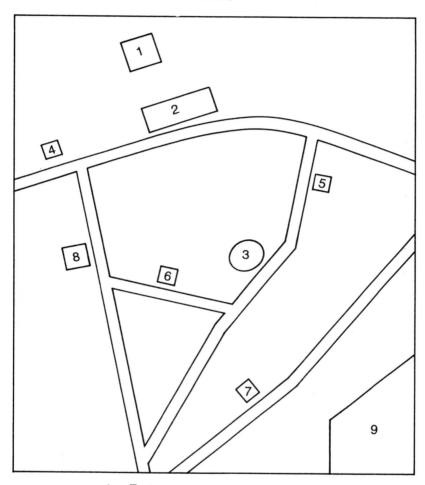

1. Fort
2. Citadel
3. Circus
4. Temple of Diana
5. Temple of Apollo
6. Temple of Jupiter
7. Temple of Saturn
8. Home of Apollos, Diana
   and Selenece
9. Settlement of the Arverni people

Key to Jerusalem:

1. Herod's Temple
2. Antonia Fortress
3. Palace of Herod
4. Royal Gardens
5. Palace of the Hasmonaeans
6. Calvary
7. House of Caiaphas
8. Synagogue of the Freedmen
9. Church of Jerusalem
10. Lodging place of Apollos and Jerahmeel
11. Pool of Bethesda
12. Pool of Siloam
13. Damascus Gate
14. Essene Gate
15. Tekoa Gate

JERUSALEM

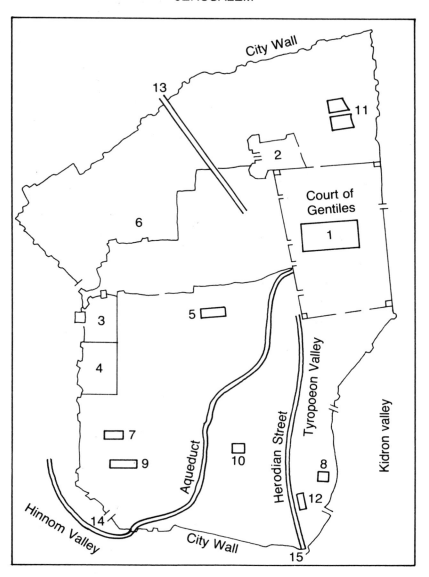

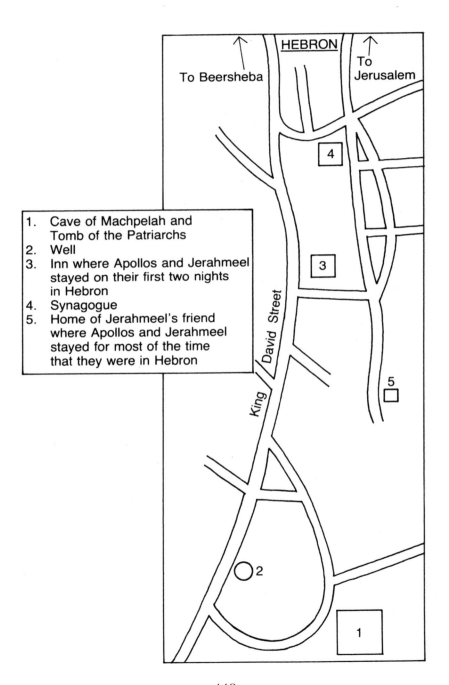

1. Cave of Machpelah and Tomb of the Patriarchs
2. Well
3. Inn where Apollos and Jerahmeel stayed on their first two nights in Hebron
4. Synagogue
5. Home of Jerahmeel's friend where Apollos and Jerahmeel stayed for most of the time that they were in Hebron

HEBRON

To Beersheba

To Jerusalem

David Street

King

BEERSHEBA

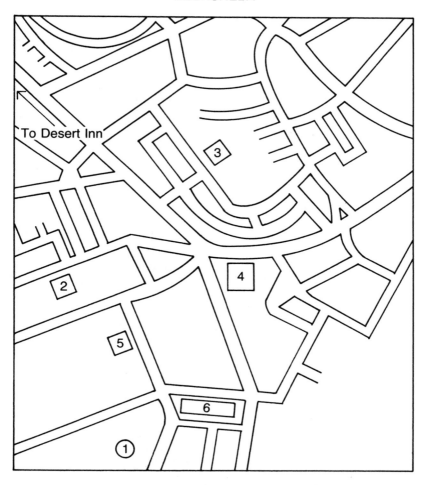

To Desert Inn

1. Abraham's Well
2. Home of Benaiah and
   Haggith
3. Magistrate's House
4. Synagogue
5. Inn where Apollos and Jerahmeel
   stayed on their first night in
   Beersheba
6. Market

EPHESUS

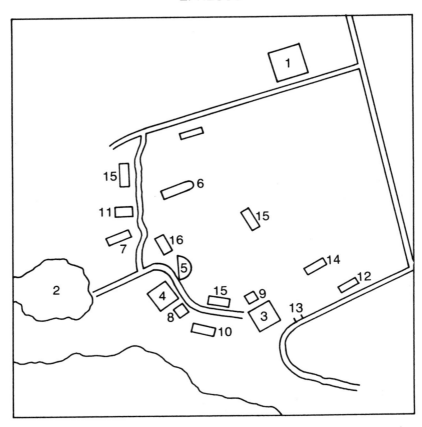

1.	Temple of Diana	9.	City Hall
2.	Harbour	10.	Lecture Hall of Tyrannus
3.	Public Market	11.	Home of Aquila and Priscilla
4.	Market Place	12.	Home of Diomedes and Calliope
5.	Theatre	13.	Magnesia Gate
6.	Stadium	14.	Smaller Churches
7.	Main Church	15.	Synagogues
8.	Library	16.	Gymnasium

APPENDIX 4

Biblical References

1. Mark ch 1 v 4–6
2. Isaiah ch 53 v 7–8
3. Acts ch 8 v 26–40
4. Judges ch 16 v 23–30
5. Genesis ch 20–21
6. Genesis ch 26
7. 2 Chronicles ch 14 v 13–14
8. Exodus
9. 1 and 2 Maccabees
10. Joshua ch 19 v 1–2
11. Genesis ch 46 v 1
12. Genesis ch 22 v 19
13. Genesis ch 21 v 30–34
14. Genesis ch 26 v 32–33
15. Matthew ch 14 v 10
16. Genesis ch 13 v 16 to ch 15 v 5
17. Genesis ch 18 v 18
18. Genesis ch 14 v 1–20
19. Exodus ch 2 v 16–22
20. Exodus ch 18 v 13–27
21. Esther ch 3 v 16–17
22. Joshua ch 2 v 1–24
23. Ruth ch 1 v 16–17
24. Matthew ch 1 v 2–6
25. 2 Kings ch 10 v 15–31
26. Jeremiah ch 35 v 18–19
27. Nehemiah ch 3 v 14
28. 1 Chronicles ch 2 v 55
29. Judges ch 1 v 16
30. Psalm 87
31. Luke ch 3 v 7–9
32. Matthew ch 1 v 6–11
33. Judges ch 5 v 17–22
34. Judges ch 4 v 9
35. Genesis ch 41 v 45–52
36. Genesis ch 38 v 6–30
37. 2 Samuel ch 15 v 17–21
38. Genesis ch 25 v 4
39. Genesis ch 36 v 1, v 10–15
40. Psalm 51
41. John ch 1 v 35–41
42. Luke ch 7 v 18–23
43. Genesis ch 23
44. Genesis ch 25 v 9
45. Genesis ch 49 v 31
46. Genesis ch 50 v 13
47. Genesis ch 50 v 26
48. Numbers ch 13 v 22
49. Numbers ch 13 v 22, 28, 33
50. Joshua ch 10 v 1–27
51. Joshua ch 15 v 13
52. Numbers ch 14 v 6, 10
53. 2 Samuel ch 2 v 4
54. 2 Samuel ch 5 v 3
55. 2 Samuel ch 15 v 7
56. 1 Maccabees ch 5 v 65
57. 2 Samuel ch 5 v 6–8
58. 2 Kings ch 16 v 5
59. 2 Kings ch 18 v 13 – ch 19 v 37
60. 2 Chronicles ch 36 v 11–21
61. Nehemiah ch 2 v 1–20
62. 1 Maccabees ch 4–7
63. Mark 6 v 17
64. Leviticus ch 16 v 1–34
65. Leviticus ch 12 v 1–8
66. Luke ch 21 v 1–4
67. Matthew ch 6 v 1–4
68. Acts ch 6 v 9
69. Acts ch 7 v 54–60
70. Acts ch 12 v 2
71. Acts ch 5 v 12
72. Acts ch 12 v 17
73. Mark ch 15 v 21
74. Acts ch 13 v 1
75. Acts ch 2 v 1–42
76. Acts ch 12 v 20–23

77. Acts ch 13 v 55
78. John ch 2 v 1–11
79. 1 Kings ch 17 v 17–24
80. 2 Kings ch 5 v 32–37
81. John ch 11 v 38–41
82. Mark ch 3 v 31–35
83. Luke ch 2 v 25–35
84. Mark ch 16 v 1–6
85. John ch 20 v 5–7
86. 1 Corinthians ch 15 v 4–7
87. John ch 20 v 5–7
88. Matthew ch 28 v 16–20
89. Acts ch 1 v 4–11
90. Deuteronomy ch 18 v 15
91. Isaiah ch 9 v 6–7
92. John ch 18 v 36
93. Hosea ch 6 v 2
94. Psalm 22
95. Jonah ch 1 v 17
96. Matthew ch 12 v 39–41
97. Psalm 14 v 1–3
98. Romans ch 3 v 10–12
99. Matthew ch 5 v 21–22, v 27–28
100. Genesis ch 4 v 3–5
101. Isaiah ch 53 v 1–9
102. Isaiah ch 53 v 12
103. Luke ch 23 v 40–42
104. Luke ch 23 v 44
105. Matthew ch 27 v 51
106. Matthew ch 27 v 52–53
107. Luke ch 22 v 19–20
108. Micah ch 5 v 2
109. John ch 1 v 43–46
110. Isaiah ch 9 v 1–2
111. Luke ch 2 v 1–7
112. Luke ch 1 v 14
113. Isaiah ch 7 v 14
114. Matthew ch 1 v 20–21
115. Matthew ch 2 v 13–15
116. Matthew ch 2 v 1–17
117. Hosea ch 11 v 1
118. Jeremiah ch 31 v 15
119. Acts ch 11 v 27–28
120. Acts ch 2 v 46
121. Acts ch 13 v 1
122. Acts ch 11 v 26
123. Acts ch 15 v 39
124. Acts ch 13 v 7
125. Acts ch 16 v 16–40

126. Numbers ch 20 v 4–9
127. John ch 3 v 14–17
128. Mark ch 15 v 17
129. Mark ch 15 v 21
130. Mark ch 15 v 33–34
131. John ch 19 v 28–30
132. Mark ch 15 v 33–34
133. John ch 19 v 23–24
134. Psalm 16 v 8–11
135. Joel ch 2 v 28–32
136. Mark ch 2 v 1–12
137. Acts ch 19 v 23–41
138. Luke ch 19 v 1–9
139. John ch 8 v 1–11
140. John ch 4 v 5–42
141. Mark ch 10 v 46–52
142. Mark ch 14 v 3–9
143. Mark ch 1 v 40–45
144. Acts ch 4 v 36–37
145. Acts ch 16 v 11–13
146. 2 Thessalonians ch 3 v 6–15
147. Acts ch 6 v 5–6
148. Acts ch 1 v 7–9
149. Acts ch 8 v 4–5
150. Ezra ch 10 v 10–11
151. Luke ch 10 v 25–37
152. Acts ch 8 v 5–25
153. Acts ch 10 v 1
154. Acts ch 9 v 40
155. Matthew ch 8 v 5–13
156. Acts ch 10
157. Acts ch 21 v 8–9
158. Matthew ch 27 v 16
159. Luke ch 23 v 18–25
160. Luke ch 23 v 33–43
161. Mark ch 15 v 6–15
162. Isaiah ch 53 v 6
163. Mark ch 14 v 51–52
164. John ch 19 v 26–27
165. Acts ch 15 v 36–41
166. Acts ch 18 v 18
167. Acts ch 18 v 2
168. Acts ch 20 v 5
169. Acts ch 16 v 1
170. 2 Timothy ch 1 v 5
171. 2 Corinthians ch 8 v 6
172. Acts ch 19 v 9
173. Zechariah ch 9 v 9
174. Zechariah ch 12 v 10

APPENDIX 5

Bibliography

The Holy Bible Authorised Version; Cambridge University Press

The Holy Bible New International Version; Hodder and Stoughton 1979

The Jerusalem Bible General Editor Alexander Jones; Darton, Longman and Todd 1976

The Holy Bible and the Apocrypha Revised Standard Version; Thomas Nelson and Sons Ltd. 1959

The Good News Bible Today's English Version; The Bible Societies/ Collins 1976

The New Bible Dictionary Organising Editor J. D. Douglas; Inter-Varsity Fellowship 1962

Oxford Bible Atlas Editor Herbert G. May; Oxford University Press 1989

The Lion Encyclopaedia of the Bible Organising Editor Pat Alexander; Lion Publishing 1986

Larousse Encyclopaedia of Ancient and Mediaeval History General Editor Marcel Dunan; Paul Hamlyn 1963

Larousse Encyclopaedia of Mythology Editor Felix Guirand; Paul Hamlyn 1959

The Joy of Knowledge Encyclopaedia Mitchell Beazley Encyclopaedias Ltd.; Rigby International Ltd./Winfray Strachan Ltd. 1981

Pauline Places by Ronald Brownrigg; Hodder and Stoughton 1988

I, Claudius by Robert Graves; Methuen 1979